Hands upon
The Anvil

Sara Powter

Bible Quotes from King James Version

ISBN: 9780994578235
Paperback

ABN 99 768 734 831
Pacific Wanderland Publications
Kincumber Australia NSW 2251

saragpowter@gmail.com
www.sarapowter.com.au

1st edition 2020 printed by Ingram Spark, Australia
2nd edition 2021 printed by Kindle, an Amazon Company
3rd edition 2021 Pacific Wanderland Publication
printed for Woodslane, Warriwood NSW by SOS
4th edition 2022 (revised) Amazon Australia; & Kindle
5th Edition 2023 - revised and modified, Amazon Australia; & Kindle

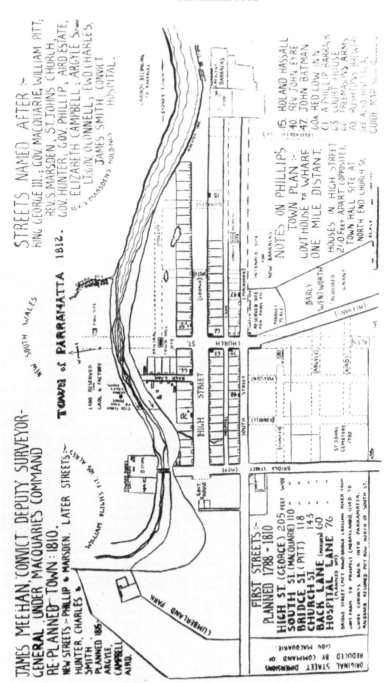

Australian Historical Novels

Unlikely Convict Ladies Trilogy

Dancing to her Own Tune
(co-authored by Sheila Hunter & Sara Powter)
Amelia's Tears
A Lady in Irons

The Convict Stain Collection
(All stand-alone books)

No More, My Love
The Vine Weaver
Scotch at The Rocks *{Sequel to The Vine Weaver}*
Waiting at the Sliprails
(The following are coming soon)
Convict Shadows of the Past *(2024)*
In Defence of Her Honour *(2024)*
Gentle Annie Soames *(2024)*
I Can't Stop Tomorrow *(2024)*
Madeline's Boy *(2025)*

Early Colonial Days Trilogy

When Upon Life's Billows *(2025)*
Tuppence to Pass *(2025)*
Saddler's Song *(2025)*

The Lockleys of Parramatta

Hands Upon the Anvil
Out Where the Brolgas Dance
Diamonds in the Dirt
The Earl's Shadow
Once a Jolly Swagman
Jonty's Journey

Shelia Hunter's
Australian Colonial Trilogy

Mattie
Ricky *{Jonty's Journey is a sequel}*
The Heather to the Hawkesbury

Family Tree and Character list at the end of the book

TICKET OF LEAVE.

NO.

COLONIAL SECRETARY'S OFFICE.

NEW SOUTH WALES.

Twenty eighth day of January **18** 20

IT is His EXCELLENCY the GOVERNOR'S Pleasure to DISPENSE with the Attendance at Government Work of *Inn Keeper and Storekeeper* who was tried at *Kent Assises* Convict for *seven years* arrived per Ship *Shipley* *Moncrief* Master, in the Year *1820* and to permit to employ *him*self (off the Stores) in any lawful Occupation within the District of *Parramatta* for *his* own Advantage during good Behaviour; or, until His EXCELLENCY'S further Pleasure shall be made known.

By His Excellency's Command,

Major EC Grace

Behold,
I have created the smith
that bloweth the coals in the fire,
and that bringeth forth
an instrument for his work;

Isaiah 54:16.
King James Version

Acknowledgement of Country:
In the spirit of reconciliation, I acknowledge the Traditional Custodians of country throughout Australia and their connections to land, sea and community. We pay our respect to their Elders, past and present and extend that respect to all Aboriginal and Torres Strait Islander peoples today.

<u>Thanks</u>.
I wish to thank my beloved husband, Stephen,
for his patience in answering my never-ending questions;
also for answering 'Does this sound right?' questions.
To my dad, who said I could do anything I set my mind to.
My mother, Sheila Hunter,
inspired me to write by writing three books herself.
Sadly, she never saw hers in print and will never know that I followed her lead… at least, not this side of Heaven.

Thanks also to my convict ancestors.
Who were ripped from the arms of their loved ones,
And sent forever to the other side of the world.
I appreciate their sacrifice and their faith more every day.
Their faith in God still lives on through many of us.
I am astounded that their faith survived the rigours
of the convict life they were all forced to endure.

Thanks also to my husband, Steve,
And to Roby Aiken for your patience in correcting my punctuation and
Noreen Robertson for doing the final read-through edit.

Table of Contents

The grammar and language in this book are
Australian English spelling

Kindle Editions are X-ray enabled.

Chapter 1   The Blacksmith

"*S*onny, quick, under the table!"

Eddie scurried under the workbench, not questioning why.

Lieutenant Simmons stomped in, slamming the door open.

Sitting safely under the filthy workbench, Eddie shivered and held his breath. He was scared that he might bump a hammer or the set of tongs that he was kneeling on and give away his hiding place. He stayed still, relieved that Mr. Tindale had seen the soldier coming.

Lieutenant Simmons loudly asked, "Where's that little rascal, Eddie?"

Mr. Tindale said to Lieutenant Simmons, "Eddie hasn't turned up to work this morning, so I don't know where he is. I'm busy." He kept beating the horseshoe he was making.

Lieutenant Simmons grew red. His anger was visible.

Mr. Tindale's shoe tapped Eddie on the knee, just motioning that he would keep him safe. He kept belting the red-hot horseshoe and making a lot more noise than usual. The heat of the building was overpowering.

Lieutenant Simmons turned on his heel and walked out once again, banging the side door.

After what he considered time for the man to go, he said, "Cor blimey, that was a close one." He slid out from under the workbench, brushing off the soot that covered the room. "He's on the warpath this morning, Mr. Tindale. I don't like that, Lieutenant Simmons. I saw my brover Charlie crying this morning. He does like the young boys he does; at least, he likes them to belt up som'fin. If my dad knew what it was like, I reckon he'd fair thump him, 'n that would be bad 'cause, me Dar were a convict he were, and even though he runs a local pub and is the keeper of the stores, I reckon he'd still get into big trouble. So I'll just keep me mummer shut and keep trying to hide."

Mr. Tindale said, "Okay, Eddie, but back onto the bellows; I need this metal hot, and you know what that means: hard, hot work. I don't pay you to sit. I'll not be telling your father, but son, Charlie should."

"Yes, sir; sorry, sir!" Ed jumped to grab the top arm of the bellows and started pumping.

Mr. Tindale was the blacksmith in the town of Parramatta. He was hard-working and well-liked. He took Eddie on as an apprentice even though the child was just six and very small. Now, he was ten years old, a good worker, and was good at the bits he could do. He took pride in his work. He liked him as soon as he came in looking for work. He could see he had good strength for his age; he'd need that to be a blacksmith. Mr. Tindale couldn't do both the bellows and the smithing; it took a lot of stress off Mr. Tindale, so he said yes and gave him a job. He had to tie a rope on the top bellow handle so the lad could work them. He was just able to reach it these days.

Eddie arrived promptly in the mornings as soon as all his chores were done. He had to muck out the stables at the 'The Jolly Sailor Inn' that his Mama and Dar ran. It was a good job; he was used to holding and talking to the horses. Even on cold mornings, he had companions. The horses knew him as he'd been doing it for two years; working hard was nothing new in the colony; every child had to pull their weight. Eddie was no exception.

He was the second son. His older brother Charlie was always in trouble with the Lieutenant, but this morning, he saw Charlie coming out of Lieutenant Simmons's rooms early, too early, and that wasn't a good sign. "I don't think that Dar can help but know now," Charlie said to Mr. Tindale.

"One day, there will be strife to pay," said Eddie.

Eddie jumped up and started pumping those bellows. The room started getting very hot as the fire flared. Mr. Tindale put the callipers in the fire with the new horseshoe. It proceeded to go bright red. He left it in until you could see the little sparks coming up off the top of the metal, then pulled it out again and started forming a new horseshoe. He was so skilled he could make them fast.

Eddie couldn't wait until he was old enough to be able to lift the big hammer. He was keen and could work the small hammer in record time; however, the big hammer was just too heavy for his small hands. With a little hammer, Eddie could make nails; he was doing quite well and with passion. He could do these quickly and get them to an excellent sharp point.

This was good because many houses were being built, so the demand for nails was growing, not to mention horseshoe and roof shingle nails. Who knew that there were so many sorts of nails? Each had a different shape. Eddie being able to do this meant that Mr. Tindale could keep working on the more essential things like coach springs, tools, lamp hooks, and all the bits that go with horse harnesses; they were fiddly, and Eddie couldn't manage those.

Mr. Tindale had realised that Eddie was also a very quick learner and thought about possibly sending him to school.

Major Grace had approached him last week and had sown the seed. He was still getting his mind around things. He knew that Eddie could already read, as he'd been going along to the Charity School in Parramatta, run by Reverend Marsden's daughter.

He heard about a new school starting in Sydney, the Cape Academy, although that meant Eddie would have to live in during the week. Ed had friends like Timmy Miller and some other Parramatta boys who were also going, and he was sure he could work out a bed for the lad.

Tim was another young lad who lived locally, possibly going as well. He'd won some scholarship. Timmy Miller's parents ran one of the other local Inns, a better quality one, too, and he was a friend of Eddie's. They could share a room with his nephews, his sister Caroline Evans' three sons. Eddie, Tim, and Caro's boys were of much the same age and should get on well together. Education would benefit them; they would need it in their lives far more than their parents ever would. It would also keep Ed out of Simmons's way. Possibilities would open up for them. He wasn't sure what Mr. Cape would be teaching, but he'd do what he could to get Eddie out of the situation he was in. Life in this new world was very different from England. Possibilities here were open to all, regardless of birth. So unlike the old country, where you were born into one class and had no hope of getting out of it. "Let's see what time will do to these boys," mused Mr. Tindale.

Pumping the bellows gave Eddie time to think. It was easy to work; it was hot but easy. He wondered if he'd like to be a blacksmith all his life. He kept running through job ideas. "It could be worse jobs. I don't think I'd like to work with dead people, so I was pleased that Dar didn't let me work for the undertaker." He'd found this job for himself four years before. "No! I think life as a blacksmith would be good. Hard work but good work."

It was a dark room, other than the fire, and there was a bit of light coming in the window, but the slab-built blacksmiths' shack with the big stone fireplace and the shingle roof was not what you'd call homely.

Mr. Tindale and his wife lived in the house at the back. She was a jolly person who made the best of everything around and the best-ever biscuits.

Eddie and Timmy would often be seen at the door when she'd been cooking them, and Mrs. Tindale, being a sympathetic person who loved children, always gave them one each and sometimes one for George, another friend in town and of course Charlie too. Eddie was the eldest of the three boys and looked out for the two smaller ones.

Mrs. Tindale sweetened them with the juice of fruit from a tree in her yard and honey. This tree had lots and lots of pink berries on it; they tasted like apples but with a seed inside, but you had to eat a lot of them to feel full.

She told Eddie they were called Lilli Pillies. She took the seeds out and put the pulp in the biscuits, and then she added some honey from one of the local bee hives.

Eddie was also able to watch Mrs. Tindale grind the barley and oats to make flour.

Eddie had never seen someone doing that before because Mama always had bags of flour from the stores, but she had more people to feed at the pub with all the coaches and travellers stopping. Being the keeper of the stores meant that Mama and Dar could always get what they needed. Dar and Charlie would help unload the ships coming up from Sydney and put them in the old stone storeroom; there were bags of flour; there was rum; there was salt meat in drums, and sometimes there were even eggs. The outlying farms often sent in more grain; there were live chickens, cows, sheep, and goats, and these often were only kept overnight as they were usually orders for people. Twice a week, there was milk, butter and rum, and this had to be stored in the underground basement of the Stores building so that it wouldn't go off or the rum stolen. The cold storeroom was built under the inn like a cellar, and only Dar had the key.

Eddie didn't like rum; he'd seen what it did to people who had too much to drink and then got drunk and started belting each other up. Living in a pub, he'd seen people like this all his life. His short life had been an adventure already. He'd seen the soldiers, most nice, but some cruel; he'd seen the carriages; he'd seen the convicts in the chain gangs; some of them were really scary, but he stayed clear of them. Dar explained that they were mostly the very worst kind.

Eddie was pleased when the day was done. He counted the nails; he'd made six different sorts and a box of each. He was pleased, as was Mr. Tindale.

"Eddie, you've done so well you can go home early. Take some of those little nails for your Mama. They are good to put things up on the walls, you know, notices and the like," said Mr. Tindale.

Eddie packed up and was heading out the door when Mr. Tindale said, "Hey Eddie, send your Dar in to talk to me sometime; I have something I would like to talk to him about."

Eddie called a cheerful, "Okay, Mr. Tindale, and thanks for looking after me this morning." He headed home. Eddie got to thinking as he walked out the door. "I wonder what Mr. Tindale could want with Dar?" And he gave a shrug.

Eddie took a quick detour past Mrs. Tindale's door in case she had more biscuits. Sure enough, she had. She handed Eddie a couple of biscuits in the cloth and said one was for Timmy and one for Charlie. Timmy was working as a stablehand/groom after school at Dar's Inn and often came to the blacksmith to get new horseshoes made.

Both Charlie and Eddie knew Timmy very well; he was only eight, and he was a funny little character, hanging around Eddie whenever he could. The boys loved each other and were good mates. They often found a quiet corner in the garden, sat down, ate their biscuits, and talked about the day. Ed would wrap it up for Charlie and stuff it in his shirt if they got a spare one.

After they had finished the biscuits, they decided to go for a quick swim in the river, as both were hot and dirty after a long day at work. It would be good to go to bed smelling clean, not that the Parramatta River was very clean anyhow. It was tidal, sometimes you got a bit sticky from the salt, but that was better than being covered in soot and horse poo.

Soon, two wet, dripping little ragamuffins scampered up the banks and headed to their homes. Charlie's packet was still safely stuffed in Ed's shirt. He knew there were more chores to be done when they got there.

Timmy had three younger brothers and sisters, and Eddie had five, which meant a lot more work, screaming and noise; that was home, safe and secure, and loved their families.

Timmy's favourite job was when he was called to hold the horses' heads when the gentleman arrived to collect someone from the Ferry or collect stores. He got to take the beautiful horses around to the stable to Charlie, and together, they would take the saddles off and feed them. Timmy loved this job, he loved horses, and he loved people too.

By the time Eddie had arrived home, he had finished dripping, and he raced through the kitchen, greeting his Mama and the two girls who worked there with her, pausing briefly to kiss his Mama on the cheek. From there, he ran out to the taproom to find his Dar leaning on the counter and talking to a big bearded gentleman. Without saying a word, he walked up to his Dar and just stood next to him. Without pausing the conversation, Dar looked down and pointed to a stack of glasses that needed washing. Eddie went and got some water from the well and started washing them. He could tell from the number of glasses that it had been a busy day and that Mama and Dar were tired.

Ed wondered how many were staying the night tonight and how many hammocks they'd have to put up in the stable. The rich ones would stay at Tim's Dar's Inn.

The glasses were done, and he went to find Charlie. He was already in the stable hanging the hammocks and asked how many they had to hang.

"I brought you something." He handed him the parcel from his shirt. It was his way of showing he loved him. The boys were close in more than just age. Only eleven months separated the boys.

Charlie said, "Twelve Ed, twelve tonight, and the lady inside too, that's gonna be a crush tonight, Ed. That's nine of us inside and twelve out tonight. Another big meal; it will be stew and bread again tonight. The lady will have our bed, so we will all be on the floor in front of the fire, but I think that I'd rather be there actually, not quite so cramped," said Charlie.

Charlie and Eddie kept hanging the hammocks on the big hooks in the stable up in the hayloft.

Eddie told Charlie, "I saw you crying this morning, but don't worry, I won't tell Dar about Lieutenant Simmons. What did he belt you for this time? He's horrible. He came looking for me, but Mr. Tindale hid me under the workbench and left angry. I think he must have seen me as you left."

Charlie looked up, startled.

The young lad said, "I just wanted you to know that now I know what's going on, so you'se not alone." Eddie said, "Tell us if I cun help in any way, Charlie."

Charlie bent his head and said, "Thanks, mate, that actually helps. He'd er, um, wanted his boots clean to shine, and I didn't have time to get them to him last night. So I snuck in early this morning, but he still caught me." He blushed.

Eddie thought he wasn't telling the full story.

Charlie and Eddie continued to hang the hammocks. They then restocked the firewood for the brazier, drew the water from the well, and got everything ready for the night.

Eddie finally was able to give Dar the message from Mr. Tindale. Later, they had to help their Dar move one of the drunk men and get him into a downstairs hammock in the stables. This was often very funny as some men became very silly when they drank too much rum.

The taproom was cleaned and ready for use the next day. The boys rolled out the bedding so the children could sleep on the floor in front of the fire. Charlie and Eddie helped the little ones to bed, crawling in themselves, and they fell fast asleep as soon as they put their heads down.

Snores sounded from the stables, and possums grunted in the trees outside. The fire inside crackled as the six little bodies slept soundly on the floor.

Chapter 2 Education

*E*ddie was up before the wharf bell rang that morning, which was strange as the bell was supposed to ring half an hour before the ship departed. It should still be dark.

He yawned, stretched and elbowed Charlie as he had to light the fire for breakfast, and now the late bell meant panic all around, for the passenger ship was due to leave soon.

Liza was up, too, as she had to milk the cow. He headed out to do his chores, packing up the hammocks and mucking out the stable with Timmy and Charlie. He then watched the passengers who hoped to catch the first ship hurry to gather their goods, grab something to eat and scurry down to the wharf. The passenger boats could only stay at the wharf for a few minutes, so their speed was essential.

Stables done and hammocks rolled and stowed for the next use, he headed off to work, his arms still tired from all the hammering and making nails the day before. He looked forward to going to work and chatting with Mr. Tindale all day.

Mr. Tindale also taught him to spell more challenging words than he was learning at school. His mentor was determined that Eddie wasn't going to stay a blacksmith all his life, or if he did, he'd be a good businessman, too. It was a hard life; Eddie wasn't so sure about this as he didn't mind being a blacksmith. He knew he'd have to learn to read correctly and do sums just to send out the bills, and he could already count up to fifty; Mama had seen to that. He needed to count the stores, the bags of wheat, the bottles of grog, the sacks of potatoes and onions, and the number of glasses. Yes, he needed to be able to count, but he wasn't so sure about this fancy reading stuff. He could write his name; Mama had seen to that, too. She had made him copy and copy and copy until he could do it neatly. Eddie was surprised when Mr. Tindale said he wanted to have a long talk with him when he'd finished his day's work.

Mr. and Mrs. Tindale had no children and treated Eddie as they would've done their own. Major Grace had paid a few visits to the forge of late, but the Tindales ran a profitable business, and Ed could tell they made lots of money Blacksmithing. It was a lucrative trade.

Mr. Tindale sat Eddie down on a log seat inside the blacksmith shop. "Now, Eddie, this long talk we need to have. I've decided that I'd like to pay for you to go to school in Sydney Town, and yes, I realise this means living away from home, and yes, I know you're only ten, and you're going to be lonely, so Mrs. Tindale and I have decided that we're going to send Timmy with you, would you like that? You're both to go to the new school in Sydney Town that Mr. Cape runs. I've already spoken to Timmy's dad, and he is happy for Timmy to go as long as you go, too. He'll be only nine, but he is very clever, and I think it would be good for you. You will need to learn all sorts of things that your folks won't have learned. Our town is growing so fast that many new possibilities will be open to you both that your parents couldn't have. Both of you are clever boys, and I want you to learn as much as you can. What do you think?" At that moment, there was a knock on the blacksmith's door, giving Eddie no chance to reply. It was Eddie's dar, Charles Lockley.

"May I come in, sir?" said Charles to Mr. Tindale.

"Certainly," said Mr. Tindale, "Come in. I'm just talking to Eddie about my idea. I thought I'd run it by him first before I said anything to you. He hasn't answered me yet. I think he's in shock. What do you say, young Eddie?"

Charles said, "What's this all about, Mr. Tindale?"

Mr. Tindale looked up sheepishly, "Well, you see, we've taken a shine to your young lad. Mrs. Tindale and I have no children. Blacksmithing is a good business, and Eddie would make a good blacksmith, but he needs to know his words and needs to know his numbers, more than just counting. Well, we've been talking, and we'd like to send your young lad and young Timmy Miller to the new school in Sydney Town called Cape's Academy. It means living away from home during the week, but my sister's got room for them both, and they can stay there free of charge, although I'm sure she'll get them to do some chores. So, Mr. Lockley, will you let him go? Will you let us pay? Please?" said Mr. Tindale.

Thomas wondered how he'd phrase the next topic. He took a breath and just charged in. "There's another thing. I'd like to have your Charlie as my new apprentice because even though he's nearly twelve, he could do with some more skills than just odd jobs for Lieutenant Simmons and working around the pub. Simmons is a mean man, and we got to look after young Charlie, too. I won't tell tales out of school, but that man shouldn't be let around any boys; he's evil." Mr. Tindale said.

Charles sat himself down beside Eddie. Stunned and speechless.

"I don't need an answer now; they can't start until the new year, Eddie will be eleven by then, but I'll need to know by the end of the month to make arrangements. My sister is keen. I've checked with her, and she's only got the three boys at home. Her husband is a Master Mariner and is often away, so there's plenty of room. As I said, they will have to do some chores around the house, but that won't hurt them. Good for both of them and they are good friends so that they won't be alone."

"Sir, I'm, well, stunned is an understatement," Charles said.

"Why don't you go and have a chat with Timmy's dad?"

Charles and Eddie left the blacksmith shop in shock; he'd barely said more than "good morning" to Mr. Tindale before. Eddie had arranged this job himself four years before, and as Mr. Tindale was a free settler, their paths didn't cross often. This is not how he expected the conversation to have turned out; he thought Eddie would get the sack.

Eddie asked if he could race ahead and see Timmy. Charles said, "Yes," so he ran on. Charles wandered down the street and didn't hear the horse until it was nearly too late. He quickly sidestepped out of the way and kept walking. He thought he'd call in at the Rear Admiral Duncan Inn and talk to Timmy's dad, Bill Miller before he went home and spoke to Sal. He'd have a better picture of what all this was about. Charles was still in somewhat of a daze, and his feet took him down the dusty road and around the corner to the Rear Admiral Duncan Inn. Bill Miller was out in the street filling the horse troughs for the day and getting ready to open. He looked up as Charles approached.

"G'day mate," said Bill. "Don't get to see much of each other, do we?"

"Hello, Bill," replied Charles. "Nah, too busy on the docks with stores and grog. Also, passengers stay over when it's an early timetable. Makes life crazy, with bodies everywhere, but it's all good money." Charles wandered onto the verandah and leaned on the railing. "Eh, Bill, what's this about Mr. Tindale sending our boys to school? First I've heard about it," said Charles.

Bill stood up and stretched his back, "Well, it sort of follows a conversation I had some time ago with Tindale. I needed horseshoes on the bay mare, and we just chatted while he was shoeing her. Timmy is one bright child who knows his numbers already and can write more than just his name. Don't know where he learnt, but he can do it. I mean, the kid is only eight. So Molly and I were talking and figured we could afford to educate one child, and it would have to be Timmy, as he has already started, thanks to Miss Marsden's school. She got him to sit some test, something over my head. We looked around for somewhere local, and there was nothing here, at least nothing we could afford. The King's School is way too much. I was just saying this to Tindale, and he goes and tells me about this new school in Sydney. Well, Molly and I have some savings, but not enough for four children to educate, let alone the two boys to board, as well as any school fees. Well, I said to Mr. Tindale that we would have to let the idea go." Bill started scrubbing again, but the story wasn't yet finished.

After a bit, Bill said, "Well, Mr. Tindale said, 'Let me think it over for a bit. Come back in a few weeks. I might have an idea'." He scrubbed a few more inches and then continued. "Well, I never gave it another thought, Charles. Put it clean out of my mind, I did. Next thing I know, Tindale comes up with his harebrained idea. The only difference is that he's paying the bills for board with his sister. Well, Molly and I couldn't have that, so we thought we could chip in a bit. So we have enough to give Timmy something to live on and pay for his travel back every weekend, and Tindale is sorting his accommodation; that way, we are both happy. What do you think? Good idea?" Bill stood up, horse trough cleaned.

Charles now had a clearer picture of what the idea was. He said, "Yes."

He and Sal could also contribute to transport and some living costs that wouldn't be a problem, and then Mr. Tindale wouldn't have to pay for all the costs. In that way, he would also be helping educate his son. Still leaning on the railing, Charles said, "Well, Bill, I've got a hand it to you. Capital idea! I think we can come to the same arrangement then. It looks like we've got two boys going to be educated; not bad for a couple of convicts, is it? It wouldn't happen in old England. Who would have thought that being sent out as a convict could benefit a family?"

Bill didn't answer, but he smiled.

Charles lifted his eyes and looked up the street. This town of Parramatta was growing fast; the roads were wide, the buildings strong and solid. The colony was growing fast. Charles mused, saying, "Yes, education would be needed in this new life. All men could be equal here, not just for work but in any job you wanted to do, too. Convict and free, side by side, shoulder to shoulder." Charles sighed. He thought back to his schooling in England. He'd skip classes whenever he could. Now, he wished he'd listened more. He didn't realise how lucky he'd been to have some education. At least he could read and write.

Bill also lifted his eyes to the street and saw Timmy racing to meet him. He just had time to open his arms wide to catch his son, who had launched himself into the air, trusting that he would be caught safely.

"Par, Par, did ya hear?" Timmy said. "Eddie and me, we is going to school in Sydney Town. I'se just been speaking to Eddie, and he's so excited, and when do we go, how long does it last, and what I wear?" The lad was full of joy and excitement, the joy of youth. For Charles and Bill, they were just letting it sink in. Both were thinking about how the wives would cope and what they'd say.

Charles was also thinking about Charlie. His mind was in turmoil. He would talk to Sally after the children were asleep.

Chapter 3 Preparations

*T*immy and Eddie found more time to seek each other out over the months ahead. Mrs. Tindale often made the boys all sorts of treats; they would sneak off and eat them on the river edge. There was much to discuss and much to ponder over. They owned very little, so packing would never be a problem.

Each mother, Sally and Molly, had made a bag for their boy. They called them duffle bags. They could use these bags for travelling to and from school and take their clothes to Sydney Town. They only had to carry their good set of clothes and some spare smalls, linens, and clean shirts; they owned nothing more. Neither child had shoes. These would have to be worn to school but must be purchased in Sydney Town as Parramatta had little choice, and it was more expensive anyway than in the big town.

Eddie was full of questions and spent the mornings asking Mr. Tindale, and in turn, Mr. Tindale was so patient in answering every question he could. He worked extra hard over these months, building up a good stock of nails for Mr. Tindale so that he would not fall behind with orders while he was teaching Charlie to fill his role. Charlie was able to come along most afternoons and start learning his new trade. It would take some time to gain Eddie's skills.

Charlie was a stronger boy and was able to help with the bellows and nails and manage the small hammer for some of the first blows on the horseshoes, but it wore him out quickly. Working in the pub and taproom was not such physical work as blacksmithing. Even the barrels full of rum rolled smoothly. This was hot, hard work. The good thing about working for Mr. Tindale was that Charlie felt safe. Lieutenant Simmons was unlikely to come and drag him out of the blacksmith shop in front of Mr. Tindale.

He wouldn't have the free time that he used to have and couldn't sit dreaming on the wharf or watch the carriages cross the new bridge, but this was not a loss for Charlie. This is when Lieutenant Simmons often found him wherever he hid. He had nowhere to run on the wharf and wasn't strong enough to fight him off, so he was usually either just picked up or dragged along to the Lieutenant's room or, worse, into the mangroves. It was no use screaming, as that would only bring on another beating. Or worse, he just did everything he could not to be found alone.

Liza and Anna now had his job. Tim was still there helping them until they left. They were safe as Lieutenant Simmons didn't pick on girls. However, Charlie told them to stay in sight of the windows so Mama could see them. He also told them to stay together and not to wander as there were still convicts around who were real "bad eggs." They were only six and seven, so too young to do much around the pub. Liza's job of milking the cow would now have to be done by Anna, and Liza would have to help Charlie do the stables and hang and then roll up the hammocks when needed. They were old enough to do these chores. This also meant that the girls who used to look after the littlies could not keep an eye on Wills and Luke, so Sally must now do this and get the sewing done as well as cook the meals. Charlie thought he might suggest to Mama to ask one of Timmy's sisters to come and look after the little ones.

Eddie would miss his little sisters, but the adventures ahead were too good to pass up.

Christmas was next week, and the blacksmith's forge was even hotter than usual as it was so hot outside. So hot that any metal left outside burnt his hand when he picked it up. Eddie was sad that Christmas was Sunday this year as last year, he had two days off in a row. Sundays also meant that the Government wharf was off-limits as it was used for the Catholics to have church services, and many of these were convicts and something called "The Irish." They spoke funny, though. Mama and Dar said all the children had to stay well clear of them. Eddie laughed at this. One day, Mama said she too was actually Irish, at least her own ma was. Eddie and Charlie never understood why, as both their parents and Timmy's parents were convicts. True, they had their Tickets of Leave, but they would always be classed as convicts, and the only problem he could see is that these people were Catholics. Maybe that was it. Eddie watched the Catholic service on the wharf from the house. When the people left after the service, he felt it was okay to sit on the jetty for a while.

The taproom was closed on Sundays, so his family had gone to the early service at St John's. The rest of the day was reasonably free. Sometimes, people were staying overnight, but this depended on the tides. The river was shallow at low tide, so the ships could only make it up the river on the high tide. He knew the sailboats needed deeper water, but a new little paddle-steamer ferry could travel in shallower water. He'd waved to the new Captain but had not yet spoken to him.

Eddie was always pleased when the church was over, as he hated seeing the chained convicts. The soldiers all sat together at the back, including Simmons. He hated knowing he was being watched. Not that they scared him, but that he knew that his dad used to be one. Not that he was ever in a chain gang. He didn't like imagining him in chains. "I do hope Dar will tell me the full story one day," he thought.

He liked going to church. It was cool inside, and he loved sitting and looking at the roof and the pretty windows. The urgent chores had been done before church, and as there were no ships today and as the taproom was not open, the house was quiet.

Eddie quietly walked up to Charlie and whispered, "Charlie, they're gone; let's sneak away now."

Charlie put the stick down that he was whittling and stuffed the knife back in its sheath on his belt. "Yes, let's," he said quietly.

The two boys quietly snuck through the stables and grabbed their fishing poles and a tin of worms they had collected earlier. They were not supposed to fish on Sundays, so they were hoping not to get caught. They had a secret path down to the river bank, where they hoped not to be seen.

Eddie whispered to his brother, "Oh darn, I forgot to bring some food."

Charlie groaned. "Oh, I forgot too; I was so keen to get away. I forgot, too."

The boys made sure that both parents were on the verandah and with the little children. Having evaded them, they walked down through the trees and carefully placed the tin of worms on a rock.

"Charlie, I'm gonna miss this, sneaking out and going off. I'm sure that Mama knows, but she wouldn't tell Dar. Sometimes I'm scared if we catch some fish how they would explain them." Eddie looked at Charlie admiringly as he grabbed a worm and threaded it onto the homemade hook.

Eddie didn't like hurting the worms either but knew that the fish loved them. One day Eddie thought he'd love to try to make a good fishhook for Charlie. One day, when he was a good blacksmith, he mused. He might ask Mr. Tindale if he could try.

Charlie grabbed his pole and slithered down to the water's edge. He swung it, hoping that his hook missed the treetops. "Hey, Eddie, did you see that? I got it out full length. See how you can throw yours."

Eddie grabbed his pole and carefully held the bit of rope with the hook as he slid down the bank.

Eddie set his feet on the rocks and also swung his pole. "Charlie, I got it out, not as far as yours, but still better than last time when I got it tied up in the trees."

The boys squatted on their heels and sat silently. There was a tiny movement in the water at the same time; there were two yelps. Eddie had just been moving as his feet were getting tingly, and he nearly fell in. He managed to regain his balance.

Charlie excitedly had brought a big bream to shore. "Cor Eddie, I

don't think I've seen one that big for ages. Do you need help with yours?"
He reached over to help his little brother.

"Gee, thanks, Charlie. I nearly fell in, and I would have been in big trouble as Mama told me not to get too dirty. Drag it up the bank, Charlie, and measure it. Is it same as yours?"

Charlie placed the two big breams next to each other to discover they were the same size and both beauties.

Eddie said, "I don't know how we're gonna explain these, but I don't care, let us try again."

He tried to get up the bank, but Charlie said, "Just pass the hook; I'll bait it for you." Charlie did so and handed it back to Eddie. Then he did his own hook and passed his pole back to Eddie to hold for him.

Once more, Charlie slid down the bank, took his pole from Eddie, and threw out his line. Eddie did so, too.

Once more, the boys squatted down and hoped for more bites; once more, there was a small swirl in the water, and both boy's hooks were attacked at the same time, only this time Eddie overbalanced and splash, in he went.

Charlie flipped his fish up onto the bank and grabbed Eddie's collar. It wasn't deep, but it was slippery, and there wasn't much to grab onto.

Eddie came up, grinning. "Hey Charlie, I didn't drop my pole, and it's a whopper."

Charlie dragged Eddie up the bank while he held on to a branch. Eddie sat dripping on a rock and handed Charlie the fishing pole with the fish still bouncing on the end. "Eddie, did you see the size of this chap? Cor! It's huge," gasped Charlie. "I don't think I've seen one this big. It's not a bream. I think they call these flatheads, and they have big barbs on the side of them, so be careful."

Charlie scurried up the bank and held the pole down to Eddie to pull himself up with. They decided not to take this one off the hook as they were not going to be able to sneak in with Eddie dripping wet, and they did not want to get spiked. The fish wiggled and flipped but stayed on the hook. It was so big that Charlie had trouble holding it. He said, "If we wrapped the line around the pole, we could each carry an end of the pole. I'll carry my two bream, and you carry yours; that way, we should be able to make it home easily."

The boys left the bush protection and made straight for home. There was no sneaking around; they just marched straight up to the house and straight for Dar.

Charles saw the two boys coming from the direction of the river and inwardly smiled. Knowing that they were not supposed to fish on Sunday and knowing it was really the only time they got. He would have to sound angry but thought, "No, I won't punish them severely."

"Well, my lads, what you have got there? One, two, three very nice bream and what's that? Wow, that is one huge flathead. Eddie, it's nearly as big as you."

With a big smile on his face, Eddie proudly boasted, "Dar, it was so big it pulled me in. I'm sorry that we snuck out, but I won't get to go fishing for a while, and I asked Charlie to take me. I wouldna gone alone. I know it's too dangerous, Dar."

Charles bent over and lifted the big fish with some difficulty. "Boys, there will have to be some punishment, but no, not a belting; that's too harsh. You can choose your own punishment, but it has to be worthy of what you have done. Charlie, you carry those three into Mama, and I'll bring this fellow in. We'll let her into the secret, but don't tell the little ones."

The three Lockleys walked into the house, Eddie still dripping. Charles and Charlie placed the four fish, two still flipping, onto the kitchen bench.

Sally Lockley turned around and was just about to say something when Charles said, "Sal, let's consider these as a farewell dinner from the good Lord. Eddie and Charlie have been on what will be their last adventure for a little while, and I've let them choose their punishment, but I'm not going to throw these four beauties away because it's Sunday. Let's eat the evidence for dinner as there are only the eight of us, and no one else will know."

Sally looked at her husband lovingly, knowing that she should be angry, but also secretly, she was thrilled, as she loved fresh fish.

"Eddie Lockley, you go and get off those wet clothes. Look at that puddle you have made of my clean floor." She sounded angry, but the boys knew her well and knew that it was for the younger children that she sounded gruff. She turned back to what she was doing, and they saw her smiling.

Eddie quickly peeled off his clothes right there, down to his smalls, then grabbed up the sodden bundle and went outside to the wash bucket.

Charles and Charlie eventually got the flathead off the hook and despatched both it and the bream. Charles carried the flathead outside and "thwack," cut off the head with the axe. He did not want anyone to get spiked with those nasty barbs. Charlie pulled out his knife from the sheath on his belt and started scaling the bream on the kitchen bench, only for his Mama to see what he was doing. "Stop that this minute, young man."

Charlie stopped and looked at his Mama. "Oh Mama, I'm sorry, I didn't think. I'll finish this outside." He bent down and started picking up all the scales from all over the kitchen floor and table.

"Oh, be off with you, son," said Sal.

Charlie grabbed the three bream, his knife and a big plate and left the kitchen grinning. As he reached the door, he looked over his shoulder and said, "Thanks, Mama, I'm really sorry."

Sal could hear lots of water splashing, knowing that there would be a mess to clean up out there, too. She was just happy that her boys and family were all well. She wasn't looking forward to Eddie leaving, but oh, what an opportunity. She was sad that Charlie couldn't go too, but he could work with Mr. Tindale and get some smithing skills. She could hear Charles discussing their choice of punishment, and after much discussion, they thought that they would sit on the verandah for the afternoon and card wool, making rolls of wool for spinning later. Sal knew they hated doing this as they would rather be active. Sally heard the back door open, and she turned around to see two clean, wet boys and four cleaned fish.

Charles was nowhere to be seen, but she could still hear him outside.

Sal said, "Charlie, you put those fish on the big china plate and cover them with a bit of salt and a wet cloth. I'll get to them soon. Eddie, you go and pull on Father's work shirt and hang your clothes."

Eddie ducked out of the room while saying, "Clothes are washed and hung in the sun, Mama; they shouldn't take long to dry in this heat." He came back moments later in an oversized shirt that dragged on the floor. He giggled. "Mama, it's a bit big."

Sally turned around and smiled at him, "Come here, silly, I'll help." She rolled up the sleeves for him, found a short length of rope and tied it around his waist. "That will have to do you until your own clothes are dry. I've nearly finished your two new shirts to take with you, but you're not putting those on now. Go find Charlie and get started on whatever punishment you've worked out with Dar."

Eddie said, "Mama, Charlie and me, we thought that we'd sit with you on the verandah and do some wool ready for you to spin. We's not gonna be together much for a bit and, even though it's punishment. We's thought it'd be nice. Also, it's hot." Eddie went and dragged out a big brown bag, picked up an empty basket as well, and stopped to collect some big wire combs. Eddie had been carding wool for his Mama for as long as he could remember. It wasn't a horrible job, as it smelt nice and, well, sheepy, but it was a hot job and not one he usually would have chosen on a hot summer afternoon. So therefore, it was punishment but also a job that needed to be done.

He settled himself on the corner of the verandah where there was a gentle breeze. The heat wasn't so fierce today, but still hot. Some days, it was so hot just sitting still was an effort, but after the burn in the blacksmith's forge, this was a cool day for Eddie. Mama was lucky to have been able to get a fleece from Mrs. Macarthur's farm. Sometimes it was nice to have Dar as the stores' keeper as it meant they had some special privileges, and this was one. They were lovely long staples of fleece with no burrs.

He placed the bag, which was nearly as tall as he was, against the wall and let it fall over. He reached in and grabbed a big handful of scruffy fleece and pulled. He teased out the twigs and placed them aside so they could later be burnt, then carefully pulled out lengths of the fleece and placed them on the carding comb. He did this a few times until all the comb was covered, then, with the other side on top, pulled them in opposite directions. The wool was supple in the heat, and making these fluffy balls of wool for Mama was necessary. It was work, but it meant they would have warm sweaters when it got cold. Usually, Eddie would be doing this in winter when the wool was cold, and it was hard work. Today, in this heat, all the grease in the fleece was soft and much more manageable.

Shortly, Charlie joined him on the verandah, and the two sat there chatting happily, both with carding combs making many rolls of fluffy wool.

Soon, the little ones joined them. Liza, Anna, Wills and lastly, Luke toddled out after them all. Lukie wanted to play with the balls, and Charlie kept having to pull him away from the basket. He was getting frustrated. Finally, they gave him a fistful to play with.

"Oh, Anna, keep baby away from these. Put him on the swing, will you," said Charlie.

Six-year-old Anna grabbed Luke's hand and walked up the verandah a bit further. Dar had made a swing for the little ones, and it hung on the verandah under cover from the sun and rain. It was like a horse and was made in two bits. With two branches as handles and footrests, Luke loved and would spend hours "riding horsey." Mama had put some possum skin on the seat, and it looked like a saddle.

Seven-year-old Liza lifted Luke onto the seat and pushed him to Anna. The verandah was full of giggles and chatter of the six children. Luke would often give a whoop of joy. Wills was helping his two big brothers by pulling out the handfuls of fleece. He was an old hand at this as he often helped Mama with this job. He wasn't strong enough to card the wool yet, but he knew how to lay it on the combs and get it ready to do.

Charles stuck his head around the corner of the verandah and saw his brood all well occupied. He decided that he'd continue working on his surprise for Eddie as all was well there. Something to take with him to school. Charles was a skilled leatherworker, and he decided to make him a special school satchel to carry his school books. Although he'd never bothered with school much, he could read and write well enough. Even his handwriting was quite neat. His mother had insisted, but he just wasn't interested. So he often just didn't go to school. The village children he played with weren't pushed, but his mother always wanted better for him. He'd had a friendly lady teacher who explained the value of learning, and he'd seemed to have an aptitude for retaining knowledge and was reasonably proficient. He just didn't manage to get there often, so his education was limited; thankfully, he'd liked figures, and it was why he was able to keep track of the stores for the town. His problem was mostly lack of practice. Eddie would have an opportunity that he never did. He knew other boys would have a satchel, and Bill made one for Timmy out of rawhide.

Charles had bought a tanned Kangaroo skin and cut, punched, stamped and coloured it until it not only shone but was a truly beautiful piece of work. Better than he could have bought. It was a satchel he would have been proud to carry himself. He had carved Eddie's name in it so no one could steal it from him. It also had a buckle on it from an old saddle that he'd polished until it glinted in the sunlight, and it was big enough to fit in quite a few books and other items he'd need for school. Charles knew that this was the last chance he'd get to finish it off as Eddie left this week.

The afternoon passed pleasantly, with all the children happily sitting on the verandah, Charles in the stables at his workbench and Sally in the kitchen. Unknown to the family, she had been able to obtain a fresh cut of mutton, and she'd been trimming it and preparing a farewell feast for Eddie. With the four fish, the boys had caught, the homegrown vegetables, and the mutton, they would sit down to a banquet rather than a stew from salt meat again.

Charlie and Eddie went to bed stuffed full and chose to sleep on the verandah as it was still quite hot.

Eddie leaned over to Charlie and whispered, "Thanks, Charlie, for coming fishing today. It has been a wonderful day. I'm going to miss this sort of fun."

Charlie tried to speak, but he choked up, so he just squeezed his little brother's hand. Eventually, he said, "I'll miss you too, bro, but you'll be back, and we'll have more adventures."

They lay listening to the cricket, cicadas, and frogs and drifted off to sleep.

Chapter 4   Final Days at the Forge

"Cor, what's they damned black cockatoos up to? Somethink disturbed them this morning. Must be a snake in the tree or somethink. Time to get up, though, Charlie." Ed groaned as the birds woke him.

The sun was peeking over the horizon. There was a pink cloud floating in the sky. Eddie lay on his blanket, soaking it all in, knowing he had to get up to get his chores done before work, but he was going to enjoy this moment.

At that moment, the ship's bell sounded, and he nudged Charlie again. "Charlie, wake up."

"Don't wanna. Leave me alone," mumbled Charlie.

"Bell's gone," said Eddie, "We gotta get movin'."

Groaning, Charlie rolled over and threw off his blanket, "I know, I know, but I was in the middle of a really good dream." He was up on his knees. "What's wrong with the cockies? Have they gone nuts or something? Who needs a ship's bell to wake up?" Charlie was grumpy and full of silly questions.

Eddie laughed and said, "Maybe there is a storm coming, or more than likely, they can smell smoke."

"Come on, Ed, get moving."

Eddie laughed. "Look who's talking."

Eddie scurried inside with his blanket, threw off his nightshirt, and pulled on his now-dry clothes and raced into the stables to muck them before Mama had breakfast ready.

Charlie followed, but more slowly. "Slow down, Ed." He picked up Eddie's blanket and nightshirt, folding his and Eddie's and placing them on the shelf where they were stored. He also donned his clothes and headed outside to do his chores. Charlie dunked his head in a bucket of water. He was now fully awake. He flicked his hair back, wiped his hands over his face and headed to the wood heap, saying, "The fire won't start itself, so I'd better get moving." He grabbed an arm full of split wood and kindling and headed back inside.

Even though it was summer, the only way to boil water or cook was on the wood stove, so they needed a fire. In the mornings, Charlie's first job was to light the kitchen fire and put on the kettle and a pot of water. He could hear the little children whispering not so quietly and knew that he only had moments before his father put his head around the corner and asked for his morning cuppa.

Charlie headed out to the stables. "Hey, Eddie, do you want some help? The wood is so dry that the fire almost started itself. I brought up extra water last night, so I can help if you like."

Eddie wasn't visible to Charlie, but he knew he was in there somewhere. He peered into the first stall; just Tess and her stall were done, then the next one was empty, so he kept moving down the stalls. "Empty. Empty. Eddie, where are you?" he said.

Sniffles were heard… "Eddie, is that you? You never cry. What sup mate?" said Charlie.

"Oh nuffin'," said Eddie, "I'm just going to miss all this. Who'd a thought, eh? I love these horses and this place. This isn't a chore; I jus' love them."

Charlie walked over to him, sat beside him in the straw, and then put a hand on his shoulder. "Come on, let me give you a hand this morning, just 'cause. You can eat, then get down to Mr. Tindale's early."

Eddie wiped his nose on his sleeve. "Thanks, Chip. That would be great."

"Don't call me that. I hate it. Mama is the only one who does," said Charlie. They got into the work and had the remaining stalls cleaned and a pile of dirty hay ready to take out to the garden. They filled the barrow and pushed it outside, unloading it in a heap next to all the previous morning's piles along the far side of the garden to weather before adding it on. That done, Charlie reached under his jacket, pulled out a handful of clean straw and wiped out the barrow before taking it back to the stable.

Charlie pushed it back, saying, "Hey Eddie, it's been nice doing this together, and quicker, too. Why didn't we think of this before…?"

Eddie shrugged and followed him up the path back to the shed. He ran ahead, opened the stable side door and held it for Charlie. "Thanks, Charlie; I always had trouble with doing that. Let's see what Mama has for breakfast." The boys ran back to the house, pausing briefly to wash in a bucket of water outside the door, and left there for the dogs. Wills heard them coming and opened the door for them. "Charlie, Ed, you should see what Mama has made for us all. She has saved up the eggs and has bartered for some smoked ham. I almost wished you'd go away more often, Eddie," said four-year-old Wills innocently.

The three boys stood at the kitchen door in awe of the smells wafting their way. Fried onion rings, too.

Eddie sniffed back more tears. "Mama, oh, thank you." He flew across the room and hugged his Mama.

Charles and Sally both looked up, and he smiled. "Sal, you were right. They didn't notice that we did not eat any eggs all week." Charles laughed and went back to reading the Gazette that the boat had brought up that morning. He could read it; his education was coming back to him. It was getting more comfortable the more he tried, so whenever he saw a paper, he'd grab it if possible. Sal rarely had a chance to read nowadays. She'd taught the children to write their names, but they had no paper and no books. They had to practise on a slate with chalk until it looked neat. Miss Elizabeth Marsden taught those she could, but not all could get to her classes. She'd taken on the Lockley's two oldest boys and Tim Miller.

The family settled down for another sumptuous feast and chatted all through the meal. Knowing that they all had a full day's work in front of them, they ate quickly and left for their various duties.

Eddie ran all the way up the hill to the forge and arrived breathless. Mr. Tindale laughed as he entered. "Whoah there, young Eddie, What's the rush?"

Eddie told him of the happenings of the past twenty-four hours in a rush. Mr. Tindale laughed again and listened in awe about the size of the fish he'd caught. Eddie hardly stopped for a breath; he just talked and talked all morning, even when pumping bellows at the very hot fire. They laughed and chatted until noon. Mr. Tindale put his hammer down and told Eddie to follow him.

Mr. Tindale walked out the door and called for Mrs. Tindale. She emerged from the door carrying a basket covered with a crisp white cloth. As it was summer, it was unbearably hot inside the buildings, and Mrs. Tindale had prepared a special picnic for the three of them. She walked over to the verandah of the house, where there was a sound of water running.

Eddie was amazed. Mr. Tindale had somehow made a waterfall running down the woven little branches off the verandah wall. It was very cool, with the breeze able to blow through it and cool the area. Eddie looked over the verandah, his eyes following the water as it ran into the drain before going into the shop and realised it was the water used in the forge. He was so hot after pumping the bellows all morning. The coolness of this spot was amazing. Although he'd washed his hands, he let the water trickle down his fingers and rubbed them over his little red face. He did this repeatedly until he'd cooled down. "Oh, Mr. Tindale, this is just magic. You are so clever," said Eddie admiringly.

Mrs. Tindale sat on a wicker chair and placed her basket on the verandah before her. "Eddie, I thought for your last meal for a while, we'd have a picnic. I have some boiled eggs and some cold mutton as well as some special cakes for you. It's just a little treat." Mrs. Tindale sighed as she looked at him. She so wished he belonged to them, but taking a deep breath, she caught herself and brightened her smile, saying, "Eddie, you've been such a great help to Mr. Tindale; it's the least I could do."

Eddie didn't know who to look at, Mr. Tindale, who had a massive grin on his face, or Mrs. Tindale, who was a bit teary. So he said nothing. He just grinned back at both of them, with a mouth full of cold boiled egg.

Mrs. Tindale then handed him a little cloth bag. Eddie opened it and gasped as it was full of his favourite biscuits. "Oh, Mrs. Tindale, what have I done to deserve these?" asked Eddie.

"It's for tomorrow, Eddie," said Mrs. Tindale. "It's not much, but I do know you love them so. Make sure you share them. We also have another surprise for you. Mr. Tindale is taking the day off and is going to Sydney Town with you. It will also give him the chance to see his sister, so you boys won't be travelling alone."

Eddie grinned and tried to say, "Fank you" through a mouthful of another egg. He swallowed. "Thank you so much. Do you really mean it? Are you really coming with us, Mr. Tindale? Seriously? I was wondering how we was gonna find our ways around Sydney Town and to your sister, Mr. Tindale. We were only talking about it yesterday," Eddie said gleefully.

Mr. Tindale rested against the wall of the house and said, "Never you mind, Eddie, your father and I have it all worked out, and I will accompany you both on the boat, stay overnight, and return on the following day. It will give me time to see my sister and settle you boys, and also obtain some items I need for work. Does this suit you young, sir?" Mr. Tindale was laughing. He saw utter relief across Eddie's face. "I'm sorry, Eddie, I should have told you earlier, but I didn't think we'd get all the orders finished. However, we finished the last of the nail orders this morning, and we have two more things to finish this afternoon, so young man, we'd better get cracking." He stood, bent over and lightly kissed the top of his wife's head and tousled Eddie's fair hair.

Eddie wiggled his fingers in the water wall again. Then, running the wet fingers through his hair, then over his face, he jumped off the verandah and scurried back into the forge.

Mr. Tindale and Eddie chatted about Sydney Town all afternoon until the last two jobs were finished. They spread the coal in the forge fire. Scattering them made the fire cool quickly, and the coal would then relight quickly when a new fire was started in a couple of days. Eddie just stood and looked around. His mind absorbed all around him.

As Eddie was leaving, he said, "Thanks so much, Mr. Tindale. Thanks for taking me on when I was a kid, and thanks for the schooling, too. I hope I don't disappoint you. I've learnt so much from you." He turned to walk down the path and threw over his shoulder, "See you tomorrow morning." He stopped and turned again. "Mr. Tindale, I really do thank you." He ran back, gave him a quick hug and fled home.

Chapter 5   Down the River

Woken just before dawn by the rooster from down the road, Eddie flew out of bed, nearly treading on Charlie in the process. "Sorry, Charlie," he muttered as he raced out the back door. It was the last morning for a while that he'd be able to talk to the horses. "Hi, beautiful boy, move Bobbs; I've got to get in to clean you up." He pushed past the big horse and dragged in a bundle of clean straw, which he dumped in the far corner and then swept up the piles of dirty stuff with a big broom. When it was all near the stall door, he opened it enough to push the steaming pile out. He also pushed out the broom with a clatter and returned to the clean pile in the corner. He scattered this around the stall. Once satisfied, he picked up a brush and walked over to the enormous draught horse. "Hey, Seaweed, quit moving. I can't reach all of you anyway, but it doesn't help when you shinny around like that," Eddie spoke to the horse in a calm voice, not worried that someone would hear him but so that the horse would not be startled. After he'd brushed most of him, he put away the brush and left the stall. Next was the feed trough and fresh water. He knew this should have been first, but he also knew that Seaweed would not let him brush him unless the food was yet to come. Not so the other horses. He finished the rest of the stalls, spending a bit of extra time with each horse and giving each beast an extra cob of corn; it was his way of saying farewell.

Charlie came in after lighting the fire. "Hi, Ed. Anything I can help with?"

Eddie had just finished feeding the last horse and said, "Thanks, Charlie, I've just finished the last one; I just have to get rid of the muck. Wanna help with that?"

"Yeah, why not? Bring the barrow here; you hold it, and I'll fill it." Charlie could use the pitchfork easily and soon had most of the fouled straw in the barrow. Once the first few loads were in, Eddie grabbed the broom and a scoop to pick up the last of the muck. This done, Charlie handed the pitchfork to Eddie and grabbed the barrow.

Eddie stowed the broom on the wooden hooks but carried the fork and a rake and followed Charlie. The boys chatted happily while they emptied the barrow. Then they refilled it from one of the previous, now dried, piles and spread it around the vegetable patch. The chores done, and the boys returned to the house. Mama and the children would be up; breakfast would be waiting. They scrubbed their hands and faces with the water from a bucket outside the door. Although it was only about an hour after dawn, the day was already hot; the water was cool from the night and delightfully refreshing. "Come on, Ed, we'd better get moving before Dar comes looking for us," Charlie said. "You've got to get some food into you before you head off."

Eddie found the clean rag Mama hung at the back door for them. He rubbed his face so hard it was bright red. He emerged grinning broadly and said, "Race you." And quickly ducked inside before Charlie realised.

"Mornin', Mama, Mornin', Dar, jobs all done for the last time for a while, Charlie helped with the heavy stuff, and we put a load of old stuff on the vege patch too, so we're starvin'," he said breathlessly.

Charlie entered, also clean and shining from a rubbing on the cloth. "Clean hands, Mama, so we're ready to eat."

Sally ladled a big spoonful of cracked grain porridge into each of the four big bowls, two medium bowls and some into two little bowls. Anna took one of the small bowls and started feeding little Luke. Liza took the other one and, set it before Wills and handed him a funny bent spoon. Charlie had whittled this for him so he could feed himself, and Wills loved it.

"I cun do it, Liza, gimme it," said Wills. She handed Wills the spoon and watched him dip it in the bowl and see how hot it was. "Ooh, nice Mama, wots in it?"

Sal looked at her little son and said, "It's honey, Wills. Do you like it?"

He nodded, slurping it up.

"Look, there is some clotted cream, too. Would you like a bit?" Sally spooned some into each of the bowls; she then sat down and waited for everyone else to collect their bowls. Charles, sitting at the head of the table, waited until they were all seated, then bowed his head. He said Grace, giving thanks for a healthy family and food to eat, as he usually did before each meal; this time, he added, "… *and Lord God, we thank you for the opportunity ahead for young Eddie and ask that you keep him safe. Amen.*" He looked up and smiled at Eddie, who then almost attacked the porridge.

Sal could tell Charles was full of emotion and also that Eddie was barely holding it together, as was she. All the children chatted nonstop. Sal and Charles laughed occasionally and chipped into the conversation when asked a question. All knew that this would be the last full family meal for quite some time.

Sally rallied and hurried the smaller children. Wills finished his porridge and, banged down his spoon with a grin, and said, "More pees, Mama."

"No, not yet, Wills, maybe later; we all have to go and see Eddie onto the boat. Remember, he's going off to school today. Lukie, good boy, you ate it all up. Anna, thank you, and you're a good girl for keeping him clean."

All the older children scurried about carrying plates and washing them up. Liza and Anna were putting them away on the gingham cloth-covered shelves. This done, Charlie and Eddie went to finish getting all of Eddie's things together and trying to fit them into his bag. The clothes were no problem; he didn't have many, a few shirts, including the two new ones Mama had made him, his good church pants and his smalls. Mama had also put a little brand new Bible in the bottom and gave him instructions to read it often and remember to take it with him to church. He also packed his one woollen jacket as it could get cold. He had neither shoes nor socks, so he didn't need to pack these. The things he could not fit in were some school things and his blanket. He was just heading off to find some string or rope when he heard his father's footsteps.

"Eddie, I have something for you. I've been working on it for a while and finished it last night. I do hope it's big enough for you for school." Charles handed Eddie the kangaroo leather school satchel he'd made for him.

Eddie held it and teared up. He threw himself at his father and wrapped his arms around him, "Oh, Dar. It's perfect. I never seen'd one near as good, even in the shops. I bet the other boys will be jealous of me. Now, I won't need to tie my books in some rope. I was just gonna go find some. Oh, Dar, you dunno just what this means. I won't stick out at school. Oh, Dar, thank you so much." Eddie hugged him again.

"Eddie, I thought you'd like to know that Timmy's Pa has also made him one. Silly, but it is the sort of thing the other boys will tease you about if you don't have the proper bag. Remember also, Eddie, that we have not bought these, we have no money for that, and some boys at school do not have a satchel or even a jacket. So you remember, you and Timmy will have to look out for them too. When you think you're worse off, remember there will always be someone worse than you." Charles continued, "The thing is, I'm glad that you are not going alone, and not just going with someone, but your best friend. Most other boys will have no one. So you remember to be kind, just as nice as you always are."

Charles was proud of his children; both Charlie and Eddie were sons of whom any parent would have been proud. They rarely got themselves into trouble, and if they did, they had a good excuse, or it was to provide the family with food.

"Charlie, I saw you sitting over there. I know that it's sad you can't go too, but we do not have enough money to send two children, and Eddie, being younger, will find it easier to learn. What's more, I need you here, and you need to learn to run the Inn. We'll work out a way you can get to Miss

Elizabeth's school more often. I'm sure Eddie will teach you when he returns, and we will try to get some slates and chalk so we can all learn properly. What do you think?"

Charlie said, "Oh, Dar, I do know. I'm not real sure I'd like to go away. Nah, Ed can have this for himself. I am happy to stay and help; don't you worry about me; I'm good with it."

Charlie had been sitting in the corner watching Eddie for a bit, chipping in occasionally with titbits of conversation. "Dar, I'm just a bit sad that he's going 'cause I'll miss him. We get on so good. Wills and Lukie are a bit young to hang around with. Believe it or not, he watches for me, and I'll miss him."

Charles walked over to Charlie, who was sitting on a seat in the far corner of the room. He put his arm around the boy and said, "I know, mate, we all will. I'll just have to make more time to spend with you. I'll try to get someone to help out with the outside chores and gardening; then, you can learn the ropes on how to take over the Inn. Would you like that? You will be helping Mr. Tindale too, so you will be busy, as well as schooling yourself."

"I look forward to it, Dar. I always liked the smithy, and e'en though it's hot, I can't wait until Wednesday when he comes back and fires it up again." Charlie still didn't look too excited.

Charles stood up from the bed. "Well, boys, now Eddie is packed, we'd better be off. Let me take that, Ed. You'll have it for the rest of the day."

He picked up the duffle bag his mother made and the blanket, leaving Eddie to carry the new satchel, now stuffed with all the school things. They walked into the now quiet kitchen and out the back door and headed toward the wharf. As they were making their way down the grassy slope, they saw the boat coming up the river towards them.

It was now about 9 o'clock, and the sun was up and gaining strength. Trickles of perspiration were already running down Sally's back and beading on her forehead. Her hand was also sweating as she was clutching Lukie's little hot hand as he toddled down toward the water. It was too hot to carry him, and she was thankful that his walking skills meant she didn't have to today. However, she held him firmly, as she was sure he'd head straight to the edge of the wharf if she let him go.

Fair-haired Charles, too, was feeling the heat. He'd learnt to wear a flat straw hat when he was working outside. He still burnt easily. He didn't look forward to moving all the barrels into the cellar later today, but at least it was cooler down there and out of the sun.

The girls held Wills' hands. He walked down the slope between them. He was enjoying this unexpected outing without fully understanding what a "goodbye" was.

Charlie and Eddie stood quietly on the quay with the bags between them. The little ship edged closer to the wharf. There was much activity on board as the Captain readied the rope to throw to the waiting hand on the jetty. The ferry was tied off, front and back, and the gangplank lowered. The passengers on board collected their bags and got off in an orderly fashion. Charlie and Eddie watched as the gangplank bounced as one particularly heavy passenger went "clop, clop, clop" down the gangplank.

"Charlie, look at that," said Eddie quietly, "Do you think it's gonna break? If he's not careful, he'll be ending up in the drink." At that very moment, as he stepped onto the wharf, the gangplank fell off the edge of the ship. Thankfully, the crew on the wharf were watching and saw it moving and grabbed it before it fell into the water.

"Well, that was close. Mr. Falconer-Meade, you're lucky you could've been a goner," said the deckhand. He and one of the crew grabbed the plank and put it back on the edge of the boat. The rest of the passengers alighted without incident.

He was a big man. He turned to Charles and said, "Hey, sir, where can I get a bed for the night? I'm only here for the night before I have to get the coach to Windsor. I'm looking for a person by the name of Fishbon. You don't know him by any chance?" The big man was bright red and puffing, possibly because it was so hot and perhaps because of the incident on the boat ramp.

"I'll come and chat in a bit, sir, but we have to catch the ferry." Charles turned to walk down to the boat.

The ten-minute bell rang, and the boat was readying to leave.

Charles turned around and pointed to Bill Miller, who was just walking down the grass embankment with the family. Charles said, "That man over there has a bed, and you might be able to stay with him at the Rear Admiral Duncan Inn. I've only got hammocks for visitors."

Bill Miller, at that moment, stepped on the wharf and was instantly accosted by the big man. "Sir, I believe you might have a bed for the night," the big man said. "Can you help me?"

Bill, who was much more concerned with getting Timmy on the boat, was a little frustrated over this. This was not the time he wanted to deal with some stranger, so he turned to him and said, "If you wait in the shade and, I'll be here in a bit. I'll come and talk to you after I put my boy on the boat. I won't be long; the boat will be only here for ten minutes. Looks like you could do with the rest anyway." With that, Bill picked up Tim's bag and walked away. The big man stepped off the wharf and gratefully sank onto a log seat under a tree.

Molly Miller and Sal Lockley gave each other a quick hug and said hello. Bill and Charles shook hands.

With ten children now on the wharf, the four parents had to keep an eye out.

Baby Ellen was on Molly's hip, but Luke, Sam, Gracie and Wills were shuffling around, and somebody had to keep hold of them at all times. With five children under six, they had to be watched continuously.

Liza and Annie watched Wills and Luke, but Sam and Gracie were heading towards the wharf's edge.

That moment, Timmy looked up and realised how close they were to the edge; he grabbed the backs of each of their shirts.

"Cor, that was close," says Eddie.

"Glad I saw them; they are little escape artists; those two are double trouble, can't take your eyes off them for a moment. They'll be in one scrape after another; don't know what Pa and Ma are gonna do without me." Timmy sighed.

Timmy turned back to Eddie and said, "Nice satchel, Eddie. Did your Dar make it for ya? Look what my Pa made from me. Like yours, Pa made it strong, so they should do us for a while. He got the leather from Mr. Ellis. Looks like they are both roo skin."

With precious minutes ticking by, Bill and Charles hugged their boys. The boys, in turn, hugged all their brothers and sisters, and lastly, they hugged their mothers; both were teary.

Mr. and Mrs. Tindale arrived at the wharf with Mrs. Tindale carrying a large basket and a bag; Mr. Tindale had his small brown leather suitcase. They greeted everyone, all the men shaking hands, and Mr. Tindale shook hands with Eddie and Timmy. "Are you ready, boys, for a big adventure? Because that's how you've got to look at it. You have to both work hard and remember that there'll be lots of time for fun. Mrs. Tindale and I will try and come up sometime to show you around Sydney Town. You'll notice a lot more people there than there are here, but you'll soon get the hang of it."

With this, he turned around and kissed his wife's cheek. "See you in two days, Pet," he said, and he took the basket from her, picked up his brown bag and headed towards the gangplank.

Eddie and Timmy grabbed their bags and followed hard on his heels. Once on board, they stowed their bags in the cabin and found a place along the railing so they could still see their families.

They sat watching the scuffling of the Captain as the gangplank was stowed, ropes cast off, and the boat pushed away from the wharf with a long pole. The little steamer ship left the wharf. Thankfully, now the tide was running out; it was carrying the boat with it. It was going to be a slow trip back to Sydney Town unless the onshore breeze died down. The boys didn't mind. They had never been on a boat before, and Mr. Tindale made them feel comfortable and safe. He put a hand on each shoulder, drawing them close.

Eddie could see that the family were still on the wharf. He waved, but he could also see a familiar figure on the top of the grassy embankment, that of Lieutenant Simmons. He wasn't watching the boat; he was looking at

Charlie and knew there was now nothing he could do. Dar and Mr. Tindale now both knew what was going on and that they would keep a better eye on him. Keeping him busy and out of the way was the best thing that he could do, and Charlie would certainly be kept busy. He'd be working with Mr. Tindale at the blacksmith's, he'd be learning how to run the pub, and he had all the everyday chores to do, as well as Eddie's.

As the boat reached a bend in the river, the family started to leave the wharf. Charles, Sal, Bill, Molly and the children turned to go home.

Sally noticed Margaret Tindale alone on the wharf. "Mrs. Tindale, would you like to come and have a cuppa or cool drink with us?" She smiled at her.

"Thank you, you're so kind, dear; I'd love that. I'd love to help with the children, too. A cool drink sounds perfect." Margaret Tindale picked up little Luke and carried him up the hill on her back.

The big man stood up and followed Bill and Molly Miller back to the inn. He was huffing and puffing in the heat, carrying his bag. Both Molly and Bill were busy with three children under four; they couldn't help him. His suitcase was certainly big for just one night, so they figured that he was on a long trip. Bill turned to the big man and said, "I hope you don't mind a horsehair mattress 'cause that's all we've got. They are slab beds but got no bugs, so you won't get bitten or nothin'. An' the sheets are crisp and clean. We're nothing fancy like Sydney Town, but we're the best in town. So don't expect a lot, but we got good food, and it's clean, so I hope you sleep well. You could go to the Union Hotel. The beds might be better, but she's rough. It's where most of the town's trouble occurs. Let's go up home now and have a cuppa tea and find somewhere shady to sit. We'll sort you out."

Bill and Molly led the way back to the Rear Admiral Duncan Inn. Everyone now had sweat running down their faces and backs; it was going to be a scorcher. The boys were lucky; they were on the boat, and there was a sea breeze. Sal looked back from the top of the hill to see if she could see the ferry, and she could see the top of the mast and a belch of smoke just above the tops of the trees. She stood looking for a while, as did Bill and Molly and the children.

The big man had found a tree and was standing in the shade; he did this whenever possible. "Is it far to this Inn, sir?" said the big man.

Bill turned and looked at him and saw that this man was struggling in the heat, and said, "It's only a couple of blocks; can you cope? I can ask Charles to borrow the cart if you can't. What'd you say?"

Puffing, the big man said, "I'll be right. I can do it," and proceeded to walk in the direction that Bill pointed.

The boat was now not visible behind the taller mangrove trees, so the young family quickly caught up with the big man who had not yet introduced himself. He looked like some important government man, and being an ex-convict, Bill decided that whoever he was, he'd better be nice to him.

The trip back to the inn was slow, not just because of the big man but because little two-year-old Sam had decided he wanted to walk. Bill took the bag from the passenger. It was hot, it was dusty, and everyone was thirsty by the time they reached the Inn.

Molly put little Ellen in the basket, and she lay straight down and went to sleep. "Poor mite, she's worn out by the heat," said Molly. "How about I get everybody something cool to drink? Would you like something, sir, a long cool drink? I have a big jug of lemon myrtle and Lilli Pilli water in the pantry. It's made with local honey, and the children say it's delicious. It's certainly refreshing." She poured three big mugs and two small ones. She handed one each to Bill and the big man, and they all sat down in the cool kitchen. Molly made Gracie and Sam sit on the floor and handed them their cups.

The big man initially sipped the cool drink, then drank deeply, enjoying every mouthful. He finished his mug very quickly and asked if he could have another. "This truly is delicious," said the big man, "what's in it?"

Molly said, "The local people eat this funny fruit as big as your finger and green. It has little balls of pulp in it and tastes a bit like lime, so I juice them, then heat the juice with some honey and these Lilli Pilli fruits and mix it with water. The children love it, and it's refreshing. It's easy to keep cool in the pantry, too. I keep it in a big ginger beer keg, so there's plenty more if you want it." She handed him a second mug full and watched as he drank it.

He seemed some shades paler now than the red he was when he first arrived. He had caught his breath. "I should introduce myself. My name is Falconer-Meade. I have come to find someone." He took another gulp. "Thanks, ma'am; now I do feel better. I was beginning to feel that I was a goner. I don't cope with heat well, and today is hot, extremely hot. I wish to meet Mr. Fishbon. Any ideas where I can find him?"

Bill said, "There's a Mr. Fish-something up in Marsden Street that could be him. He's only been here a week, but I heard George talking about him at the bar last night. My friend George is here to meet somebody from the Hawkesbury River. Something about some message from home. I'll go and see if anyone knows where he's staying." They went into the taproom.

The Rear Admiral Duncan Inn was much bigger than the Jolly Sailor and had two floors. The taproom was a long room that took the whole width of the building. It was surrounded by windows, which today were all open. The ground floor was built of stone, the top floor of timber; the kitchen was joined to the taproom by a short corridor. Off this was a narrow staircase down to the cellar. It was built on the side of a hill. There was a second door into the cellar from a narrow lane where the carts could unload the kegs. The family did not have to go past all the men drinking in the bar. Molly was able to keep the children away from the men. She suggested that the man follow Bill and talk to the men in the taproom, as they may have information on Mr. Fishbon.

Mr. Falconer-Meade stood up, bowed slightly and said, Thank you to Molly, not only for the cooling drink but also the information and then followed Bill down the corridor into the taproom.

Molly heard the men's voices get louder as the door opened, then quieten again. She thought to herself, "I'd love to see the look on their faces when they see that giant of a gentleman walk into their bar."

In the heat of the day, Molly still had to prepare meals, so she started the fire to get it hot enough to cook the bread and midday meal. She checked the loaves that she had set to prove last night; she placed them near the oven. It was so hot that they were nearly spilling over the top, and she wondered whether they should be knocked down and let rise again but knew there wasn't time. With the dry timber, the fire roared into life, and she placed the tins in the oven.

Gracie and Sam were still sitting on the kitchen floor, playing with the ball. Rolling it back and forwards to each other, it was too hot to do anything else, and the floor was lovely and cool. Molly wondered what Tim was doing, how far up the river the boat had gone, and how he was enjoying the trip.

Sally was in her kitchen a few blocks further down the street; she was thinking the same thing only about Eddie; both were already missing their boys. Margaret Tindale was sitting at the kitchen table with her, drinking tea.

Sally realised how lonely she was. She had Luke up on her lap and enjoyed the childish cuddles that only a baby can give.

"Oh, Mrs. Lockley, you are so blessed. We could never have children. We prayed, but it just never happened." She bent and kissed the top of his fair head.

"Please call me Sal. Everyone does." She looked into the other lady's face. "Mrs. Tindale, Margaret, I'd be honoured if you would come as often as you wish. I'd love the company, too."

Meanwhile, on board, the little ship, the two boys and Mr. Tindale enjoyed every moment of this adventure. Over the last few months, Mr. Tindale made the trip often now that the ferry was a steamship. He introduced them to Captain Stephen Roberts.

Eddie recognised him as the Captain he had waved to most days.

Mr. Tindale pointed out landmarks, bays and houses, told the boys what the birds were and instructed them what the sailors were doing on other ships. They were well out of the tidal section of the river. In the bay, the wind was coming just about straight towards them. If they had been in a sailboat, they would have had to tack down the harbour. What should've been at least a four-hour trip on a sailboat was only going to take a couple of hours. On the nearly new paddle steamer, less than two, if the wind was behind them. The boat also had a mast and could carry a sail. Today, they could head straight down the harbour, but they would not use the sail today. The boys were having an adventure. Everything was new, and Mr. Tindale knew so much about everything, and he didn't mind answering their questions. Mr. Tindale said, "Boys, boys, let me catch my breath. Let me answer one question before you ask the next one."

They all laughed. The wind was picking up, now turning from the North-East. They could feel it buffeting the little boat.

The Captain yelled, "Thomas. Bring those boys here. You're the only passengers on board, and I'm sure they'd like to steer for a bit. How about it, boys?"

Mr. Tindale nodded his head and said the boys could go. "You would like to, wouldn't you, boys? I would've loved to at your age. Off you both go."

Eddie and Timmy couldn't believe it; they scrambled up to the Captain and, one at a time, were allowed to take turns in steering the ship.

Eddie found that he could feel the wind pulling the steering wheel, making the boat slew to one side. When the wind blew a little harder, he found it hard to hold the wheel. "Captain, can you just put one hand on the wheel as it is so heavy, and I'm not very strong," said Eddie. "Timmy, you're gonna need some help doing this, but ooh, feels good; you can feel the wind, and you can feel the boat move."

Timmy was bouncing around from one foot to the other, obviously anxiously awaiting his turn. "Eddie, do you think we can do it together? You think we can both hold on as I don't think I can hold it myself, but I so wanna have a go."

Eddie, standing behind the wheel stepped to the side and said, "Yes, come on, Timmy, we can do it together."

The Captain, standing behind both boys, holding onto the top of the wheel, just grinned. He loved kids, he had seven himself, but they were grown and left home. Whenever there were children on board, he let them steer. It was even better when the sail was up.

They were entering the widest part of the harbour, and the wind changed direction.

There was a shout from Mr. Tindale. "Whale Ho!"

The Captain shouted, "Thomas, quick. Grab them." To the boys, he said, "Quick! I have to steer around it. It could knock us over."

The boys quickly scampered back down to Mr. Tindale, who was standing at the railing holding out his hands. Mr. Tindale placed them at the railing in front of him and put his arms on either side of them. This stopped them from moving as the ship hit the waves. It also meant that they could concentrate on watching the whales.

"Where are they?" said Timmy. "I can't see any whales. What's a whale anyway? I never saw one before." Timmy was looking at the water in front of him and looking for some big fish.

Mr. Tindale tapped him on the shoulder and pointed, "Tim, over there, look. See that big black thing in the water; that's a whale."

"Cor, no! That's an island, isn't it?" he said. "Cor, no, it's gone." Tim stood in awe at where the big fish had been.

Mr. Tindale then pointed to more further away, "Eddie, Tim, look, there's more. Oh, look, it's jumping."

The Captain was listening as he yelled, "That's called breaching. I've seen them do that, but not often inside the heads, let alone in the harbour. You're lucky. Never seen them do that in here before; they must know you boys are on board."

Mr. Tindale exclaimed, "Wow, look there, there's a baby one; I bet that it's just been born."

The boys scrambled over to the other side of the little boat. Mr. Tindale followed more slowly. They all stood watching the whales and saw the newborn baby whale a few more times until the little boat had moved further down the bay.

"Cor," said Eddie, "It's huge. Are you sure that's a baby?"

They saw a couple give a big spurt of water. Then they were gone. A few minutes later, they were seen some distance away.

Some gulls landed on the mast, and a bigger white bird was seen to land on the water. It landed on its feet, skidding to a landing.

The boys watched, intrigued and laughed as they watched one try to take off again. It ran on the water before gaining flight.

Soon, the little boat turned again into the lee of a headland, and the wind died down. They had a few stops to make before Sydney.

Mr. Tindale thought this would be a good time to lift the cover off the basket. He wondered what goodies his Margaret had placed in it for the trip. The first thing he saw was a large container of the boys' favourite cookies. He knew she had included these. Next was a rag tied in a knot; once opened, he found it was full of hard-boiled eggs. This, he also knew, was Eddie's favourite thing. He kept digging and found what he was looking for, a crisp, clean cloth, slightly damp, and with a cloth wrapped around a large pile of bread slices with fresh creamy butter on them and placed in pairs. There were also some slices of pickled beef, some brawn, as well as eggs.

Margaret had also included another little bundle of Lilli pillies, raw and sweet; they were delicious, and a small tub of honeycomb cubes covered with another little bowl. "Boys, are you hungry? Mrs. Tindale has given us a picnic, come and see what she has included."

Timmy was there first, "I'm famished, Mr. Tindale, oh she's so good. There wouldn't be any of her cookies, would there be?"

"Oh, Timmy, you have to eat good food before the treats, you know that, but yes, there are plenty for you both," said Mr. Tindale.

Timmy grinned at Eddie and said, "Ed, this is the best day ever, and I never want it to end." He turned to Mr. Tindale and said, "And sir, you're the bestest, too." He plonked himself right next to the basket and then made room for Eddie to sit next to him. "Ed, sit here."

Mr. Tindale handed out a slice of bread each and then told them the options from what was in the basket.

"I'll have some meat, please and an egg," said Eddie.

Timmy said, "I don't care, Mr. Tindale, I love it all." Timmy put out his hand and was given two eggs, one of which he handed to Eddie. Mr. Tindale handed a thick slice of pickled meat to Eddie.

Timmy cracked the egg on his head and sat peeling it, throwing the eggshell overboard. Once peeled, he nibbled off the end.

Mr. Tindale said, "No, look." He squashed his own peeled egg inside the folded bread and took a bite. Both boys followed suit, and all three sat munching their lunch. Eddie took a bite of the slice of meat alternately with his egg. Mr. Tindale finished his meal and reached into the basket for the cookies and fruit. He laid out the little parcel of fruit on his lap and handed some to each boy. "Eat up; Mrs. Tindale also included these for you. Look what else she has included for you." He pulled out the big jar of cookies.

With a "Coo" from Eddie and a "Wow" from Timmy, Mr. Tindale handed them each two cookies. "When you've finished these, Mrs. Tindale has included an apple for each of us. She bought some, especially for the trip. A real treat."

Thomas looked at the honey and then at the two small boys; there was no place to really wash them if they got it everywhere, so he decided that the honey could be given to Caro. It would be a treat for them all later. Once their immediate hunger was sated, they sat back and watched the passing bays, animals and boats. The boys sat one under each arm in the same place where they had eaten their meal. They fired questions at Mr. Tindale and the Captain all the rest of the way to Sydney. They made a few stops to collect or drop things off at various wharves, but no other passengers joined them. The rest of the trip to Sydney Town was full of new things to look at; the boys stayed close to Mr. Tindale as he explained all the different points of interest. He pointed out to them the new stone windmill with canvas sails. He explained how the entire top could swivel to catch the wind. There were shipbuilding wharves and dry docks or slip yards where a ship could be repaired. Arriving at the wharf at Sydney Cove, the dockworker threw the ropes and pulled the ferry in.

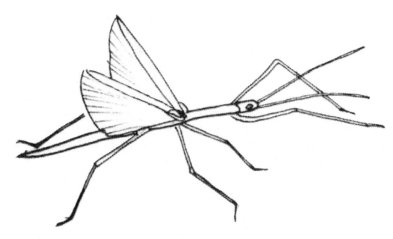

Chapter 6   Settling In

*T*hey lifted down the gangplank for the three passengers to alight.

The boys watched as they had at the wharf in Parramatta, but this time from the boat side.

Mr. Tindale pointed to his sister, Mrs. Evans and two younger boys, who were awaiting their arrival. She was excited to see her brother. The boys were hopping from one foot to the other, excited about the two new boys coming to live with them.

Eddie and Timmy collected their bags from inside the cabin and followed Mr. Tindale down the ramp onto the wharf. He greeted his sister with a laugh and a handshake, then a big bear hug, then greeted the two boys formally with a handshake, then bent down and grabbed them both, hugging them too, both boys laughing hard. Eddie and Tim stood back quietly, watching the family greeting.

Mr. Tindale turned around and introduced first his sister, then the two boys, Stevie and John. He explained that Phillip, the eldest lad, was at school and he'd meet them afterwards.

The happy group walked off up the hill along Pitt Street, Mrs. Evans on the arm of her brother. They lived in a new two-story stone house, a short walk to the school and everything else in town. Her husband was the captain of a supply ship; he enjoyed the space and comfort of home on his regular returns.

Sydney was a place of much activity. More than once, there was a yell from behind them. They all had to move quickly out of the way for a cart, a dray, or a carriage coming up from the wharves. It's just as well it had not been raining, or they could all have been covered in mud.

The four boys were chatting away with Eddie and Timmy, beginning to enjoy the adventure before them. As they walked up Pitt Street, they occasionally stopped to rest in the shade of a tree and put down their bags. Stevie told Eddie that they'd been given the day off from school to meet the "new" boys and show them around the town a bit.

Eddie and Timmy were so excited, looking around and asking many questions. After the slow walk up the hill, they arrived at the Evans household. The group had stopped at a large stone house set back slightly from the road. There was a large gum tree on the street, and the boys stood in the shade and caught their breath. Eddie and Tim stood looking amazed. All were looking forward to a cool drink.

Mr. Tindale and Mrs. Evans walked to the front door with the four boys following closely. A mob-capped girl opened the door and greeted them with a smile. The boys followed the adults into the cool hallway. The girl led the way into a large front room where she had drinks waiting for them all.

"Yummy, lilli pilli punch with honey, and it was even cool," thought Eddie. "Mrs. Tindale makes this too; only she also adds Lemon Myrtle leaves, giving it a lovely lemon flavour."

The boys all loved it, finishing the pitcher quickly. The boys discovered they, too, had a cellar and were able to keep large pitchers of water cool. Eddie asked the girl's name and found that it was Effy, and she was the maid. Timmy's eyes grew,

He turned to John and said, "You have a maid?"

John said, "Oh yes, but she's a convict; lots of people have them."

Timmy and Eddie just looked at each other, thinking they had really 'gone up in the world'.

Eddie thought that at least there were no convict chain gangs here. He saw them all too often in Parramatta, as did Timmy. He had even seen them flogged. He heard that there were still convicts in the sandstone quarries, and they had to do hard labour although they weren't chained together. They were often skilled craftsmen and masons who had committed crimes.

After Effy had served the drinks, she asked Eddie and Timmy to follow her. She took them up to their room. Stevie and John were hard on their heels, chatting all the way. They had each grabbed a bag on their way out of the room. All five young people headed upstairs.

Effy led them up the turning staircase and opened a door into the front room. There were two sets of double bunks and a single bed in the large, airy room. It had a built-in cupboard along one wall and a large chest of drawers.

Stevie said, "Eddie, you and I get to have the top bunks and John and Timmy the bottom ones." They each had comfortable mattresses on them and colourful covers on the beds. Eddie and Timmy were stunned.

They usually had to share a bed with their siblings at home; it was more often a spot on the floor before the fireplace. In summer, it was a screened section of the verandah. They quickly unpacked their things; neither had much. They then joined the family downstairs.

Mr. Tindale and Mrs. Evans were still sitting in the front room chatting. Stevie and John were sitting on the floor, waiting for the other boys to finish and come downstairs. On their arrival, Stevie asked permission to show the two new boys around. All four boys went out to explore.

Stevie said, "Let's first go up to the school and meet Phil. His Latin lesson should be finished by now, so he can come with us."

They walked under the large gum tree and out onto the street. They dodged the carts of fruit and vegetable sellers. They often had to hop over the piles of mess on the dusty road.

The two Parramatta boys' shoeless feet were used to dodging the rocks and occasional piles of horse manure deposited on the road by passing horses. In the city, bullock wagons were passing every few minutes. There were many horses, carriages and gigs, not to mention the herds of stock that were being shepherded from the docks to the town markets. Small convict children with small wooden barrows and a flat wooden paddle had to go along the streets to collect the manure and take it to the Farm Cove dung heaps. Even so, there were so many animals that the job seemed never-ending.

The four boys walked further along Pitt Street and turned the corner into King Street. Their eyes were flicking everywhere.

A short way down this road, a few boys were emerging from what was the school.

Stevie and John waved, and one of the boys waved back. Phil looked happy as his Latin lesson was over, and he was looking forward to meeting Eddie, who was nearly the same age as he was. Timmy, aged almost nine, was in between Stevie, nine and John, eight.

Phil saw his little brothers and greeted them with glee. "I'm so glad that's over. I'm not sure why I have to learn Latin, but that's it for the day. Let's go home and dump this bag. My tongue is hanging out for a drink."
He then turned to Eddie and Timmy and greeted them, and welcomed them to Sydney. The group of boys almost danced back to the house, with the younger ones staying under the large gum tree in the shade, awaiting Phil's return.

Eddie was thinking to himself, "Latin, I have to learn Latin?" He was a little concerned. "Where am I ever going to use that?"

Phil bounced out the front door, having changed out of his school clothes. Phil suggested that they go down to Mrs. Macquarie's point and watch the harbour ships and boats. It was cool under the trees down there. It was just too hot to play ball or any other game. They walked down the hill towards the bay, then up the grassy slope to sit under the low headland's leafy tree. Phil and Stevie pointed out many of the new buildings. They sat watching the boats that were sailing on the harbour. There were people fishing, some collecting oysters on the rocks. Ladies were sitting under parasols watching the sailors unload the cargo, and a bullock team and large wagon, just about to leave the dock with a full load of goods for the Government Stores building.

Eddie quizzed Phil for information about the school.

Phil answered all his questions, telling him not to worry too much as Mr. Cape assessed each student and asked them where their skill level was. So he expected Eddie, Timmy and Stevie to be in the same class, if not John's class. Phil had been learning from his mum, and a teacher, Mr. Fishbon, started him on Latin before he left for Parramatta. So, he was more advanced than others of his age.

Phil said that there was a range of subjects. "There is Latin, of course, French and Greek; Mathematics; Debating, that's like planned arguing, and it's fun; Astronomy, that's studying the stars; they teach that because if you want to be a sailor, you need to be able to navigate. There's Geography, that's studying other countries, so it's good also if you want to be a sailor, you have to know the skies; and of course, there's Grammar, Spelling and Reading. Sounds horrible, but Mr. Cape makes them fun as we put this together and put on plays, you know, like acting."

He paused to look at Eddie's face as his jaw had dropped open.

Phil continued, "Last year, Mr. Fishbon sometimes came and taught Latin as a special teacher and some mathematics too, but they have so many students there now that Mr. Cape has had to bring in more teachers full-time. We have exams only once a year, in December, but they give spot tests every week." Phil said, "I love school, but not languages. Do you know that some words are 'girl' words and some are 'boy' words in some languages, but you get the hang of it after a while, and it's not that hard? It sounds stupid, really…." He shrugged his shoulders. "But that's why we go to school, I suppose."

Eddie was thinking to himself, "What have I got myself in for?" He said to Phil, "I thought it would be just be Reading, Writing and Mathematics; I don't know how much use I'll get out of Latin, French and them other ones you told me about… but I'll give it a go." He sighed, "That Mathematics, yeah, I can see the use of that, and the Reading and Writing too. I've already done some of them; I can see I'll need them. The Astronomy will be fun coz I love watching the stars, and I'd love to know more about them." Eddie sighed again.

Phil was lying on the ground next to him, chuckling. He had already decided he liked Eddie a lot. He was a game kid who'd go far in this life. Timmy, too, was a good kid. He hadn't said much to him yet, but he had confidence in him that boded well for school.

The school was not free, but it was cheap enough. Most students were free settlers or sailors' children. Mr. Cape allowed some of the street kids and convict's children to sit in the doorway listening in. Three boys often came: Ricky, Tad, and Will, who had a limp; they were nice boys but scruffy. They didn't hang around after class, so he couldn't find out much about them.

Mr. Cape had piles of slates and chalk for them to use. He told the teachers not to shoo these children away, as it would be the only education they would get. He was kind, and all the children adored him. He would not allow any talking in class. The repercussion for disobedience would be the cane across the knuckles. As that hurt, none of the children would misbehave, not even the street kids.

The five boys lay on the grass for some time, talking and getting to know one another. Stevie, Timmy, and John were a little further down the hill from the two older boys. Stevie was a wealth of knowledge about boats and people.

John knew all sorts of things about the plants, trees and crawly things. He loved bugs and anything that had wings.

Timmy said, "Look, John. What's that sitting on the stem of that tree trunk?" It was greeny-brown, and it looked like it was wobbling.

John was so excited. "Oh Timmy, look, it's a stick insect, and it's a boy one."

Timmy, intrigued, said, "Oh, come on, how do you know that?"

John said, "Because it's skinny, of course. The mummy ones are much bigger and fatter, so this one is a daddy one." John put his finger out and let it crawl onto his hand. It was a big one and was so large that it nearly reached his elbow. "They don't hurt, Tim; here, put out your hand."

Tim came closer, and John let the green creature walk onto Timmy's arm. "Oh eek, John, it tickles. No, it scratches."

Timmy was even brave enough to pat it.

Phil saw it and pointed it out to Eddie, who couldn't resist coming over and having a look, too. Phil very gently eased out one of the wings so he could show the boys. It was pink. The wing was small compared to the length of the insect, less than a quarter of the overall length. In awe of it, they decided to let it go back to the tree. John once again let it crawl back onto his arm and released it onto the tree.

Phil decided that it was time to go home, so the five boys reluctantly started moving down the hill to the docks to make the walk up the hill. It was still so hot. Eddie looked westward towards home; he could see puffs of smoke on the mountains to the West.

Back in Parramatta, Charlie realised how much he was already missing his little brother. Liza was helping, but because she was little and a girl, he had to help her more than she helped him, but she was some company.

"Oh, Liza," said Charlie, "thanks for helping with the chores; I suppose they will be left to us now that Eddie has gone."

Liza, who'd just collected the eggs, said, "Charlie, I'se just pleased to be able to help out. I'se not been big enough before. As you know, I help Mama wash and look after the little ones, but now I feel I am helping."

The heat of the day was overpowering. The sweat was trickling down the middle of her back.

Charlie, too, was sweating heavily as he finished mucking out the stables and taking it to the muck heap, then spreading some of the old fouled straw onto the vegetable garden.

Charlie called to Liza, "Hey, Liza, come and help water the vegetable garden. All the leaves have gone soft."

Liza came around the corner of the stable carrying a wooden pail sloshing with water. She had spilt more than half by the time she eventually arrived at the garden. "Sorry, Charlie, but I tried to carry more. I'll just have to make more trips." She put the half-full pail in front of Charlie and looked down apologetically.

Charlie had seen a damaged barrel that Dar had cut in half. He went to the stable and got it, dumping it at the end of the vegetable garden. "There, Liza, you bring along lots of half buckets of water and fill them; I'll do the watering, then we'll swap."

Liza ran off with the pail she had and started the job of filling the half barrel. At least she could run on the return trips. It was hot work, but she chatted nonstop as she worked.

Charlie found a bent beer mug and watered each precious plant. After a while, he'd drained the barrel and realised it would be easier to swap jobs. "The, Liza, come here, we'll swap jobs. You'll find this easier."

Liza came over to the barrel, and Charlie showed her what he was up to.

He picked up the wooden pail and walked off to the water trough. Charlie could easily carry full buckets of water and quickly filled the barrel for Liza and then continued to help her water the plants. This done, they walked back to the stable and washed up in the trough. Their feet were muddy, so they ended up jumping into the water trough fully clothed.

As they were giggling loudly, Sal heard them and came outside. Rather than get angry at them, she laughed. She had Anna and the two little boys with her.

Charlie and Liza were still sitting in the trough, although now quiet. Sal walked over to it, picked up Luke and sat him in Charlie's lap. Wills and Anna followed. Soon, all five children were enjoying a cool dip. Sal was nearly as wet as they all were. "Mama, you are soaked, but oh, isn't it nice and cool? It's been so hot today; I've had drips running down my back all day," Charlie said.

Liza, who was now dripping wet as she had just dunked her head underwater, said, "Well Ma, me feet was covered in mud after watering the sad veg'ables, so I needed a wash, as did my clothes."

Sally just laughed, "Why were the vegetables sad, poppet?"

"Acause their leaves were floppy like this..." she made a sad face.

Sal giggled; she loved enjoying some fun times with the children. They were all so fair that their almost white hair and fair skin was red. It had been such a hot, hot day; this was just what they all needed.

There was no breeze; although the sun was nearly at the horizon, it was still hot. It was so hot that Sal was worried that there could be fires. It had been dry for so long; all the leaves crunched as you walked. Every drop of water was precious. Sally mused aloud, "Is that smoke I smell?" She turned and looked west to see if there was anything visible.

Charlie hopped out of the tub and made sure that Anna and Liza watched the little boys and sped, still dripping, up the road to see if he could see any smoke. There was. The sunset was going to be marvellous, but it was not for a good reason. He turned back. "Mama, yes, there's smoke, but it's up on the hills. There's no wind, so let's hope it stays up there."

Sal was standing in the middle of the courtyard, looking worried. Sal sent Charlie into the taproom to get Charles and to tell the other men. Fire. How they hated these fires. There was no predicting where they would go or how far. The fun of the last few minutes evaporated as fast as the water. Charlie had already stopped dripping, and the girls were lifting the little boys out of the trough.

Sally said, "Liza, take the littlies to the verandah. Wait until they stop making puddles before you take them inside. Anna, can you help Liza start getting tea ready?"

Liza and Anna took the chubby little hands and slowly walked to the shady verandah. Luke tried to snatch his hand from Anna, but she held it firmly as she was used to him running off. Liza and Wills dawdled towards the shade of the tree at the end of the verandah, and Wills tried to crawl up onto the edge but couldn't quite make it. Liza gave him a boost, and he left soggy footprints along the wooden boards until he plonked himself down next to Mama's rocking chair. He looked very pleased with himself. Liza, then Anna and Luke joined them, making four puddles where they sat. Chatting and giggling away, they didn't understand the danger of fire. They were finally cool after a scorching day.

Charles had come outside with about five men who'd been inside with him. One was Mr. Falconer-Meade, the big man who'd arrived on the ferry. He'd walked down from the Rear Admiral Duncan Inn, where he would stay the night. He wanted to talk to Charles about trying to find Mr.

Fishbon. He was also sweating profusely. He still wore a jacket, and Sally took one look at him and got him to sit on the side of the large trough the children had just vacated. The other men had walked up the road to see where the fire was and check if there was any wind, for if so, the fire could grow fast. Charles sent Charlie to the military barracks a few blocks to inform them. Charlie didn't want to meet up with Lieutenant Simmons, so was dawdling on the hot Parramatta streets. As he walked, he heard a horse clip-clopping behind him, and he moved aside to let it pass before he realised it was Major Grace. Charlie was so relieved, as the Major was a good friend of his Dar's. Charlie greeted him and passed his Dar's message on.

Major Grace said, "Come on, lad, it's far too hot to walk; hop up, and I'll give you a lift back."

Charlie was up in a flash and holding on behind the Major. He turned the poor hot horse, who plodded back down to the Inn. Major Grace handed Charlie down, who went to the horse's head and held the bridle while the Major went to find his Dar. Charlie took the horse to the trough and gave it a long drink. Fires were not usually worrying, and it was common to see smoke from the aboriginal fires, but they did not usually light them when there was a strong wind or in scorching weather.

However, this was not a typical day, and the fire was now much more significant than a normal fire. He could see the curling plumes of red-black smoke already. It was growing by the minute.

Major Grace went to find Charles; he was in the taproom. "Lockley, you wanted to see me?"

Charles greeted Major Grace, "Hello, sir. Would you like a drink?" They sat on the verandah edge along with some of the other local identities.

Old Ted, one of the old timers, said, "I remember how it was so hot in the summer of '91 that the parrots and bats were falling dead from the trees. So many dead in the river that the freshwater was undrinkable."

Geordie Jim, the carrier, chipped in, "I remember when in '99 the woods between Sydney Town and Parramatta were completely on fire, the trees burnt to the tops, and every blade of grass was destroyed."

Charles and Major Grace discussed what could be done if the flames jumped the river at Emu Plains. Thankfully, the harvest was in; the stubble was burnt after the harvest. There was much-cleared land now between the mountains and the towns, but there were still pockets of bushland where the fire could take off again. Major Grace decided he'd better head back to Lancer Barracks and prepare the troops, as they were needed to fight the fire if it got close to town.

Charlie had been watching for him and, as he moved, had brought his horse over from the shady stables. The Major mounted and flicked Charlie a coin as thanks. "Here, lad, catch."

"Coo, Major, thanks heaps." Charlie said gleefully, "I hope the fire doesn't get over the river. It's hot enough today as it is. Don't want to be out fighting flames in this."

The Major rode back to the barracks.

Charlie took his newfound wealth in and handed it over to Sal. "Look, Mama, Major Grace gave me this."

Sally took the coin he offered, then handed it back. "Well, my little Chip…sorry, Charlie, I think it's time you started to save a bit, don't you? Who knows when you might need some money to buy something you want. Make this the first of your savings."

Charlie stood open-mouthed, looking down at the sixpence coin in his hand. He had a tin hidden in the stables. It would go in there. "Thanks, Mama," was all he could manage to say.

By the time Major Grace returned, news of the fire had reached the troops. They were beginning to prepare the drays with barrels and fill them with water. There were piles of hessian bags to soak and thick clothing to get ready. There was not much they could do if it got too big, but they knew that belting out the flames with wet bags was how they could at least protect some of the houses, the Church, and the Store. The rest would just have to burn. Government Store was the most important building, as it held the entire area's food reserve.

Over the years, they had seen the frequent fires the Aboriginal people lit. Initially, the Major had wondered why, but since living near the bush, he found that areas that had been burnt were less susceptible to the raging bushfires that tore through the landscape every summer. The Aboriginal people used fire to clear the bushland and make hunting easier; it was their way of caring for the land, and it worked.

Back at the Inn, Sal, Charles, and the children were also preparing for the possibility of fire. Filling empty kegs with water and putting old bags in more buckets filled with water so you could beat out flames and place them around the buildings, especially if the building had wooden shingle roofing. Being on the river was a bit safer, but there were always spot fires, which could be beaten out with the wet bags.

All the hay needed to be covered, and piles of dry manure dampened. The horses had to be readied for not only release if the stables burnt but if they were required for use. They had to be saddled or harnessed.

Charlie set about at least putting bridles on them all. "Well, that's one job done," he muttered.

Charles walked into the shed, "Well, my boy, there's not much else we can do now but wait. We need rain, and that would help, so pray. But it would need to be a deluge to put that fire out. It's hot enough for a storm, so let's hope we get one. If we get lightning, though, it will start more fires."

Sometimes, the waiting was the worst thing. The sun was still some hours away from setting, but the sky was already red, and the wind was now picking up.

The heat was stifling.

Luke was too hot even to wander off.

Liza had placed a bucket of water on the verandah, and the four small children were just playing in that, dipping in their hands and wiping their faces.

Charles and Charlie went outside to look at the sky and see how bad it was getting. The fire was turning the sky darker every minute they watched. It was a big one.

Chapter 7   Church and a Bush Fire

$\mathcal{E}$ddie, Tim, and the boys were finally settling down to bed. It was their first night in a new house, a new bed, and a new life. He was used to sleeping rough on the floor or curled up with his brothers and sisters, but to have a bed to himself was strange. It was also so hot. At home, when it was this bad, he could go outside and try to sleep on the verandah, but here, there was no verandah, and the windows were glass; although open, the room was still hot and stuffy.

John had fallen asleep as soon as he lay down, but the other boys had talked until Mrs. Evans had come in. "Okay, boys, that's enough talking for tonight. We must be up for church tomorrow, so please sleep now. My, it's hot in here, though. Phil, if you can't sleep, take the boys down to the basement; it's nice and cool in there."

Phil said, "Thanks, Ma, we might do that. Night!"

The other three echoed, "Night!" "Night." and "Night Ma."

Eddie could hear Steve tossing and turning and said to Phil, "Where's that basement? It's so hot."

Phil responded, "Grab a pillow and blanket; trust me, you'll need it."

Soon, there was a scuffling and the sound of four pairs of feet heading downstairs. There was a heavy door at the bottom of the stairs that Phil opened, and a draught of cool air met them.

"Oh," said Timmy, "it's almost cold down here. No wonder you said to bring a blanket. Now I'll be able to sleep." The four boys settled down and were soon fast asleep, wrapped tightly in their blankets.

The next morning, Effy greeted them with, "Good morning, everyone, it's time to get up. I'm getting the breakfast ready, so you have about ten minutes to prepare for church. Hurry."

Four sleepy boys groaned and sat up. Her bright, cheery wake-up call soon had them moving. They each grabbed their pillows and blankets and shot upstairs in a race. Mr. Tindale was met on the stairs and had to lean against the wall for the four speeding boys to pass.

He laughed. "At least you got some sleep last night. It was so hot that I almost joined you, but I'm past sleeping on the floor. Hurry, boys, or we'll all be late for church."

When the boys reached the bedroom, John was still asleep. The room had cooled a bit overnight but was still hot. Phil shook him, and he sleepily awoke. "Errr, is it morning already? I was having a nice dream about swimming," he said.

Phil reminded him, "It's Sunday, and if you want something to eat before church, you'd better get a scurry along." That got him out of bed in a flash, and soon, five freshly washed boys with combed hair dressed in clean clothes were sitting at the dinner table. Eddie and Tim had tried on Phil and Stevie's spare shoes the night before, and although they pinched a bit, they weren't too uncomfortable. They'd never worn shoes before, and they did not like the feel.

Mr. Tindale and Mrs. Evans were already there, and Mr. Tindale stood in his place to say grace. In a deep and respectful voice, Mr. Tindale intoned. *"Bless, O Father, Thy gifts to our use and us to Thy service, for Christ's sake. Amen."*

All said, "Amen." As he sat, Effy offered barley porridge to each and ladled it into their bowls. There was also a bowl of fresh thick cream and honey for a topping. The boys tucked in. Mr. Tindale and Mrs. Evans had a small bowl each, followed by some bread and some of Mrs. Tindale's Lilli Pilli Jam. "Oh, Thomas, Margaret's jam is delicious. Let her know how much I do love it," cooed Mrs. Evans.

"Yes, I'm spoilt," he said. "She is a great cook. I should be really fat. Just as well, I work hard. It burns it off."

The food was eaten, and the dishes were stacked by the boys to be washed later by Effy. The entire household left to go to church. Effy pulled the door shut after her. St James' church was a lovely stone building, but quite plain. There was some building going on behind it on most weekdays, but on Sundays, the area was quiet. Reverend Mr. Hall, the minister, was waiting outside and greeted everyone as they entered.

Mrs. Evans led the family to her pew. Reverend and Mrs. Hall and their five stepdaughters entered and went to their pew. The five boys giggled and were sushed by Mrs. Evans.

The girls were dressed in similar dresses and walked in height order, with the youngest walking behind her stepfather's father.

Reverend Hall stood aside when he reached the front. "In you go, girls and mind your manners." His wife followed them in, looking up and glaring at Mrs. Evans. Caroline mouthed "Sorry" to her friend.

Reverend Hall walked to the front and started the service. Mr. William Merritt both conducted the choir and played the organ. Everyone stood and sang the first hymn, Rock of Ages.

Eddie and Timmy couldn't help looking around while they were singing. The church had a different feel to St John's in Parramatta. This one didn't have pillars holding up the roof and was just one big building. You had to step up into the pews, which were enclosed in a sort of box. Everyone had their place to sit, and you had to wait until the gentry were seated before you could start. The hymn finished, and Reverend Mr. Hall continued the service with lots of prayers. Timmy was wiggling in his seat, then a waft spread and the nearby boys grabbed their noses.

"Eddie, I couldn't help it, sorry. I really couldn't," said poor Tim.

Mr. Tindale, with a smile on his face, shushed them. The odour reached the Hall girls, and one by one, they looked around at the boys just behind them.

Tim was sitting, head down, looking contrite. Mr. Tindale and Mrs. Evans looked at each other and just smiled. Next were the prayers, and they all knelt on the hard wooden kneelers. They were all used to it, but kneeling for so long was hard for small, active boys. John and Stevie flopped onto their heels. Mrs. Evans tapped their heads; they knelt up properly. The prayers were over, Phil said, "Phew" under his breath as he stood and sang the Te Deum. This was one of Eddie's favourites, and so he sang lustily. The other boys joined in and made a joyful noise to the Lord. The choir sounded heavenly. Eddie was in awe. The heat was building, and the smell of the sweaty bodies was getting hard to bear. Reverend Mr. Hall had yet to give the sermon. They all sat on the hard pews and listened for what seemed an age. Reverend Mr. Hall started. "The sermon for today is taken from 2 Corinthians 5:17. *Therefore if any man be in Christ, he is a new creature: old things are passed away; behold, all things are become new.*"

Eddie doesn't remember any more; his mind started wandering.

Reverend Mr. Hall went on and on and on. Timmy was hot and still needed to visit a privy. Phil, Eddie and Stevie were anxious for it to be over, and John had fallen asleep on his mother's lap. FINALLY, he finished.

Eddie thought, "I shouldn't feel like this. I pray to God. Mama said to keep my prayers short and to the point. God knew what I meant. Surely he can say what he means in ten minutes? Even Reverend Mr. Marsden didn't go on this long." It seemed an age Eddie turned to Phil. "I didn't know someone could talk about nothing for so long. It must be nearly lunchtime."

Phil smiled and whispered, "Welcome to my world; you'd better get used to it; he does this every week."

After Reverend Mr. Hall had finished giving any of the weekly notices, he then turned to Mr. Merritt. "If you could lead us in the last hymn, please, with the choir singing the first verse." This caught Eddie's attention. He loved singing; maybe he could sing with them.

Mr. Merritt affirmed with a bow of his head, lifted his arms above the keyboard and, while sort of conducting with his head, played *"Praise to the Lord the Almighty the King of Creation."*

The choir sang, and then, on the second verse, the boys and everyone else joined in. During the last verse, Reverend Mr. Hall walked down the aisle and stood outside the door to say goodbye. Mrs. Hall and the girls left first, then the other front pews' occupants, and finally, Mrs. Evans and Mr. Tindale led the boys outside. Effy, who had been sitting at the back with the other convicts, joined the family and suggested the boys hurry back with her so they could change into more relaxed play clothes.

Although it was still morning, it would be another sweltering day. Church had lasted over two hours. Very hard for small boys to sit still for that long, especially in the heat. There was the smell of smoke in the air and not a breath of wind. Surely, the rains had to come soon. The five boys and Effy hurried home to prepare the Sunday midday meal and the boys to change and dip in the cove. It was the last free day until the school week started, and all were keen to explore. They had decided on a trip to the park on the headland near Sydney Cove. There was a carved stone seat under the trees and a lovely swimming hole not far from it. This was a favourite haunt of the Evans boys on a hot Sunday afternoon. It soon became a favourite of the two Parramatta boys, too.

In Parramatta, Eddie and Timmy's families had sat through Reverend Marsden's long sermon and were sweltering in a breathless, hotter-than-normal church. The fire was getting more prominent, with a pall of smoke now visible and beginning to settle on the town. The weather was getting hotter. The ground was too hot for the children to stand on, so they sat under the big tree just outside the church, waiting for their parents. The grass was so dry it crackled. The leaves were falling from the gum trees. The smell of eucalyptus mixed with smoke was making eyes water. The family of magpies didn't move when the children joined them under the tree; they, too, sat panting, gasping for air. It was just too hot. Charlie still had to do his morning chores before church, as the animals still needed feeding and the stables needed mucking out, so he'd got up at dawn and had most of it done before the family were ready to leave. Liza had Luke sitting between her legs; he flopped back and lay down. She moved so he wasn't touching her.

Charles, Sal, Bill, and Molly were walking towards them with Major Grace. On Sundays, the taprooms were closed. It was as close to a day off as the men got. There were still people staying at the Inns, more at the Rear Admiral Duncan Inn than The Jolly Sailor. There was day staff who could help feed them.

They walked down to the river bank and sat in the shade of the new bridge. The new sandstone bridge still needed some finishing touches but was nearly complete. Under the new bridge, it was cooler than almost anywhere else in town. You could have a dip and then sit in the shade.

Thankfully, there were some trees along the river, too. It was a wonderful spot to spend a few precious hours. Charlie and his sisters, Liza and Anna, and Timmy's six-year-old sister Gracie, Anna's best friend, all paddled or swam in the salty water. They had seen sharks in this area before, so they didn't stay in the water long. Bill pointed out a snake swimming across the river, so after relaxing for some time, the families said farewell and returned to their homes.

Charles and Bill have been keeping their eyes on the smoke, which was getting darker and spreading. The fire was now coming over the top of the range and down the mountainside towards the town. Smoke was beginning to settle in the valley, and the heat was unbearable. Throughout the town, everyone was inside if possible. No one ventured out except to feed their animals, many of whom had been brought into the stables. Even the parrots were silent; the kookaburras were not laughing, and magpies were looking for water with their beaks open, panting. Such was the heat that many of the noisy flying foxes fell dead from their branches.

Major Grace was waiting on the verandah at the Inn when Charles and Sal arrived home. He had seen them at church, but they had gone before he could talk to them. He said, "Charles, I've sent a man down to Sydney on the ferry to bring back more troops. Hopefully, some will arrive on a special run of the vessel before nightfall, as tonight is high tide, and the ferry should be able to get up the river. If they make it, they would help protect the town if the fire gets closer." He hoped it wouldn't, he added, "I'd rather be prepared than sorry." He watched the smoke settle and figured the ferry would not return tonight as he could see the smoke as low as the water.

In previous years, days like this often finished with a violent storm. Let's hope one will come this time. They could feel no moisture in the air; everything was dry. Even the green leaves on the gums crackled when you picked them. Dry, bone dry. Dust and heat. The horses stood with their heads down, too hot to move. Charles and Major Grace chatted for some time before the Major excused himself and once again returned to the barracks.

The milking had been completed early in the morning by Sal. The milk from yesterday was sitting in the somewhat cool cellar. It still had to be skimmed, and the butter churned. This was a popular job on a hot day as everyone could sit in the cool but dark cellar and take turns turning the butter churn handle. Even young Wills and Luke tried to 'have a go', but as the butter started balling, it got harder and harder, so Sal took over. The children were content to sit and listen while she told them a made-up story while she worked. Saturday's milk they drank on Sundays or gave it away. Sunday's milk would generally be made into butter on Mondays, as they usually didn't churn on Sundays.

By the time the butter had been churned, turned out onto the marble slab, then patted, blocked and set aside, it was time to milk the cows again. Sal went to do this. Liza had to feed the chickens and gather the eggs. Anna took the little boys into the kitchen and gave them some damper with fresh butter and honey. Neither was very hungry; both were so hot they sat and ate quietly; Luke was smearing his all over himself. Charlie had gone to find out if there was anything he could do to help Dar. He also had to refill some of the buckets that leaked. He had no energy.

Old Tom arrived. "Mrs. Sal, I've come to tell ya that I thinks that there's a big storm comin'. The ants are building high towers on their holes, and them black cockies is screeching, an' the termites are startin' to fly. That's a sure sign. Don't worry about the fire; this storm will knock it out. I jus' comed down to tell you so you'd know."

Sal knew Old Tom had knowledge of nature and that he could read the signs better than anyone she knew. She said, "Thanks, Tom. Can I give you a meal while you're here? There is a fresh stew on the boil and a fresh batch of bread and new butter."

"I'll jus' take some for later, Mrs. Sal, if that's ol' right," said Tom. "I won't have to venture out durin' the storm tonight." He took the plate Sal gave him. He turned to go, holding a plate brimming with stew; as he reached the door looked back and said, "Thanks, Missus Sal, you don't worrit about the fire now; the storm will come. I know it. You get the things out of your basement; it will bring lots of rain, lots and lots of rain." The door banged shut as he left and went down the steps to the dusty road.

The smoke grew thicker during the afternoon as the breeze dropped. The smoke settled on the ground. Breathing became hard, all activity ceased, and some held damp cloths to their noses. The evening drew the day to a close. By dark, the air had changed, and you could feel a difference, moisture.

Sal walked to the door to call Charles in to eat; Charlie was already washing in the trough and was dripping wet. "Sorry, Mama, but I was so hot and dirty. I'll dry off before coming inside," said Charlie.

Sal called Charles, and he came around the corner. "Just us for dinner, love. Major Grace has mobilised the troops in case the fires get closer. He's even sent someone to Sydney to get help. Didn't say who he'd sent. Hopefully, they will bring some reinforcements either tonight or tomorrow on the first ferry. The rest will have to come by road. I hope the fires don't jump ahead. Thankfully, the wind has dropped, so we should be safe tonight at least." Sal told Charles of Old Ted's visit and how he was sure a storm was coming.

Charles ran his fingers through his fair hair, then said, "I've never known Old Tom to be wrong about the weather. If he says a storm is coming, then there will be one. Before bed, I'll lift stuff off the cellar floor. Charlie can help. Let us eat." They went inside arm in arm.

Chapter 8   A Storm is Brewing

𝒯he ferry docked in Sydney Cove at the Phoenix Wharf in the
circular bay. Captain Roberts ushered the few passengers off the ferry. He
could see the smoke settling out west and knew that there would be no way
he could make the final trip for the evening, as visibility would make it
dangerous. The smoke was too thick; it would settle on the water, making
navigation unsafe. He secured the boat and returned to his cottage for a
meal and bed. He was greeted warmly by his wife, who asked, "Home, love?
Not going out again?"

He shook his head. "No, love, the smoke has settled. It's too thick
for a night passage. I don't want to get caught out there." He hugged her
and went indoors to change. He was muttering to himself. "Blasted
Simmons. I don't like that man. Throwing his weight around as though he's
actually important. I can only go as fast as the boat goes."

Simmons had headed straight to the Barracks near Hyde Park to
Major Humphrey Downes to let him know Major Grace's orders. Job done,
he headed to the Barracks Mess for some tucker. He had arrived in time for
the early evening meal from the Barracks kitchen, and he could smell fresh
bread from the bakery next to the Officers' Quarters. He had some stew
and ale and would hopefully get a tot of rum or two at the nearby inn.

He spent some time chatting to some of the other soldiers. He
boasted about why he'd been sent to Sydney.

They slowly drifted away from him, each making excuses to leave.

Simmons looked around him, thinking, "I'm only here for the night; I'm not going to spend it in the Barracks with this stinking, snoring lot." He had been cut by them, shunned. "I've done my job. I'll go and find that dratted boy."

He was still angry at Tindale for taking Eddie out of his reach. He knew where Tindale's sister lived. He thought, "I'll just go and have a look. I might get lucky, and he might head outside for a cool walk tonight; who knows," he mused to himself. He could smell the smoke from the fires here now; it wasn't as thick in Sydney, and it was nowhere nearly as hot here as in Parramatta. He wandered down from the barracks to the wharf and waited until dark.

Sometime later, Simmons headed back up Pitt Street to Tindale's sister's house. He had not planned on sitting on the docks for so long.

As he moved from the quay, he heard a distant rumble and knew a storm was brewing. He walked up the hill, the storm not far behind him. "So much for sleeping out tonight," he thought; he swore to himself, "I'll have to find somewhere dry to sleep. Hope I don't have to go back to the Barracks."

The storm was moving closer.

Flashing lightning wasn't far away, and the rolling thunder drew closer. After a few spots of light rain landed on his face, he stood under the large gum tree outside the Evans' place.

It was now completely dark.

A flash of lightning showed a face in the top window. "Ha, found him." A lecherous grin appeared on the man's face.

The same flash of lightning showed up his hiding place in front of the house.

He saw Eddie was watching him. Aghast, Simmons stepped back under the tree.

Eddie loved storms and was looking out the window to see how close it was. From upstairs, he could clearly see flash after flash of lightning in the sky, closely followed by the thunder as it growled loudly.

Again, another bolt of lightning flashed nearby, and with a slight movement, it illuminated Simmons just as he moved to stand under the tall gum tree in front of the house.

His shift of stance had caught Eddie's eye.

Eddie gasped. "Noooo," he said. He blanched and started shaking. "Why? Why has he followed me here? I thought I'd left that behind." He looked again but couldn't see anything in the darkness.

The other three older boys woke with the thunder and all crowded at the window to watch if it hailed or rained; the Evans boys also loved watching hail bounce in the front yard. They all hoped it hailed hard.

The storm sounded like it was nearly overhead. Four small faces peered out the window when a lightning bolt struck the tree in front of the house. John slept on.

All shouted.

Eddie's eyes remained fixed on the tree outline. He had almost forgotten the storm. It was like an explosion.

With a massive crash, the tree out the front split in two.

All jumped back from the window.

Eddie had not told the others that Simmons was outside.

Three startled boys gasped as Eddie said, "It fell on him."

"Who?" they echoed.

They had not noticed Ed had no longer been watching the storm but had his eyes fixed on the driveway.

Eddie, still somewhat shaken, said softly, "It was Lieutenant Simmons. He was standing under the tree, just watching the house. I saw him in a flash a minute ago. I'm sure he's dead. He couldn't have lived with that huge tree falling. I have to tell Mr. Tindale. He'll know what to do."

He turned and just looked at Tim.

Tim returned his glance with a troubled look.

Eddie and Phil raced downstairs and knocked on Mr. Tindale's door.

When it opened, Phil said, "Uncle Thomas, the lightning struck the tree outside, and there was a man under it."

The shock hit, and Eddie said with a tremble in his voice, "Simmons," was all he could muster in a strangled utterance.

Thomas Tindale looked at Eddie. The boy was sheet white and shaking hard.

Mr. Tindale grabbed his dressing gown and drew it on over his nightshirt.

Phil continued, "Uncle Thomas, Eddie said the man is dead, but he might just be trapped. He can't have lived through that. We gotta go and look." Phil was shivering in shock now, too.

Mr. Tindale and both boys knocked on his sister's door and told her what had happened. Her room was at the back of the house; she had only heard the thunder.

"Oh my," she said, "Thomas, put on Douglas' overcoat and see if there's anything we can do, but be careful."

All four hurried down the stairs.

Mrs. Evans grabbed a tin on the way down.

Phil knew this was her "Ouch box," as John called it. It had lots of bandages and some ointments in it. As they reached the door, Mrs. Evans stopped and handed the boys some oilskin jackets. "You'll need these, Tom. Go, but do be careful. The storm is just starting. I'll stay here."

Mr. Tindale lit an oil lamp and carried it with him. The force of the storm had not yet fully hit. It was raining and was getting heavier.

When they reached the tree, they saw that the lightning had cleaved it neatly in two. Both sides were lying on the ground. A couple of dead birds were on the ground nearby, and a pair of boots were clearly visible from under the trunk's thickest section. They weren't moving. Simmons was obviously dead; no one could survive that. The tree was enormous.

Mr. Tindale put his hand on Eddie's shoulder, drew him close and said, "It's over, son. He's gone, lad. There's nothing we can do for him tonight, and it's too dangerous for us out here. We'll go inside and deal with him in the morning. Eddie, it's finished."

Eddie crept closer and hugged him.

Mr. Tindale drew him to him and comforted the shaking lad. He wanted to pick him up and hug him. He would have but then would have had to explain to Phil. The poor boy was only a child.

Phil had been looking at the dead birds, poking them and didn't hear what his uncle had said to Eddie.

Mr. Tindale called Phil and turned to Eddie, who was still standing next to him and clearly in shock.

All three headed inside just as the rain and wind started in earnest. They made it inside just as another bolt of lightning struck close by. They all jumped and closed the door quickly behind them.

Mr. Tindale took the boys' oilskins and sent them to bed.

Phil went first.

It allowed Mr. Tindale to squat down, hug Ed again, and ask him quietly if he was all right.

"I think I will be Mr. Tindale. I just got a shock seeing him there." Ed's voice was no longer shaking, but he was shivering.

"Go to bed, lad; we'll discuss it later." He watched as Ed slowly climbed the stairs.

Ed nodded and climbed the stairs.

He turned and mouthed, "Thank You."

Phil and Ed both had wet hair, which cooled them down, and the air was finally beginning to ease from the heat of earlier in the day.

Mrs. Evans had appeared. "Caro, can you please help me put these coats out to dry?" Mrs. Evans understood he wanted to talk to her and followed him to the kitchen.

"Caro, I have to tell you about Eddie and the real reason I've sent him here." He continued, "A soldier named Lieutenant Simmons was, um, more than brutal to both Eddie and his older brother Charlie. I don't know precisely what's been happening, although I have a fair idea; both are petrified of him, and Tim is too. It was Simmons standing under that tree when it was hit by lightning; he is now dead. I have no idea why he was even here, as he was stationed with Grace in Parramatta. I saw him on the hill when we left. Eddie saw him under the tree outside tonight. The poor child is in shock. He knows that he's dead as he saw it happen. He's going to need extra care to get over this. At least now he and his brother are both safe. As are the rest of the boys in town. Oh, Caro, this is a blessing in disguise."

Caro hugged her brother, "Tom, I knew there was more than you told me, but I'm glad it's over. This storm sounds like it's going to be a big one. So let us sleep while we can. It could get worse." She hung the damp coats over the back of the chairs.

They said good night to each other and left the kitchen.

Mr. Tindale put another log in the firebox of the stove. He watched it flare while it caught fire. He then turned down the vent to let it burn slowly overnight. It was still hot in the kitchen from the day's heat, but the stove needed to be hot for the cooking and hot water the next morning. It would also dry the coats. He blew out the lamp and left the kitchen.

John remained asleep through the night without stirring; the other four boys barely slept at all.

The storm raged all night, with lightning, flashes, thunder, rain and wind. Mrs. Evans slept intermittently, worried about Eddie and how he'd cope with the morrow.

Mr. Tindale was up before dawn and opened the door to survey the carnage. The storm had passed in the early morning, and the sun shone through the remaining clouds. Not only was the tree down, but there was stock everywhere, so he presumed the fences were also down. Many buildings had lost roofs, and shingles were all over the yard. He eased himself past the remains of the tree and walked to Hyde Park Barracks to report Simmons' death and to get some help removing the tree and his body.

On arrival at the Barracks, Thomas was greeted by the guard and directed to the Major's office to the left as he walked in the front gates. The waft of fresh bread greeted him. He walked past the bakery and into the Major's office. He cheerily said, "Morning, sir! Bit of a blow last night, eh?"

The Major just nodded. He had a lot to do this morning, and he was worried as he expected Simmons to have stayed in the Barracks, and he hadn't. He'd have to send out a search party for him, too, then clean up his mess again. He sighed. More trouble.

Mr. Tindale continued. "I've come to report the death of one of the troopers, not one of yours. One Lieutenant Simmons, from Parramatta, took shelter under the big gum tree in front of my sister's house on Pitt Street. Lightning struck it, and it split the tree asunder. Simmons was killed instantly. He's completely under the trunk, so there's no hope. It happened about an hour after dark last night. We only know it was him as a young lad staying with us recognised him only a few moments before it happened. Simmons was stationed with the 48th in Parramatta, and we don't even know why he was here."

A slow smile crept across Major Downes' face. Trying to hide it, he stood and walked to the window, watching the troops mobilise; he then turned and looked at Mr. Tindale with a look of relief still on his face.

"Simmons was sent by Major Grace to summons troops to fight the fires if they came close to Parramatta. I checked the smoke this morning, and the storm seems to have dealt with them effectively. However, Simmons was not a popular man. Although he should have stayed at the Barracks last night, he did not appear. He would have caused trouble if he had. I thought I'd have to send a search party out to find him. I don't think anyone will grieve too much from his passing; he had no family here. I am not overly worried, as he usually causes trouble when he is around. I'll send around some men to remove both the tree and the body. I still have to send some men to Parramatta, but I'll probably now only send about thirty instead of the eighty I was going to send out. The first ten can go on the morning ferry, the others by road with the fire cart. Parramatta may need help cleaning up after the storm, too. If it hit hard enough to extinguish the fire, there could be damage. The rest can be on clean-up duty. We may need everybody we can get. Sorry, I didn't mean that as it came out." His eyes smiled. "We have to check the safety of the boats and wharves, but I'll prioritise this job. Hopefully, there will be no other reported deaths, but it's early, so we may hear of more."

Still smiling, Major Downes put out his hand to shake; Mr. Tindale knew he was dismissed.

Thomas turned and walked back out into the morning sunshine. He mused, "It's going to be another sweltering day, and probably a sticky one. High humidity means probably another storm tonight. I'll have to leave and get back to Margaret. I'll call by the school on the way back and see what's happening. Hopefully, no damage was done there. I bet Cape will be there checking to see if there's any damage." Thomas arrived at the school gate soon after dawn.

Sure enough, Mr. Cape had just arrived to check for damage.

Thomas greeted him, "Morning, sir. I was hoping to bring Eddie Lockley and Tim Miller to meet you today and enrol them, but I have to head back to Parramatta. The boys are staying with my sister, Mrs. Douglas Evans, and will attend with their boys. I know they will behave, as they know what a privilege this is for them. Their fathers are fine, upstanding men. They run two of the best Inns in Parramatta, and Eddie's father is also Government Stores Keeper for the town." Thomas smiled at the young teacher. "Sadly, I have to leave and get back to my wife and see how she fared in the storm."

They chatted for a while about Parramatta and the boys.

Mr. Cape nodded and said, "Tindale, don't worry; just send the boys along, and we'll get them sorted. I'm thinking that we may need a working bee of soldiers before we do any schooling." He surveyed the immediate area and saw how much debris and large branches were strewn around the school. Even with fifty boys, this would take some clearing. "I'll go get some troops. Don't want the lads injured. Tell them not to come up until noon.

First, put them to work cleaning up their own house. Good day to you; I must go away now and get on with the cleanup." He turned and walked into the building.

Mr. Tindale walked back along the street and was pleased to see that some soldiers had started sawing up the tree in front of the house. There was also a cart to carry away Simmons' body when they could reach it. "Hi, men, thanks for coming so fast. I hope no one else was injured last night."

"Don't think so, sir," one replied.

"This one is just a freak accident, wrong place, wrong time," said Mr. Tindale.

As he passed them, he heard one mumble. "Or not," mumbled the soldier, "Couldn't a happened to a nicer guy," he said sarcastically.

Another said, "Finally got wot's cummin' to him. 'Bout time he got his comeuppance."

A third said, "Good riddance."

The remaining soldiers only acknowledged his comment with a grunt and kept working.

Mr. Tindale thought, "I couldn't agree more with all of you," but he said nothing.

Two of the soldiers had peeled off their jackets and were on either end of a long, double-handed saw.

With long, smooth strokes, the hard green timber was eaten away quickly. Most of the smaller branches were already gone. Workhorses dragged away the larger ones.

Soon, what was left of the body would be accessible. With the pool of ooze, there was zero chance of life.

Mr. Tindale went inside; he'd keep the boys well out of the way.

Mrs. Evans greeted him. "Hello Thomas, did you get everything sorted with Mr. Cape? I see the soldiers have already started work. Major Downes is certainly prompt."

"Yes, all sorted, Caro, and with a smile on his face. Simmons was both well-known and very unpopular if the soldiers' comments are anything to go by. Even the Major smiled when I told him." He paused before saying, "I'll have to leave Caro and return to Margaret. You have many helpers here; she has none," he said. "Mr. Cape is getting some troops to help with a big branch at school. He doesn't want the boys until noon."

"Oh good, I understand; I expected this. So don't worry, Tom." She turned to walk into the parlour. "Come in and grab something to eat before you catch the ferry. I'm sure Margaret will be fine."

Mr. Tindale followed her, saying, "I told Cape about the two boys and explained the situation. He's looking forward to meeting them. Can you get them up and out cleaning up in the backyard, away from the tree? It's a mess."

"Will do, Tom," she said breezily. She walked upstairs, woke the boys, and rejoined him in the kitchen.

Effy had made tea and handed Thomas a cup. Strange to have a cup of hot tea in a hot climate, but it was cooling.

He and Caro sat in the parlour and waited for the boys.

Soon, they were all up, dressed and ready. Eddie was the last to appear.

Mr. Tindale took him aside and said quietly, his hand resting gently on Ed's shoulder, "I've seen Major Downes at the Barracks, and he's got things well in hand. Look out the window, Ed. From what I heard as I walked by, I don't think he'll be missed either. It's over, Eddie. Finished. I'll let Charlie and your father know when I see him later. Bill too. Charlie starts with me tomorrow, so we'll talk. I'll be travelling back with ten of Downes' men. I'll make sure that Major Grace also knows the details. I'll leave a message and get him to come, and I'll fill in the details." He gave Ed's shoulder another squeeze. And he left Ed watching the tree being removed.

He turned to everyone else and said brightly, "What a storm it was last night. Trees are down everywhere, and many homes have lost shingles, if not roofs. I hope the ferry is still running; it's about half tide now, so I'll have to leave soon." He sat at the table. "Eat up, then help clean up out the back. Leave the front to the soldiers; stay well clear. Do you all understand?" His eyes locked on Eddie's.

Ed had joined them at the table.

Five heads nodded; most had mouths full.

Thomas continued, "I also saw Mr. Cape this morning on the way back from the barracks. He said not to come until noon. You'll all be doing a school clean up for an hour or so of the small branches then school. He's expecting you two. Phil will show you where to go." He turned to Phil, and he said. "Show them to his office, please, Phil."

Phil nodded.

He turned to Mrs. Evans, "Caro, you'll need to get these two some shoes. You should have time to buy some before school. Is that all right?"

She agreed. "I'll take them on the way back from the ferry."

He turned to Eddie and Tim, "Mr. Cape is firm on the dress code. Shoes are a must, so no bare feet. Satchels and clothing should be clean, neat and tidy. Hair brushed and neat at all times. Mrs. Evans will get you two what is needed."

They had all finished eating and sat, awaiting permission to leave the table. He was pleased with both boys' table manners. They were surprisingly good.

His tone softened, "Now, the vegetable garden won't clean itself, and the backyard needs sorting too. You can all go to the bootmaker on the way back from seeing me off. I'm leaving on the first ferry. I have to make sure Aunt Margaret is all right," he said to his nephews. Then he turned to Eddie and Tim, "I will look forward to a letter from you each as soon as you can write one. I'd like a letter each week that you don't come home. I expect that you will write to your parents each week as well. This way, I'll be able to follow how you're progressing by how you write your letters."

They both nodded.

"Oh, and you won't have to pay postage; just hand them to Captain Roberts. He'll drop them into your folks, Eddie. I'll collect them from there. All right?"

Again, both boys nodded.

Effy arrived to clear away breakfast. The storm was almost forgotten, and the talk was about school. Mr. Tindale finished his cup of tea and went upstairs to pack. He caught Eddie's eye and called him over. "Are you all right, lad?" he inquired.

Eddie nodded, unsure if his voice was steady. "Thanks, sir, but I think I'll be okay. It's just a shock. One minute he was there leering at me, then he was gone."

Mr. Tindale nodded. "Talk to Mrs. Evans if you need to; I've filled her in."

Again, Eddie nodded, and his eyes filled with unshed tears. "Thanks, sir."

After the other boys had finished eating, they raced upstairs to change out of the clean clothing they had put on, expecting to go to school and put on work clothes. Eddie followed and changed quickly. First, they had to escort Mr. Tindale to the ferry.

Mrs. Evans was waiting downstairs for them.

They all left to walk downhill to the quay. All around them, there was storm damage, branches were broken, and shingles strewn around.

The boys cleared the street as they walked, stacking piles of smaller branches to be removed later.

Thankfully, the boats were undamaged, and Captain Roberts was already on board the ferry, bailing out the last of the rainwater.

There were one or two other passengers. All were talking about the storm. Everyone was anxious to get home to Parramatta and see if their homes had been damaged. The ten troopers arrived and assisted where needed.

Captain Roberts greeted everyone cheerfully and ushered them up the gangplank. With everyone on board, the ropes were cast off, and the ferry pulled out. There was a cool, brisk breeze on the water, and it would be behind them, so it should be a fast trip. Thomas would tell him en route home.

Old Tom knocked on the kitchen door at the Inn. "Mrs. Sal, I'm just returning your plate. I really enjoyed my tucker last night. I tol' you that we'd get a storm and that it would kill them fires. No smoke this morning. Look." He turned and looked Westward. The sky was clear and blue. "I'm heading away for a bit, just wanted you to know, Missus."

Sal walked outside with him and also looked. "Yes, Tom, that storm was wonderful. The rain was so heavy that I hope it's put all the fires out. I'm sure there will be some stumps left burning. I hope we'll get more in the next few days, but I'm also thankful that it's been so dry that there wasn't enough rain to flood everything. We're still high and dry here. Take care on your travels, Tom."

"Thanks, Missus. I'll try. I'm heading south for a bit; I gotta show a pommy bloke a farm I know about. Gotta meet him down there." He doffed his hat and walked off. "Just so ya knows where I is, eh."

Sal had insisted that Tom let her know if he was heading off somewhere so as not to worry about his absence.

Charles had left earlier to walk up to the Lancer Barracks to talk to Major Grace. He'd heard from Bill that Mr. Falconer-Meade had returned without finding his family. He'd come from England to search for his son Matthew and his wife. He'd come to see Mr. Fishbon, a teacher at the new King's School. Mr. Fishbon knew Matthew in England.

Charles reached the barracks, and Major Grace was just emerging from his office. "Hello, Charles. Is all okay down at the Inn? Bad storm last night and looks to be plenty of damage, but hey, no smoke."

This man was a gentle giant, towering well over six feet. He was firm and fair in his judgements, and his soldiers both liked and admired him. He had golden hair, the same fantastic colour as the three Lockley men. They had similar fair hair and blue eyes, but the Major's was a shade tall darker. Charles stood much the same height as the major.

Eddie had inherited his father's bright blue eyes and the blonde wavy crop of hair but looked like his mother. Charlie was a young version of Charles. It was why Sally called him Chip when he was little; he hated it. He was a "Chip off the old block."

Charles said, "We are all fine, thanks, Ned. No, I've come to see you about one of the ferry passengers from a couple of days ago; he goes by the name of Mr. Falconer-Meade. He's looking for his family. They are missing. His son Matthew, wife Martha, came out early the year before last, and then, after some time, silence. It had been over eighteen months since he heard from them. There used to be monthly letters. I was wondering if you could get your men to keep an eye open for them?"

Major Grace said, "Charles, get him to come into the office and give me the names and dates again. I'll inform the next Parade. The word should spread; we should hear something soon if he's around this area."

Only when no one was listening could they call each other by first name. They had been friends since soon after their arrival, some ten years before. It was a very unusual friendship and seemed very lopsided.

Charles thanked him and left for the Rear Admiral Duncan Inn to find Mr. Falconer-Meade. He knew how much he had already missed Eddie, and he had been gone for only two days. He hoped the man would find them.

Bill was sawing a fallen tree when he saw Charles coming, and he stopped work. The night before, he had spoken to Charles about Falconer-Meade and his missing son. "Morning, Charles," called Bill, "Much damage?"

"Nah, all good down at our place," replied Charles. "A few small branches but no real damage. Now the stores are in their own stone building, I don't have to worry about them, and our basement didn't flood this time, so good there, too. How about you? Only this, or did you get flooded?"

"A bit," Bill replied, "but no damage."

Charles looked up and nodded a greeting to Mr. Falconer-Meade, standing under the verandah with his neat leather bag beside him. "Good morning, sir; I've just been up to see Major Grace about your missing family. He'd like you to come and see him before you catch the ferry. You can leave your bag, and I'll walk up with you. He's in the office now."

Mr. Falconer-Meade nodded his acquiescence, placed his bag on the corner of the verandah and stepped down to Charles. "I appreciate this, Lockley. I'm apprehensive about my boy. It's just not like him to be silent. As you know, I will return on the ferry this morning. I have to also return home to England. Meade Park needs constant care, so I must get home as soon as possible; I've been looking for him for over a month. I'll just have to trust that he can't get word to me and that they are all right. So I appreciate your effort." He looked so sad.

They slowly walked to Major Grace's office, and Charles waited outside while he spoke to the Major.

They soon emerged into the bright sunshine. It was already getting hot and sticky, and only a few hours past dawn.

Mr. Falconer-Meade shook Major Grace's hand and bowed, then walked over to Charles. "He will pass the word through all the troops and landowners. Hopefully, something will come from this. I'm beginning to have my doubts."

They walked out the barracks gates just as Bill passed with his dray. He had brought it around to fill with the fallen timber. He stopped and offered them a lift, which they willingly agreed to.

Mr. Falconer-Meade may have been a big man, but he was agile enough to heave himself into the dray.

Charles hopped into the open back. They trundled past the Rear Admiral Duncan Inn to collect the gentleman's bag and continued to the jetty.

Charles stayed with them and said he'd make sure he was able to get the ferry. They arrived early and stayed on the dray in the shade of a tree until the ferry arrived. Charles slipped off the dray and cleaned a few small branches off the wharf. There was no other damage from the storm. They didn't have long to wait as they could see the belch of smoke coming around the river bend. It would be about fifteen minutes before it arrived, so they waited.

Black and white pelicans and tall white birds were feeding along the river's edge. There were swirls of fish in the shallow water's edge. Occasionally, one would jump. Presently, the ferry chugged around the final corner.

Standing on the deck was Mr. Tindale, and they each lifted a hand of acknowledgement.

Captain Roberts edged the little steam ferry into the wharf and cast a rope around the pylon, looping it perfectly. He tied up the rear. Charles caught the rope he was thrown, and he tied it fast to another pylon. Captain Roberts slid down the gangplank for the passengers to alight. First, the passengers were handed down by Mr. Tindale, then the troops.

Mr. Tindale alighted last, farewelling Captain Roberts. He smiled and greeted the men. "Rough night here last night?" he questioned.

The three nodded in agreement. Bill said, "Lots of rain, noise and thunder. most seemed to have missed town this time, but it was enough to put out the fires by the looks of it."

"Lots of tree damage in Sydney Town. Only one death that I know about by the time I left. I'll tell you about it later," said Mr. Tindale.

Captain Roberts joined the small group, and they chatted and compared storm stories. Soon, he ushered Mr. Falconer-Meade on board and set off back to Sydney.

Charles, Bill and Mr. Tindale retired to the dray, still in the shade of the tree.

"I'm so glad you are both here, you especially Lockley; I have a story to tell you." He looked at the faces of both fathers. "Some time ago, I realised that Eddie and Charlie were both petrified of Lieutenant Simmons, Tim too, but to a much lesser extent. I didn't fully understand why, although I knew him as a bully and goodness knows what else. Eddie would shake whenever I even mentioned him or if he came to the forge. Look, it's a long story, but he was abusing them. I think it was, um, more physical, but truthfully I'm not sure. He was an ugly character."

He paused, looking at Charles. "Did you note I said *was*? Last night, just as Caro and I were heading to bed, Phil, her eldest son and Eddie came to my room. Eddie was sheet white and shaking, and Phil was in shock. Eddie hadn't been able to sleep and was standing at the window watching the storm roll in."

"Yes, Eddie loves storms," said Charles with a smile, nodding.

"Well, he'd been watching the approaching storm through the

upstairs window for some time. Then, in one of the flashes, he saw a man near the tree in front of the house. On another flash, he saw his face before the man stepped backwards. It was Simmons. He was just standing still, looking up at the house." He paused and looked at Charles.

Charles angrily flushed. "Yes, I knew that something was going on. I asked them, but neither boy confided in me. I could only try to keep them out of his way."

Mr. Tindale continued his story. "While the four older boys were watching, another lightning bolt hit. Only this time, it was a direct hit on the tree, cleaving it in two and instantly killing Simmons." He was looking at Charles as he said this to watch his reaction. He could only guess at how he felt.

Charles blanched. "Seriously? He's dead?" He let out a huge sigh.

Bill sat silently, just listening, looking from one to the other. He'd been oblivious to any danger for his son.

Mr. Tindale continued. "At dawn the next morning, I went to the Hyde Park Barracks and reported the incident to Major Downes. A huge wind directly hit the town, and debris was everywhere. He had already mobilised the troops and sent some directly to Caroline's house. He also arranged a cart to remove not only the tree but also the body. As I left, they were just getting him out. We took the boys away before they fully uncovered him, but you could see his boots and a puddle of gore. The soldiers had seen his face and identified that it was indeed Simmons. He was not liked by anyone there; even Major Downes smiled when I told him, and you should have heard the soldiers' comments about him. No one knows if he has a family, nor do they care."

Thomas paused and looked at both men before continuing, "So your boys and all the other boys are now safe." He looked over at Bill and saw that he understood. There was not much anyone could say. All were deep in thought. "Would you like me to tell Charlie, or do you want to?" he asked Charles. "He knows that Eddie has spoken to me about him."

Charles said, "In that case, Mr. Tindale, I think it would be better for you to tell him the full story, but I'll let him know he's dead. I'll take pleasure in that, great pleasure. It was well known through town that all the boys would scoot when he was seen around. What do you think, Bill?"

Bill agreed. "I think if you tell him he's dead, Charles and leave the details to Mr. Tindale. Everyone, including Major Grace, will be pleased he's gone. Charles, you can tell the Major, can't you? He said he'd sent someone to town for more troops; I gather he sent Simmons. There is no other reason he'd be there, is there? I'm just glad he's dead."

Charles said, "I'll take delight in letting the Major know if that's all right?"

Mr. Tindale said, "I'll certainly tell Charlie what happened." They talked a bit longer, and then Mr. Tindale said, "I'd better go and see how

Margaret fared after the blow last night." He turned to Charles, "Send Charlie to me at about noon. I'll probably have the forge ready for some small jobs I must complete. I'll see how he copes with the news first. I'll get him prepping the jobs for tomorrow if I need to do any repairs for Margaret. It will give him time to think it all through."

Bill offered to drop him off at the forge on his way, as it was getting hotter every moment. He nodded ascent and took Mr. Falconer-Meade's seat; they headed off.

Chapter 9   Life Anew

Charlie headed off to the forge. He was munching from a chunk of cheese in one hand and a fresh, thick slice of bread in the other. He wasn't hurrying; it was too hot, but he wasn't precisely dawdling as he wanted to hear the full story, Eddie and Simmons. He couldn't believe that he was dead. "He's really dead." He skipped, then mumbled to himself as he walked and ate.

On arrival at the blacksmith's shop, Mr. Tindale was waiting for him. The fire was not on, the forge quiet. He was sitting sorting nails into piles.

Charlie knocked on the doorpost and walked in. Mr. Tindale greeted him. "Hello lad, looking forward to a bit of hard work? Eddie said to say hi and sent his love."

Charlie shuffled as he stood. "Yes, sir, I am and thanks."

Mr. Tindale motioned for him to sit on the stump seat next to him. "Well, we're not going to, at least not yet. I thought we had more important things to talk about today, so no hot work just yet," he paused, "now you know Eddie has told me a bit of what went on with Simmons? I won't elaborate or ask questions, but I will tell you it's now all over. He's dead. Gone! Did your Dar tell you much?"

Charlie shook his head. "He only said he was dead, and you'd tell me how …" Charlie looked directly at him. The honest, trusting look of a child. He searched for understanding in the older man's eyes. "… that you'd give me the full story. But he's really dead, sir? Really gone?" He suddenly thought fearfully. "Eddie didn't do it, did he?"

"No, lad, Ed had nothing to do with it. But he did see it happen." Mr. Tindale put his hand on his shoulder and said, "… and yes, lad, Simmons is gone and squashed flat at that. I'll tell you the entire story, just as Eddie told me...."

They sat talking for over an hour.

Charlie had tears on his cheeks that he wiped away on his dirty shirt. Occasionally, he would let out a sob, more from relief.

Mr. Tindale gave him the time and space he needed. There were long silences, but they were not uncomfortable ones. They formed a bond that day that would be with them all their life. Mr. Tindale was impressed with Charlie. There was a depth of character in the boy. He knew he would enjoy working with this quiet lad. He already knew from Eddie that he was a hard worker.

Margaret came in with a mug of steaming tea and some of her special cookies.

Charlie had eaten some before and relished the thought that he'd get them more often. He smiled wanly and took two. "Thanks so much, Mrs. Tindale. Eddie sometimes brought me one, and they are delicious. Thanks again."

He nibbled his first biscuit, pocketing the other one for later.

As it was now mid-afternoon, Mr. Tindale told him he could go home after he'd finished sorting the dropped box of nails that Mr. Tindale had been working on when he arrived. A simple job, but all he could have coped with today. "Poor child." he thought, "His emotions are in turmoil."

He sent Charlie home with the instructions to help out there. He'd done nothing more than sort the nails at the forge, then swept the shop and leaves from outside. There had been no actual damage from the storm. There were no urgent orders, and Mr. Tindale felt that Charlie had much to consider. Tomorrow, he would be earning his lunch.

"Come prepared for a full, hot day tomorrow, Charlie. We have to start you from scratch, so we'll start early. Come as soon as you have finished your morning chores, but make it as early as possible. Off you go, lad, and smile. Today is a new day, a fresh start. Deep breath, Charlie; you are free."

Charlie nodded and smiled.

Charles saw Charlie walking home mid-afternoon. He stood in the stable yard and waited. When Charlie got closer, Charles just opened his arms. It was not something he often did, but he saw Charlie needed a big hug today.

Without changing his stride, Charlie walked into his father's arms and just stood there, being loved and accepted. They stood silently, just savouring the fatherly compassion. Then the tears started. Charlie's tears of relief soaked into Charles's shirt. Great racking sobs of pain, finally released.

He stood there until Charlie pulled away slightly.

Charlie sniffed.

Charles ruffled his son's hair. "Come on, son, the stables aren't going to muck themselves out, but let's do it together. Talk if you want; I'll listen. Charlie, no matter what happened, I love you. Just know that."

Charlie just nodded, picked up the wooden muckraker, and silently started on the stables.

They worked in silence for a while, then Charlie turned to his dad and said, "Sir, I'd like to tell you everything, but can we sit behind the stables where we won't be disturbed?"

The rest of the jobs could wait a while. They would get them done, but this conversation couldn't wait. Charles walked out with his arm along Charlie's shoulder.

The soldiers were still working on removing the big tree. The body was gone by the time they returned. As Mrs. Evans walked all the boys past the remains of the stump, Eddie looked over and saw a pool of blood, and he shivered.

Mrs. Evans said, "Boys, just don't look; it will all be cleaned up before you return from school. In the meantime, we have some things to do. Now, have you all got your satchels? We won't be back home before school starts." She was carrying a cloth-covered basket.

All five boys answered, "Yes, Ma," or "Yes, Mrs. Evans." They headed down to the slop shop or bootmaker to see if they could get some ready-made shoes from Mr. Iles. He looked ancient due to his hunchback and gnarled hands; however, he was probably only about forty.

Many children wore horrible, cheap shoes. These, however, would mean they could go to school.

Charles and Bill had each given their sons some money for shoes, but it wasn't much.

Unbeknownst to them, Mr. Tindale had already spoken to Caro and told her to buy the boys, not the cheap, ready-made ones that their fathers had supplied money for, but to purchase each boy a pair of proper lace-up ones. She was also to buy them some knitted socks rather than them having to wear toe rags. She had already intended to do this before they arrived, but Tom handed her £1 to cover the costs. He didn't tell her that this was from Major Grace; that remained his secret.

On arrival, the front window had boots and shoes of all shapes and sizes: shiny black lace-up boots and tiny yellow leather dancing slippers for ladies. There were top boots, half-boots, slip-on shoes, and shoes on the bottom shelf that looked about the right size. These shoes were odd in that they had neither left nor right shoes, and they were cheap and nasty, mostly worn by convicts. The boys expected that they could afford these things, and they were not looking forward to it.

Neither boy had ever worn shoes nor boots before but had heard their parents talk of blisters even while wearing toe rags to stop them from rubbing. The boys were not looking forward to having to put up with these.

Mrs. Evans opened the door, and a little bell rang as she did so. The three Evans boys waited outside with the bags.

Eddie and Tim came in with her and saw a wizened old man emerge from a back room.

"Morning, Mr. Iles, we've come to get these two some shoes for school, please. Neither have ever had them before, and they must wear them to school today. What have you got in stock?" she asked.

Mr. Iles motioned for Tim to climb up on an elevated chair and sit down. Mr. Iles lifted Tim's dusty foot and placed it on a funny cross-stick with measurements etched on it. Then he grabbed the other foot and did the same. "I always measure both feet as too many have different size feet. Who knows why the Good Lord made it so, but He did. Well, now... let's see. I made a pair about two months ago for a boy, but he'd grown too much by the time his mother came in to collect them. Look." He walked over to the window and picked up the shiny black half-boots with laces Tim had already admired. "How about these, lad? They are just the right size for you, a bit big, but it's better to get them that way and put some cloth in the toes until you grow into them. What do you think? Would you like to try them on?"

Tim nodded, awestruck. They were the shoes of his dreams. "Oh, Mr. Iles!"

Mrs. Evans tapped him on the shoulder and handed him some hand-knitted socks. "Try these. They are much more comfortable than toe rags."

Mr. Iles handed them to Tim to help him put them on. Then he unlaced one of the boots and slipped it on his foot, then the other one. "Careful now, lad, they will feel very strange for a bit, but your feet will get used to them. Take it a bit easy until your feet get used to it. Hold my hand as you step down." He put out a gnarled, brown-stained hand with bent fingers, and Tim balanced himself on it as he stepped from the steps.

Tim didn't say anything but wrinkled his nose and tried them out. "Cool, Eddie, oh wow. The socks. The shoes. Oh, and they're black and shiny and ... and ... oh, I never thought I'd have boots like THIS."

He went to Mrs. Evans and just hugged her. "Thanks so much, Mrs. Evans, oh. Wow. Just thanks."

He turned to Mr. Iles and hugged him, too. "They're great; thanks, sir; the socks make them comfy."

He jumped up and down, grinning.

Mr. Iles turned to Eddie. "Your turn now, lad, up you get."

Eddie hopped up into the chair and looked down at his filthy feet. He'd been walking through water puddles and mud, and although he'd wiped them on the grass, they were still dirty. "Sorry, sir," was all he could say. He looked sheepish.

Mr. Iles just laughed. "Never apologise for hard-working hands and feet. They are normally a sign of honest labour. If you think they are dirty, lad, you should see some I have to work with. Your feet are strong and healthy and ticklish; I'll bet." He ran his thumbnail under Eddie's foot and tickled him.

"Ahh," said Eddie. "Yeah, I'm real ticklish on my feet. Liza is doing it all the time to wake me up."

Mr. Iles chuckled, as did Mrs. Evans.

He liked this bent man with huge hands. He had an infectious smile that just made you want to smile back.

Mr. Iles tried to straighten up and uncurl a bit, but years of bending over a shoe last and making boots had made his back permanently curved.

He measured his feet; then he scratched his head. "Now let me think. I'm sure I have some boots here that would fit you. Where did I put them? I had some kangaroo leather given to me, and I thought I'd try boot-making. It's thick and soft, but I'm unsure how it will wear. Where did I put them?" He mumbled to himself and shuffled over to a wooden crate on the floor.

Eddie had been hoping for a nice pair of lace-up boots like Timmy but thought he'd have to have some of those ugly boots with no left or right foot like the convicts wear. He watched silently but eagle-eyed.

Mr. Iles opened the wooden crate, and there were many drawstring hessian bags, each with a pair of shoes. "These are the test shoes I make. Trying out new styles. I know I have a pair in here somewhere...." He pulled out bag after bag. Opening some, but feeling the weight of some and putting them aside, "Ahh, this is them."

He turned to Tim, "Lad, put these back in there for me, please."

Tim plonked himself on the ground next to the crate and put them back in the box as neatly as possible.

Eddie was still sitting, quietly waiting for Mr. Iles to open the bag.

Mr. Iles tried to untie the lace holding the bag shut but handed it to Eddie. "Here, lad, you'll have to do it; my old fingers can't manage it today."

He handed the bag to Eddie but turned to Mrs. Evans and winked at her.

Eddie easily opened the bag and went to hand it back, but Mr. Iles said, "No, lad, you pull them out."

Eddie did. "Oh, sir, they are beautiful."

He hadn't pulled them out but had put his hand in the bag to feel them. "Mr. Iles, they are so soft." Eventually, he removed them and sat them on his lap. They were a deep red-brown and soft; they were a pair of short boots with brown leather laces. Unlike Tim's boots, which were firm leather, you could tell these were soft as they flopped sideways.

"Come on, lad, let's see if they fit." Mr. Iles took one and loosened the laces.

Mrs. Evans handed him some socks for Eddie, and after they were on, he eased one boot onto Eddie's foot. "I hope they are also a bit big for you so you'll get good wear from them. Boys' feet grow so quickly at this age."

He looked at Eddie and smiled. "Perfect fit, lad. Now, let's have a walk around."

"Both of you, walk back and forwards, and let's see how they go." He squatted on the wooden crate and looked at how the boys walked. "Good," he said. "You may still get some blisters, but they shouldn't be too bad. If I were you, I'd wear them just for school and church until your feet get used to them. Try not to wear them in water or get too dirty, but they should just wipe clean. Rub with some beeswax occasionally, which will help preserve them. Hopefully, they will be able to be handed down to your brothers and sisters when you've grown out of them." He smiled at Mrs. Evans and said, "Out you go, lads and show them to the Evans boys. Mrs. Evans and I have some finance to do."

Eddie remembered that he had the money from his Dar and Mr. Miller had given him Tim's Pa. He handed that to Mrs. Evans and whispered, "I don't know how to thank you. I really don't."

He disappeared after Tim and could be seen showing off his boots to the other three boys.

Mrs. Evans and Mr. Iles discussed the prices of the boots and reached a reasonable total that both were happy with, less the coins Eddie had given her. Mrs. Evans paid the five shillings, collected her basket and the boy's two forgotten satchels and left.

Mr. Iles had a massive grin on his face, being able to sell two pairs of boots and expensive ones at that. That's more than he'd usually make in a week. His missus would be pleased.

After Mrs. Evans joined the boys, she said to John, "Where should we go and have a picnic lunch? You've been left out of everything, so you can choose."

John thought about it a bit and said, "I love watching the ships unload, and if we sit in the park on the hill, we can watch. There are some rocks there, so we shouldn't get muddy."

Mrs. Evans agreed, and they headed off down the street to The Rocks to sit on the rocks and eat their early picnic.

The overnight rain and the heat made the day very humid. No one wanted to do much, and they knew they all had to walk back up the hill.

They sat together to eat their picnic lunch. The five boys realised it would be soon time for school.

Eddie and Tim had once again pumped the other three for information.

Mrs. Evans sat listening.

They all walked back up George Street together, only parting company when the boys left to head to their school on King Street.

Mr. Cape stood at the door of the school. He was marking off the boys as they arrived. He greeted Phil, who introduced Eddie and Tim.

"Good morning, sir; I'm glad to see the school building is unharmed. Sir, this is Eddie Lockley and Timmy Miller. They are living with us for a while."

Eddie and Tim waited in front of Mr. Cape. They had expected an older man, but he was a young gentleman about thirty years of age with big sideburns down the side of his face. He smiled at them and said, "Well, gentlemen, what an adventure we all have had." He smiled, showing his top teeth. "I look forward to hearing all about your stories. I met Mr. Tindale earlier this morning; he's filled me in on a little of your histories."

He winked at Eddie and smiled. "I hope you are prepared to work hard and learn from this opportunity you have been given?"

Eddie answered for them both by just saying, "Yes, sir." He wondered exactly what Mr. Tindale had told him.

Mr. Cape turned to Phil, "Take the boys to my office, please, Philip. I won't be long; only three more to arrive."

To Eddie and Tim, he said, "I'll be about 10 minutes, then we'll grade where you both are at and place you in your classes. So just sit and wait for me."

As they walked through the hall, they peeked into one of the classrooms. There were already boys in there copying work written on the board. There was only the noise of chalk scratching on slates. Phil opened the door at the end of the corridor and showed them in, pointing to two chairs on the side of the room. "Sit in there and stay quiet and still." He waved as he left, then went out, leaving the door open.

There were fifty boys enrolled at the school. Most of them were already in the classrooms; you would have expected to hear chattering, but there was silence. No one talked.

Soon, Mr. Cape came in and sat at his desk. He had some slates on his desk and a couple of chalksticks. "I'll just see where I should place you two and where you should start you. Don't worry; this isn't a test. Now, please write your names. See, that wasn't hard. Now write your numbers …."

After twenty minutes, the boys filled three slates on both sides. Mr. Cape sat and read them. "All right, lads, follow me. I'll put you in the same class until you settle in. You'll find mixed ages in each class because some boys have started late and some early. We work at each student's pace. By the end of term one, you will probably have caught up to the rest of your age group. If you are having trouble with anything, and yes, boys, I mean anything at all, not just school work, come and see me. I am happy to work one-on-one with you and help you catch up."

By the end of the school day, they had their first Latin lesson and learned the importance of Mathematics and neat writing. They had learned to find England on the giant globe that Mr. Cape had in the classroom, and they listened to Phil in a Debate with some of the other boys. The topic was "the importance of discipline." Overall, they had fun, if you can call schooling fun.

Tomorrow was more Latin, Mathematics, Astronomy, Grammar, Spelling, Shakespeare, and Languages.

The school bell rang, and Mr. Cape dismissed all the classes, and the boys walked out in an orderly manner until they reached the gate. Eddie and Tim removed their new boots and socks. Shoving the socks into their satchels and tying the laces of their boots in a loop, they then hung them around their neck. The five took off up King Street and belted around the corner into Pitt Street and home.

The tree had gone entirely. Not a leaf remained on the road, and only a split stump in the garden. The area was wet, where someone had washed away the blood.

They stopped, looked at the stump of the tree, then walked past slowly and went inside. Eddie stood and looked at the wet pavement; he shuddered and followed them inside.

~

This was to be the routine for the next years.

Eddie and Tim settled in with the Evans family.

Each had their chores and helped around the house. Both obtained occasional jobs as messengers for Major Downes so they could have some pocket money.

Ed didn't know that Major Grace had arranged this for them, but he was thrilled to bring in some money so he could help. Major Downes discovered that he was quick and honest, just as Ned Grace said.

Ed only kept enough money for his ferry trip home. The rest he handed to Mrs. Evans. He would allow no argument.

About once a month, they would use their savings to get home after the school day on a Friday. They could only go on the days when the high tide in Parramatta was late Friday afternoon. Captain Roberts greeted them warmly and let them help with the ropes, especially when docking.

Every other week, he would deliver letters for them.

At the end of two years, Tim was taller than Eddie. However, Eddie's physique was much broader and stronger. Sadly, Eddie's voice broke at this time, and he was no longer allowed in the church choir. He had loved the singing and was sad that it would be some years before his voice stabilised.

Ed had surpassed Tim's height by fifteen, eventually standing over a head taller than his best friend. His speaking voice was deep and rich; his physique drew the eye of many a lass. Every chance he got, he'd still work at the forge, and his muscles rippled with the health and vitality of youth.

Eddie knew his school days were drawing to a close.

He hated being noticed, especially by the girls, and ogling him, they did. Every time, he blushed and looked away. He could feel their eyes following him and boring into him. It bothered him greatly. The skinny, gangly boy had grown into the most appealing, tall, blonde, handsome man.

He pined for the heat and dirt of the forge. He wasn't that interested in Latin and other Languages. Debating was interesting, but not for him. He enjoyed the other subjects, especially Geography, Astronomy and Shakespeare. He had also loved the choir, but he'd been thrown out when his voice broke. He'd recently been accepted back as a baritone.

Tim had turned out to be an excellent scholar and was doing brilliantly.

Eddie had passed every test and exam he'd sat, but his mind was hankering for the outdoor life.

Mr. Cape's School had grown so much that he'd been offered a new post at the Sydney College. Next year, the College students would all leave the King Street building and transfer to the new College Street School.

Ed wasn't sure he'd be there, though.

He was ready to go back and work with Mr. Tindale.

He'd kept his hand in blacksmithing during holiday times. The business had grown so much, and Charlie could only work with him half the time as Dar had hurt his leg. Charlie was needed at the Inn for the heavy lifting. Mr. Tindale had given him such an education. He now had to work out how to use it. He and Mrs. Tindale came down to visit as often as they could. They now had a girl named Maryanne to look after the animals, which freed up Mrs. Tindale to come. She would always come with a container full of her special cookies.

He'd talk to Dar when he arrived home. A few other boys were also making the trip home to Parramatta; they had also been at school with him, and they were all friends: Frederick (Freddy), Ken, Bobbie, George, James, and Ben. Many could not afford the fees at the King's School in Parramatta and so had decided to live with various families in Sydney and attend the school there. They hated the twenty-mile walk if they missed the ferry.

Freddy was brilliant at Debating; he should go into Parliament, and Mr. Cape said he should think of Politics too; Ken, he said, should be a Doctor, Bobbie an Architect and Ben an Accountant. John was destined to be a Naturalist. Hopefully, he would get a job at the new Museum being built next door. The other boys had their lives mapped out for them. Even Tim said he would do Law with Stevie and Phil. They were all doing one day a week as apprentices.

Eddie had grown very tall but was still "filling out." It will be interesting to see if they end up in these roles. It would be interesting to see where he'd end up himself.

What he could see ahead of him was the forge. This wasn't a problem. He loved the work. He'd wanted to see the forge and the business grow. He looked at his now soft hands and missed the calluses that used to be on them.

He asked to see Mr. Cape.

Mr. Cape stood and just scratched his head. When he met with Eddie, he said, "You're good at many subjects, Eddie. You work hard and succeed, but you don't excel. You have more common sense than all the boys in the school together, and you are a powerful leader. Yet, Eddie, I can't see you as a politician, doctor or any other profession. I know you will succeed in whatever you try. I can only encourage you to keep with Mr. Tindale until you know what you want to do. See what opportunities arise and grab them with both hands."

Eddie felt in limbo.

He hadn't told Mrs. Evans that he would not come back next year. He knew he wouldn't return, and so did Mr. Cape.

He would talk it over with the Major and then decide.

Ultimately, an urgent note from home the day before school finished decided his future for him.

Charles had fallen from the loft in the barn and broken his leg. Eddie needed to return home and go back to the forge. He was saddened for his injured father but delighted to return to what he loved. He looked forward to getting his hands roughened by the work on the anvil.

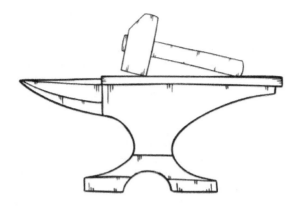

Chapter 10   The Anvil and Jenna

*F*ive years had passed since Eddie left school.

He had loved it and made many good friends, good friends that would stay with him forever: Jim Martin, George Thornton, the Evans boys and Tim. Tim was still there; he wanted to be a lawyer.

There were now six boys from Parramatta who travelled together after school. Mostly, they managed to catch the ferry. Occasionally, they had to walk the twenty miles, which took over five hours, but they were often able to hitch a ride on a passing cart. Sometimes, they would stay the extra night in town and catch the morning ferry back on Saturday morning.

Mr. Tindale had welcomed Eddie back to the forge. By the time Eddie was sixteen, he had reached full height and towered over his mentor.

Mr. Tindale discussed his future with Charles. Mr. Tindale said, "Charles, I have decided that after Eddie turns twenty-one, I want him to become a junior partner. Ed had kept his hand in whenever he was home and for holidays. I have no children, and I want Eddie's future secured. It also will mean I can ease off a little."

Charles was laid up for months with his broken leg and was only on light work for months more. He was fortunate he didn't lose his leg. Thankfully, the fractured bones did not poke through the skin. Charlie and Eddie did all they could to run the Inn. Ed took the burden of doing the books from Charlie. With Charlie running the inn, he had not been able to come to the forge, and Eddie was again needed on the anvil.

Eddie worked hard, and nothing was too much trouble. He was working full time with Mr. Tindale in work he too loved. He was nearly twenty-one, and Mr. Tindale said he would be made a junior partner in the Blacksmithing shop for his birthday.

The years had been good to the Lockley family. The business was still brisk. His father could walk again but now had a limp.

Liza was engaged to be married to the saddler's son Albert Ellis. Bertie, as she called him, had finally come up to scratch. He had been mooning around after her for some years. Almost since they were children. He was the same age as Charlie. He would often be hanging around the stables late in the afternoons when Liza was doing the mucking out. He helped whenever he could, and they had become close. Bertie had worked at the Inn as a child with Tim.

Charlie and Eddie were both enjoying life. They worked, they fished, and they swam together. Neither sought the company of the rough-drinking lads nor chased girls either. They preferred a quieter life; their family and their church friends were all they needed.

Eddie had learnt much in the past five years on the forge. He could remember needing to stand on a log to reach the handle of the bellows. Now, he could work the bellows and heat the work simultaneously.

Mr. Tindale handed all the heavy work to Ed while he did the books and the shoeing of the horses. This was something Mr. Tindale loved as he adored horses. He had a knack. He could calm a fretful horse and have him stand still while he shooed him. He would sing to them, and they seemed to respond.

Eddie would stand watching him, and he loved watching their ears. From back on their heads to forward and nuzzling the smithies huge dirty hand. They instinctively knew they could trust him.

The forge was a happy place to work, and many people would come and sit on the log seats and talk. In particular, three came often: Old Tom, who was old but never seemed to get older, "Have-a-chat" Harry, and Lawrence, who only had one eye, and they called him "Leery Larry" behind his back. The Lilli Pilli tree had grown even bigger over the past ten years, and Mr. Tindale had made a beautiful wrought iron garden setting and set it up under the tree near the log so anyone could come and sit in the shade and watch the forge. It was far enough away not to feel the oppressive heat of the fire. The three old men felt special to be invited whenever they wished and came often. Ted and some even older characters also appeared for a free mug of tea.

Early on in Eddie's smithing career, he had been set to make horseshoe blanks. These were some of the most common items needed, coming in many different shapes. Farm horses, carriage horses and draught horses pulled the heavy town carts and drays from the troops' horses. There were racing shoes, pony shoes, draught horseshoes, and others, all needed blanks. The roughs were always in stock. Ready to quickly mould into the correct shoe shape that was needed. Many of these had samples displayed on a board on the wall. The blanks of the most common sorts were in wooden drawers, and they could be finished quickly and placed on a waiting horse.

It was nice meeting all the different people from all walks of life. He loved watching people. No two were alike.

Everyone was friendly to the smithy because if you weren't, they may be 'too busy' to fit you in. Eddie and Mr. Tindale enjoyed the friendship of many of the important people in town. Everyone eventually came to the smithies shop, from the Governor to the convicts, farmers to ladies in their buggies.

Mr. Tindale taught Eddie to 'read' people. He learnt there were so many different sorts of people. Most nice, but some to be avoided.

Over the years, the actual shop had changed little. It was still a timber-framed building. It could open entirely on one side, with a big door folding back onto the outside wall, but with a door to the side for quick access if the main wall door were closed. There was a massive anvil to the rear of the building, and the forge and bellows and two smaller different-shaped ones for special purposes.

Mr. Tindale had built workbenches and storage cupboards over the years. He kept the inside clean and as tidy as possible. The outside was a shingle roof and hand-hewn timber slats with gaps along the top to let out the heat. Sadly, this also meant the bitter winds would tear through the building in winter. Working at the forge in winter was nice as they could warm up from the fire. Most days were busy.

Each day, Eddie went home content. Life was good.

Mr. Tindale stuck his head through the side door. "Have you finished the wrought iron lacework that Mr. Miller ordered? I said you'd drop them down today. Is that all right?"

"Yes, sir, that's fine, Mr. Tindale. I'll be done in a bit and will take them down about noon if that's all right. Three are complete; this is the last one. Tim's home from Sydney, and I'd love to catch up with him if that's all right. I've completed all the orders and will restock the wheel rims when I return this afternoon." Eddie smiled at Mr. Tindale's request, as he already knew this was what he was planning to do but wanted Old Tom to hear the polite request.

Ed looked around while he was working. Part-completed wheel rims were also needed. They would be fitted, trimmed and joined to hold the wooden parts of the spoked wheel together. Some of these pre-formed loops were also commonly stockpiled, but they were down to the last one. Cask strapping was always in stock and could easily be cut to length and riveted. The Cooper, Mr. McGuinley, would come and collect long lengths of this and cut to size what he needed.

Eddie continued working and completed the last of the fancy wrought iron decorations. Each of these would become new sign holders. They were beautifully done and intricate coils of spiralling metalwork, giving a classy touch to the growing Rear Admiral Duncan Inn.

At noon, Eddie set off with the four newly completed twisted wrought iron frames. Although heavy, he slipped them over his shoulder effortlessly and sauntered up the hill.

He whistled as he walked, waving his hand in greeting to many of the town locals. They all waved back and occasionally stopped for a quick word.

Tim greeted him on his arrival. "Well, here's a sight for sore eyes. How are you, Eddie?"

"I'm fine, Timmo! How about you? Home for a while, or just a few days?" enquired Eddie.

"Just a few days this time, but I will be moving back soon as they want me to set up an office in Parramatta. I'll be living at home and working here in town. How is blacksmithing going?" He sounded excited.

"Say, that's fantastic, Tim. It'll be so nice to have you back again. I missed you so much after I left school, and you stayed on. How are the Evans family? Everything still all well?" asked Eddie. "I was hoping we could catch a bite to eat while we chatted; anything around?"

Tim said, "Sure is! Of course!"

"I'd better give these to your father first, Timmo. Is he here? I'll hand these over to him."

The two young men went inside to find Mr. Miller.

Eddie carefully removed the wrought iron frames from his shoulder, placing them against the wall. "Are these as you wanted, Mr. Miller?"

"Eddie, they are perfect." Mr. Miller said. "I'm getting the sign writer to redo the signs, and I thought I'd like new frames. What do you think?"

"They'll look good, sir. Anything to bring in new customers. Many more farmers are moving into the area, and I'm sure they will bring in more trade. My Dar is also refurbishing the Inn. He is building more sleeping rooms on the stables for those who don't want to share the barn. People are getting fussy these days. Gone are the days of all the hammocks strung in the loft. They all want beds in private rooms. I wonder where it will end. He has grandiose dreams of building a sleeping wing."

Tim asked if they could both have something to drink. "Pa, Eddie has always been partial to the Apple Cider. Is there any cool? I'll have Ale, please."

Bill Miller handed the two boys the tankards. Eddie drank deeply. "Go easy, lad; that stuff still has a kick. If you're that parched, I'll get you a jug of Molly's lemon punch."

He left the room and returned with a large pottery jug of cold lemonade. "Here, lad, get that into you. I bet that smith's shop is a hot place, and nothing better to quench the thirst than this."

Eddie loved this drink and had much of it when he was young.

Two tankards later, Eddie said, "Oh, that's hit the spot, sir, just what I needed and just how I remembered it too."

The boys sat and chatted for some time, but soon, Eddie stood to head back to work. "Come down to the shop when you have a spare moment, and we'll chat some more. I have to head back now."

Eddie stepped down off the verandah and turned to go. He could hear something approaching fast. He turned to look and saw a herd of goats racing down the street and heading directly for him. Coming up the street from the opposite direction, he could see a person walking on the road.

The person was dawdling, looking down, lost in thought. They did not realise they were in danger.

He ran!

Eddie and Tim were both yelling.

The person raised their head.

Eddie was nearly there, and so were the goats.

He grabbed and dragged the person aside, only to find that the enormous stone horse trough was much closer than he expected.

Splash. They both tumbled in just as the goats sped past, and the pair sat up, spluttering.

"What the... exactly why did you do that?" came an exasperated howl.

It was a girl... dressed in old work trousers, and she had lost the old felt wide-brimmed hat she'd been wearing. Her honey-gold hair tumbled down around her face. Her hat had been trampled by the goats and flattened. Suddenly, she giggled, then threw her head back and laughed.

They were both sitting in the large stone horse trough.

Eddie was stunned. He looked at her. "Dripping wet, she would be about half my size," he thought.

"You should see your face; that was so funny. Oh look, my hat, it's flattened, but I'll fix that." She leaned out, grabbed it off the ground and dragged it into the trough. Dunk, dunk, then bang and a few well-aimed punches and slopped it back onto her head. "Well, it didn't get damaged and is now a lot cooler, as am I. I'm Jenna." She put out her hand to Eddie.

Eddie found his voice, "Hello, I'm Eddie. I'm so sorry, but I suppose getting wet was better than being trampled by marauding goats."

Again, she giggled, but not a silly girlish giggle, but a deep, joyous sort of musical laugh. "You have a strand of straw in your hair; I wonder where that came from. Bend over." She reached over, brushed her hand against his cheek, and removed the offending strand.

Electricity shot down his cheek.

"Well, you've made my day, Eddie, whoever you are. I'm new in the area, well, sort of. My family have settled in Emu Plains, and I had to come to town for supplies. It's my first trip here, though. Normally, it's my oldest brother's job, but he's busy. Pa is short-handed at our Inn, and I've been sent to town to collect a huge load of supplies." She paused, feeling her top pocket. "And just out of town, my horse lost a shoe, so now I have to find a blacksmith," she said without stopping to take a breath. She carefully removed a soggy list and flattened it out.

They had finally removed themselves from the trough and were standing in the street, both dripping wet, the puddle around them getting bigger by the moment.

At this comment by Jenna, Eddie mockingly bowed. "At your service, ma'am. I am the blacksmith, or at least one of them. Where have you left your brave steed?" He chuckled. "May I escort you to it?"

He offered his arm to her and joyfully went in search of the said horse. All thoughts of work fled.

They left a trail of puddles and wet footprints as they walked off. Of the goats, there was no sign.

He towered over her; she only came up to his shoulder. She had a smile that would make clouds fly away, so sunny it was. Her amber eyes danced with joy when she laughed. He couldn't take his eyes off her. He did not even remember that Tim was still watching.

Tim smiled, shook his head and walked inside.

Jenna was a country girl who was also familiar with hard work. He discovered she was eighteen and was one of John and Martha Turner's seven children on the Arms of Australia Inn at Emu Plains.

Since the road was built across the Blue Mountains, many people were heading west, which meant more farmers and travellers needed goods. Emu Plains was in the foothills. The last stop before the climb started.

Jenna's family Inn was a very popular place. Many travellers would stock up on supplies like flour, sugar, salt and horseshoes. It was these that Jenna had been asked to get, along with tool heads, nails and assorted other smithed goods, as well as barrels and the rings for them. She didn't expect to have to get a shoe for her own horse.

Jenna's horse, she called him Phillip and her dray was tied up outside Major Grace's office at the Barracks.

They unhitched him, and they walked slowly back to the blacksmith's forge with the lame horse and the empty dray.

Eddie was still feeling tongue-tied with this amazing girl. He had never been one for a lot of small talk, and she just chatted happily about many different things that interested him. He wanted to see across the mountains. He wanted to know what possibilities there were for him in life. He already had a feeling that this girl would be part of these dreams. Hopefully, she'd be sent in for supplies more often, or he'd find reasons to make deliveries out that way. He might even need to stay over sometimes at their Inn. He'd find some excuse. He sighed.

They arrived at the forge, and by this time, that was mid-afternoon. Mr. Tindale appeared with a steaming cup of tea for Eddie. "Looks like I'll need another mug. Who is this young Eddie? And why are you wet?"

"Mr. Tindale, this is Jenna Turner. We had an incident with a herd of goats, and both ended up in the horse trough just down from the Rear Admiral Duncan Inn. She's come to buy supplies from Emu Plains, but her horse has cast a shoe. Her folks run the Arms of Australia Inn."

Eddie looked down at her and handed her the tea that Mr. Tindale had brought for him. "Do you mind an old tin mug?" he asked with a smile.

She said, "Aww, come on, Ed, that's all I have a drink from. We're not fancy out at Emu. See how I'm dressed? Just down to earth, common folk." She took a sip. "Mmm, hot, strong and sweet, just how I like it." They settled for a while until the tea was finished. "Thanks, Mr. Tindale."

Mr. Tindale had joined them. "I believe you need supplies?"

"Yes, sir," she said. "Good! Straight down to business. All right."

She pulled out the now dry list. "Pa needs… six spade heads, twenty pick heads, and twenty axe heads. He said shears, callipers, and tongs; I can see various kinds. Darn, he didn't put what sorts; I suppose one of each of those, then. Irons and welding irons, assorted vices; the holding sort not bad manners," she laughed. "Six different sorts of hammerheads. Also, one hundred horseshoes, mostly the packhorses ones, and the other assorted blanks, clinchers, rasps…." She checked her list. "…and Pa said nails, lots of nails. What have you got in nails?"

Mr. Tindale showed her the sample board.

She looked and said, "I'll have six boxes, please one each of those and…." She also chose horseshoe nails, roofing nails, long nails, and a small box of tiny ones. She kept looking. "Oh, look, a box of mixed heads; throw those in too. Oh, even more hammerheads." They were of various shapes and sizes. "Where are you up to with costs now, sir? I still have to get food supplies. One of my brothers works for the saddler out there, so we're good for leather goods."

He tallied everything up, and she dug into a leather pouch and handed the money to Mr. Tindale.

That sorted, he said, "I'll have your horse done in a moment."

Ed got to work on the new shoe while Mr. Tindale prepared the hoof.

Jenna watched, having seen this done before, "I never tire of watching the skills involved in doing such a simple job," she said. She sat with her chin on her hands, watching Eddie work. "I used to sit and watch our farrier whenever he came."

Eddie's muscles rippled as he swung the hammer on the hot shoe. The sweat trickled down his forehead from the heat of the fire. He'd stripped off his wet shirt and put on his thick leather apron. His muscular arms were bare, glistening with sweat. He worked quickly, aware her eyes never left him, and they weren't always watching his work. He lifted his head and smiled at her.

She met his sky-blue eyes in a steady hold, then smiled.

He smiled back, his eyes alive. He discovered he didn't mind her watching him. He actually enjoyed it. Yes, he liked it.

Mr. Tindale had filed and smoothed the hoof after removing the old shoe.

Eddie finished the new one and asked him, "Ready?"

Mr. Tindale said, "Yes."

Eddie brought it over in the tongs while it was still hot. He fitted it for size and set it on the hoof. It seared onto the hoof, and it set flat. Mr. Tindale then nailed it in position. "There, Mr. Phillip, all done. That should feel better," he said as he let the leg go and patted the horse.

Phillip shuffled, getting used to the feel of the new shoe. Eddie led the horseback to the dray and harnessed it up. He had started loading the order on the dray while Mr. Tindale finished the shoeing.

"Let's load up the rest of the goods, and I'll take you down to the store to get the rest of your supplies. Is that okay, Mr. Tindale?"

"Sure thing, Eddie; you can't let a lass like this do that on her own. She won't know where to go either. I'll see you tomorrow, Eddie." Eddie turned and smiled at Mr. Tindale and mouthed "Thank you" to him with a massive grin.

"Up you go, Miss Jenna," He handed her to the dray seat. "Eddie will see you, right? You can trust him; he is a good lad. His father runs the Government Store, so you'll get things at a good price." Mr. Tindale raised a hand to wave and walked into the shop.

Mr. Tindale looked into shelves and drawers and then at money in his hand and said to himself, "I don't think life is going to be the same from today. I think Ed has met his match in that small person." He picked up a chalk piece and started writing on the board what needed to be replaced after Jenna's large order. He added a few bits and then spread the forge coals to let them die down for tomorrow.

Eddie and Jenna set off in the dray to the Jolly Sailor Inn. "It's getting late, Jenna. Where were you planning to stay? Do you mind if I take you home to Mama? Also, you can talk to Dar about the supplies you need. You can stay with us tonight, at the Inn. So you'll be safe, saving you a bit of money. Do you mind sharing with the girls?"

She said, "Thanks, Ed. That would be great. I share with my sisters at home."

On arrival at the Inn, Eddie got Jenna to drive the dray straight to the stables. Charlie was just walking out. Eddie asked him to unharness the horse. "Hey, Charlie, his name's Phillip," he said. "Can you then stable him for the night, please?" The three chatted briefly before Eddie took Jenna inside to meet his mother. "Mama, this is Jenna Turner from the Emu Plains. Her folks run the Arms of Australia Inn. Is it all right if she stays tonight? She has to get stores to take back with her tomorrow. Can I leave her here while I go and talk to Dar?"

Sal nodded and turned to greet Jenna. She liked the look of this bright-eyed lass.

Eddie walked out to look for his father.

Charles limped up from the cellar and greeted him. "Hello, son, did I hear voices?"

"Yes, Dar," he said, "I've bought somebody who needs some stores. Any chance she can get some cheaper?

"Ooh, it's a 'she', is it? This is new. Where did you meet her?" Charles asked.

Eddie blushed, but he continued his explanation. "Yeah, her name is Jenna Turner. She's from Emu Plains. Dar, it's a funny story." Eddie told his father the story of meeting Jenna and the goats. "Her horse needed a shoe, so I took it to the forge and fixed that up. Mr. Tindale and I have been able to supply some of the ironwork she needed, but I'll have to make some wheel edgings and take them out next week. The nails, hammer and pick heads, horseshoes and spades are on board already." He paused, thinking of the attractive young lady he had rescued.

His father smiled at his son. He'd not seen him gush so effusively ever before.

Eddie continued, not having noticed his father's interest. "Apparently, there is a rumour around that something is happening over the mountains. There's new land and stuff; I know farmers are heading out there, and I heard of new towns, too. There's a slow trickle of men heading west. New land grants and such. Jenna said that's why her Pa sent her in; they need stock."

He excitedly talked as he had when he was little, hardly pausing for a breath.

Charles looked at him with one eyebrow raised questioningly. "Turner, you say," said Charles. "I wonder if she's Jack Turner's daughter. He came out with me in '20. He was the one who helped report the rebels on board. We both were given our 'Ticket of Leave' from that. I know he went out that way somewhere after he married. I might have a chat with this lass of yours."

Eddie almost blushed. "Oh, Dar, She's not my girl," he grinned. "Well, not yet, but she's so nice. I hope she is Jack's daughter; that would make things much easier. Let's go and find out."

Charles looked amazed. Eddie had never shown much interest in anything much more than his work. No girl had ever turned his head before. He knew just how fast that could change, and Ed was the same age he was when he first saw Sal. One look across a yard was all it took.

They walked back into the kitchen and found Sal and Jenna laughing while preparing the evening meal, Charles limping and using a stick.

"Hello, Miss Jenna," said Charles, giving her a mock bow, "Now, would you, by any chance, be Jack Turner's daughter?"

She gasped. "Yes, sir."

"We came out together," he said quietly.

"Oh, my goodness! Mr. Lockley, sir, yes, Jack is my Pa. I didn't realise you were 'that' Mr. Lockley. Pa talks about you and THAT incident all the time. He fell on his feet thanks to you and Major Grace."

"Well, this makes things different. You're almost family. Anything we can do for you or your family, well, we'd be honoured," said Charles. "Let's have a look at this list of stores you need, and we'll see what we can sort out. Eddie, head up to Mr. Tindale and ask if Charlie can fill your place tomorrow. I want you to take Jenna home tomorrow. There will be too much on her dray to travel alone. There are still some ruffians on the road, and I'd rather you go with her and take the guns, too. You might be able to shoot a roo on the way home. Take the pistol, too. Just in case, make sure you have enough shots. Off you go, Ed. I'll get Jenna's list sorted." He shooed Eddie out, and then Charles ushered Jenna to the table and sat down with her to review her father's requirements list. "Now, lass, I believe you had a damp introduction to my son. I do hope you weren't hurt?"

"Oh, Mr. Lockley, yes, but it was so funny. I was walking down the street, minding my own business, off in some dreamworld, and also worried about finding a blacksmith to re-shoe my horse when I got crash-tackled by a tall stranger and ended up drenched in a horse trough." She laughed again. "Rather than hurt, it was just so funny, and I sat in the trough and just laughed. I was hot anyway. As we were falling in, I realised why he did it, because about thirty goats ran down the street. I would have been head-butted and flattened if he hadn't. So he really saved my life." She gave him a beaming smile. "An original way to meet a girl, I must say. And he was just the man I needed. A blacksmith. After the goats passed, we emerged, dripping wet and walked down the street to Major Grace's office to get my horse and dray. Pa had said to leave it there until I sorted out the supplies. Pa knew Major Grace from the ship." She realised something. "Oh, you'd know him then too."

"Yes, lassie, I know him," said Charles, "He's one of those true gentlemen in this colony. Yes, he's a good man and, dare I say it, a true friend. You can trust him. He was on the ship with two other battalions, the 59th and 63rd. He is in charge of the 48th, and they were sent directly here. He's been here ever since."

"Anyway," continued Jenna, "As we walked up the street, we left a long line of wet footprints and puddles, and we laughed most of the way there. We were still laughing on arrival at the Major's office. He greeted us with a look of surprise. He, too, enjoyed the story after we told him what had happened." Jenna took a mouthful of her tea. "We took Phillip, that's Pa's horse, and the dray and walked up to Eddie's blacksmith shop," she took another gulp of her tea. "Eddie then introduced me to Mr. Tindale, who helped me with more of Pa's order while Eddie set about making a new shoe, then Mr. Tindale finished him up."

Sal had joined them by this stage and sat listening. She liked this girl as soon as they met. Sal chipped in. "Charles, I had tears rolling down my face when she told me the story. Oh, it must have looked so funny."

Charles was, by this stage, wiping his own eyes.

Jenna was giggling again.

Anna, Wills, and Luke all stuck their heads around the door and asked if anything was wrong. After Charles introduced them, Jenna repeated the story, and the three newcomers joined in laughing.

Twelve-year-old Luke asked, "I wonder what happened to the goats? I want a few goats, Mama. Can we get some goats, too, please?"

"No, Luke," intervened Charles. "You need fences to keep goats in, and even then, they escape." By this time, Charlie had joined them.

Charles turned to him and said, "Charlie, I've sent Ed to Mr. Tindale's to ask him if he'd mind you taking his place tomorrow; I'm sending Eddie to escort Jenna home. It will be too dangerous to drive all that way to Emu Plains with the load she'll have on. Hope you don't mind, but Luke and Wills, you can pull your weight and do Charlie's chores tomorrow and then some." He turned to Sal. "I have some other things they need to do for me. It will keep them out of mischief." He turned to the younger boys. "Did you hear that? Full chores tomorrow, so no school for you both. I'll send a note. I'll mind the taproom." He then turned. "Anna, you can milk the cow."

Both boys were punching the air in glee.

"Right, now, lass, that's them all organised; where's this list?"

Jenna pulled it from her pocket again and handed it to Charles.

Charles took it, and he sat reading it. "Hmm, ahh, ah-ha," he said. "Yes, we can do all this. We'll have to pack it all carefully. Did you bring some ropes?"

Jenna nodded, "Yes, sir, and there's an old sail that Pa bought, so the supplies are both covered and watertight. It will cover the whole dray."

"Good," said Charles.

Eddie walked in as they finished. By now, the lamp was lit, and the table set by the younger children.

Sal stood and asked, "How would you like to give me a hand, Jenna? We can chat while we work. We have a few at the counter who'd like some stew, and there's a lot of us." As they left the room, Charlie, Charles, and Eddie sat down.

Charles looked at Eddie. "Well, lad, I hope you don't mind, but you're now free to take Jenna home."

Eddie smiled ear to ear, then blushed bright red. "If I would, Dar, I'm looking forward to it."

"I wonder why," Charles said quietly to him. "I like her," he whispered.

Ed did not reply to his comment but smiled. "So do I," he thought. He turned to Charlie. "Charlie, I spoke to Mr. Tindale, and he's looking forward to you coming up again. All three of us might have to put in a few hard weeks to replace all the goods the Turners have bought. I'll have to take a few wheel rims out next week as we didn't have the right sizes."

Charles stood and went to usher out the two younger boys. "Come on, you two rascals. Time to wash for dinner." He turned back to the two older boys. "Come on; you two can come as well. Scrub." To Charlie, he said, "Charlie, go and change that shirt; it smells. Put your church shirts on. And Eddie, you're filthy. Even after your dip." He turned smiling to himself. "We have a visitor, an important visitor, don't we, Eddie?" He nudged him with his elbow, and Eddie blushed again.

"Oh, Dar," was all he could say.

They all scrubbed in the cool water and certainly looked somewhat cleaner. The two elder boys stripped off their shirts and gave them a rinse in the water and a rub with the soap. "Hang them on the verandah rail, boys; in this heat, they will be dry by bedtime," said Charles. "Inside all of you, and mind your manners tonight, please."

The meal was a great success, even though it was only stew. Everyone talked and laughed, finally stumbling into bed late.

The candle had guttered, then spluttered out before anyone noticed how late it was. Liza and Bertie had even come along after they had eaten, as Bertie had walked Liza home. She had stayed for a meal with his family.

Liza and Anna said Jenna could share their bed. She collected a little bag she'd brought in from the dray and followed them. Soon, the remaining lamp was extinguished, and the house was silent.

The next morning, the cockerel crowed just before dawn as it normally did; kookaburras, cockatoos and numerous other birds joined them. Somehow, for Eddie, everything was fresher and more joyous. He came from his room whistling, a towel across his shoulder.

Soon, the house was full of activity. After a visit to the water drum outside, where, one by one, they all washed their faces, everyone went about the morning duties. Charles called for Jenna and Eddie, and they walked down to the Government storehouse. Charlie was harnessing Jenna's horse and dray and would bring it down on his way to the smithy's shop.

Charles was responsible for ensuring they were safely stored and ordering stock to keep the supplies needed. Since transportation was due to end, he could sell to anyone and re-order when required. Major Grace had nominated him for this position as he knew he was trustworthy and educated. Most people preferred to buy their bulk supplies from Charles as the Government Stores' prices were lower than from the shops.

Jenna had not expected to be able to do this and was surprised at how much more she could get with her money. She turned to Charles. "Oh, Mr. Lockley, how am I ever going to fit all this on? And how am I ever to thank you?" Her eyes were wide open. "Phillip will earn his keep if he gets this home safely."

The pile of bags at the big barn doors kept getting bigger. Eddie heard Charlie arrive and start loading the stores around the already laden dray. He'd carefully placed all the heavy iron stores down the centre of the dray so that it would balance evenly. They set the heavy grain bags, along with salt, along the sides and all the smaller items in the centre so they would not fall off. Then, they placed the flour bags on top. Once everything was loaded, Charles, Jenna and Eddie wrapped the sailcloth over everything and roped it down. By the time this was done, they were all ready for breakfast. They all hopped onto the bench seat, and Jenna then drove back up the hill to the Inn.

Sal awaited them and greeted them with, "Porridge is ready, and I've made you two a packed lunch to take. There is bread, cheese, and ale, and a few other things. You'd better hurry and eat so you can get on the road before it gets too hot. Inside with you all. The others have already eaten and gone." She ushered them inside and served them immediately.

Barley porridge and cream with some honey is delicious. "Thanks, Mama," said Eddie. "We'll be off now."

He gave her a quick hug and turned to his father.

Charles had laid a long package on the table and unwrapped it. Inside were two rifles and some ball and powder. He measured out some of the ammunition and tied it in two leather pouches. One for the ball and one for powder. Then he unhitched a pistol from his belt. "You'll take this too, Ed. You know how to use them all, but be careful; they are both loaded," Charles said. "Keep the pistol on you and the musket under the seat. You'll be right. I'm sure you won't need them." He placed the two chosen guns next to the oilcloth wrapper. "I told Charlie to saddle Bobbs. Don't forget you will need him to get home." He rolled up the remaining gun and moved it off the table.

"Dar, can I just take the pistol? Otherwise, I have to take the saddle holster." Ed said.

Charles sighed, "I supposed so. Off you go now. Jenna, it's been a real delight meeting you. Don't be a stranger, and send my regards to your Pa and Ma. I hope we get to meet up again sometime. I'll tell Major Grace what he's up to, although he may already know. He's a silent one, that man, but a good man."

Sal came from the kitchen, and they all walked out to the dray. The two horses were stomping and eager to get moving.

Eddie handed Jenna up into the dray, and he hopped on Bobbs. Charles untied Jenna's horse, Phillip, and handed her the reins. They moved off up the street at a walk. Both turned back and waved farewell; Phillip was already straining to move the heavy dray. He was a big gelding and was strong. He could not take off with the heavy load or hurry. It would take most of the day to get to Emu Plains as they'd have to walk the entire way. Hopefully, they would arrive before nightfall.

After travelling for a few hours, Eddie asked if she needed a stop and a drink. "There's a nice place to stop near Eastern Creek. Would you like a bit of a stop? It can't be for long, but we can give the horses a drink."

Jenna said, "I'd love that, Eddie, and I think Phillip is ready for a break too."

Around the bend, they came to a spot that was obviously used for resting horses. They had just passed the turn-off to the Government stockyards at Rooty Hill. Someone had also made a trough of sorts, made from a hollowed-out log, and placed it in the shade of a large tree. "I might need to go for a wee walk too, Ed. I won't be long." She hopped down and headed into the scrubby bushes.

She had been gone about three minutes when Eddie heard "Edddddie, Edd. Oh. No! Eddie," in a somewhat panicked voice.

He had hobbled the horses at the trough and checked the load. When he heard her, he raced to see what was wrong. "Jenna, where are you?" he called. She was still not visible.

"Behind the fallen wattle tree, Ed. There's a snake at my feet, and I can't move. I just wee'd next to it, and it's not happy. I didn't see it until I stood up."

Eddie could hear the fear in her voice. He carefully walked towards her, stomping hard on the ground to cause vibrations. It worked, and the snake slithered off.

"Oh, Eddie, thank you so much!" she said. Her voice was still shaking. She hopped up on the fallen tree and jumped down into his arms. He had just meant to give her a hand but didn't mind a hug. He bent to kiss the top of her head, but she lifted it at that moment, and he kissed her forehead instead. "Thank you, Eddie, for being here. I'm not that keen on snakes. Actually, I hate snakes." She shivered, still in his arms. "I hate them with a loathing. I would have had to stand there all day. That's twice you've saved me." She moved from his arms but grabbed his hand. "Once more, and I'm yours for life, you realise." She turned to him with an immense grin on her face. "Oh, Eddie, you should see your face. You are so funny. I was only kidding, you know."

Eddie was still holding her hand, "Actually, I might even like that, you know." He held her hand as they walked back to the dray. "Let's get out of here. You have a quick drink while I find a safe tree myself." He walked off towards a large gum tree.

By the time he returned, she'd hitched Bobbs to the back of the dray and said, "Come on. Up you hop. We can't talk much while you're riding. Wanna take the reins? I'm still shaking."

He hopped up beside her and took the reins from her. "Gee up, Phillip. Off you go." The horse now rested, started and moved back onto the dusty track.

Jenna started humming as she settled back. "Oh, it is nice to rest my arms." She shook both arms to relax them. "If I loosened them, he would just stop, so I've had to keep my wits about me. Poor Phil. The load must be heavy to pull on these tracks. I sing to him when I'm travelling alone; he seems to like it. What songs do you know?"

Eddie suggested a few; they started off singing quietly for a while but then moved on to some songs from the inn. Eddie admitted that he had been in the Choir at St. James when he was in Sydney. So they threw in an occasional hymn; finally, they fell silent until Phillip struggled at another hill.

Eddie handed Jenna the reins and jumped off. He would go to Phillip's head and grab the bridle, leading him up the incline. "Come on, boy, you can do it."

Jenna hopped off, too; although she was so small, it didn't make much difference in weight, but she also went to Phillip's head and patted him. "Come on, old boy. Not many more to go before another rest." She turned to Eddie. "There's another rest spot at Ropes Creek. I thought we'd stop there for another break. We'll then attack what your Mama has packed for us."

"Sounds fine, Jenna. It's also hot now, so a nice shady spot will be perfect." They walked Phillip up to the top of the hill, and both hopped back on the hard dray seat.

They could see a creek in the not-too-far distance, and both were looking forward to the stop. They discussed anything that came to mind; they agreed on most things, but on some, they had opposing views.

Jenna, as Eddie had already realised, was an independent woman. Most girls in the area were. They really didn't have a choice. Life was tough for everyone.

Eddie was still surprised that her father had allowed her to come to Parramatta alone. Let alone wear men's breeches. Many women had to chop wood, draw water from a well, and sometimes wash in the local creeks. In some cases, the women had to "keep the home fires burning," as it was said, while their husbands were either away, in gaol or had even died.

Jenna, therefore, had determined ideas on the ability of females. They discussed this for quite some time. Jenna was getting somewhat "iffy" and a bit upset with Eddie until he said, "Next time, scare off your own snake."

Jenna looks up at him. "I'm sorry, Ed; I didn't mean to upset you. I just get so angry that I'm not supposed to have a thought in my head just because I'm a girl. I get so annoyed. I'm not the sort of girl to sit and paint in watercolour." she sighed.

"Oh, Jen, I understand. Mrs. Evans and her husband used to talk about this often. She had three boys to bring up virtually alone as Mr. Evans, or Captain Evans as he actually is, is often away for months at a time. I lived with them for five years, and she was such a capable woman and was often somewhat irked when her beloved husband returned home and, without consultation, just took over everything she was doing. I would see her sigh, just like you did, and shrug her shoulders. She knew it was no use arguing about it. She hated that she was then only supposed to pay calls to friends, play the piano, sew or paint watercolours. She hated sitting so idle." Eddie looked down at Jenna. "We men forget that you women have to go through the pain of childbirth, and that takes strength."

"Are you serious, Ed? You mean that?" said Jenna. "Every other man I know thinks women should be at home, just bearing children and cooking, twiddling their fingers. We can do all sorts of things by ourselves, but I prefer working together as a team. It's how Maa and Pa manage, and it works. I'll never marry until I find someone who won't crush me." She sighed again. "My Pa has needed me to help him at the Inn on more than one occasion, so he knows I'm capable of most things that my brothers, Marc and Alex, can do. Marc is often away, and Alex is at work with the saddler. I can fill in for them. I can fix saddles, shape a new spoke and do basic woodwork repairs. I can fix a new shoe and things like that, but Ma also taught me to cook, sew and other girly things, and I love them too. Marc, Alex, and I love to fish and swim, too, so we often go together when we can get some time off. I have learnt to play the piano and read and write, as Maa said, one day. She taught me. I was probably going to have to play in church. It turned out I had some skill, and now I quite enjoy it. I only get to practice if we go to Windsor, though, as we don't have a church near us."

Eddie said, "When I lived in Sydney at school, I also learned to play a bit. More to pick out a tune when the Choir Master was away. I love to sing as you may gather. I was a boy soprano when I was a kid. Then my voice broke, and I got thrown out of the choir." Eddie fell silent.

Phillip's steps grew shorter and slower, but they were nearly at the creek. Eddie pulled the dray up under the tree and tugged on the brake. He hopped off and started to loosen Phillip's traces. Jenna, too, jumped down and went to untie Bobbs. Both horses drank and started nibbling the green grass growing under the trough.

Jenna grabbed the bag that Sal had supplied and dug into it. "Oh Ed, your ma has packed hard-boiled eggs, some bread and some twists of … I think it's salt." She tasted it. "How luxurious! I've never seen it done like this. What else is there? Ooh, cider, oranges, and cheese. You know, have you ever tried salt on the oranges? Pa loves a pinch of salt on them. He half peels them in a spiral like this." She grabbed a folding knife from her pocket, chopped off the top of the orange, and peeled it halfway. Then she said, "Then he cuts it like this," chopping it in a cross pattern down to the peeled section. "Then you sprinkle salt on it and chomp." She took a bite. "Hmm, yum. And then there are the eggs. I love salt on those, too."

Eddie said, "I hope there's some for me. Let's sit under the tree and unpack the food." Jenna threw the peel into the bushes and grabbed the bag, heading to the shade. Sal had sliced and buttered the entire loaf of bread, but she'd wrapped it in a damp cloth and put it in with the hard-boiled eggs, cheese, and other goodies. Jenna grabbed one of the blankets that she had been sitting on, as the wooden dray seat was not that comfortable. She got Eddie to spread it out for a picnic.

Eddie sat the cider bottle in the creek to cool down and went to sit in the shade with Jenna. They enjoyed their feast, and both lay back to enjoy the peace, tranquillity and shade. They both dozed off only to be awoken by the whinnying of the horses. Eddie rubbed his eyes, noticing a coach coming down the roadway at speed.

Jenna also sat up and looked. "Oh, it's the mail coach," she said. "My, it's late. It normally should be through here mid-morning. Something must have happened. We'd better move along, Eddie; there could be some trouble up the road." They hopped up and quickly packed up and got back on the road.

They could smell the late flowering oranges from the Orchard Hills trees as they drove closer to the river. It was a delightfully sweet smell and a waft of eucalyptus from the gum trees. As the breeze moved, different scents carried in the air. They chatted nonstop, occasionally breaking into song, especially when Phillip came to a hill. Ed's deep baritone complemented Jenna's contralto.

After one song, he said, "I often break into song when smithing an intricate piece; it helps me concentrate. Occasionally Mr. Tindale joins in."

Some hours later, they could see the trees lining the riverbank in the distance. They had made good time with few mishaps. They should reach the river by dusk and should be able to cross it before twilight.

Phillip had just crested a hill, and there was a large hole that neither saw. The front left wheel caught the edge of it and made it over okay, but the back wheel caught it and went straight in. It was a big hole, and the wheel had buckled under the weight of the dray.

"Oh no," they said in unison.

Eddie hopped down, "Hold him, Jenna; I'll see how bad it is."

She could hear him muttering to himself.

"We'll be able to move the dray, but I'm going to have to pull off the wheel to fix it. One of the spokes broke. Thankfully, all the tools you bought from Mr. Tindale are what I'll need to repair it, but I have to dismantle the wheel. That means we must unpack some of the load as they are all underneath the dry stores. Let's move the dray first; we'll see if we can get it off the road and under that tree. You go to Phillip's head and get Bobbs to pull too."

They got Bobbs loosely tied to the dray, and Eddie said, "Ready? One, two, three, go." With a big tug, the two horses managed to get the stuck wheel out of the pothole.

"Yeah," said Jenna. "Did it. Come on, Phillip, you get a rest for a bit. You too, Bobbs."

Eddie walked beside Bobbs, who was roped to the dray. He was straining at an odd angle, so he needed some encouragement to pull.

They directed the dray with its wobbling wheel off the road.

"I'll just get to work and find something to hold the dray up. Jenna, can you find some chocks for the wheels? We'll leave the horses tied to it until it's safe." They each walked off, looking for the needed items. Eddie found a couple of big flat rocks and a big round one, and Jenna found three that would do for chocks. Eddie had to make four trips to get them to the dray, but eventually, the wheels were chocked, brake on, and the big rocks were sitting nearly under the axle. "Jenna, can you get Phillip to move just one step? That should take the dray up onto the rocks. Ready? Now…"

Jenna released the brake and got Phillip to move just one step. "Gee up, Phil," she said.

He took one step, and the dray went up on the rocks. She quickly pulled on the brake again, then went to Phillip's head. "Will I take him out of the harness so he doesn't move the dray?"

"Yes, thanks, Jenna, that would probably be a good idea. Let him graze. The hobbles are in the back. Can you do them both?"

She said, "Yep, no worries, Ed. Leave it with me. You get on to the wheel. Hope it won't take long, or we won't get home before night." She went to deal with the horses while Eddie unpacked some of the dray stores so he could access the tools he'd need to remove the wheel.

It took an hour to access the tools, remove the wheel and assess the damage.

Eddie was sitting with his head in his hands when Jenna saw him. "What's wrong, Eddie? Can't you fix it?" She asked, sounding concerned.

"Yes, I can fix it, but I will need to make a new spoke. To get it in, I have to completely dismantle the wheel and then somehow get the rim back on again, so we'll need to make a fire. It's going to take ages. Jenna, we won't make it to your home tonight. I am so sorry, but I'm glad you were not here alone. Okay, let's get cracking. Wood for a fire, and we'll need water. Thankfully, there's a trickle in the small creek. We'll have to use one of the horse's nose bags to carry it, but it's the only thing we have. I have to find a branch and make a spoke, then remove the wheel trim; oh, you don't need to know the details, let's just get on. Wood first, I'll need a lot of wood. The entire rim has to be hot. And Jenna, careful of snakes. We can build a fire over there, so I don't have far to carry the wheel. It's safe enough as it's nowhere near the bush."

Once they had some wood, Jenna said, "Ed, I can make a start on the spoke, and you can fine-tune it."

Eddie pulled off the wheel rim, and Jenna started making a new spoke with a branch he'd found. She whittled the ends to the right size with Eddie's knife while he reassembled the bits on the ground. It fitted; that was the easy bit. Jenna had a small fire going to one side and had the ring fire ready for the wheel trim. It had burnt down enough but was still hot. The rim was sitting next to the fire, ready to be heated.

"Okay, Jenna, I'm ready. Let's put the rim in the fire. Let's hope I can get it back on." He looked exhausted.

Jenna said, "Eddie, you are amazing. There is no way I would have known what to do. I would have just had to sit here until someone came. Then I would have had to stay with the stores and just send a message to Pa to come and help. I'm so glad you came." She gave him a half hug and said, "Okay, let's get this thing finished."

They carefully placed the rim on the coals and stacked more wood on top. The rim was soon hot enough, and they were ready to remove it, but first, they needed water. Jenna had emptied the horses' nose bags and filled them with water, ready to quench the heat. They needed to pour water on the rim once it was on the wheel, and as the water hit the steel, it shrunk the metal trim onto the wheel; this kept all the bits together and made the wheel stable.

Eddie normally did this at a fully equipped blacksmith forge where everything was at hand and ready. Here, he had to use branches to remove the hot rim from the fire and drag it onto the wheel. Then, together, they had to hammer it onto the wooden wheel while it was still scalding hot. He had the hammers ready, a small one for Jenna and the big ten-pounder for him. "Are you ready, Jenna? Water, hammers…" He prised out the rim with two big branches and some of the new callipers. "Okay, stand clear here it comes. Let's hope it slips straight on. It should, as it came off."

As he set the hot rim on the wheel, it burnt the timber as it should, and it sat on with only a bit of hammering to do. "Jenna, just hit your hammer on the side of the rim, and I'll hit it on here, then pour the water over your half when I say. Okay? Ready? Now…" Bang, bang, the rim slipped on. "Water now, fast, not too much, but all around your half of the rim."

She was in awe of how he knew just what to do. She'd seen it done before, but not by the side of the road. She fell back on her butt. "Wow, that was amazing, Eddie, now to get it back on. Can you see to do it?"

There was no moon tonight; it would become dark quickly. "I got more wood while you worked, so we have a stack. We'll have to stay here tonight and move off tomorrow morning. Just as well, we didn't eat all the food your Mama sent. We have the blankets from the seat, but I'm not sleeping on the ground. Sorry. No way." She had a big grin on her face. "Come on, let's get finished. What tools do you need to finish? I'll put the rest back in the dray."

He pointed out which ones to leave and brought her the rest. "While we're waiting for the wheel to cool properly, let's make the load flat, and you can sleep up there. What do you think? Should keep the snakes away."

"Oh? It's almost like a mattress, but it will smell floury. Just as well, your Dar put the flour on the top; we only have to flatten the bags."

They removed the rest of the sailcloth covering and adjusted the load.

Jenna placed tools on the back of the dray while Eddie put them away. The few that were required to fit the wheel would fit under the seat with the unused guns.

They worked away until the load was flat enough to sleep on. Then they covered the load again with the sail, and Jenna laid the blankets on top.

Eddie lifted her down and held her a little longer than he should, just enjoying the closeness.

She laid her head on his chest momentarily and hugged him back. She lifted her head, and he gave her a peck on the lips, then released her. "Not like a gentleman should treat a lady he's known for a day," Ed said to himself.

She sighed contentedly.

"I'll get the wheel back on now so that we're ready to go at first light. There's enough grass for the horses, but they will need water. Is there enough in that creek?" He walked over to the wheel, felt the rim, and saw that it was cool enough to work on. He lifted it and rolled it over to the dray. He manoeuvred it onto the hub and fixed it with the pin to hold it on. He stood looking at it with his hands on his hips and said, "Done."

Jenna walked over and slid her arms around his waist. "Thanks, Ed."

He put his arm around her and bent and kissed the top of her head. "I can't believe I only met you yesterday. I feel like I've known you forever. Come on, let's eat before the fire goes out. What's left?" They walked to the fire, holding hands. "What's for tucker woman?" he said laughingly. He laid back on the grass with his arms behind his head and relaxed.

Jenna handed him some bread she'd toasted over the fire on a stick. "There are some eggs left, too; squish one on the toast. There is some cheese left and a bottle of ale. We'd better leave some bread for the morning, but we almost have a feast."

They sat down and ate their feast while chatting.

As the fire died down, the darkness finally fell. The birds had also settled down for the night.

Once the leftover food was stowed, Eddie said, "Up you go, girl, you'll be safe enough up there. I'll grab a blanket and sleep down here. I'll be able to keep the fire going." He stowed the food under the seat with the tools. Then he checked on the horses. They were fine, and he returned to the dray.

Jenna had scrambled up on the dray bed and said, "I've made room for you too. It's not like we're undressing. There are too many snakes around to be safe down there. They are nasty brown ones out here. Come on, you too." She patted the blankets.

He shuffled his feet shyly. "No! Really, Jenna, it's not right. I can't. I won't. What's more, I only met you yesterday."

She said, "Rubbish, Eddie, we're only going to sleep, and I mean sleep. I'm not that sort. But I don't want you down with the snakes, not to mention spiders. So you're coming up, okay?" She was now standing on the dray, hands-on-hips and looking down at him.

He shrugged, threw a few more logs on the fire, and then hopped up on the dray. They settled down on the flour bags and covered themselves with a blanket.

The peace lasted about five minutes until Jenna threw off the blanket. "I'm hot. I'll just lie on top." She threw her arm about her head and turned her face away from him.

For Eddie, she was just too close. He lay listening to her breathing. He thought to himself, "I am not going to get a wink of sleep with her this close." His butt was sore from riding, his back stiff from the primitive blacksmithing and repair, and that wasn't all.

Her breathing was deep and even.

He closed his eyes to at least rest, but sleep didn't come. He could smell her sweetness. He lay looking up at the stars, then listened, trying to pick out different cicada sounds and crickets that John had taught him about. He could hear frogs and some rustling in the trees.

After some time, Jenna rolled in her sleep and put an arm across his chest. She rolled closer, and he put his arm under her head and pulled the blanket over them a bit as the evening had cooled.

The crescent moon was just coming up, and he could see her face as she slept.

He moved a little so she was more comfortable; she snuggled into him in her sleep, so he wrapped his other arm around her, too.

He closed his eyes and slept.

Eddie woke to a kookaburra above him in the tree singing his morning call.

Jenna was still wrapped in his arms but was stirring.

He didn't dare move. His arm was numb, but his heart was full. He'd never felt like this before. He looked down at her adoringly. She was as beautiful in sleep as she was awake.

She opened her beautiful amber eyes when the cockatoos set off with the dawn chorus. "Morning, sleepyhead," he said as she opened her eyes.

She sat up. "I'm so sorry. Did I sleep like that all night? I'm used to sharing a bed with Cathy and Vicky." She rubbed her eyes, then bent back over him and kissed him on the nose. "But it was nice waking up next to you, though." She hopped down from the dray and dragged the blanket from him, folding it and throwing it back up on the dray seat.

He sat up, still wishing he could hide under the blanket.

She headed bush.

Eddie stretched his numb arm and slid off the back of the dray. He had actually slept well, cuddled up to Jenna. He had a grin on his face as he walked to the coals of the fire and kicked them together. He put on some kindling and blew on it. He soon had it roaring. Not that they needed it; some toast would be nice, though. They had finished off the eggs last night, but there was still some cheese. They'd have to do with creek water to drink. He'd take the cider bottle and fill it.

Jenna was walking back through the scrub, "Oh good, you got the fire going. I'm going to wash my face. Yeah, no snakes on my wee walk this time. Your turn. I'll toast the bread while you're gone."

When he returned, she had thinly sliced the cheese and somehow melted it onto the toast. It looked delicious and bubbly.

They soon had their scant meal, put the fire out with water from the nose bags, packed up and put Phillip into the harness.

"We have to reverse Phillip to get the dray off the rocks. Up you get Jenna, I'll take out the chocks and get him to reverse." Eddie shifted the rocks and went to Phillip's harness. "Come on, boy, back you go." Phillip reversed a few steps, and the dray jerked as it came off the pile of supporting rocks. "Now, let's see if this fix of mine works. Pull on the brake while I crawl under the dray and remove the rock pile. I don't want Phillip to take off while I'm under it."

"I'll hold him steady. Can you just kick it flat, then I'll move the dray?"

"Okay," said Eddie. "I'll kick off the top one." He slid his leg under and kicked the top rock off. He checked that the axle would clear it and moved out. "Okay," he said, "Walk him forward; I'll put the rest by the tree. If I leave them here, some other vehicle may hit them if they take the road wide. I'll put those chock-rocks and some smaller ones in the actual hole so that it won't be so bad. Thankfully, I left out a spade. There's some loose gravel just off to the side, so I'll push that in and try to fill it."

Jenna watched as he cleared the last of the rocks. The sun was now above the horizon. The birds had mostly flown off on their foraging hunt for the day.

Eddie finished moving all the rocks, walked back to the dray, unhitched Bobbs from the seat, tied him to the rear, and then climbed up beside her.

She offered him the reins.

He said, "No, you bring him home. I want to keep my eye on the wheel repair. So just go slowly for a while to make sure it's solid."

He hung over the side of the dray and watched the wheel bounce over the ruts in the road. He sat up and smiled. "All good; it's as solid as a bought one."

Jenna offered the reins again, but he shook his head.

"Nope, I'm just going to sit back and relax. Give my arms a rest." He grinned again, and she smiled back.

The early morning mist was rising off the river, and the dew was still on the grass. Birds were out foraging for worms, bugs and spiders to feed their squawking babies. There was a companionable silence as they just enjoyed the surroundings. Each was occasionally pointing something out to the other.

They had kept Phillip at walking pace in case they hit another pothole. By mid-morning, they had arrived at the river, and Eddie was pleased they no longer had to cross at the old ford.

There was only one rough spot, where he'd hopped down and walked beside the loaded wagon. He had watched the wheel as it bumped its way along the rough road and said, "I'll be happy when this gets fixed properly. I do hope we make it. Thankfully, we are nearly there."

Jenna said, "Come on, up you get, or we'll not make it before noon if you walk. Pa will be able to replace it while this one gets repaired. We have a spare cartwheel at home. I'm so keen for you to meet everyone. It's like a crazy place at our house. Marc is sure to be there as he's Pa's biggest help. He's the same age as you. Alex is working with Mr. Parker, so he will be home later. Vicky and Cathy help Maa; Nick and Calum, that's what we call Malcolm, will be doing schoolwork as Maa is strict about them learning to read and write properly. Pa knows your Dar can read, and so he learnt. He made us all learn as well. I'm glad he did now."

Jenna said, "Look over there. You can see the road to the prison. Oh, look, there's a road gang heading out. Up there on the hill is where they are going to build the church, and this is our road." She pointed to a left-hand turn-off.

After they turned the corner, he could see a new stone building with lots of pillars and a verandah. The cedar shingles still had the orange-red glow to them as they hadn't yet had time to weather to grey.

"Oh, nice," he said.

"I'll drive past the house, and you can drive into the yard, and we can unload directly from there. Hopefully, everyone will be here and can all lend a hand."

He glimpsed the curtains moving, and soon the front door flew open, and two boys flew outside, closely followed by two older girls and a lady. They were all waving, and Jenna stood up and waved back. "I'm back, safe and well."

As they drew to a stop at the front of the building, Jenna handed the reins to Eddie and jumped down, throwing herself into her mother's arms and kissing everyone else. She then turned to Eddie and, with a wave of her hand, "Everyone, this is Eddie; Eddie, this is the crazy mob, but I love them heaps."

An older man walked around the corner, and a younger version of himself followed him.

"Pa, Marc, this is Eddie. Ed, if you follow Pa, he'll show you where to go." Thus dismissed, he followed the man around into the yard. She disappeared inside with the others.

Eddie stopped just near the small well in the backyard and handed the reins to the man.

"Is here okay, sir?" Eddie asked.

"Yes, lad," he replied. "There's fine. Well, now, lad, what's Jenna got herself mixed up with now? I thought of sending someone with her, but she's an independent lass. I dare say there's a story. We were expecting her yesterday."

Eddie hopped down. "First, Mr. Turner, let me introduce myself properly. I'm Eddie Lockley, Charles' son, so I'm not exactly a stranger." They shook hands. "It's a long and funny story, but in short, her horse went lame, and we helped. Dar supplied the stores you needed, and when he found out who she was, he wouldn't let her return home without an escort... Me."

Eddie showed Mr. Turner the wheel. "Dar insisted I come with her. I'm glad I did, as we hit a pothole and a wheel smashed yesterday about an hour from the bridge, and by the time I got it fixed, it was too dark to drive home. So we stayed by the side of the road." He pointed to the damaged spoke. "Here, sir, I did the best I could, and I'm sorry, but I had to use some of the new tools that you have bought. Sorry about that. Jenna made the spoke, and I put it in. I also got the buckle out of the wheel rim."

They looked at the repair job, and Mr. Turner turned to him and said, "You did this? On the side of the road? How? You need a blacksmith to repair these normally."

"Well, you see, sir, I am one. I'm the person who re-shod her horse. Mr. Tindale, the blacksmith, is my boss, and I happened to be in the right place at the right time, and well, the upshot is I'm here after Dar got worried about Jenna returning by herself. Jenna can fill you in on the entire story, which became a lot more complicated than it should have been, but she's safe, as are the stores. The only thing we didn't have in stock was the wheel rims. She said they were only for stock here, so I can bring them out next week if that's all right." Eddie was nervous and talking too much again.

Mr. Turner could see that. He smiled to himself.

"That's fine, lad. If you're Charles' son, and you certainly do have the look of him, then I know my Jenna was safe. He was about your age when I first met him. We were a lot dirtier, though. Fancy that. I knew we'd catch up again sometime." He smiled. "Thank you for taking such good care of our girl. She keeps us on our toes and does that one. No stopping her. We called her Jennifer Martha when she was born, as she was like a little phantom. We didn't know she was on the way until she was nearly here. Alex shortened it to 'Jenna' as he couldn't say it properly, and so Jenna stayed."

He turned to Marc, who'd been listening from the stable. He was sharpening a scythe with a wet stone. "Eh, Marcus, Eddie here is Charles Lockley's son. I told you about him. We came out together in January '20. Can you stable the horses, then come and join us."

Marc nodded. "Sure, Pa."

Eddie went over to Marc and shook hands. Each was admiring the other's honest face. Both were as dirty as each other, as Eddie had not been able to wash properly since repairing the wheel. He said to Marc, "This is Bobbs; leave him saddled, please, as I have to be off home soon, but if you could feed and water him, I'd appreciate that."

Ed turned to Mr. Turner and asked if he could wash up first. H   e pointed to the pump and a half barrel under it. "There you go, lad; I'll get something to dry yourself with."

Jenna stuck her head out the back door. "All okay, Ed? Come in when you're done. Breakfast is nearly ready. We timed it well. Maa has the kettle on as usual, and she's put some ham and eggs on for us. I'm famished. So move along."

"Yes, boss!" Eddie replied laughingly. He washed thoroughly, rubbing himself with a scrap of clean, coarse rag.

Mr. Turner returned. He stood watching, "Bossy thing, isn't she?" He didn't wait for a reply but walked inside.

Eddie followed and was greeted by, "Oh. The hero of the hour," from Mrs. Turner. "Jenna said you fixed a wheel on the side of the road."

"Yes, Maa, he did, but we're famished. Can we eat first, then tell the story?" Jenna grabbed his arm and ushered him to the long kitchen table. "Let's eat first, then we'll talk," she said to him while pushing him into a seat.

Mrs. Turner served fried.eggs and ham with some toast and butter.

"The best food I've eaten for a long time, Mrs. Turner. Much thanks," said Eddie.

"Okay, finished? Now I'm going to tell everyone about my trip," Jenna announced. She turned to Eddie, "Now, this is my story; I can embellish it as much as I want. So Shhh from you, you're my hero."

Eddie smiled but blushed.

Jenna went on to re-tell her saga of the goats, snake and finally the wheel, embellishing liberally and totally embarrassing Eddie, who had blushed accordingly when the accolades of thanks came from them all.

He sat grinning at her all through her story.

She left out the bit where she had slept in his arms, but by the time she'd finished, everyone was in awe of Eddie and his skills.

Jack was the first to say something and stood to do so. "I knew my Jenna would fall on her feet; she always does. But I can never thank you enough for keeping her safe. I'll have to send Marc next time." He looked at their disappointed faces and the looks from each to the other. He smiled. "Marc would have gone this time, but we needed him here."

Instead of sitting down again, he poured another cup of tea and handed it to Eddie. "Down that, lad, we'll get on with unloading the stores while you say your goodbyes. I hope that next week you can stay overnight here when you return with the wheel rims." He winked at Jenna, then walked out.

They all left the table, with the younger ones clearing and washing the dishes.

Mrs. Turner ushered Jenna and Eddie to the other end of the room. "Have a seat for a bit, Ed," she sat in a rocking chair, "I've not had a chance to thank you myself and to think you are Charles's son. I shouldn't really be surprised. He's already done so much for Jack that his son would be the same, so not unexpected." She was watching them and caught a glance between them. "Hmm," she thought, then smiled. They chatted for a bit more before Ed excused himself as he had to leave.

Jenna was almost bouncing from one foot to the other. "Maa, can we send a few things back with Eddie? His Mama sent us with masses of tucker, so we weren't hungry."

Mrs. Turner agreed and went into the pantry. As they walked outside, Jenna said, "Sad that all adventures have to end."

He turned and looked down at her. "Actually, Jenna, I'd like to make some excuses for more visits. Would that be all right?" Eddie asked nervously.

"Oh Coo, Ed, would it ever. I'd love to see you…often. But you'll have to ask Pa." He nodded.

Jack was nowhere in sight, so Eddie quickly bent to kiss the top of her head, but she lifted it at that moment, and he got her full on the lips.

They smiled, so he gave her another one a bit longer, just as Marc appeared.

"That's enough of that; she's my little sister." He was laughing, so they knew he was joking. He looked at Eddie, "I look forward to getting to know all your family. Maybe a picnic next time. Like, we could all meet halfway down the track to town? Bobbs has had a drink, but not too much. I also gave him a rub down, so he's ready for a run. Pa's just coming."

Jack came back to the dray. He'd been stashing the heavy food stores away. "Eddie, thanks for supplying all this and the hardware. So much more than I hoped." He was about to hump another bag on his shoulder. "I forgot to get some shed S hooks with points to hang things on so the rats can't eat them and six crowbars. Could you bring those too when you come, please? All the travellers want to buy solid tools; our smith never has enough stock."

Eddie made a note of it in the little notebook he always kept with him, then looked at Jenna and, with a bend of his head, motioned for her to go.

She did.

"Of course, Mr. Turner, but I'd like to ask you something if I may." Eddie fell silent, somewhat worried. How to ask?

"Well, lad?" said Mr. Turner.

"Well, sir, I'd like to court Jenna, sir, if that's all right, sir?" He tried to be confident. "I know I've not known her long, but a lot has happened in the last two days, and I'd like to have the chance to get to know both her and the entire family better. It'll be hard as I live so far away, but I'm sure Mr. Tindale and I can work it out." Eddie tried not to shuffle his feet and stood still. His nerves were getting the better of him. He flushed.

Mr. Turner was silent for a while, rubbing his chin. Finally, he said, "Well lad, I like Charles, best man I know other than the Major. And if you're even half the man he is, I'd be honoured to know you better. As to courting, well, she's a handful. But you're welcome to come as often as you can. I figured there might be a few bits she wasn't telling us. Let me say this. If you hurt my girl…" he paused, "But, I'm sure you won't."

Eddie sighed with relief. "Thank you, Mr. Turner. She's a lady, sir, and I treat her as such. I respect her, and I promise nothing happened that wasn't right. But you're correct, she's a whirlwind, but she takes my breath away. I've never met anyone with half the passion for life that she has. I don't want to break her. sir, I like her just as she is." He continued. "I'll take it slow, sir, and treat her right."

Bill nodded, pleased with what he'd said.

Ed finally took a long breath. "You know you're always welcome at our Inn if you're in town. That is, any of you. Dar would love to catch up with you again. I'd heard about you long before I met Jenna. This place is a bit of a small world. Thank you again, sir. If I may go and talk to Jenna, then I'll be off. I'll see you on Saturday."

Mr. Turner agreed. He was smiling as he walked to the dray and grabbed another sack of flour.

Jenna had been helping Marc unload some of the smaller things she'd bought. She put them in the stables and tool room. Some she couldn't even move as they were heavy; the boxes of nails and single items were all put in their place.

Ed caught her eye, then walked over to Bobbs and untied his reins from the fence. Jenna came over and looked at Eddie.

She whispered, "What did he say? Can you come?"

Standing behind Bobbs, he just bent down and kissed her quickly. "Yes. I can come often. Is that to your liking, madam?"

"Oh, yes," she said. "I'd like it very much. I'll see you Saturday then?"

"Yes, you'll see me this Saturday and most other Saturdays if you wish."

She did a happy dance on the spot and squealed, "Yes!"

Marc came out of the shed at that moment, and Eddie hopped up into the saddle.

Eddie just reached down and stroked Jenna's cheek, then turned Bobbs. He waved to Marc and said quietly to Jenna, "Until Saturday."

She stood watching the tall, handsome man ride off. He turned once to wave before he was out of sight.

Chapter 11   Good Things Happen

Summer came and went. Time for Eddie and Jenna slowly passed as he couldn't make it out to see her every week. Sometimes, Jack Turner and Jenna would come into Parramatta and stay overnight, sometimes even for two days, while Jack caught up with Charles. Mr. Tindale often released Eddie early these days, but if not, Jenna would sit watching him work. If there were deliveries out West, they were always planned for a Friday afternoon, and Eddie would deliver them and head on to Emu Plains for the weekend.

Jenna often came in during the week and sat watching her beloved. She didn't mind the forge's noise; she loved hearing the hot metal quench in the water. Even more, she loved to watch him hammering the red-hot steel things. His body was dripping with sweat from the heat, and his muscles rippled with each hammer swing. In the year they had been courting, he had reached his majority. When he turned twenty-one, Mr. Tindale had called him in and had him sign papers to make him a partner in the business.

Eddie had never accepted much payment from him. He considered that fair, as Mr. Tindale had paid for all his education. It was like Eddie had two sets of parents, both of whom he loved deeply, and there was, of course, the Major. He, too, was special. He always made time to talk and looked out for him as a child. Charlie, too, was treated like their son. He was now courting Gracie Miller, Tim's sister. He still came to help out when there was a big order. Wills and Luke, at fifteen and thirteen, were pulling their weight at the Inn. Liza was about to marry Bertie and would be living with his family. Anna was "walking out" with Timmy, and they were to be married when Anna turned eighteen in November of the next year.

On the first Saturday in early November, they rode through Emu Plains. Ed suggested they cross the ford and ride through the orchards along the river on the other side. Eddie was riding his new horse, a stunning pure black stallion that his objectionable owner had poorly treated. It came in lame with the man, and he ended up abandoning him at the blacksmith shop. He threw up his hands and said, "I'm not paying for that. He's a foul-tempered brute, that one; you can have him. He's thrown me twice this trip. Tell me where I can get a decent hoss I can ride. I'm Orf…." The man walked off and did not return.

Eddie could see that this horse was highly strung and probably badly treated, but, oh, so magnificent. Over two weeks, he'd been at the smithy holding yard. Ed had broken through his fear barrier and bonded with him. The holding yard was outside the shop in view of the forge. Eddie would talk to the horse while he was working. Every break, he would walk to the fence and just look at him. The stallion would always shy away. After the first few days of this, Eddie stepped inside the yard. He stood still. After doing this a few times in one day, the horse stepped towards him. By the second day, on entering the yard, the horse, now named James, came over to Eddie. On day three, when Eddie entered the yard, James was waiting for him and nuzzled him. He knew he'd won. He was still a very highly strung animal and would flinch with sudden noises, but the forge noises never seemed to worry him. Neither did Eddie's singing or whistling.

Eddie had often ridden James out to see Jenna. She'd been allowed to borrow Phillip, and they rode through the orange orchards on the river edge. All the trees were in flower; it smelt heavenly. It was the excuse he used to get her to come.

As they rode across the ford and up the riverbank, he fell behind her and flicked Phillip's rump with his reins. The horse took off. Jenna held on tight but yelled, "Eddie, save me, save me. I don't know what happened to him." Eddie, of course, knew, and Phillip had done precisely what he'd hoped he would do. Ed knew James could catch him up without trouble.

Eddie cantered alongside and said, "I'll save you if you marry me. Will you?"

"Yes, of course, I'll damned well marry you; just get me off this horse," shouted Jenna.

Eddie reached over and grabbed Phillip's harness, stopping him. Then he reached over to Jenna and kissed her. He got off and lifted her down so he could kiss her properly, which he did. They walked down the orange grove hand in hand, the horses following them.

"I don't know what got into Phillip. It's not like him to go off like that."

Eddie chuckled. "I flipped him with my reins like this."

"Oh, Eddie, that's cruel," she said laughingly. "You'll pay for that."

He said, chuckling, "Oh, now that sounds like fun. When? And talking of when, how soon will you marry me?" He produced a small leather pouch. "I thought this might come in handy today. See if you like it. Your Maa said this is something you talked to her about once."

She opened the pouch, and inside was a gold ring with three rubies embedded into the band. "Oh, Eddie, it's perfect."

He took it from her and slipped it on her finger. "Bargain sealed."

He took her in his arms again, lifted her chin and traced her lips with his finger. He stood looking into her face, devouring her with his eyes. "I love you so much. Never change, my love." He bent and gently pressed his lips to hers. His gentle kiss was returned with a passion that surprised him.

Jenna murmured against his lips, "You'll have to ask Pa yet if we can, you know."

"All done," said Ed, while still holding her, giving her lots of small kisses as he talked, "I asked him when he came into town last week. We had a long talk." He swung her around, shouting joyously, "Yesss." He was so joyful, he almost yelled it. "I love you so very much. You know that, don't you? You bowled me over, quite literally, the day I met you, and I've been off balance since." Their kisses deepened, keeping her well-occupied for some time.

"Pa never let on. He did look at me funny sometimes, but I never suspected." She reached up to pull his head down to her again. "You mean they knew? Both of them?"

Eddie nodded. "Jen, when I say "when" I need to tell you what I hope." He kissed the tip of her nose before continuing. "Mr. Tindale and his wife are going to move to Sydney to be closer to his sister, and he has asked me to run the smithy shop by myself. They want me to live in their house in the guest room at the back. I asked if it were all right for us to live there after we were married. He said that it was sort of what he'd hoped. This way," he kissed her, "their house is looked after, and we don't have to live in the Inn. What do you think?"

He heard "Ah-hum." but she couldn't answer properly as her lips were occupied.

"So that's a yes?" he asked.

"YES! Absolutely," she said.

"Sort of having our own place, without having to pay for it except work hard. I'm fine with that. We'd be caretakers but would be living on-site. You'd have to look after the garden, the chooks and hives."

He kissed her again, holding her tight. "But, sweets, they move in six weeks."

Jenna was stunned; she pulled back, still in his arms. "Six weeks. Are you serious? Eddie, I'd love that. And our own place; well, almost. So does that mean we can get married soon?"

He picked her up and spun her around. "Yes, love, in a few weeks. Is that all right?"

"Yes," she squealed, bouncing on the spot.

He chuckled. She was as excited as he. They had slowly walked to the river bank and were now sitting on the grassy edge. The horses were cropping nearby. "Well, the banns take three weeks, and there's a bit of time before that to let the family know. It's November now; how about we aim for the first weekend in December? Is that enough time to get something sorted?" Eddie lay on his back with his arms behind his head.

"That's only five weeks away, but yes! Yes, yes, yes, Five weeks is plenty of time." She leaned over a kissed him. It was no gentle peck but a searing, passionate show of affection.

"Hmm," he put his arms around her. "I like that. Do it again." They were occupied for some time. She curled up close against him, wrapped in his arms.

Eddie was going to find these next five weeks hard, but then she'd be his. He looked down at her and gently brushed a tendril of hair from her face.

She reached up and ran her fingers up his neck and into the thick blonde hair, slowly pulling him down to her. Her kisses did more than just stir his desire for her. He opened her mouth to him, and if he thought that her kisses before were passionate, he was beginning to realise what marriage to this woman would do to him.

She allowed his hands to wander over her body. He was about to unbutton her bodice when James came over and nuzzled him. "Oh, leave off, James. I'm busy."

He rolled onto his back, breathing heavily and waiting for some of the heat of his desire to pass.

Jenna giggled. "I think he's telling us we'd better head back." Phillip had wandered into the water, and Jenna looked up to see him roll in the river. "No, Phillip, now the saddle will be wet."

"Oh good," said Eddie as he sat up, "You can come up in front of me. What a good excuse?"

He heaved himself up on James. Jenna put her foot in the stirrup and sat in front of Eddie side-saddle. She was cradled in his arms. She reached up to pull his head down and kiss him again. "Oh, I think these are going to be the longest five weeks."

Phillip was still standing in the river. He was dripping wet; the saddle skewed. Eddie walked James in and leaned down to grab the reins. They walked home at a leisurely pace, enjoying the closeness. Just before they came in full view of the house, Eddie dropped Phillip's reins and smacked his rump again, this time sending him home. He trotted off, leaving James to follow. Eddie changed direction, though, and headed to the path along the river bank. "I just want to have a few more moments with you." He stopped James under a tree and lifted Jenna down. "Just one last kiss before we go back and face the music."

Sometime later, they both came up for breath. "Hmm, Eddie, have I told you I love you too?"

"No," said Eddie, "and it's just as well. As I would hope you would not behave like this with anyone else." Eddie laughed.

"Actually, Ed, you're the only one I've ever even kissed. And the only one I have ever wanted to kiss as well. I like it. Do it again."

"Oh, you minx." He willingly obliged. "And Jen, you are the only one I have ever kissed too." He dragged himself out of her arms. "Come on; we'd better be getting back." He heaved himself up onto James and, pulled her up, and settled her into his arms again. James plodded back to the Inn; his riders gave no direction, seemingly otherwise occupied. On arrival, it was suspiciously silent. Jenna looked puzzled. She slipped down off James' back, and Eddie took him into the stable yard and released him into the holding pen, still saddled. Jenna was about to say something, but Eddie just said, "I'll fix him later. Let's go and see where everyone is." They walked to the house arm in arm. She fitted neatly under his shoulder.

He opened the door for her, and as she entered, the family yelled, "Surprise." She later discovered that her Pa knew that if Phillip returned without them, she'd said, "Yes." His swim had been accidental but worked perfectly into Ed's plan.

She was somewhat annoyed that she didn't get to tell everyone herself but was so happy that it really didn't matter. She turned to Eddie and gave him a gentle love punch, telling him he was mean. He bent down and whispered, "Sweetie, but they had no idea *when* we're getting married; tell them *that* bit of news."

He chuckled. She spun around. "Maa, Pa, Oh, and we're getting married in about five weeks," said Jenna

"Five weeks, what do you mean five weeks?" said Martha. "How can we get ready for a wedding in five weeks?"

Jenna said, "Maa, we can talk about this later, but that's what we're hoping for. Eddie is taking over from Mr. Tindale, and they are moving to Sydney. So this will give us time to have a week-long honeymoon before we take over the smithy shop." She hugged her mother. "We get to live in their guest room too, so we won't need even to set up a house. Oh, Maa, I'm so excited. Only we have to be married before they leave."

Marc was still shaking Eddie's hand. "Oh, you're brave to take her on. Don't get me wrong; I love her dearly. But she's a handful."

"I know," said Eddie, "and I love it." He grinned. He was watching her as she moved around the room; his heart was rejoicing. Oh yes, she'd certainly keep him on his toes.

Alex had finished work a little early and was able to join in the festivities. There was much back-slapping and goodwill.

Jack was standing off to the side, leaning on the mantlepiece, smiling to himself.

Eddie walked over to him. "Thank you, sir, for everything. I hope you don't mind a quick wedding. There's no need for it for *that* reason, but it means that we can have a break before I take over as the smithy full-time by myself. So we have a mere five weeks. They want to leave on December 12. Dar always said that once you have made up your mind, don't draw things out. I'll have to check when with Reverend Mr. Bobart if he can marry us that week. Do you mind coming to Parramatta for the service?"

"Son, if you're willing to take her on, why wait? Trust me; it's the waiting that makes it hard. Once you've made the decision, tie the knot fast. You already have our blessing. It's a pity the church here is not yet built, so Parramatta will be fine. Windsor is too far from us all." Jack said, "Eddie, you set what plans you think best; we'll fit in. Jenna is a fortunate girl. I've grown to not only admire you as much as I admire your Dar but to love you like another son. Just look after my girl, and we'll get on fine." Jack, once more, patted his shoulder and congratulated him. "Our plan worked well, didn't it? Did she have any idea?"

"No, sir," Eddie said. "She was stunned. She was worried that I had not asked you first. She didn't want to say yes before I had." Eddie turned to look at her. "She's one great girl, sir." Their eyes met, and he smiled. "She's the happiest person I know, and I love her dearly."

"I'll let you into a secret, son. Martha has been busy making a special dress for her wedding for some time. We had hoped you would not want to wait too long. It's nearly finished, so everything will be ready for her. Five weeks will be plenty of time. Jenna's been working on her own box since not long after she met you. It seems she knew, too. I guessed something was afoot that first weekend. Sadly, she has no dowry but herself."

"Sir, in all honesty, nothing happened that first weekend nor since; that was not good and proper. Although I did accidentally give her a kiss." He stood looking at Jack, somewhat embarrassed, "And nothing like 'that' will happen until we're married." Ed looked lovingly at her, "Sir, she's dowry enough as she is."

Jack said, "One of the drawbacks of coming out as we did in chains is we had nothing, but we have our faith, our health, and our freedom, and we have the Inn, now we have a little money for emergencies. We would not have had any of this in the Motherland. So, in all, what your folks, Martha and I went through to get here turned out worthwhile for our families. You have a good education, thanks to Mr. Tindale, and you can go far. You can turn your hand to many things. In this place, we all have the ability to socialise with people from all walks of society. Jenna will grow into a strong woman like her mother. She's a diamond, and I have noticed that many of her rough edges have already smoothed off. Martha was also a bit of a strong-willed girl, but she matured. Children are a settling influence. Martha and I did not have family here to help us. We worked hard and turned to those who could help when needed. Likewise, we helped them, in turn. That's how life works out here."

Jack drew on his pipe. He blew a curl of smoke. "Each then grows strong as we pull together. When this Inn was built, many of us thought that no traffic would come our way, but we knew a road would eventually follow when the mountains were crossed. You watch; the road will become better and better, and more and more people will be crossing those mountains to farm. Soon, it will be able to take big carriages. Who knows what the future will bring, but I want to do my bit to set my family in place to achieve a good place in life." He looked back up at Eddie, "And you, young man, are a man of the future. My Jenna will be a good helpmate for you. She'll be there beside you wherever your life leads. Well, that's enough of the serious talk for tonight." He slapped Eddie gently on the back. "There's a party going on. Come and help me tap the casks."

Chuckling, Jack turned to Martha, "Ale, woman, or cider, I'm not fussy. Just hand me something to celebrate with. Our daughter is getting married, and we're getting a new son."

Martha laughed and handed him a tankard. Jack slid his loving arm around his wife. He lifted her chin and gave her a gentle kiss. "I love you, you know?" he whispered.

At that moment, there was a knock on the front door. Mr. and Mrs. Parker, Alex's boss, arrived, and a few other neighbours also came in. All this had been arranged in the time that Phillip arrived home without Jenna. Word had spread fast in the small village. Each new visitor came with something to either eat or drink. Soon, the house was full and overflowing.

A carriage arrived, and more guests came in. Alex and Marc had gone out soon after Eddie arrived and attended to James. They completed some other urgent chores and rejoined the party. On their return, they rolled in a new barrel of ale and tapped it with the men clustering around to catch the excess in their tankards. All enjoyed a heady brew. Even the young folk drank but were only allowed one jug to share. The party continued well past the regular bedtime. During the evening, various members disappeared to do some chore or other, then returned. So the cows were milked, chickens locked up, stock fed, and the party went on. Eddie was able to get Jenna aside a few times for a quick kiss. He stood with his arm around her waist as often as he could.

At one stage, he managed to walk her outside to watch the setting sun over the nearby mountains. Again, they were sprung by Marc, but Eddie good-naturedly told him to "push off" and continued to kiss Jenna. She willingly obliged until Alex also caught them. She laughed and dragged him back inside.

Everyone had gone by about nine. They each drifted off to their various beds. Eddie is to share the room with the four Turner boys, and Jenna will share their big bed with Vicky and Cathy, as usual. The house had only three bedrooms, and when female visitors sometimes came, similar to Eddie's parent Inn, the children slept on the floor. This was normal for the time, and like the Lockley Inn, the visiting men slept in hammocks in the stable or loft.

The next morning, the chickens were up before anyone else. The rooster was sworn at a few times before anyone emerged. Eleven-year-old

Calum and twelve-year-old Nicky were up first and began milking the cow as usual. Martha and Jack emerged next and set to preparing food for the mob. After about twenty minutes, Jenna and the girls appeared giggling. They quickly disappeared outside and washed; Jenna returned with a wet rag and snuck into the boys' room. Soon, a gasp and laughter were heard, and a bleary-eyed Eddie then the rest of the boys appeared. Jenna had dripped cold water from the well on his face and woken Eddie, then greeted him with a kiss. "Good morning, husband-to-be. Time to arise." To the other boys, she just ripped off the sheet. They were soon up and dressed.

Breakfast was a quiet affair, but the effects of last night's imbibing of the ale soon wore off, and the normal chattering returned.

Jenna and Eddie kept looking at each other, and both had smiles plastered on their faces. Martha said, "Okay, you two, you can have the morning off. Eddie has to leave at midday. I need some honey from Mrs. Walker, so you must drive out on the Windsor Road and collect it. Take the buggy, as you'll need to carry it back. I've ordered a small barrel full, so you can't carry it on the horses." That got them moving, and soon they were leaving with Phillip, now harnessed into the buggy.

"You know we may have to call one of our children, Phillip. He's been so instrumental in our relationship." Eddie looked down at her, "Can you believe we're going to be married? Has it sunk in yet?"

"No," she said dreamily. "Hmm, Phillip. I'd have to spell it differently. I don't want everyone to know we named a child after a horse. But without a horse, we may not have met. That and a loose shoe." She leaned her head against his arm. "Five weeks. I can't wait."

"Well, we are going to Jen," he said empathetically. "I promised your Pa that I'd treat you like a lady, and I will," Eddie said stiffly.

"Ohh, Ed, I didn't mean *that*. No, we'll wait. To me, that's all about respect and trust, too. No, I just mean that I'm really looking forward to December. That's all." she said breezily. "At least I'll get to see more of you now we're engaged, and I can kiss you when I want, which is often. Like now." She pulled his head down to kiss her. "Next Saturday can sort of be a dry run. Soon, I won't have to keep saying goodbye to you and wait for ages to see you again. That's what I meant by I can't wait." She snuggled against him again, and this time, he put his arm around her.

"Oh! Sorry Jen, Saturday? Huh?" he said a bit guiltily.

"Yes, silly, Liza's wedding," she said and shook her head.

"Oh! Yes, is that this Saturday? I've had my mind on other things. I wonder what?" He swallowed, "Yes, it's so hard waiting, but it will be worth it. Let's think of other things. We've got the morning free, what can we do? I was thinking just about…"

She snuggled up under his spare arm, wrapping her arms around his waist. She never found out what he was thinking about as she drew his head down and kissed him again. She said against his lips, "Let's get the honey first and then see what happens."

Eddie returned to Parramatta on Sunday afternoon, and he called by St John's Church to see the Reverend Mr. Bobart and see if they could arrange to have the Banns read and book a date for the ceremony. He was shown into the Reverend's office and sat waiting. After some time, Reverend Mr. Bobart meandered in, nibbling on a biscuit. "Sorry to keep you waiting, boy. I had to do a taste test of the new batch of cookies. Bessie will be in with some soon. Now, what can I help you with?" He sat at his big red cedar desk and leaned back in his chair.

Eddie knew this man well as he was a regular member of his congregation. "I'm sorry I have not been at church much of late, but when you hear what I've come to discuss with you, you will understand why. You see, sir, I've come to discuss my marriage with you and to sort out a date. Miss Jennifer Turner from Emu Plains has accepted my offer, and due to the Tindale's wanting to leave for Sydney in mid-December, we hoped to be married the first Saturday in December. I know that's only five weeks away, sir, and she's not in the family way, so the only reason for the hurry is I would get a week off before the Tindales leave." His eyes were on Mr. Bobart's face. He waited anxiously.

"Well, my boy. First, I will say congratulations. I've met your young lady a few times over the past year, and I like your choice. I believe your fathers were, let's say, roommates for a time. I know they were both granted 'Tickets of Leave' for their brave actions on the way out here. Let me see." He opened a big book on his desk. It was obviously his diary. Speaking to himself, he said, "I have Mattins, then a wedding at 10 a.m., hmmm. I think we can fit you in at 11 a.m. on Dec 4. How's that? I'll want to meet you both here next week unless she can come in earlier. We'll get all the particulars and prepare the Banns."

A knock at the door was followed by Bessie bringing in a tea tray. The aroma of fresh, warm biscuits arrived with her. "Thank you, Bessie, that will be all." She departed, softly closing the door behind her. "You must try these, Eddie; they are outstanding."

Eddie took one of the warm biscuits and took a bite. He'd always been partial to these sweet treats since Mrs. Tindale used to spoil him with similar ones when he was a boy. His eyes opened. "Oh sir, you are right; these are delicious. What's that flavour?"

"Bessie calls them Wattle-seed and honey. She has made friends with some of the local women, and this is one of the foods they eat. It's toasted and then crushed wattle seed, but not just any wattle seed. Bessie trades flour and salt for some of the native foods and fresh fish. We've been getting some amazing food. We could learn so much from these people. I do wish relations were better." The Minister helped himself to a third one. Eddie took a second. They sat, drank their tea and ate until the plate was empty.

Eddie looked guiltily at it and apologised. "I'm sorry, sir, it seems we finished off the lot."

Reverend Mr. Bobart roared with laughter, "Oh, not so, lad, she's made about nine dozen of them. Seems we're not the only ones who like them. I don't see many of them, so I think she gives some away. I think they will all be gone by Saturday." He stood up, as did Eddie.

"Thank you, sir, thank you very much. Jenna and her family will all be here Friday night for the wedding on Saturday. So we'll see you here on Saturday. What time would be convenient…?"

Reverend Mr. Bobart flicked his eyes over the diary. "Ten o'clock would be good, or as soon after that as possible. Liza's wedding isn't until a bit later, so you should have time to get everything done and get back home." They walked out into the hall, and he opened to door for Eddie, who had collected his hat from the hall stand, then gave a quick bow and left. James was waiting patiently outside. Ed unhitched him and rode the short distance home. It was a path that he'd taken each week for the walk to church on Sunday mornings. Reverend Mr. Bobart's wife, Elizabeth, was the first teacher he'd had. She was Reverend Marsden's daughter and taught the "Charity children" to read and write. He had much to thank this family for, and now he was to marry in this church. Eddie had much on his mind and was unaware of the trip home. James knew the way and found it unerringly. They were walking into the stable yard before he realised.

Charlie was just coming out of the shed. "G'day Ed. You're late. Everything all right?" he asked.

"Oh, everything is fine, Charlie. Congratulate me. She said yes." Eddie grinned from ear to ear.

"Oh, wonderful, Eddie. That's such great news. I was sure she would. What about her family? All good there, too?" asked Charlie.

"Yep, all good. Mr. Turner warned me of 'if you hurt my girl', but I expected that. He's a lot of bluff and puff, and I have lots of time for him. I can see why Dar likes him so much." Eddie had dismounted, and together they attended to James. They chatted for a while and then walked into the house when Luke shot out the door to the water drum. "I'm guessing it's nearly mealtime. I must admit I have totally lost track of time today." They hung up the brushes and bridle. "How's work been?"

They kept talking as they walked indoors.

"Well, look who the horse brought in," greeted Sal. She gave him a hug and a sloppy 'mama' kiss on his cheek.

"Errk, that was a wet one, Mama," he complained, but still, he grinned.

"You look happy for yourself. And you're late. At least you've washed up. I'm just about to serve. Go sit yourself down." He bent down to kiss the top of her head. She said, "Oh, go-awn with you, shoo." He went, but not to the table. He stuck his head out the back door to call his father. "Dar, grubs on."

Charles lifted his head and said, "Hello, boy, I didn't hear you came back. All okay? Good trip?" His old injury to his leg still troubled him somewhat. Eddie helped him stand and opened the door for him to enter.

They were the last two at the table, Eddie holding Charles' chair for him as he sat. The food on the table was wafting delectable smells around the room. "Before we eat, I'd like to say something before we say thanks. Jenna accepted my offer, and we're getting married in five weeks on December 4 at 11 a.m." He raced his words and then sat down. There was still an empty place, but they knew who that was for.

"Well, blow me down," said Charles. "I knew you wanted to marry the girl, but that's quick. I know you're sure and all that. Is she 'in the family way'?"

Eddie blushed and said, "No, Dar. Absolutely not; she's not that kind of girl. We haven't, well, you know. No, it's to do with the Tindales. I'll explain over dinner. Let's say 'grace', then I'll tell you all about it."

Charles thanked the Lord for their food, and Sal served. Each passed their plate to her, and she filled it, serving hers last. "Okay, now spill, Ed, what's the rush?" she said as she sat.

Eddie took a mouthful and chewed. He gulped ale and swallowed. "They want me to take over the smithy full time, and they are moving to Sydney to be close to his sister. Since Captain Evans' ship went missing, Mr. Tindale wants to be closer. It's, well, more than six months overdue, and he'd already been gone for twice that long. Now, there's little hope of him coming back." He took another mouthful.

The family knew that Captain Evans' ship was missing. They also knew how sad Eddie was, as he'd lived with them for the five years he was at school. He'd grown to love them. He finished chewing and swallowed. "Phil is now of age and can look after the family, but he's recently married. Mrs. Evans is finding it lonely now that all the boys are at work all day. Only John lives at home with her now; he's somewhat, um, vague. Mr. Tindale has only been doing light work for a while as his hands are not coping with the hammering, and he said it's time to pass on the work. We'll be working as a partnership, and they will come back occasionally, probably more often, for the first few months to see how we're coping. But they have also said we can have the back guest room at their house and live there." He took another bite and swallowed. "So we are to start off living in a house, with a garden, the shop and everything in the house we can use too."

Charlie was the first to comment. "Once again, you've fallen on your feet, Ed. And no way I'm not jealous. You took the time to teach me so much after your schooling. I can read anything, and thanks to you, even my writing is nearly perfect. I think it's wonderful. You've worked hard to get where you are. I'm in awe of your hard work and your skill. I worked with him part-time those five years you were away, and it's a tough slog. I learned so much from him, and it's good that it's worked out this way. It's hot but honest work, though, but, man, look at you. Your hands are enormous. You are physically twice the man I am." He slapped his back and made Eddie nearly choke.

"Careful. I'm fragile," said Eddie. Everyone roared with laughter. Eddie was six foot two inches tall and built like a mountain. Piercing blue eyes and a mop of the most fabulous wavy, long, thick, fair hair that never seemed to stay in place. His years as a blacksmith developed his muscles so much that all his shirts had to be hand-made for him. It's no wonder Jenna had fallen for him.

Sal looked adoringly. Although still fair, Charlie had her slightly darker hair colouring, although he looked more like Charles, and Ed had his father's colouring but looked a bit more like her father.

Sal often thought about her mother and wondered what had happened to her back in England, or maybe she'd gone back home to Ireland. Perhaps she would write and see if she could come out here where it was warmer. Possibly Charles' mother and sister could come too. The last convicts came to New South Wales last year. Some were still being sent to other parts of Australia, but not here. There were still 'lifers' on 'Tickets', so labour was cheap, if not free, and help easy to get. She thought, "I'll talk to Charles tonight." She smiled to herself.

Charles looked at her, and his mind wandered back to when he first saw her. She was in a line of women coming from the Women's Factory. Although she was as dirty as the others, she had dignity and poise. She stood out from the rest. Somehow, she'd managed to wash and groom her blonde hair; it stood like a glowing beacon amongst the filth of the other women. It's what he first noticed. Then their eyes met, and she gave Charles a shy smile. He could see the fear on her face. He had to find out who she was. He and Jack had recently arrived but were never assigned as convicts *per se*. Only days after arrival, they were told they would be given their 'Ticket of Leave'. He and Jack Turner were with Major Grace on the way to arrange their paperwork.

Charles asked the Major, "Can you help her?"

The friendship between the three men was awkward. Two were still convicts, and the Major in the army officially overseeing them.

The Major called to the soldier in charge of them. "Private Reid, that one; tall, blonde, history, please?"

"Her name's Sarah McCarthy, but she answers to Sally. And she's a bit toffy-nosed and educated somewhat, too. Don't like the fact that she's a convict and got locked up. Reckons she's as innocent as an angel. Don't they all?" the soldier replied.

"Well, send her to me. She'll do as my housekeeper," said Major Grace. "At least she's clean." He returned to Charles, "One of the privileges of rank is I can take which convicts I like. She'll be safe now. Now let's get this paperwork signed and find you a job." The three men entered the office, and Major Grace finished registering and signing the certificates. "I'd hate to think what would have happened that day onboard if you two had not acted quickly. It's why you're both getting these." He handed them each their documents. "Pity I can't make it a pardon, but you both found guilty. This is the best I can do. This means you can't go home, but here, you can make a new start. I bet you'll both do well."

Jack thanked the Major, took his certificate and went to leave. "I've heard of a job in Camden, sir. May I check it out? The Governor said Mark Duffy is looking for help at his store."

The Major added, "Of course, but get the man to drop me a line when you're settled." Jack nodded and walked outside.

Charles took his certificate. "Thanks, sir; for me, it pleaded guilty or die, so, not an option to do anything else." Charles, too, walked outside and, talked to Jack and say farewell.

Private Reid had followed them up to the Office, and he had the blonde woman with him. She was pushed inside.

Charles looked at her. She was beautiful but so scared. He wanted to be able to comfort her. After Reid departed, Charles went back indoors, and the Major invited him to sit down and then made tea for them all. Then the Major told her she was safe, and she wept. Charles knelt before her to comfort her and assure her she would be safe. Sarah, no, that didn't suit her; Sal, yes, his Sal. They would both protect her. Soon, she was in his arms, sobbing in relief. Charles Lockley and Jack Turner had tried to stay in touch, but because Jack now had a job way down south at Camden, they had lost touch. It was only through Jenna nearly getting trampled by goats that they reconnected again. Charles had initially got work in the same house as Sal, as a stable hand with one of the Major's friends. Major Grace had given them both men references, which meant that all they had to do was decide where they wanted to work. He was employed to drive a coach and look after the Perry White's household and garden at his house, Glenmere. Charles could turn his hand to most jobs but loved gardening and leatherwork and did them well.

It wasn't long before Charles applied to marry Sal. As the application had to go before Major Grace for approval, it was a technicality. They often met with the Major, Perry, and his wife, Katy and discussed their growing faith. Sal soaked in everything she could. The unusual group became friends. Charles and Sal married only weeks after their arrival, but she still had to serve her time with the Major and Perry White. Charles Junior arrived nine months after their wedding. Eddie was born eleven months later and named after Major Edward Grace, as he was born on his birthday.

Edward was also Sal's Grandfather's name, although the Irish version, Eamon, they didn't tell Major Grace that. In succession after that, Elizabeth called Liza; Susanna, known as Anna, William, as Wills; and Luke John, Luke from the Bible and John after Charles' Pa. Therefore, Major Grace always had a soft spot for Eddie.

The Major had retired but only lived down the street in Phillip Street. Surprisingly, he had not returned home to England when he retired. Charles often wondered why he didn't. He had never married, so Charles and Sal adopted him. There was a knock on the door, and the Major walked in. He had a permanent dinner invitation with the family on a Sunday evening. He told Sal and Charles he would be late, so he just walked over to the empty chair and seated himself when he arrived. He loved the acceptance of just being one of the family. "What's this I hear, my boy?" He nodded to Eddie. "Getting married, I hear. She's a fine lass, but she'll keep you on your toes. Life will never be dull with Miss Jenna."

Sal served his meal. "Ned, how did you hear? Eddie has only just told us."

Ned chuckled. "You know this town. News is circulated before the person making it knows." Seeing their stunned faces, he added, "Actually, it was Bessie from the Rectory; she brought me down some biscuits she had made and let the cat out of the bag. As I removed my boots outside, I heard you all talking about it, so I knew you'd told everyone. Congratulations, my boy!" After giving thanks, he tucked into his meal with gusto. The table the family sat around had been the one that had belonged to Perry White. It was given to Charles as a parting gift when they left. Sal knew Ned didn't cook for himself. Bessie and Sal both took him meals and cakes. He enjoyed the family occasions when he could enjoy good food and friendship. They had as much to thank him for as he did them. He just fitted in. He could be himself, just Ned, and was on first-name terms with all the family over dinners.

After dinner, Eddie motioned for Charlie to follow him. "Hey, mate, I just want to officially ask if you would stand up with me at the wedding. You know, to be one of the witnesses? Jenna is going to ask Marc to be the other one."

His brother grinned. "I'd love to Ed. Thank you. Now I'll tell you something too. I asked Mr. Miller if I could marry Gracie today. I haven't spoken to her yet. I know she'll say yes, but I want to think of something special. How did you do it?"

Eddie told him of the galloping horses through the orange orchard and the rest of the story. He blushed, and then they both laughed.

"Oh! That's fabulous. I bet it will get better with the telling over the years, too," said Charlie. "I have to think of something special for her. Don't say anything to the rest of the family, not even Jenna. You know how girls talk. But if you get any ideas… let me know."

Chapter 12   Weddings and Things

*L*iza and Bertie's wedding was on Saturday. After the ceremony, the house was in mayhem, and everyone was invited back for an outdoor feast. Old Tom had stuck his head in the kitchen and said, "Mrs. Sal, the rains are coming. I feel it in my bones."

November so far had been a series of perfect days, cool nights and warm days. It had not occurred that it could rain, but Old Tom was rarely wrong. Charlie had already thought of this and had cleared out the barn. He placed the stock food bags as seating around the edge of the barn. He said to Eddie, "We won't be able to all sit-down, but we can put the tables in there; all the young ones will have to eat standing. We'll hoist a sail over the yard."

Charles and Sal came to look and agreed. If nothing else, it would be ready if needed. The barn loft was prepared for people to sleep in. The Turners were all coming, as Mr. Parker, Alex's boss, was going to look after the Inn at Emu Plains and the animals for the night. They'd all arrive late on Friday. Charlie said to his father, "Mr. and Mrs. Turner can have our room, and we'll all sleep here with all the other boys. Jenna, Vicky and Cathy can choose, but I think they'd rather squash in with the girls. Some will be on the floor, though, but still no rats or snakes inside."

The Tindales were already packing and sorting. One day after work, Mrs. Tindale called Eddie in and said, "Eddie, as we're moving into Caroline's house, we're not going to need more than our personal items and clothing. I know you will be living in the house as just a caretaker, but I want you to know that most of the furniture here will come to you if our nephews don't want it. We don't know what the future holds, but this will give you and Jenna a great start in your married life. Not many couples have this opportunity. We would not let anyone else stay here, but this is almost your second home anyway. You have become the son we never had, and we love you dearly. Tom would not hand his beloved forge over to you otherwise."

Eddie looked stunned, stunned but thrilled.

"Now, having said that, it's not what I brought you in here for. I have something for you to give Jenna. Caroline only has boys, and I have come to love Jenna as I love you. So I'd like her to have this to wear on her wedding day. It's my gift to her. Something she can keep forever, to remember her special day." She was holding a long, flat floral box. "Tom commissioned Douglas to buy those for me when he was on one of the tea runs to China. He bought these for me, and then later, Tom bought a matching set for both Caroline and me, and they are larger. So I don't need two. This one is for Jenna with my love. I'll keep the ones Tom bought me."

Eddie took the box from her and carefully opened the lid. Inside was the most beautiful necklace of small white pearls. "Oh, Mrs. Tindale, these are beautiful. How can I ever thank you?" He captured her in a gentle bear hug. She was like another mother to him; he cared for them both dearly. "There is no way I would ever have been able to buy anything like this for her. I shall certainly let her know. Can I bring her up on Friday evening, and you can give them to her yourself? I'd really like that."

"If that's what you'd like, Eddie, then yes, I'd like that too. Bring her after you've had dinner. You'll have a lot to do on Saturday anyway."

She kissed his cheek just as Mr. Tindale walked inside. "What's all this?" he laughed. "Kissing my wife and you newly engaged," he teased Ed. "So she has given them to you? I'm sure Jenna will like them."

"Oh, sir, she'll love them. But I'll bring her up here on Friday night for you to give them to her yourselves. She won't believe her eyes. I'll suggest she doesn't show them until our wedding if that's all right, though."

Friday arrived soon enough.

At dawn, Mr. Parker arrived at the Inn to man it if anyone arrived. The Turner family loaded themselves into the wagon with its new cover and harnessed Phillip. They set off with hampers of food and the old sailcloth in case of rain. It was just as well, as the rain was torrential for more than half the trip into Parramatta. Jack pulled on his oilskin coat and a wide-brim hat. Everyone else sat under the sailcloth cover. Jack had made a couple of curved poles and turned the cart into a sort of wagon. It worked. They remained dry, as did all the food they were bringing.

The Jolly Sailor Inn was a hive of activity. The tables were ready in the barn, the decorations were up, and helpers were everywhere. Old Tom was sitting inside the barn, seemingly overseeing everything. He changed the placement of a few things until he was satisfied. He was a funny character. He was eternally old; in reality, he would only have been in his fifties. Even when a child, Eddie always thought he was old; however, he hadn't changed much in the intervening eleven years. He was slightly bent over, but his toothless smile and a friendly word for everyone were delightful. Bill Miller had told them how Tom had arrived on the convict ship with him. So he must be in his sixties now. Sadly, his two close friends, "Leary" Larry and "Have a Chat" Harry, had died, as had Ted. The man who had befriended him and taught him many of the quirky skills he had gathered. He spent much time with the people in the stables at all the Inns. He no longer drank a lot. He said it gave him gout, so he all but gave it up. Occasionally, he would have a rum to celebrate something, but he said, "Gimme a mug of sweet black tea, and I'm happy." His remaining teeth were black, but it was from chewing tobacco, which he spat out in a stream wherever he wished to. As he sat watching the goings-on, he was occasionally asked, "Tom, hold this," or, "Tom, pass that." He felt useful. He was happy. He was certainly both trusted and liked, if not loved. Few knew his story, but all were sure he had one. Bill had never spoken of his past either. No one ever asked.

Sal watched Tom from the kitchen. Charles stuck his head in the door to ask if Sal needed help. She shook her head. "All organised, thanks, love." Sal beckoned him in. "Look at Old Tom. He's in his element; why he's actually happy? I don't think I've ever seen him smile before. We'll have to put our heads together and see if we can find him something to 'do'."

"Are we ready for tomorrow? Do we have enough food? I have extra kegs in the cellar. Bill has some fresh ginger beer; he's bringing that over, too. I wonder how much we'll get through and to think we have to do this again next month," said Charles without taking a breath.

Sal turned to him, "Oh Charles, we have what we have. No one will complain, and if I know them, they will all arrive with more. At least with only four weeks between the weddings, any leftover drinks from this will be able to be kept for Eddie and Jenna's wedding. And we'll be old hands at it. Why don't we think about holding other wedding parties here, paying ones? We could whitewash the inside of the barn and get more tabletops and… oh, all sorts of things." She looked at Charles. "I think we could make a bit of money from this." She looked down and kept busy. She had sown the seed, now to let Charles mull this over. She smiled to herself. He would return to her in about a week with this idea, thinking it was his own. She'd let him. They were always looking for more income. Liza's wedding party in the shed gave Sal the thought of starting somewhere to have parties for other families. "I bet he'll think hard about it, too," she smiled.

Just on dusk, sounds were heard in the yard. Sal looked out the kitchen door to see a flat-top wagon-like cart pull into the stable yard. Heads popped out from under the cover, and "Hellos" and "Cooees" were shouted by many. Eddie was beside the cart, handed down Mrs. Turner, and returned to Jenna. He lifted her down but didn't release her, sliding her down and keeping hold of her waist before giving her a hug and a passionate kiss. "Ooh, Eddie, not in front of everyone," she said. She hid her red face on his chest.

"Why, love, we're allowed to now." He kissed the top of her head before lifting her face and kissing her again, another long, deep and passionate kiss. She slid her arms around his neck.

Cathy, aged nearly fifteen, just said to Vicky, "Oh yuck. I'm not letting any boy do that to me."

Fifteen-year-old Wills came and helped her down from the wagon. He blushed as he took her hand. He squeezed it gently.

She looked at him open-mouthed. She may rethink that idea, after all.

Eddie released Jenna and lifted Vicky down from the cart. "Don't kiss us, Ed," she said, giggling.

Ed looked at Vicky, his future sister-in-law, and thought, "One day, this girl will be a beauty." But he still preferred his Jenna. Jenna was… vivid. He saw Cathy's mouth drop open when she saw Wills and Luke behind him. He thought, "How can all three be so different from Jenna?" He laughed and quickly let them go. The two younger boys hopped down and took off with Luke.

Sal emerged from the kitchen, still rolling up the apron she'd just removed. "Martha, it's so good to see you again. Come inside. The kettle is boiling, and you'll need a wash-up. Bring in your things, as you're both sleeping in the boy's room." The women went inside, leaving the men and young people to sort out the wagon's contents.

It had been raining off and on most of the day. However, the rain had ceased about an hour before. It was now hot and muggy. The stars were beginning to appear by the time the wagon had been emptied and stored behind the shed.

Charlie and Jack walked over to the shed. "Jack, I've just had an idea. We could bring one of the flat wagons into the yard later tomorrow and use it as a stage where the musicians can sit or stand. It's big enough, and we could have some dancing too. We have enough lanterns and plenty of room. That's if the rain holds off."

Jack replied, "Fabulous idea, Chas. We'll remove the poles and clean ours up tomorrow." He turned to Charles, "…now you said you have plenty of ale? I could do with a drop or two. How about it?"

The four younger girls all went in to help their mothers with the meal, and the men went to find a drink.

Marc and Charlie were the only ones left in the yard. They saw Eddie and Jenna walking hand in hand towards the Tindales.

All the younger boys went in the other direction, with Wills saying, "Come on, let's go to the wharf."

"Let's follow them," said Charlie to Marc, pointing to their fathers.

"I could certainly do with a drink," said Marc. They wandered off towards the Inn, too.

Saturday dawned bright and sunny. Everyone was up at dawn. There were chores to do and many hands to do them. The girls were all bleary-eyed as they had talked long into the night.

Sal and Martha prepared a large pot of grain porridge with cream and honey to top it off. This was followed by freshly cooked bread and fried eggs. Martha brought a basket full of them from her friend, Mrs. Walker, out on the Nepean River. With at least seventeen to feed, there was no place to sit, so food was served from the kitchen and eaten on the verandah. The four parents sat inside at the table, discussing the plans for the day.

Charles and Sal had drawn up a list of last-minute jobs, and Martha helped Sal allocate these to the various people who came back for seconds. Liza, Eddie, and Jenna were conspicuously absent from chores. Both mothers knew that being Liza's special day, she was already going to be occupied enough. Eddie and Jenna were due up at the church at 10 am to see Reverend Mr. Bobart, and by the time they were through there, it would only give them time to come back and dress for the wedding. There were plenty of hands to do what was required.

More and more of their friends and family arrived. The kitchen was a hive activity; food was prepared and taken into the cellar to keep cool. Kegs were readied for tapping, and tankards, plates and bowls sitting on the tables were also readied for use.

Mrs. Evans and the three boys had arrived on Friday's Ferry and stayed with the Tindales. Ed introduced Jenna to them the night before.

Just before everyone was ready to leave for the church, Old Tom appeared and asked for Mrs. Sal. On being told she was nearly ready, he sat and waited.

Sal, dressed in her Sunday best, came onto the verandah. "Hello, Tom; how can I help you? I thought you'd be at the church already."

"Well, I be thinkin', Mrs. Sal. I'm not that keen about weddin's an' if it's alri't with you, I'd like to stay here and mind everything till you return. Got one of those feelin's 'o mine," he said shyly.

"Oh, Tom, there's no need for that. We'd love to have you at the church." Sal stopped for a moment. "Tom, don't you have anything to wear? You can borrow one of Charlie's shirts."

"Well, no, Missus, I don't, but that's not it. I jus' think that someone should stay an' keep an eye on things. So if it's alri't, I'll jus' sit in the barn and wait for everyone to return. You know me, I jus' got a feelin' in my bones, an' you know when that happens. Well, I'll bide my time 'ere. You go orf an' enjoy your weddin'." Tom doffed his hat to Sal and turned to go into the barn without waiting for her reply.

Charles appeared dressed and ready. "What did Tom want? Isn't he coming?"

"No," said Sal, "he's got one of his feelings, and so he's going to stay and look after things here."

"I'll take him some ginger beer," said Charles.

Charlie appeared at the side of the house in a gig. He had borrowed it from Bill Miller and done it with white flowers and ribbons. He had harnessed James into it. He had a new bridle and reins, all in shiny black; he, too, was dressed for the occasion. His mane and tail were plaited neatly; his coat shone inky black. Charlie had added a plume of white cockies feathers to James' head.

"Dar, I thought you and Liza could arrive in this."

Charles stood looking standing with his hands on his hips. "Oh lad, you've done us proud. Liza will look like a queen arriving in this."

Charlie hopped down and flicked James' reins over the railing. He grabbed an old rag and wiped a few mud spots off the side. "Drive slow out the yard; it's still a bit muddy in patches. Jack and I have also cleaned their cart, and all the rest of us will go in that. So we'll all arrive clean. I'll get him to help me harness Phillip into it."

Eddie and Jenna were late in getting back but were dressed and ready in time for a quick snack before the service.

Martha had brought what she called finger food, so there was no need for cutlery. There was a bacon and egg pie, hard-boiled eggs, homemade sausage, some apple turnovers, and a large pile of oranges. With so many youngsters, they could eat like an army of soldiers. Soon, this pile of food had all but gone. Everyone but Liza and Charles piled onto the cart and headed off. Sal kissed Liza as she stood watching everyone load up. Charles handed her in the front with Martha and Jack.

Charles had his arm around Liza's shoulders. "Come on, girl, our turn now. Last time you'll be here as a single lady."

Liza turned to him and said, "Oh, Daddy," and burst into tears. She was the only child who called him that, and he loved it.

He enfolded her in his big arms and gave her a bear hug. "Nuff of that, my Blossom. Now smile."

She did…

He grinned and then said, "Okay, now hold it. Because these will be some special hours to remember." He also had a lump in his throat but didn't let on. He gently pinched her cheek lovingly. He heaved himself up beside her, and, waving to Tom, they drove off. He walked the gig out of the muddy yard. "Okay, James, to the church we go." He flicked his reins and said, "Gee up, boy."

James decided he liked this carriage and high-stepped, prancing his way up to St John's church.

Liza giggled at James' antics. She relaxed.

He was such a wondrous horse.

Old Tom's hunch was right. He was just settling down to his bottle of ginger beer when he heard voices.

Captain Roberts, the ferry Captain, was walking up from the wharf with a very roly-poly man and a lad. Tom stood, watching them get closer. He knew Roberts well. A memory stirred in Tom; he reminded him of someone, and he shrugged, trying to shake out the memory. He lifted his arm in acknowledgement and tankard in hand and sat on an empty half barrel to await their arrival.

They took some time before they left the vessel. Finally, the two men and the boy, about twelve, arrived. Tom poured some ginger beer for them. Captain Roberts was an invited guest, but the tide had delayed his arrival, so he said he'd miss the service but wait for the festivities with Tom. The only passenger on the ferry was this one gentleman. He introduced himself. "My name is Falconer-Meade; this is my grandson Joshua. I've come looking for my son Matthew."

As soon as he said his name, Tom stood looking at him with his mouth dropped open. Finally, he said, "So that's who you remind me of. I knew a man named Maffhew Falconer-Meade, oh some, let me fink…'bout ten…no twelve years ago who had your look about him, somethin' about the way you walked, I fink. I had a fair bit to do wiv him and his Missus. We spent a week or two looking for farms. He was with his wife and baby. He had some gran' idea that he was gonna buy a big farm and run stock. He came to check out this area and was gonna return to buy this farm I know'd about. I never saw him again. He never comed back. I dunno really what really happened to his Missus and the little boy, but I'd heard later that Maffhew died of some illness. Last I heard, they was still in Sydney. I dinna know how to get in contact wiv them, and over time just forgot. Maffhew said the kid had a funny name, something too long, so they called him Tad, as he was a little tadpole of a thing."

Mr. Falconer-Meade mopped his head and then his eyes. "Do you mean I have another grandson? Tad. I wonder, could it have been Theodore by any chance? That's a family name."

"By Jove, that's it, Fee-a dore; no wonder they called the little mite Tad. Wot a mouthful for a little tacker?" Tom smiled.

Mr. Falconer-Meade wiped another tear away with his handkerchief in his hand. "Do you know, sir, that this is the first I've heard about him in those twelve years? I came here about a year after his last letter and could find no trace of him. That was about eleven years ago. But if you say they were last in Sydney, I might head back and have a longer look there. At least I now have somewhere to start. I've been looking for Matthew, not his wife and certainly not a child. My, my. He'd be about fourteen now, too. 'Tad' well, at least that's a start. Thank you, good sir." He shook his hand again.

Captain Roberts had been listening while sipping his ginger beer.

"You know, I have an idea. There's a lad I know about in Sydney. He has been working with some of the 'lost boys', I call them. He's getting a bit of a name for himself; he goes by Ricky English. He went to Eddie's school when he could. No idea if that's his real name, but it's what people call him. Nice lad, very different from the typical street kid. Last I heard, he and two other young lads he'd befriended had some idea of helping some other street children. I think one is called Tad." He sat thinking. "Your friend Fishbon helped set him on his feet as a wee tacker. Chat with Fishbon; he's back in Sydney now with his wife; they have a house there. He teaches now at the new school on College Street. They know Ricky quite well. A few boys sit with them in church." Captain Roberts continued. "This Ricky makes the boys come to church with him each week. It's how I know him. We go to the same one. One lad is a fabulous artist and draws all the people in the church. He has a skill that one. We each have our own talents; some develop early, and it seems that Ricky is keen to dig them out in his friends. One of the boys has a bad limp, too. I can't remember which one, but they are nice lads. They never cause any trouble. Much more likely to stop it than cause it. I have a lot of time for the three of them. Even Mr. Landon has taken to him."

Mr. Falconer-Meade plied Tom and the Captain with many more questions. Sometime later, they could hear the joyous shouts of many voices descending upon them. "Sounds like the weddin' party is coming home," said Tom.

First to arrive was Charlie driving the cart with Jack, Martha and his parents on the back, along with Reverend Mr. Bobart, his wife and the Tindales, and Mrs. Evans and Major Grace upfront with Charlie. Following them were Bertie and Liza in the Ellis's brougham. The Miller's in the gig, with James, still prancing, but his plume of feathers had fallen over his nose, and he looked funny, and all the others on foot.

Thankfully, the day had remained clear, and the sun was still shining, the sky spotted with white fluffy clouds. The mud in the yard had dried up and was now mostly firm underfoot.

Charles lifted Sal off the cart; they walked over to the three men.

"See, I wus right, Missus. I knewed I had to be here. I wus jus' the right man that this gent needed to speak to. I knewed his son Maffhew some twelve years ago," Tom said. He took a good swig of his tankard and grinned a toothy grin. "If I hadn't stayed, I mighta missed him."

Charles looked at the newcomer. "I remember you," he said. "You were here about ten years ago; I remember that day. Old Tom here knew your boy? Well, small world. You arrived the day our boys went off to school."

"Yes, sir, but it was eleven years now. Mr. Thomas here not only knew him but told me I have a grandson I knew nothing about, Theodore Falconer-Meade, apparently known as 'Tad.' I shall return to Sydney reinvigorated to go on with my search. I can only stay another month or so; if I can't find him this time, I'll have to come back again sometime later. I would extend my time if there is any chance I could find him." He turned to the Captain, "Looks like you have return passengers, sir."

Captain Roberts said, "It's a full moon tonight, so we leave about six. Will you go back to The King's Arms?"

"Thank you, good man. I held my room, as it's been my base, so, yes, I'll be back there. I'll scour the streets if I have to. I now have three people who may direct me. This is wonderful news. Absolutely wonderful." Mr. Falconer-Meade laid his hand on the shoulder of his silent grandson. Joshua just smiled in reply.

Captain Roberts said, "In the meantime, we have a wedding party to attend." They joined the rest of the guests.

Sal went indoors to don her apron, a nice new one edged in lace and helped prepare the afternoon and evening food. Soon, streams of food were emerging from the cellar and kitchen. The entire village seemed to have descended upon the Inn forecourt. Throughout the afternoon, people came and went. More food arrived with more people.

Charlie and Jack set the wagon in a place where it was both out of the primary access way but still visible to everyone. The Fiddlers climbed up and started playing. One man played the spoons; another drummed on an old keg. Soon, many were up dancing and singing too. Everyone was having a wonderful time. The music continued well into the evening.

Captain Roberts and the Falconer-Meade's departed after the meal. Charles and Sal walked them down to the wharf. They waited until the ferry left and disappeared around the bend. Charles took Sally in his arms and said, "You know, love, I don't tell you often enough how much I love you. I do, you know. Very much," he said lovingly. He lowered his head and kissed her.

"I love you too, my dear one," replied Sal. She laid her head on his shoulder. "Can you believe we have a married daughter? Where did those years go? I don't really feel older, just more tired than I used to be." She lifted her head. "I love you, Charles, so very much. I think back to that day when I saw you first. I was in a line of other convict women. I often wonder what made you notice me. Why me? I've asked before; you know you've never really answered. The Major was wonderful to us back then, wasn't he? I feel so sorry he has no one."

Charles shrugged, bent and kissed her slowly. "God led you to me."

They stood in each other's arms for some time, and then Charles said, "We'd better head back, my love." He kissed her cheek. "Just remember I may not say it often, but do I love you. I'd be lost without you."

They walked back with his arm around her shoulder, tucking her under his arm. The music was drifting down to them. About halfway back, he swept her into his arms again and danced with her in the descending twilight. He was about to kiss her again when Charlie and Gracie met them on the road, not far from the barn.

Charles looked at Sal and smiled.

"Hi, Dar and Mama; we wanted to catch you before you went back. Looks like you have to plan for another wedding. Gracie has said, 'Yes' to me. I couldn't resist; I asked her during the service. I'd asked Mr. Miller a week ago for permission. I just had to find the right time. But I couldn't wait. So, I leaned across and asked her right in the middle of the wedding. She said yes, just as Liza did."

Charles congratulated them and shook Charlie's hand. "Congratulations, my boy!"

Sal hugged Gracie and kissed her cheek. "I'm thrilled, sweet girl. Just thrilled."

Gracie looked adoringly up at him. She glowed. "Par said we have to wait until I'm eighteen, but knowing we're engaged is enough for the moment. He's been special to me since we were little. We wanted to tell you but not announce it tonight as it's Liza and Bertie's night. Ma guessed already, and she told Par."

Eddie and Jenna were waiting for them. Knowing what Charlie had told him earlier, Eddie had also twigged that he'd proposed and been accepted; such were the smiles on their faces. The fact they were holding hands as they walked to meet his parents gave them away. He'd whispered his presumption to Jenna as they had wandered down to the returning four.

As they got closer, Eddie walked beside Charlie; he quietly said, "Did it, eh?"

"Yep. In the middle of the wedding, just as Liza said, "Yes," so did Gracie. I'm over the moon. Mr. Miller said we have to wait until she turns eighteen."

Eddie swung around, grabbed Gracie, and kissed her on the cheek. "I'm over the moon, Gracie. Congratulations to you both! Shh, I won't say anything."

Jenna laughed. "Now we have to find someone for Marc. He's the last one standing."

As they returned, they nearly bumped into Marc; he was dancing with Bertie's sister Amelia, or Milly, as everyone called her. She was a vivacious redhead with greenish almond-shaped eyes. Jenna watched him throughout the evening, and he could hardly keep his eyes off her. She nudged Eddie. "We're too late. He's caught," carefully pointing towards Marc. "Looks like we're keeping it all in the family. Haha, Bertie's sister. He can't keep his eyes off her."

Eddie laughed and watched Marc for a while.

Tim had swung Anna onto the dance floor. She looked up at him adoringly; he drew her close into his arms. Ed knew that it had always been Anna for his best friend. Even when they were children, he adored her.

Marc got the courage to ask Milly to dance again and, this time sat down next to her. She was nineteen and was Liza's best friend. Now, Liza had married Bertie; she was almost family. She worked in the saddlery with her parents, making bootlaces and other decorative leatherwork. She had marvellous carved leatherwork skills. Her artistry made her father's saddles so popular.

Jenna was guessing that the spare room in the Tindale's house may be used often by Marc. She laughed and whispered to Eddie. "I think we'd better set up a guest room once we're married. Looks like we'll need it." She grabbed Eddie's hand and dragged him up to dance. George Ellis took up his fiddle and played a jig, and all the young folk joined in. The older folk and parents were all sitting this one out. Sal and Bertie's mother, Charlotte, had made a large cake, and together they brought it out of the house.

As the cake was brought out, the musicians fell silent, and Charles climbed up on their cart. Although it was a warm evening, a fire was lit to the side, burning enough to brighten the entire area. The moon was now just above the horizon and was getting lighter. Charles was clearly going to say something. A hush fell.

Charles cleared his throat. "Ladies and Gentlemen, oh and everyone else too," Everyone laughed. "Now I know I'm old. I have, no, we have a married daughter." He looked to Sal, "Can you believe it, my love?"

She shook her head.

"But seriously, folks, we've come today to celebrate the joining of these two young people, Elizabeth and Albert, better known to us all as Liza and Bertie. I don't want to spoil their thunder, but you're all invited back here in a month, as we will do it all again."

There were gasps and a few saying, "Huh?"

"You see," Charles continued, "Eddie and Jenna will be married on December 4th. Our dear friends, the Tindales, are moving to Sydney to be with his sister, Mrs. Evans." He nodded towards Caroline Evans, "You all know why."

A general shaking of heads and words of sadness echoed through the crowd.

"So as they will become the caretakers, but we thought we'd get them married off first. What do you think?"

There was a roar of good-humoured laughter and hoots with replies of "Yes."

"Now, the toasts! Everyone, please make sure your tankards are full."

Many moved towards one of the grog tables and refilled their mugs.

"Ready?" said Charles. "So first, I give a toast to our Queen. To Her Majesty, Queen Victoria!"

Everyone drank deeply. "Yeah!" Or "Hear, hear!"

"Now I give a toast to the bride and groom. Please fill your mugs and drink deeply for this one."

"Yeah, you bet," emanated again from the crowd.

He turned and winked at Charlie… "Now, as you know, weddings are infectious. There was a proposal in the middle of the wedding, but I'm not going to tell you who it was, but there will be at least two more weddings next year. I'll be broke," said Charles. Hand to his forehead, feigning anxiety.

Again, there was a roar of laughter. It did not take long before everyone realised it was Charlie and Gracie, as Tim and Anna had already announced their engagement.

At this point, Charlie found his voice. He spoke loudly, his arm around Gracie, "Actually, Dar, we've been talking with Tim and Anna. November next year will actually only see one wedding."

The crowd hushed… waiting to see if there was more.

He continued, smiling, "But there will be two marriages. We're going to have a double wedding."

There were more gasps, and these four young people received many congratulations, slaps, handshakes and kisses. Liza and Bertie were amongst them, laughing and dancing happily. She was so excited.

Jenna again leaned over to Eddie. "And I bet there will be a third wedding, but it will be Marc and Milly. I wonder if we can make it a triple one? What do you think? He's over-talking to Mr. Ellis now. I bet he's asking if he can court her. They only need a month to read Banns."

Eddie nodded in agreement. They kept their eyes on him. They watched as he walked straight back to her side, and he nodded to her and sat down smiling.

Jenna caught his eye and poked her tongue out at him, then winked and smiled broadly.

Eddie roared with laughter and bent to kiss Jenna. "Minx," he said.

Marc looked down at Milly, smiling. He wiggled closer to her; she reached out brazenly, grabbed his hand, and held it. "Now, sit still," she said. He grinned. Yes, he had met his match.

The Major sat watching the young people around him, and his mind flicked back to his time in London. He smiled. Why would he ever want to return? No, he loved the informality of life here. Everything was far more straightforward. He relaxed, his eyes catching on a pair of blue eyes watching him. He smiled in return. These wonderful people were his new family. Ned was as good a friend as Gerry, Rob or Jim. Of them, only Jim knew the name he was using here. Admittedly, he missed his boyhood friends.

The party continued for some time before Liza and Bertie left in the Ellis' brougham accompanied by much cheering. They were going to stay at a friend's tonight and then another house for a week while they were in Sydney. The remaining guests drifted away until there was just family left. The fiddlers had gone, and everyone left had gathered around the fire. Marc was last seen walking home with Milly and her family. They had already fallen behind before they were out of sight; they were holding hands. He said he'd be back a bit later.

Martha and Sal were nearly dead on their feet, and Cathy, Anna, and Vicky started collecting the remaining food and taking it to the cellar. Jenna and the boys began cleaning up the rest of the mess.

Jenna said, "Maa, you and Mama Lockley head off to bed; we'll get this sorted as much as possible tonight and will clean the rest tomorrow after church." She bent and kissed her mother and then Sal. "I'm so lucky I'm going to have two wonderful mothers." She walked off with a skip in her step.

Sal looked at her. "Oh, the wonder of youth. Do they ever tire?" she asked.

Martha replied, "Let's go. We'll at least get washed before the men come in."

Martha locked her arm through Sal's, and they wandered off into the house. She looked up and thanked God for the beautiful evening. Sal caught her action and simply said, "Amen." They smiled at each other and walked up onto the verandah.

Sal said, "You head to bed; I'll put the porridge on to soak." She walked into the kitchen. She'd already filled the pot with water when she'd rinsed it out earlier in the evening. She measured out the cracked grain, poured it in and put the lid on the pot.

Charles walked in, looking as tired as she felt. "Come on, sweets, bedtime." He waited for her and draped his arm around her shoulder as they headed off to bed. He quietly turned down the lamp and shut their door. Anna would turn it off when she was done.

~

Dawn came way too early the next morning. Everyone emerged blearily-eyed. The cold water in the tub outside was the first stop for every one. The chores still needed doing, and the cow needed to be milked. The church service was in an hour, and there was much to be done.

Everyone was still tired. Charles and Jack decided to take the cart so no one had to walk. They would all fit, but the four younger boys, Wills, Luke, Nick and Calum, ran ahead instead of riding. Martha and Sal watched them in awe. They had all had less than five hours of sleep, but they had all had a fabulous time at the party.

The church bells were peeling as they drove up to the church. Reverend Mr. Bobart greeted them all. "Morning, all! Wonderful party yesterday; nice to see the young couple so much in love." He leaned toward Eddie as he walked past. "First time today," he smiled.

Eddie nodded and mouthed, "Thank you."

Not being a regular at St John's, Jenna started to look around her. The next time she'd be in this beautiful church, she'd be getting married herself. She shivered. She then looked over to her handsome fiancé. In a month, this attractive man would be her husband. She lifted her eyes and thanked God. The morning sun was streaming in through the three windows above the altar. Yesterday, she'd sat here for her soon-to-be sister-in-law's wedding; in a month, it would be her and Eddie.

Mrs. Meadows, sitting in the seat across the aisle, caught her eye and smiled. She was so lovely but looked so sad. She'd had a quick word with her yesterday. She was so nice.

Reverend Mr. Bobart started his sermon. Her attention snapped back. 'Love is patient, Love is Kind', he began, and she nodded in agreement. Her mind wandered off again.

Eddie squeezed her hand as he could tell she wasn't listening. She smiled up at him and shook off her cobwebs.

At the appropriate time, the Banns were read for Edward John Lockley and Martha Jennifer Turner. Eddie and Jenna grinned as their full names were added to the list.

Mr. and Mrs. Tindale looked over, and both smiled.

Jenna squeezed Eddie's hand. She was so pleased she was here to hear this. She'd possibly miss the next two times.

As they left the church, the choir sang "Praise to the Lord." Jenna loved this Hymn and had chosen it for their wedding. She could never thank God enough for the twist her life had taken and for the goats. She looked again at Eddie just as he looked at her. They couldn't hold hands as they were walking out of the church. It was just not done. They followed Ed's family out. They were standing as close to each other as was allowed but not touching. Many were standing in small groups, catching up with friends. Groups of children were playing on the wide-open lawns. Older people were standing in the shade of the big tree in the yard.

An older lady from the church was standing behind them. "Look at these young people, no respect for traditions. Marrying in such haste, and for what reason, I ask ?"

Jenna giggled but was shocked.

Eddie turned around and said, "Mrs. Jenkins, you have not met my betrothed, have you? This is Miss Jenna Turner. We're getting married next month. Did you hear our Banns read today?" Without waiting, he turned to Jenna, grabbed her elbow, and walked her out.

Mrs. Meadows followed them, and close behind her was Major Grace. As usual, friends were milling in groups on the church grounds. They walked towards Ed's parents. One shrill voice carried over the murmur of other, more gentle ones.

Jenny saw Wd frown. He said, "No matter which church you go to, there are people like this. You'd think they have better things to do. There were people like this in Sydney, too," Eddie groaned. "So much for believing in God. If they really listened about what was said in the church, maybe they would stop being catty." Eddie was grumpy. This was not like him.

Jenna looked up at him, surprised. "Ed, I'm sure she didn't mean it." Jenna stood, looking at the speaker. At that moment, she could hear the same catty voice pulling another reputation to shreds. They listened for a bit. "Oh, Eddie… I see what you mean." Her hand was over her mouth in shock.

Reverend Mr. Bobart approached them, "Are you all right, Miss Jenna? You both look upset."

"Oh, yes, Reverend, it's just something I heard," she said.

Mrs. Jenkins had hardly taken a breath; Jenna put her finger to her lips and then hand to her ear; she mouthed, "Listen."

The three stood there listening to the catty shrew, tear strips of various reputations of people in the town, including dear Mrs. Meadows, who was the sweetest, most gentle lady. Her husband died from a snake bite, and she had just emerged from mourning.

Mrs. Meadows lived alone in a cottage not far from the Lockley Inn. Major Grace lived two doors up from her and often offered to walk her home from church. She was tall, graceful and stunningly beautiful. A willowy blonde with a ready smile for everyone. Her eyes were the most incredible cornflower blue, but they were always sad. Jenna liked her immediately. She was caught looking at her, and her gaze was returned with a big, friendly smile and a gracious nod. Jenna had caught her breath when she saw her for the first time in the church. She didn't know ordinary people could look so, well, regal. She looked pretty in the dim church; in the full sunshine, she was breathtakingly beautiful. Her blonde hair was intricately wrapped around her head, with two ringlets trailing down her back. She wore no jewellery but needed none to enhance her beauty.

Reverend Mr. Bobart was shocked at what he was hearing Mrs. Jenkins say and turned to Jenna and Eddie and apologised. "I'll deal with this," he said. "I've been told about her before but never caught her at it. I've only been Rector for twelve months, but I've heard some nasty things about her. This will give me an excuse to nip this in the bud once and for all."

He turned around and tapped Mrs. Jenkins on the shoulder. "Ma'am, I think we need to talk. I'll call on you tomorrow." He bowed to her and walked away without letting her say a word.

Everyone else was leaving the church grounds. Eddie's family had already left, as had many others; they had missed her comments.

Mrs. Jenkins stood mouth open. Then she flushed. Her friends backed away from her; soon, she soon stood alone in the churchyard. Everyone remaining had turned their backs on her and walked away. She was utterly alone; she had been cut.

Christina Meadows saw Jenna approach the lady, and her compassion for the old woman was shown by Jenna's gentle touch on her arm.

Jenna walked up to her. "I know you didn't mean what you said, but words can hurt people. The Bible says the tongue is sharper than a two-edged sword." She took a breath before continuing. "Eddie and I are marrying quickly because the Tindales must move to Sydney to be with his sister. There is no other reason."

Tears ran down Mrs. Jenkins's face.

Jenna hugged her.

"I'm so sorry," Mrs. Jenkins said. "I know I need to watch my tongue, but it runs away with me."

Major Grace offered to walk Mrs. Meadows home as they lived not far from each other, so they, too, were departing.

Mrs. Meadows turned to look at Jenna before leaving. She touched Major Grace's arm and pointed Jenna's actions out to him.

Eddie was standing near them; he was talking with the Minister.

Reverend Mr. Bobart, who was still standing talking to Eddie. "My, that is one special lady you have there. Look how she's handled, Mrs. Jenkins." He stood watching them.

Mrs. Jenkins was now head bowed and still in Jenna's arms. "I'm so sorry," Mrs. Jenkins cried over and over again.

Jenna looked appealingly to Eddie and mouthed, "Help."

In awe of what he had just witnessed, the Major turned and escorted Mrs. Meadows across the lawn. He had heard the lady's words about Mrs. Meadows, yet he could say nothing in her defence. He had no right to defend her, and doing so would cause more problems than not. They could not be known as a couple. His heart raged at the injustice.

Both Reverend Mr. Bobart and Eddie took pity on Jenna. Reverend Bobart walked over to them. He simply put his hand on the older lady's shoulder and gently waved his hand towards her home. Then he said, "I shall visit at 9 a.m., and we shall discuss this more."

Mrs. Jenkins walked off utterly chastened, still dabbing tears from her cheeks.

Eddie and Jenna took this chance to escape, and by walking the opposite way around the church, they, too, disappeared quickly.

Soon, only the Reverend and his wife were left standing outside the church. He took her hand and said, "I think, my dear Elizabeth, one small problem may have sorted itself out today. Maybe others will take note. If only people would learn to love one another. They don't have to like each other; they just accept each other as they are. This petty bickering is so frustrating. It's like putting God's work in chains, too. If only they would concentrate on the needs of the poor or the spreading of God's word. It's in many churches and community groups. There is nearly always a loose-tongued person or one a little like this. The words that the tongue is sharper than a two-edged sword is certainly true."

Elizabeth stood watching the last of their flock disappear.

He paused, then said to his wife, "That young lady of Eddie's certainly puts God's love into practice; I wish more would." He sighed, and they walked back into the empty church. He shut the heavy church door but left it unlocked if someone wished to enter when he wasn't there.

Eddie, noticing that no one was around, took Jenna's hand and linked it through his arm as the Major did with Mrs. Meadows; only Ed placed his hand on top of hers as they walked back. "I'm so proud of you. That was such a hard thing to do. We've all been too afraid of her to say anything. She's hurt so many people over the years."

Jenna mumbled something, then looked at Eddie. "Well, you see, my tongue also runs away with me sometimes, and I find myself saying things that I shouldn't even be thinking." She cringed to herself. "Well, when I put myself in her position, alone and unloved, I feel sorry for her. So, well, I'd want a hug, so I gave her one. That's all." She jumped over a large mud puddle and nearly tugged Eddie into it.

He laughed, grabbed her by the waist and swung her around. "Well, I still think you're amazing." Then kissed her on the tip of her nose.

Time for the Turners to return home approached fast. As it was, they would be arriving home after dark. Sal and Martha had raided the leftovers from last night and prepared a picnic for them for both midday meals, snacks and dinner if required. Bottles of ginger beer and some cider, too.

"There is also cake leftover," Sal said, "and take the half cask of ale too. You'll need something to drink, and it won't keep. We have another one already tapped. The bouncing won't help it, but it's liquid. You can bring the empty back next month when you come," said Sal.

The men had re-erected the canopy over the cart as not only was it hot in the sun but also threatening rain later on.

Jenna and Eddie emerged from the barn after saying a fond farewell. "Not long now, sweetie, and we won't have to part." He lifted her onto the back of the cart. She leaned down and kissed him.

"Oh, leave off, you two," said Marc.

Jenna said, "You're just jealous that Milly isn't here too."

He blushed beetroot red and shut up.

Jack laughed, "Who's Milly? What have I missed?"

"Shh," said Martha, "I'll tell you later."

"No, you won't; I know you. Is she Bertie's little sister? The redhead? Is that her name?" Jack asked.

"Yes," said Marc. "Now leave off." He blushed again.

"Oooh," said Cathy and Vicky in unison, then giggled.

Then Vicky said, "Make sure she comes to your wedding, Jen. We want to meet her."

Cathy caught Wills's eye and stayed quiet. He blushed and dropped his head. He had been close at hand every time she needed a drink or food. Both were only fourteen.

"Oh, she'll be there; I doubt if I could keep her away. She knows Marc will be there. She already has him under her thumb. We were watching," Jenna teased Marc, enjoying the payback of siblings. She did love him dearly.

Alex looked over at her. He had copped his share of her teasing, too, but it was only payback for how they had both teased her over the years. He dared not let on his feelings about Mary Parker. It's one reason he loved his work because she worked next to him. At nearly sixteen, she was too young to court, but she knew his feelings, as did her father. Soon… He sat quietly, keeping his feelings to himself. He was thinking, "Next year, when she was seventeen, he could start courting her, then become engaged and marry the next year. But he'd wait; he smiled to himself.

The Lockleys all stood in the yard and watched as the cart drove off. Charles put his arm around Sal and said, "Come on, there's still more to clean up. We'd better get on with it. Get to it, everyone. The sooner it's done, the sooner we all rest. Let's just have a cold meat dinner tonight. I think there will be plenty left over. The Major will be joining us as usual, but I'm sure he won't mind."

Eddie lingered until they were out of sight. He gave a final wave, blew her a kiss and turned to help with the clean-up.

Chapter 13   Trips

*T*he next three weeks passed quickly. Eddie put in many long hours at the anvil, stocking up for the week he'd be away. The Tindales were nearly packed. Some of their luggage had already been sent by carrier to Sydney.

Liza and Bertie dropped in for dinner occasionally; they seemed happy. Everything, including the weather, seemed good. Warm days and rain at night. The barn had been kept clean and was ready for the second wedding.

The cart was nearly packed, ready for the last visit to Emu Plains. It stood waiting to be harnessed to James the next morning. Ed had ridden James bareback to the forge. He harnessed him to the loaded cart. The delivery was at Orchard Hills Farm near Mulgoa and was over halfway out to Emu Ford, so he would continue from there and have two nights with the Turners instead of one.

"I'm loaded and ready to head off, sir," he called to Mr. Tindale the next morning. "I'll see you on Monday, bright and early."

"Off you go, Ed. Take care. See you," he called back.

"Ed, wait," called Mrs. Tindale. "Can you take this to Martha, please? I promised her the recipe, and I keep forgetting to send it. I've had it written out for ages." She handed him a letter and basket. "I made some cookies for you too. Can't have you fading away to nothing."

He laughed. "I don't think that will happen in a hurry," he stated. "I'll make sure there are some left for the family. Thank you." He flicked up the reins, and James trotted off.

Mr. Tindale stood watching for a while; then, as he turned to go inside, he noticed someone else watching Eddie. "I wonder what he's doing back here?" he mused but shook his head and went inside. He had some wrought iron hooks and fancy twists to finish for Caroline; he'd get those done before he quenched the fire. He was going to take the weekend off, too.

Eddie didn't see he was still being watched. He called the Inn to collect his bag and some food. He kissed his mother's cheek, then said, "Bye, Mama, see you Sunday."

No one else but Sal was around, and she stood on the verandah waving. As she turned to go inside, a man walked down the hill from the forge's direction. This was not so unusual, but he was obviously trying not to be seen. She thought this strange. She looked at him again and made a mental note of what he looked like.

He looked up and saw her watching him and scarpered towards town, stopping under the tree outside the cottages. He was reasonably well dressed and clean, with dark trousers with an old tan, possibly leather, jacket. She couldn't see much of his face as his hat was pulled down tight. He kept looking back to see if she was still watching. So she walked into the kitchen and watched him through her window until he was out of sight.

"Charles is due back soon. I'll tell him," she thought. She shook her head. Strange! In due course, when Charles arrived back, Sal filled him in on the strange man. Neither gave it much more thought, but neither forgot.

Eddie had a quick trip to Orchard Hills and Sheridan's farm. James was fresh, and the heavy load had hindered him little. He unloaded all the purchased items and collected the money from the estate manager. He didn't like having so much cash on him but had no other option.

It was not the first time this had occurred; therefore, some years ago, he'd built a small wooden box that could be locked, into which the metal cash tin was able to be inserted. It was under the seat and camouflaged in the bench structure. He had built a similar box on the other side to balance the look. It was rarely used. He waited until he was out of sight, then stopped and locked the money away. He tucked the leather thong with the key around his neck under his shirt. It would only take about a half-hour before he reached the river and another few minutes before he saw Jenna.

James trotted off, pleased to be relieved of the weight of the load. He did look magnificent, as he had the natural gait of a trained carriage horse. He held his head up with his neck arched and looked like he was almost prancing. Eddie loved this beautiful black beast, and this was obvious to all, as his harness, bits, and traces were always polished, and his coat brushed and sleek. Sometimes, Ed would brush little square patterns on his rump for fun. James' skin would flicker as he did these gentle strokes.

Eddie had made some horse brasses for him too. James loved to hear the jingle of these as he trotted. James had a very light mouth and responded to the slightest movement regardless of whether he was pulling a cart or ridden. Not many horses were happy with either, but James was. From the day Eddie was given him by Mr. Tindale, he'd tendered this fine animal with love.

James, in turn, responded not just to Eddie but to Jenna, too. He seemed to realise that she was special. Although this may have had more to do with the carrots and apples, she snuck him.

Eddie made this trip often to Emu Plains over the past six months. Mostly, he rode but occasionally with a cart, dray or borrowed gig. James' temperament was always skittish when first harnessed. Eddie often had to take him for a quick bareback ride before harnessing him into a vehicle. He usually settled down quickly into a regular pace. People would turn to watch James prance by. He had a smooth gallop stride when being ridden, with horse and rider moving as one. He would stretch his legs, and when on the road they knew well, they'd fly. A big black horse and a big blonde man. Both were worth watching, and people would just smile and keep watching; you just couldn't stop. Eddie and James were well-known and a joy to behold.

Today, being harnessed to the cart, James pranced, sometimes even breaking into an easy-pacing gait. Both were enjoying the outing. It didn't take them long to cross the river and head along the road to the Turner's Inn. James did a natural flying change as he knew his trip had nearly ended. He trotted into the Inn yard without much instruction and stopped in his usual spot.

Jenna raced out the door in a very unladylike fashion. She jumped onto the cart's seat, threw herself into Eddie's arms, and pulled his head down for a kiss.

"Steady on, girl; you'll knock me over," he said. "Let me sort James out first, and then I'll greet you properly."

She chuckled. "I can't believe this is the last time we'll have to do this." She'd hopped down quickly and bounced from foot to foot as she was wont to do when excited.

"You know if you help, it will be done faster." He was grinning as he said this.

They got James unharnessed, and Jenna took him into the holding yard. She slipped him half an apple. Eddie pushed the cart into the shed and stowed the tack on the cart. He left his bag on the seat and said, "I'll grab that once we've rubbed him down."

Jenna was one step ahead of him. She'd collected a horse brush and was already returning to rub James down.

As she walked into the yard, James rolled in a special sandy patch on the far side of the yard. She stood and waited, knowing that he'd come to her. He stood up, whinnied and trotted to her. She gave him the other half of the apple.

Eddie arrived with some feed, and together, they rubbed him down and gave him a brush.

Jenna couldn't reach the stallion's back.

They had let him stay in this yard while he ate, and then Eddie would stable him for the night. This done, they walked back to the shed and put away the brushes.

Eddie walked over to the cart and reached into his shirt.

"Not yet; we have a visitor inside." She knew he was going to collect the money, but he took the hint and left his bag on the seat, knowing that it would make an excellent excuse to come back and collect it.

Instead of going inside, he took her to the back of the cart and said, "Now, let's say hello properly." He ran his fingers through her honey-gold hair and gathered her into his arms.

She slid her arms around his neck and moaned. "It's just as well we're being married next week," she mumbled against his lips.

Martha walked outside. "Jenna, I know you two are out here as James is snorting. Where are you both?"

They emerged from the stable arm-in-arm.

"I knew it," she laughed. "Greetings, Edward. Come and meet our visitor. Reverend William Clarke is on his way to Bathurst and beyond."

Eddie smiled; he knew this man.

Eddie bent and whispered to Jenna. "Whoops, I'm in trouble. She doesn't call me Edward often."

Jenna laughed. "Nah, she's just anxious. She's been explaining why we're getting married in Parramatta and not Windsor in his Church." She whispered as they were walking in. "I think we're in the bad books. We don't get to Church more than once a month from here. We've been waiting for our own Church in Emu for ages. However, I have always wanted to marry in Parramatta. It's just so beautiful."

"Trust me, love; I'll sort it." Eddie squeezed her hand, then dropped it.

Jack introduced him as he entered.

Reverend Clarke and Jack Turner stood to welcome him.

Eddie gave a bow and extended his hand to shake. "I've been looking forward to meeting you again, sir. As I'd like to apologise to you about the wedding." He thought if he took the bull by the horns, it would deflate the situation.

"Ah, lad, I was wondering, that's all," said Reverend Clarke. "I knew you from when I was teaching at The King's School, didn't I?"

"Yes and no, sir, and Charlie and I were altar boys and acolytes for years at St John's, so I rarely got to talk to people after the service as I was helping Reverend Marsden. Then, for five years, I lived in Sydney as I went to Mr. Cape's Academy, not King's," Eddie explained. "It was Reverend Mr. Bobart's wife, Miss Elizabeth, who was then Miss Marsden, who began my schooling. I owe them a lot."

Reverend Clarke said, "Ahh yes, I remember you now; so, you have an older brother? I remember him and your parents too; nice family."

"Yes, sir, and two younger ones as well, William and Luke and two sisters."

"Mm, I know young Wills, nice lad." Reverend Clarke smiled at Ed and turned back to Jack, thus dismissing Eddie. "Now, Jack, you were saying that you and Edward's father arrived together? Well, it seems you have both made a 'go' of things. Good on you."

They talked for some time before Martha called everyone to dinner. Jack asked Reverend Clarke to thank God, which he did in a sonorous voice.

The evening advanced slowly until Reverend Clarke said, "I have a big day tomorrow as I'm off across the mountains. I've been directed to look around this Bathurst area, so I'd better head off to bed soon. I shall bid you all good evening." He walked out.

There was almost a sigh of relief from Jenna, but her father caught her eye, and she fell quiet, somewhat chastened.

The boys' room had been quickly converted into the guest room for Reverend Clarke for the evening, and the boys were to sleep in the barn loft. This meant Eddie, too. Although there were hammocks there, they all preferred to lay out some horse blankets and cover themselves with a sheet. This was far more comfortable, especially when the straw was fresh. As Eddie was over six feet tall, he liked to stretch right out. He liked to sleep on the floor; however, he didn't do that out here as he'd often found large, shiny black spiders that would spring backwards when tapped with a stick. He'd heard they had killed people, so the loft was a better choice. Not to mention the snakes.

Jenna helped Eddie carry out some sheets, a jug of cider, and mugs.

Marc, Alex, Nick, and Callum joined them for an impromptu party. Cathy followed Jenna and Eddie, but Vicky had gone to bed. She had an early start the next morning, but none of the others did.

Martha and Jack motioned for them to keep their voices down, so all seven of them climbed the loft ladder and sat talking. Cathy had turned the lamp up as she ascended the ladder so there was just enough light to see. They sat talking about the wedding and party plans for next week.

Eddie accompanied Jenna and Cathy downstairs with the explanation of having to get his bag. Cathy took the hint and went quietly inside.

Standing at the back of the cart, Eddie and Jenna took a long time saying goodnight. But finally, she went inside to bed too. She said, "Don't forget the key," as she gave him a final kiss and then fled before her father came and told her to go inside.

Eddie carefully unlocked the box and removed the leather pouch from the cash tin. He held it in his hand, wondering what to do with it, and finally tucked it inside his shirt pocket.

He climbed up the ladder and, as he took off his shirt, carefully wrapped the pouch up inside it and tucked it under his head as his pillow.

The others had already settled down for the night. They had the lamp downstairs to sort themselves out, and Eddie was now trying to get himself settled by the dim moonlight. Finally, he lay down and fell straight asleep.

He had dreams all night. He supposed he was subconsciously worried about having so much money on him. He slept badly.

He only stirred when Marc crept out of his straw bed at dawn. He slept on.

Soon, the other boys followed, leaving Eddie still asleep.

Jenna crept up and woke him with a gentle kiss.

Her hair tickled his nose, pretending to be still asleep; he brushed it away, then he reached up and grabbed her, rolling her into the straw next to him. He nibbled her lip, then kissed her deeply, and she responded in kind.

"We'd better get out of here before Reverend Clarke catches us," she mumbled against his lips. "I brought you a mug of fresh creamy milk. I left it downstairs as I hoped I'd get a kiss to start the day." She gave him another peck and pushed him away. She whispered, "Pa said you can place the contents of your special box in his safe place." She motioned for him not to say anything. "Shh, the boys have friends coming over; one is downstairs somewhere."

He reached out to her to remove a few bits of straw from her hair. Although his mouth tasted like a chook pen, he pulled her to him for another kiss. "All right," he whispered. He released her, and they sat up. He groaned. "One week, you'll keep."

Jenna shinnied down the ladder and said loud enough for a listener to hear. "Your milk is on the cart, Ed. Come in for breakfast when you're done."

Reverend Clarke had just emerged from the door as she jumped onto the floor. She released a held breath, "Oh, so close."

Jenna greeted him, "Morning, sir; I was just taking some milk to Eddie. He's still in the loft, so I left it on his cart. Breakfast is in about half an hour. Cathy has to finish milking the cow."

The reverend said, "I'm just going to stretch my legs, then I'll be back in a jiffy."

Eddie pulled on a clean shirt, remembering the pouch wrapped in the other one, and climbed down. She was watching for him and could tell there was a bump in the top pocket. He had the money. Phew!

The Reverend walked off, swinging his cane.

Eddie picked up the milk, lifted it like a toast, and meekly drank while Jenna watched him. He still didn't like warm milk; he never had it unless it had crushed berries or honey in it.

With the Minister gone, she ran back across the yard. "You don't like milk, do you?"

He shook his head. "Not really," he said. "Not unless it has fruit like strawberries squashed into it or even honey. Spoilt, aren't I?"

"Well, I'll have to make sure I never run out of honey, won't I?" She took the mug from him, wiped the milk off his lips with her finger, kissed him, turned, and walked inside. "Come on; we must stow that packet before the others return. I don't want it left unlocked." She held the door open for him. "Quick, I can hear them."

She knocked on her parent's room; her father was waiting. "Pa, can we come in? Can you lock this up for Eddie, please?" Jenna put her hand out to Eddie for the pouch.

"Sir, I was paid for a large order at Sheridan's on the way here; I'm on tenterhooks about having all this with me." Eddie handed over the pouch.

Jack bent down, flipped back the rug and lifted a section of floorboards. He had a large key, unlocked the strongbox, placed the pouch in it, locked it again, and replaced the covering. "There now, all safe. Now, you two go off and enjoy yourselves. You have the day off, Jenna. Well, sort of, as you have a few collections to do for me. You'll need to harness up Phillip again for this one."

Eddie was relieved that he no longer had to worry about that money. "Thank you, sir. I really appreciate you keeping this secure. Where would you like us to go?"

"Out Windsor way, lad," said Jack.

They followed Jack out of the room. Jack kept talking. "Jen, you have to head down to Mrs. Walker's. We need honey, eggs and…" he kept talking, but the names meant nothing to him. Jenna waved him into the kitchen, and he went in to help Mrs. Turner prepare the breakfast. There seemed to be a lot of food for the family, but they had a visitor, and he presumed they were doing something special or expecting more. Probably also provide him with some to take on his journey.

Martha rang the gong for breakfast, and everyone came in and ate.

The day was warming up fast, so they ate reasonably quickly so they could each get on with the day and their job. Reverend Clarke bade them all farewell and left on his journey west. Jenna and Ed harnessed up Phillip, and they, too, left on their journey to Windsor and visited the various places Jack needed items collected.

Jack, with his arm along Martha's shoulder, waved them farewell, "Phew, I thought we'd never get them off; they don't suspect a thing," said Jack.

Marc, Alex and Nick arrived from the barn. "Have they gone yet? Can we set up now?" said Marc.

Jack and Martha had arranged a surprise party for them when they returned. As many of their friends were unable to attend the wedding, they thought they'd bring the wedding to them, well at least the party. So… tonight, they were going to have a shindig, as Finn and Maureen Murphy called it. It had taken a lot of arranging. Jack had organised a list of items to be collected from around Windsor. None were really needed, but it got them away. He had been planning this for some time. He said, "Jenna may suspect something, but not that the entire town was going to descend upon the family that night."

Setting up would take them hours; the couple was not expected back before mid-afternoon. The barn had to be prepared; the holding yard was to be turned into a dance area, a parking area for carts and carriages, and a temporary holding yard further along the river. Hence, they were not visible as the couple arrived back.

Martha waited for about half an hour, then rang the gong again. Soon, people were arriving from all directions. Some with food, some with drinks, many in work clothing and prepared to do some heavy work. Some forty people were soon milling around the place doing many needed chores. The women were in the kitchen, and some men were preparing an outdoor food cooking area. Children were climbing trees and hanging bunting and ribbons. Others were scrubbing rocks and logs for seats.

Martha had also made homemade Aberdeen sausage for a quick lunch. This was a recipe that she was given to her by her grandmother. It was a mix of finely diced meat, bacon, eggs, and flour with spices, then rolled into a sausage shape, covered with more flour, wrapped in a cloth tied at the ends and in the middle, and then boiled. It was delicious and easy to eat. You could slice, dice, mince, or use many different ways. She'd made many loaves of bread during the week, and others had brought more.

Kathleen Parker was busy slicing the loaves; the Murphy family had arrived *en masse,* all fourteen of them, but they were fabulous workers, and work they certainly did. Within four hours, the yard had been transformed. Lantern hooks were in many places, hanging in trees and on fences. Even the inside barn walls had been whitewashed. The stables were transformed into a food servery, and plates, cups, mugs, and cutlery were neatly stacked on wooden tables and then covered with sheets.

Everyone gathered for a finger food luncheon and cider with fresh ginger beer for the children.

Those who lived close went home and changed; those who'd come from a fair distance stayed and cleaned up and changed so that everyone was back again and waiting by mid-afternoon.

Shamus Murphy, a nine-year-old, was designated as a scout. He had to sit out of sight but near the bridge and then scamper back and warn that the young couple were nearly home. Jack thought they'd be home by about 3 o'clock.

Sure enough, about fifteen minutes after the hour, Shamus came scurrying in and said, "They are just about the cross the bridge, Missus; they'll be here soon." He raced around, spreading the word. There was a rustle, then a hush as people hid everywhere. Many stood behind the barn and the shed; some inside and some children even up trees.

Jenna and Eddie drove unknowingly into the now tidy yard. The whitewashed barn looked terrific. They were greeted by both Jack and

Martha standing waiting in the yard.

Martha walked to Jenna, "My darling girl. We could not get all our friends to attend the wedding, so we thought we'd bring a wedding of sorts to them." Jack just stood there with a grin and clapped his hands twice.

People oozed from everywhere. Yelling, "Surprise!"

Eddie and Jenna, who were still on the cart, just stood up and looked. Some eighty people appeared, and more were coming down the street.

Jenna jumped down and ran to her parents, hugging them both at once. "Thank you, thank you, thank you. Everybody is here. I can't believe it." She swung around and grabbed Eddie's arm. "Ed, everyone is here. Come on." Many he had met over the past year. Some were new faces.

Marc had appeared and had taken Phillip and the cart away. Six fiddlers from the Murphy family, some just lads, and a few others started playing on a hastily made stage in the holding yard. Someone else was even playing with spoons on a washboard. Many were milling around the overwhelmed couple. Soon, the food started appearing.

Martha had been hiding it in the small underground cellar. A keg of ale was tapped and another of cider. The party began in earnest when the barrels appeared. Bottles of ginger beer for the children and sweet cordial, too.

Guests kept arriving until dusk, each bringing more food or something to drink. Many also had gifts of preserves, hampers, cheeses or other wedding gifts for Jenna and Eddie. They were overwhelmed. There were hand-embroidered tablecloths and linen, harnesses, leather goods and tools from the others.

The Murphy's had arrived with half a sack of potatoes from his Murphy's Spud's Farm; this product was something Eddie adored. Next to cider, he thought this was the best gift of all.

By around midnight, everyone had gone. They had all had a wonderful time. After dark, Jack had gotten up on the band cart and given a wedding speech. Marc had arranged a mock wedding, and all the small children acted as attendants, all impromptu but great fun. Cathy Turner, Jenna's sister, and her best friends, sixteen-year-old Mary Parker and Colleen Murphy, had made a crown of flowers and presented it to Jenna. She looked as regal as a queen. Eddie watched her, surrounded by her friends and family. He knew that it would have been lovely to have been married close by, but the closest Church they could have used was Windsor, and it would not have fitted everyone into it. After he had proposed as they lay on the riverbank, they decided that they would be married at St John's Parramatta as it was bigger and more convenient for many of their friends and family. There was also more accommodation in town for people wishing to stay overnight. She had agreed, but he knew she wished they had a church at Emu Plains.

Martha said they would arrange all the wonderful gifts to be brought in next Saturday. She would help Margaret Tindale and Sally store all the foodstuffs in their storeroom for the young couple on their return.

This would be a fantastic start for a young couple. One that each of the older ladies would have enjoyed themselves.

The bleary-eyed family were late up the next morning, yet knowing that the cows still had to be milked and other chores to be done, as well as the clean-up, they each dragged themselves out of their cots and hammocks and prepared for the day. Cows were milked, and porridge had been eaten; they heard voices outside.

The Murphy family and the four Parkers had arrived to help with the clean-up. Others drifted in and out throughout the morning until the yard and barn were back to normal.

Soon enough, it was time for Eddie to leave.

Jenna followed him to the back of the shed, and he took her lovingly into his arms and gently touched his lips to hers, tenderly giving her many kisses. "Not long now, my love. Soon."

Marc joined them, and they pushed the cart around to the front and loaded the empty keg from last month's party after Liza's wedding. He tied it on and added his duffle bag next to it.

Jack called him inside, and they retrieved the money from the secret hiding spot, and he shoved it into his pants pocket. They walked back outside to find Marc had brought James up from the bottom yard and had some trouble as he was frisky. James would have loved to have a run before he was harnessed and was playing up. He'd been standing for two days.

Eddie went to his head and stroked his nose. He settled somewhat but still shied a bit when Eddie placed the collar on him. He stood pawing at the ground, and Eddie warned Marc to be careful. "Tie him to the hitching rail before we add the cart, Marc. He's too fresh. Alex, can you hold the shaft on this side? It's going to be a quick trip home, I'm thinking." Eddie laughed lightly. "I really should take him for a run first, but I don't have the time."

Martha came out with a bundle and a stone bottle of ginger beer. "I brought this instead of ale as I think we all had enough ale and cider yesterday. This will keep your head clear. There's a loaf of bread. I sliced it and added more of my sausage so you can eat without stopping if required." She, too, knew James was fresh. "Ed, can you also thank Mrs. Tindale for the recipe, please?" She put the items in Mrs. Tindale's basket.

"Thanks so much, Mrs. Turner. Will do. I'm still full from last night. We were eating until bedtime," he replied.

James was dancing around from his hitching rail, and his ears were back on his head. He wanted to run. Eddie had just enough time to yell, "Marc, watch out," before James bucked.

Marc jumped sideways and missed the double kick.

Eddie went to his head and spoke to him as he stroked his nose; although the words were spoken softly, he said, "James, you can be a cantankerous brute sometimes." The big black stallion's ears flicked and sat back on his head.

Ed took one look at him. He shook his head at the horse.

Jack joined them as they pushed the cart onto the horse instead of the other way around. It took some time, but finally, James was in the shafts and fully harnessed up. He was champing at the bit and pawing the yard and obviously roaring to get going. Jenna came over and stood beside Eddie as he placed the basket under the seat. He felt his pockets to make sure the pouch from the strongbox was still there and turned to Jenna. He took her in his arms and tenderly put his lips to hers. "My love, by this time next week, we will be married. Our lives will be no more farewells. But for the moment, I must say, *Au Revoir*, my sweet. It means until we meet again." He released her. James was still misbehaving and pulling. Eddie said, "I think I'd better be off. He'll pull my arms out of the sockets anyway." He turned to thank Jack and Martha, nodded to Marc and said, "I'll see you all next week." To Jenna, he merely said, "I love you," and hopped up on the seat.

Jack untied James, and both he and Marc walked him out of the yard and didn't release him until they were on the road. Alex followed Martha and Jenna, who were arm in arm. They stood watching as Jack let go of the bridle and James, still dancing in the harness, took off.

Eddie turned and waved, "You'd better all pray for me," and laughed. "I think it will be a very quick trip home." He blew a kiss towards Jenna, and they took off.

"Stay safe, Ed; see you Saturday," she yelled back as he took off.

They watched until he was out of sight and turned to walk inside.

James led Eddie on a merry dance. He tried bucking and jigging until they reached the river. Eddie managed to get him somewhat under control as they crossed, and then, as he hit the road, he took off. James could see some open road and took the opportunity to stretch his legs. They covered the mile to Penrith very quickly. Eddie was able to slow James to a walk as he had blown the initial cobwebs away. They managed to get through town without mishap. James shied a few times, but they made it through in record time. James' walk was not a slow one, and his ears were pressed back in his head. Soon, Eddie was able to give James his head. The horse took off again, and this was not an easy feat with a heavy, but thankfully almost empty, cart behind.

It took some miles before James had worn off some of his energy. They had just passed the turnoff to the Mulgoa farms he had visited two days before. The road before them was open. The air was clear, and no dust was seen from other travellers on the dusty roads. James settled to a slower trot. Once his nose was turned to home, However, he took some holding. Some hours into the trip, they'd been going along the straight section with lowish scrub along the road when James' ears flicked forward. He'd heard or smelled something and was focusing on it. His head flicked up.

Eddie, too, sensed something was different and took a firmer hold of the reins. Sure enough, out from behind a clump of trees rode three horsemen. Rough-looking characters and obviously of evil intent. James's ears flicked again, and he was listening to both Eddie and the men.

They each were masked and had guns, which were all pointed at Eddie. The lead one wore dark trousers and a leather jacket with a hat pulled down on his head. The other two were so dirty it was hard to see what they wore, but it was nondescript. He could smell their body odour. Ed focused on James and the lead man. Ed knew he had to rein in. He pulled James off to the side of the dirt road and into the long grass. He was livid with himself that he'd forgotten to put the pouch of money in the small strongbox hidden under the seat. It was still in his pocket. He'd had such a hard time controlling James that it had slipped his mind. One of the riders motioned for him to get down. No one had said anything yet. The guns said it all.

Eddie said, "Fine, but one of you had better hold his head, or he'll take off on you. He's skittish." The youngest of the riders took hold of James' bridle near the bit, and so Eddie stepped down, but instead of getting down onto the road, he stepped off into the long grass, and as he did so, he dropped the pouch into a tall tussock of dry blady-grass. As the pouch was brown, he hoped it would be entirely hidden from view. James had been pulling against the hold of the young stranger's hand on his bridle, his ears again set back firmly on his head as though he would bite. The three were concentrating on him and hadn't noticed Eddie put his hand in his pocket as he dismounted.

Ed said, "You've picked a bad candidate to hold up; I have nothing on me but a few coins. Here, you can have them." He reached into his other pocket, grabbed the coins, and placed them on the seat. "I have only food in the basket and an empty barrel on board. You should have stopped me on the way west when I was fully laden."

The meaner, older rider was still mounted. He hit Eddie on his head with his rifle's stock end. It caught him hard. The wound bled profusely. Soon, the side of his head was covered and dripping onto his shirt. Even though he was a big man, the knock had dropped Eddie to his knees. "Now, shut up."

James turned and looked at Eddie and neighed.

One man leaned into the cart, wobbled the barrel to check that it was indeed empty, and tipped out the contents of Eddie's bag on the cart tray. He checked under the seat. "Eh, there's some sort of box here." He used the stock of his gun to hit the small strongbox and smashed the wooden casing. The metal box fell out. He shook it but couldn't open it but was able to dislodge it. He shook it but could tell it, too, was empty.

They could have asked Eddie for the key but didn't.

"He's bloody right. Absolutely nuffin' 'ere. A waste of time stopping 'dis one," said number three.

As the older one who had hit Eddie said, "Well, at least he's got some food. Gimme his bag and stow the food in it. Then we'll be orf."

The man did so. He also collected the coins that Eddie had placed on the seat, stashing them in the bag.

James started straining and misbehaving when the older man spoke for the first time. He danced and twisted in the shafts. His ears again sat back on his head, and he was again champing at his bit and pawing the ground.

Eddie looked at James, concerned, wondering why he was behaving like this. He didn't say anything but thought it strange.

The youngest man was holding James. He said, "Dust! Look."

"Someone's coming," the older one said then. "Damn! Quick. Let's go. Leave the damned hoss for now. We're orf…."

Eddie thought, "I've heard that voice before; I'm sure of it." He couldn't think straight; his head hurt. He could feel the blood still running down his cheek; he now felt dizzy.

The third rider threw the bag over his saddle pommel and remounted. The younger one released James' bridle, and the three took off back into the scrub. They disappeared quickly into the shrubby trees.

Eddie waited until they had gone and leaned over and collected the pouch that he'd been kneeling on. He put it back into his pocket as the oncoming rider was nearly upon him. Eddie was still feeling somewhat dizzy but was not otherwise harmed. He stood up, feeling wobbly. There was a lot of blood, and Eddie picked up one of his neckcloths from the back of the cart and tried to stop the bleeding. He was still leaning against the cart when the oncoming rider stopped.

"Ho, sir, are you all right?" the voice questioned. "Can I be of some assistance? Have you been set upon, sir?" The well-dressed gentleman pulled up to the cart and flicked his reins over the cart sides as he dismounted.

James' ears flicked. He whinnied at the newcomer and his horse but stood still. Eddie wondered at his strange behaviour. James kept straining around, looking back at Eddie, seeming to know something was wrong.

"Yes, sir, I'm fine, bar my own stupidity. Nothing sometimes won't fix. All they got was a few coins and my food, which they stowed in my bag." He didn't dare mention the pouch. He looked around at his personal items strewn over the back of the cart. He'd turned too quickly and swayed a bit.

"Woah!" The newcomer said, reaching out to steady Ed. "You sit yourself down, and I'll bandage that head of yours. I'm a doctor, so I know what I'm doing. Sadly, I don't have my full bag with me as I've been staying with my sister, and I'm returning to Parramatta."

The doctor had Eddie sit on the step of the cart, and he went to his saddlebags. Being a doctor, he always had emergency supplies with him; bandages and a brandy hip flask were things he always kept near. He also had some basic other things, but these were the two things he looked for now. He grabbed a bundle wrapped in oilcloth, laid it on the seat, and untied it. He also took a flask from his saddlebag. He proceeded to clean Eddie up and bandage his wound. First, he used Eddie's neckcloth to remove most of the blood, then reached for another one and said, "Hope you don't mind, but this needs to be kept clean." He dabbed the wound with this clean cloth now soaked with brandy, then made Eddie lean over, and the doctor poured a bit more on the open wound.

It hurt like hell. Eddie groaned; he felt faint.

The doctor then made a small pad and bandaged his head.

Eddie's head was now pounding. His eyes were closed, and the Doctor pushed his head between his legs.

"Don't pass out, lad; you're too big for me to lift. Sit for a while with your head down."

Eddie was in no state to argue. He stayed like this for a while.

"Lad, you're in no fit state to drive. I'll tie Tess to the cart, and we'll be off. Where are you heading to?"

Eddie told him and said James had a light mouth and was still skittish. He needed to be careful.

The doctor explained that he was used to thoroughbreds and would have no trouble with him. A quick glance at Eddie to make sure he was all right and the doctor walked to Tess, his Bay mare, put away his bundle and tied her properly to the rear of the cart; then he walked around to James.

He stroked his head, first on one side, then on the other. James sniffed him, then turned his head to look back at Eddie. He threw his head up a few times, then whinnied again. He stayed still.

"Magnificent beast you have there," said the doctor.

Eddie merely grunted. He now felt ill.

The doctor then returned to Eddie and helped him up onto the seat. "I'll stow all this into the basket if that's an all right, lad." He picked up Eddie's belongings and put them in Mrs. Tindale's now-empty food basket. "That'll keep them safe."

"The sooner you get to lie down, the better, but I'd suggest we move from here in case they are lingering." The doctor took the reins, carefully steered the cart back onto the road, and headed to Parramatta.

Eddie fought the waves of nausea, thankful that it had been a doctor who had found him. His head throbbed, and his throat was dry. After about an hour of travelling, the doctor pulled under the same tree Jenna and Eddie had stopped on their first trip. He came around and helped Eddie to the ground and made him lie down for a while in the shade.

The doctor was concerned. He checked his eyes and said, "Oh, thank the Good Lord. I was worried that you may have had a brain bleed, but thankfully, you have a hard head. You will feel bad for a while. Probably until tomorrow, but you'll live. I'm going to let you sleep for a bit if you can. It will help."

Eddie lay on the grass and almost immediately fell asleep. The doctor took Tess over to the log trough and gave her a drink. Then he returned, removed James from the cart, and let him drink. He knew Tess would not wander far but didn't trust James, so he held the reins as he walked him. James, however, just wanted to check on Eddie as he saw him lying down. After about twenty minutes, he walked James back and let him nuzzle Eddie. Tess followed closely.

Eddie awoke to horse breath on his face. James' black muzzle lipped Eddie's arm.

Ed opened his eyes. All he could see was a black horse face. He reached up and, rubbing his nose, said, "It's all right, boy, I'm fine. Head like a bushfire, but I'll live." He sat up too fast; he was dizzy, oh so dizzy.

The doctor walked over to him and squatted next to him. "How do you feel?" he asked. "Close your eyes and count to twenty."

Eddie did so. Holding Eddie's chin, the doctor said, "Now open them." He watched Ed's eyes intently. The doctor breathed a sigh, "Yes, no lasting problems. I've noticed over the years that if a head wound is bad, the eyes will give a warning and won't work equally. Yours are fine."

"They might work; I'm not sure I can," groaned Ed. He rolled onto his knees, crawled a few yards away, and then vomited.

The doctor stood up. "I brought you some water from the creek for us to drink. No leeches in it, so it's good to drink. I checked since I heard the story of hundreds of Napoleon's soldiers dying from them in the water. Happened in Syria, you know. Anyway, the trough water is fine for the horses. Anyway, it's just as well that I always carry a mug and plate, and you can share my ration. I have some bread and cheese in the saddlebag, a bit squashed but tasty." He turned back to Tess, who was standing just behind him. He patted her, then reached into the other saddlebag and removed another oilcloth parcel. He sat on the grass beside Eddie and laid the parcel between them. When unwrapped, there were four slices of buttered bread, a chunk of cheese and some oranges. "There's plenty for us both, but eat slowly." The doctor reached into his belt and pulled a knife from a hidden sheath; he then proceeded to cut some cheese. He stabbed a bit and passed it to Eddie. They ate silently for a while. "Are you up to answering some questions, lad?"

Eddie nodded gently, then put his hand to his head. "I won't do that again. Yes, sir, of course, sorry."

The doctor probed gently, "How long had they been there before I came?"

Eddie answered, "About ten minutes, sir; it's a bit of a blur."

Then the doctor said, "How about we introduce ourselves? My name is Doctor Gerald Winslow-Smythe, with a Y and an E. I'm out here from Sydney after visiting my sister Genevieve Sheridan at their farm out Mulgoa way."

Eddie leaned over a bit. "My name is Edward Lockley, but everyone calls me Eddie. I'm a blacksmith in Parramatta with Mr. Tindale. I delivered a load of goods to Sheridan's at Orchard Hills only two days ago." They shook hands, and Eddie said, "Pleased to meet you, sir. I can never thank you enough. I won't say your arrival was perfect, as ten minutes earlier would have been nice, but let's say timely." He smiled. Eddie was feeling clearer every moment. He obviously didn't look it.

Eddie had missed the doctor's startled gaze and small gasp when he'd said his name as he had not been looking at the doctor.

The doctor said, "I'll get you more water; stay still."

Ed didn't think he could walk far even if he wished. He had managed to crawl back to where they were now sitting. He wasn't sure he could have gone much further. He stayed in the shade, enjoying it and the happy memories this place had as long as the snake didn't appear again.

The doctor returned.

"Thank you, sir," Eddie said as he took the large tin cup and drank deeply. "It's amazing how refreshing plain old water is," he said.

The doctor said, "We can chat as we drive now. Think you can get up again?"

Eddie nodded and instantly regretted it. "I must remember not to do that," he laughed weakly. He turned onto his hands and knees and slowly stood up. Holding on to the tree, he said, "I'll use the tree here while I can, sir, if you'd turn your back. I don't think I could make it to that stand of trees."

The doctor did so but was not far away. He put an unresisting James back into the shafts and retied Tess onto the back.

"Thanks, sir," said Ed as he turned.

The doctor helped Ed to the cart and stood behind Ed as he slowly crawled up. Every movement hurt, but it wasn't as bad as before. The sleep had undoubtedly helped.

They set off carefully until the Doctor saw that Eddie was coping well. He click clicked James and picked up his pace. The road along this section was quite good and had very few ruts. James enjoyed the new pace and held his neck high, and started to pace with a flying change.

The doctor laughed. "Oh my, you have a mighty horse here. He's magnificent, and he knows it."

Eddie agreed. "Yes, he is." His mind flashed back to that highwayman's comment, "I'm orf...." He started. It just occurred where he'd heard it before. It was the man who'd refused to pay for James' shoes, a broken harness and a new stirrup. He'd left James at the Smithy shop, saying he was 'foul-tempered'.

Eddie sat bolt upright. Instantly regretting his quick movement, "So that's why James was playing up. He recognised his voice and probably his smell."

The doctor said, "Eh? What's worrying you, lad?"

Eddie told him his suspicions, James's story, and how he got him. Mr. Tindale had reported the bad debt to the Major, then to the Clerk of the Court at the Courthouse in Parramatta and was awarded the horse as payment. Mr. Tindale then gave James to Eddie. He was legally now his.

They talked about James, who seemed to be listening as every time his name was mentioned, his ears flicked backwards. He continued his pacing as it appeared to be a comfortable gait for him. James was a big show-off.

They soon reached the outskirts of town, and James slowed to a walk. As they approached the hill just above the town, Ed gave the doctor directions. He was feeling dizzy again and was looking forward to getting home.

The doctor kept glancing at him to make sure he was all right.

Eddie was quite pale by the time they drove into the yard.

Charles was there to greet him, and when he saw all the blood, he exclaimed, "Ed, what on earth happened to my son? Charlie, Sal, come here, quickly!" he called. Both came running from different directions, as did Major Grace, who'd already arrived for Sunday dinner.

The doctor had drawn James to a halt next to the verandah. "Get the lad down, and I'll fill you in when he's settled. He's all right; I'm a doctor. My name is Winslow-Smythe. I've checked him over, and I've been keeping my eye on him. He's talking fine, and his eyes work, so all he needs is rest. Do not give him anything more than sweet water and something light to eat."

Charles and Charlie assisted Eddie inside, Sal following in their wake.

The Major had not moved to help. His mouth open in shock.

The doctor then got down from the cart and tied James to the railing. He then looked up and saw Major Grace still standing frozen on the spot. "Neddy? Ned, is that really you?"

Major Grace looked like he'd seen a ghost. "Gerry? What the hell are you doing out here?" he gasped. "I haven't seen you for nigh on over twenty years."

The doctor mounted the verandah steps in a few long strides. He shook hands, then embraced his old friend.

Charlie re-emerged and was taken a bit aback. The two men were still hugging. They broke apart when they heard Charlie's footsteps, both still laughing.

Charlie looked at them, and Major Grace introduced him to his friend. He was still in shock, so he said nothing more. "A doctor now, eh?"

The doctor broke the silence. "I gather you must be Eddie's brother, Charles Junior? I was wondering if I could possibly leave Tess and this wonderful animal James in your capable hands."

His question broke the spell. Charlie said, "Of course, sir. No worries, sir. But I'm full of questions." He jumped off the verandah and untied James' reins, and led him into the stable. Tess was still tied to the back and followed placidly. He tied James to a loop first; then, he unhitched Tess before removing James from the shafts.

Wills and Luke soon appeared to help. Both horses were quickly not only fed and watered but brushed as well. The three boys were eager to get the full story of what happened to Ed but knew that the horses had to be dealt with first.

Charlie carried in the basket from under the seat of the cart and carried in Tess' saddlebags. He didn't know if there was anything valuable in them, and leaving them out was tempting theft. There had been a few things gone missing of late. They were nearly always things James used or needed. He left the bags at the verandah door.

They washed their faces as they left the stable. The three boys joined the family and two visitors. Sal was nearly ready to serve the evening meal. The boys took their places at the table, and Anna and Sal brought the hot food.

Charles bowed his head and waited for silence, then said grace before their meal.

Everyone started talking at once. It was like a dam had burst. Questions were all around, and most were aimed at the visitor. Only Major Grace was silent.

Puzzled, Sal looked at him. He was too quiet.

The doctor related the highwaymen's attack and how he'd arrived on the scene moments later, explaining that the dust Tess was kicking up galloping was apparently enough to scare them off. He said nothing about Eddie's suspicions; that was his story. He'd tell Ned later.

Charlie was the one who asked. "Sir, you obviously know our Major. How?"

The doctor looked at the Major. "Ned and I grew up together, but our lives took different paths."

The Major sighed with relief.

Doctor Winslow-Smythe continued. "One of the reasons I came out here is to look for him while visiting my sister, Gen. I am charged with messages from home."

The Major looked surprised and subtly shook his head. The doctor gave a single nod and fell silent. He hoped they would not enquire; further, however, young boys are inquisitive. He knew these two indeed were.

Everyone else was silent too. Thirteen-year-old Luke innocently asked, "How? I mean, did you live next to each other? Were you living in the same village?"

The doctor didn't answer but looked at Major Grace.

The Major groaned and took a deep breath running his hand through his hair. "What I am going to tell you will go no further than this room. All right?" Looking specifically at the three youngest family members, he said, "Anna, Wills, and Luke, you three especially."

It was time the story was revealed.

They all nodded agreement, mouths agape.

He continued. "Gerry and I certainly did grow up together. We were educated together by tutors and later at school, but we didn't exactly live 'next' to each other. Gerald's family were...." He looked at the doctor, who nodded and inferred that it was all right to continue. "Well, they are the Winslow-Smythe's of Winslow Hall. His father is the Earl of Winslow. He has an older brother, George, so Gerry is 'The Honourable Gerald Winslow-Smythe', and my family were in the almost next-door estate to his mother. My father is...." Ned paused and looked at his friends sitting around the table, knowing his following words would change their relationship permanently, "...His Grace the Duke of Gracemere from 'Gracemere Castle' in Kent."

The family gasped, muttering, "A Duke's son." Sal gasped.

"A second son, I entered the army, and my two younger brothers went into Law. My oldest brother David, the heir, married, let us say, a lady who was promised elsewhere. To put it simply, as I had no expectations, I changed my name, applied to join the army and then came here. On the journey out, I met you, Charles and the rest is history." He bent down and stabbed his meat and overfilled his mouth. He chewed valiantly the overlarge chunk of meat he'd taken. He would not have to answer anything for a while.

The doctor began to speak. "One of the reasons I have come out here is not only to work amongst those who need medical help but to look for my childhood friend. I asked everywhere, but no one knew anyone named Gracemere or, um, any other name I thought he might have used." He looked at the Major with an eyebrow raised. "I never guessed you would have used Grace as your name," he paused. "I have to sadly let you know your father died five years ago at the grand age of eighty-one. He regretted not knowing where you were. He missed you." He let this sink in before continuing. "Your brother, David, became the Duke. Ned, he and his wife sadly never had children."

While still chewing, Ned's eyes flew to Gerry's.

Gerry paused again, letting this sink in. "Ned, I'm sorry to tell you, but your brother died after a horse fall two years ago. Your mother and two younger brothers have been looking everywhere for you and charged me with the task of looking for you out here. The army did not tell them of your name change, as, of course, they would not have known. Ned... you are now the Duke of Gracemere."

The Major's cutlery dropped onto his place, and he choked. The doctor slapped his back, and Sal raced for a drink of water. Charlie sat opposite him, just looking stunned.

Everyone else at the table sat silently. All stunned. Nearly as amazed at Major Grace. Charles was thinking, "I'm a convict who's friends with a Duke."

Sal thought nothing more than "He mustn't die now."

The doctor stood behind him and gave one colossal thump on his back, and the lump of meat flew out into Ned's serviette. The doctor dropped back into his seat. "Well, I could have timed that better. Are you all right, old friend?"

The Major nodded with tears still rolling down his face from the choke. He took the glass of water from Sal and gave her a nod of thanks. He took a sip, then a long drink. "Well, if that doesn't beat everything. So David is dead, eh? And how is the delightful Elouise coping now that she is a Dowager Duchess? I bet she won't like that. And what about Mother? Has she moved into the Dower house, or is she still holding court in the Castle?" He spoke with bitterness in his voice.

Charles and Sal looked at each other. Charles raised an eyebrow, which the Major saw. The doctor said, "Both are holding court in their respective residences, of course. Would you really expect anything different? They are both strong women. As you expected, they clashed from day one; this has not changed. Suffice it to say; they do not see much of each other. The tranquillity of the place evaporated about twenty-six years ago, soon after a certain wedding."

The Major spoke, "As you may gather, I was the person who was engaged to Elouise. It was brief, a few weeks; I was only nineteen. I took her home to meet my parents, and there she met David. I would never be the Duke, and David was heir, so she cried off and only weeks later announced her engagement to my older brother." He didn't look sad, just pensive. "Sally, that day I saw you standing proud and straight in the line coming from the women's prison, you reminded me of her, the nice side of her. Only your pride is true and strong, as I discovered. Hers was shallow and narcissistic." He paused. "I saw her for what she was long before they married. If she had not cried off, I might have absconded anyway. I think I would have found some way not to proceed with that wedding. However, David saw only jealousy in me and would not listen to what I had to say. Mother summed her up upon their first meeting."

Charles asked, "Are you going to go home, sir? Or should I now call you 'Your Grace'?"

The Major laughed, "I'm still the same person. No one is ever to say anything. Remember. Here I am, the Major and only that. Charles, to you,

I'm still Ned or Edward if you wish when we're together as it always has been." He took a small bite and chewed, then swallowed. "I will have to go, I suppose, but I don't want to. Duty calls." He looked around before addressing the Doctor, "Gerry, this family, 'is' my family now. We have been friends nigh on twenty-five years, and I value their friendship above nearly anyone else. Save yourself, Rob and Jim. Why didn't you ask Jim where I was? He knew where I was." He fell to thinking, as did everyone. A smile spread across his face. "There is another whom I will need to speak to, though," but he did not elaborate. "Gerry, I did leave a sealed letter in my army file if something should have happened to me."

Charles and Sal were still silent. The three younger ones were still sitting, staring at both men. The doctor said, "Jim had vanished when I left, Ned." He sighed, "Well, I know one thing: you won't go home alone. I'll stay here until you're ready and come with you. I just have to find a room and get my things sent from Sydney. We can talk about that later."

"Oh no, *we* won't," said the Major, "You're staying with me. I have a spare room. You can fill me in on everything else. You'll get to know my new family well while you're here."

"Talking of which," said the doctor, "I'll go and check on my patient. If he wakes with a roaring headache, that's what I expect. I'll drop back tomorrow morning and check on him. He's not to go to work, is that clear? Charles Junior, I believe you can stand in for him in that role tomorrow. Is that understood?" Charlie nodded but looked at his father, who also nodded assent. Neither said anything.

"These two men were toffs," Charles thought. They seemed normal. There is no way in England they would all have sat down at the same table for a meal, let alone become friends. In this new country, with new rules, anything was possible. Back at home, Charles would have had to bow every time the Major even walked by. Here, he was a friend and a good friend at that.

The doctor stood up, "Can I see my patient, please?"

Sal also stood and took him into the boys' bedroom. Eddie was peaceful and sound asleep. The bandages were still in place, and no blood was visible by the lamplight. The doctor put his hand gently on his forehead and felt it. "Good, no fever," he said quietly. He turned to Sal and said softly, "Let him sleep until he wakes naturally. He should be almost back to normal tomorrow, just with a sore head. Please do not give him willow bark or alcohol. Damp cloths and a dark room would be best. I think his main problem is lack of sleep. Apparently, they had a heavy night the last night. There was a party.... I'll let him tell you about that." He turned to walk out.

"Oh, he has some money in a pouch in his pocket. My sister, Genevieve Sheridan, gave it to him for the goods he delivered to her. I think that it's just shy of £15. Can you make sure it's locked up, please? He was worried about it. He dropped it in the grass when he was held up, but when he was hit, he knelt on it." He tapped his own head. "Up here for thinking. Smart boy. That much is nearly a king's ransom to some. A year's wage for him, I think he said."

Charles was waiting for the doctor's prognosis and was relieved when he said he should be fine. The doctor asked him if Tess could stay in the stables for the night and that he would collect her on the morrow if that were convenient. Charles, of course, agreed.

Major Grace stood as they came back into the room. "By your leave, Charles, we shall depart," he said. "What an interesting evening this has been! Secrets revealed to friends who, I hope, will continue to treat me as you always have by accepting me just as I am. I'll drop by tomorrow and see how the lad is if that is all right." He bowed over Sal's hand, and they left. The doctor bowed and followed his long-lost friend out the door.

Charles and Sal followed them out onto the verandah, where the doctor collected his saddlebags from where Charlie had left them. They stood and watched until the darkness swallowed them. They walked indoors to a buzz of conversation from their children.

Luke started first when they walked in. "Cor Mama, our Major is a Juke, a real live Juke."

Wills butted in, "Dar, will he continue to come here for Sunday family dinner night? Do you think he cut us now? I bet he won't."

The buzz of conversation continued over the dishes. Sal washed, Anna wiped, and the boys put everything away. Charles leaned against the bench in the kitchen, chipping in a comment here and there, thoughts running through his mind. While the children were putting the last of the things away, Sal went in to check on Eddie and make sure he was sleeping peacefully. He was.

Charles suggested the three boys sleep on the floor in the sitting room so as not to disturb Ed. They snuck into their room, grabbed their things, and crept out. With the excitement of the night, sleep was a long time coming.

Sal left a lamp burning low so she could check on Ed throughout the night. Each time she made her mind flicked back to the conversation at the dinner table. "A Duke," she kept thinking. "I worked for a Duke." She'd padded into Eddie in her bare feet and felt his head as she had done a hundred times before for all her children. The last time she went in was just before dawn. She felt his forehead, and as the doctor had, she held the lamp up to see if the wound was bleeding.

He had turned onto his side and stirred as she entered. "Hi, Mama, am I home? Oh, nice! Having bad dreams." He put his hand to his head.

"Not a dream, son, but you'll be fine. The doctor brought you home. Go back to sleep now. We'll talk later in the morning." Sal bent and kissed his cheek. He closed his eyes again and slept on.

Chapter 14   Surprises

W hen Eddie awoke the following morning, the sun was well up.

His head pounded, and as he touched it, he discovered the bandages had become dislodged as he slept. He was just sitting up in bed when he heard voices coming inside.

Doctor Winslow-Smythe had arrived, and Sal showed him into the room. "Well, my lad, how is my patient today? You're strong. I'll give you that. Most people would be laid low for a week with a knock like that." He felt his head again for fever and looked at the wound which had been uncovered. "Take it easy today. Sit or sleep but absolutely no work. Is that clear? Otherwise, you won't be getting married on Saturday."

Eddie said, "Yes," meekly.

The doctor checked out the head wound and turned to Sal. "I'll re-bandage it, but I think we should cleanse it properly first. I don't want to wash his hair, but we can clean it up if we could use more spirits." He looked closely at the wound. "It's a bit inflamed, but most of that is bruising. There's no infection. I gave it a good scrub yesterday with brandy, so I don't expect it to get any worse." He asked Eddie to stand, and together, they helped him outside to sit on the verandah. He was still in his nightshirt, and the doctor refused to let him dress. "This will make sure you don't get to do anything."

Sal and the doctor got to work with some overproof rum and cleaned out most of the blood. The fumes were making Eddie light-headed. While the doctor re-bandaged his head, Sal went and made him a light meal and a mug of tea.

The doctor finished and sat on the verandah edge. "You missed a lot last night. When your mother comes back, we'll fill you in."

Eddie tucked into a bowl full of scrambled eggs and toast as Sal arrived with two more mugs of tea for the doctor and herself. She, too, sat on the verandah. The doctor looked at her, "I think we should fill Ed in on what he missed out on last night at dinner."

Eddie, with some food in his stomach, was brightening considerably. He was munching on some toasted bread and butter. He said nothing but waited and looked from one to the other. He kept chewing.

Sal started. "Well, Ed, it seems that the good doctor here and Major Grace knew each other well back in England, but it also seems that our Major Grace isn't exactly who we thought he was. I'll let Doctor Winslow-Smythe tell the rest of the story." She looked at the doctor to continue.

"Well, before I say anything, you must promise not to tell anyone about what I will tell you. Ned, for that, is what I have always known him as since we were boys; he does not want the story to get out, well, yet anyway. I dare say you will find out why soon. So do you promise, lad? Not even Mr. Tindale or Jenna at the moment, at least until the wedding is over. When the time is right, all will be revealed to everyone." Hopefully, soon, he thought. "Only the family who was here last night know the truth so far."

Eddie swallowed and said, "Yes, of course, sir. But I am intrigued."

The doctor continued. "Well, the story goes like this…" The doctor related what had been revealed last night when he arrived at the bit about the Major now being the Duke. Eddie had just taken a mouthful of tea, and he choked.

"A what? A Duke?" Ed spluttered. "Well, blow me down, and we never guessed he was… well, a toff, no offence, sir. And you are one as well, doctor?" Ed paused. "And he chose to have a friendship with us. We're convict stock."

The doctor laughed, "Ho, that's what Ned did last night when I told him he was the Duke. I had to save his life as he choked. I should time things better." The doctor chuckled again. "Oh, we talked a lot last night. He said if it had not been for his friendship with your father and later his family, Ned would have lost heart years ago. Your family's acceptance of him, just as he was. As a soldier who'd been in command of convicts. He was amazed you'd accepted him." Gerry looked down to the river. "He'll never forget that. You are more his family than they ever were, bar his mother, whom he adores. True friends come in all packages, but they are like diamonds. We were a group of four friends, Jimmy, Robbie, Ned and myself, each coping with our own issues. Rejection hurts; Ned will never forget your acceptance of him. Remember that boy."

The three sat in companionable silence for a while. The doctor looked up and exclaimed, "Ho, what have we here? Who's this that Ned is bringing over?" His eyes rested on one of the most beautiful women he had ever beheld. She was exquisite.

Sal said, "Oh, that's Mrs. Meadows; she lives two doors down from Major Grace. Since her husband died two years ago, she's been teaching children to sew and play the piano. She's lovely. I'll go and refill the kettle."

She got up and went inside, leaving Eddie and the doctor sitting on the verandah.

Eddie was trying to get up, and the doctor said, "What's up, lad?" He laid a hand on his shoulder to make him stay seated.

He whispered, "I'm not suitably clad, sir. Can you get me a blanket from the bed at least, please, so I can at least cover myself?"

The doctor stepped inside and collected a covering from the closest bedroom and another chair. He threw the cover at Eddie. Just in time, too, as Major Grace and Mrs. Meadows rounded the corner of the verandah.

The Major exclaimed, "Nice to see you up, lad. You had us worried for a while there." He smiled. He seemed different, happier. He then introduced Mrs. Meadows to the doctor.

Sal appeared and offered everyone tea. She greeted Mrs. Meadows and gave a small curtsy as befits ex-convict to free. Mrs. Meadows had never come to tea before and had always seemed a bit standoffish, friendly but distant.

The Major and Doctor brought out two more chairs so Eddie would not have to move. Charles had heard their voices and appeared with another chair and joined them.

"Good," said the Major simply.

Once they each had their mugs, the Major looked at Sal and Charles. "You know, last night we had an, let's say, interesting conversation. Well, this opened a door that I did not think possible." He paused and looked at Mrs. Meadows. "Most of you don't know that I have been quietly courting my dear Mrs. Meadows here for months. I never expected to be in a position of, let us say, financial security ever to have more than the cottage I'm currently living in. My friend, Jack Barnes, told me I was underestimating her. I did not expect anyone to want to share my small abode. However, last night's revelations have changed that outlook, and this morning, my dearest Mrs. Meadows has accepted my hand in marriage. You are the closest thing I have to family here, and Gerry, you have always been my best friend, so I want you to wish me joy and felicitations."

Mrs. Meadows blushed, and there were congratulations all around. The Major moved his chair slightly closer to her and patted her hand. "My dear, I do have one more thing to tell you, and I wanted to do this in front of my friends." He smiled, "Well, you see, my name is not actually Grace, and when we marry, we will be under a different name. It's really Gracemere."

She looked at him. "That's all right, dear; it's a nice name too. Mrs. Gracemere is delightful." She said softly. She was obviously deeply in love with him, and her face softened as she looked at him.

The Major looked somewhat flustered.

The doctor said, "Do you want me to finish?"

The Major nodded.

The doctor said, "Well, my dear, you will not actually be Mrs. Gracemere either; you will be Her Grace, the Duchess of Gracemere."

She blanched. "I'll be what?" she looked at the Major. "Oh, Edward. You're what? You're the Duke? Why didn't you tell me?"

The Major looked bashful. "I couldn't tell you as I didn't know myself until last night, the second son and all. Gerry here filled me in. We grew up close to each other, and he knows my story. I told you Elouise married my brother instead of me because he was the eldest son and heir, and I wasn't. I just conveniently forgot to mention that he was to inherit a Dukedom." He looked at her. "Does it matter? I'm still me."

She chuckled and said, "Of course, it matters, silly; however, not as much as you think."

The doctor and Charles looked surprised. No one ever called the Major silly. She giggled. "It seems we have not been as truthful with each other as we should have been."

Now, it was the Major's turn to look puzzled.

She continued. "Well, as you know, I was married to William Meadows. But Edward, he was The Honourable William Meadows. He was a dreamer and had grand ideas of sheep farming and sending the wool clip to England. His ideas were well ahead of his ability. He was not a good farmer, and when he started to lose sheep along with all the different problems here, drought, and especially to something he called 'blowfly strike'. He had 'real' farmers at home to do his bidding. Here, he had to do it himself or employ someone. By the time he died, he'd lost heart and started drinking." She paused and looked at the Major. "I'm telling you this as it does make a difference. You see, my father warned me about this; he could see William was lazy, and I couldn't. I had some money hidden from him and bought the bungalow after he died. When everything was sold and the debts paid, there was only enough left for the tiny cottage." She took a breath and turned to look him in the face. "Ned, I'm Lady Christina Meadows, née Hunt. My father is Edmund, Earl of Riverdell. Our home is just outside Tunbridge Wells."

Now, it was the Major's time to gasp. "What? But that's the next-door County. Are you serious?"

The doctor interrupted, chuckling, "Christina? You're Christina Hunt? Little Tiny Tina? I remember you as a little girl, about eight. I can't believe you're here. You were a scrap of a thing with big blue eyes and a rosebud mouth as a child. We were just eighteen when we came to your place for the Hunt Ball," he continued breathlessly. "I remember seeing the portrait of you that your father had commissioned. Golden curls, too." He turned to Ned. "That would be about the last time I saw you, Ned, at that ball was over twenty years ago."

She merely gave a single nod of her head in acknowledgement. "Yes, I was a spoilt, precocious child. I got my way in everything and had my father twisted around my little finger. William opened my eyes to a harder life. Hopefully, I have learnt a few of life's lessons." She looked sad. "When Edward would walk me home after church on Sundays, it was the highlight of my week. I was so lonely; Mrs. Bobart was my only other friend. Even she did not know my story. I was poor, I was ashamed, and I hid. I could have written to Father, but my pride got in the way. I had no money to go home. So, I took in students to teach them to sew and play the piano. It kept food on the table but nothing more. I had put all my money into somewhere to live. I thought life was hopeless; then I met you." She sighed.

"And I moved all but next door when I retired," chipped in the Major. "You were the reason I bought the cottage. So I could be close to you if you needed something. I had been watching you before I asked to court you last year. I just wanted to be near you. To walk home with you on a Sunday made my heart swell with pride. I could touch you and talk to you in private." Ned looked at her adoringly.

Mrs. Meadows said, "When you told me about a lady named Elouise, Her Grace came to mind. She certainly was not a popular person in the area. I had no idea she was the same person you were talking about. I used to feel sorry for His Grace. Pardon for saying, but she is a shrew."

The three reminisced while the three Lockleys listened in stunned silence.

They looked at each other with an eyebrow raised or questioning look. Mrs. Meadows was an Earl's daughter. What else was going to happen?

Mrs. Meadows turned to Sal. "I want to apologise to you for never asking you to tea. I wanted to so often, but I was so shy. I had no tea to offer nor cups to drink it from. I was also so alone and would have loved to have a friend. I knew I could trust you, as Edward said I should. I never had the courage to approach you. Edward and I were not in a position where we could be seen together, and at first, I was not out of mourning. I was hoping that things would change when that passed. Now it has. Please, I would love to have a friend here, even if only for a short time."

Sal was overwhelmed, to say the least. Mrs. Meadows was just shy. "Oh my! Of course, I'd be honoured. I would have spoken to you before, but I didn't think you'd want me to as I was a convict." Sal brushed aside a tear. "That'll teach me not to judge," she thought.

Something suddenly occurred to Eddie, and he sat upright quickly. "You know, if I had not been hit, none of this would have happened. I would not have met the doctor, who then met the Major, who then proposed to Mrs. Meadows and discovered who each other was. What saddens me is that you're all now going to leave us and go home." He said excitedly. "Oh, I shouldn't move so fast," he said, touching his head.

Charles, who was sitting next to him, put his hand on his shoulder. "So, boy. You are responsible for all this? So we'll blame you when they all leave us here."

Everyone laughed.

The Major reached and took Mrs. Meadows' hand. "You know I'd like to be married before we leave, what do you think? Feel like a walk to the church and talking to Reverend Mr. Bobart? What do you think? Or would you like to wait until we arrive home? I don't want to rush you."

Mrs. Meadows said, "It can't be soon enough for me." She squeezed his hand. "I've been waiting for months already. We can have a honeymoon here before we leave. I'd like to have our real friends at the wedding and as witnesses too. A small private wedding is what I'd love. Before people discover who we really are."

The Major grinned. "Suits me, too." He turned to Charles, "Sounds like you're getting more visitors, or I should say Eddie is. We'll be heading off. Remember, shh!"

Charles nodded in agreement as the Tindales walked around the corner of the verandah. By then, Mrs. Meadows and the Major were taking their leave. To waylay suspicion, the doctor accompanied them. So Mrs. Meadows walked off the verandah with a gentleman on each side.

The doctor said, "I'll accompany you up to the church to make sure no one suspects anything."

Sal snapped back to reality. What a morning!

Mr. and Mrs. Tindale arrived to see how Eddie was. Charlie had been set to work on the orders that Mr. Tindale had. They had taken the news of Eddie's attack with shock. Mrs. Tindale could not settle until she saw for herself how he was. "I needed to see for myself how you are. Are you up to tell us what happened?"

Eddie said, "Yes, of course, but first, Dar, can you please get the pouch and basket?"

Charles went and retrieved the pouch that he'd put in his strongbox.

Eddie assured the Tindales he was all right. "I'm sure that I'll be right as rain in a day or so. I'm just sorry that I have left you in the lurch. Thankfully, Charlie can step in for me."

Charles arrived back with the basket and money pouch and handed them to Eddie, who took them and passed them straight to Mr. Tindale.

"Not a farthing missing, sir! I'm so pleased to finally hand this to you, and Missus Turner said thank you. Now to my story…." He told his story, adding some details that he had not told the doctor. His father was listening, but Sal had gone inside to make tea.

When he got to James' behaviour and his reaction to the highwayman's voice, Eddie filled in some missing details that had not jelled until that moment. "Sir, I think the lead highwayman was the man who left James at the forge. It was the way he said both 'hoss' and 'I'm orf' that gave it away. I never saw his face up at the shop, and I couldn't see it under his mask, but I will swear it was the same voice. On top of that, there's the way

James started behaving. He was bucking, propping and dancing around in the shafts while he was there. As soon as he left, he was quiet again. He recognised him, I'm sure."

While he was talking, Sal brought another tea tray. She poured, and they sat drinking their tea, talking about the strange, angry man.

Sal said, "Ed, that reminds me, when you left on Friday, a man was watching you as you left. I couldn't see his face as it was hidden under his hat, but he was wearing dark trousers and some sort of brown jacket. He saw me watching him, and he disappeared fast. I haven't seen him again."

"Dark trousers and a brown jacket, eh?" said Eddie. "Well, that settles it. It was the same person. Most around here wear light-coloured, brown or white trousers, not dark ones. I wonder what he wanted?" Eddie mused. "If he wanted James, he could have taken him then. Maybe he saw how he was behaving."

Mr. Tindale said, "As you drove off on Friday, I also saw someone watching you, and you are correct as to who it was. I recognised him as James's previous owner. He followed you down the hill from the Smithy. It must have been who you saw, Sal."

They discussed it further and, Eddie's forthcoming wedding and the Tindale's departure the week later, then the Tindales took their leave.

Charles said, "Bed for you again, my boy; you're looking peaky."

"I feel it too, Dar," Ed said quietly.

He assisted Eddie back to bed and then went to find Sal. He leaned against the kitchen bench. "Well, what a morning. Just when I didn't think I could be more surprised than last night, I'm floored. Fancy the Major getting married. He's a clever one."

Sal turned to Charles and walked into his arms. "Oh, Charles, I have seriously misjudged her. I thought she was a snob and was just shy and poor. I feel so terrible." She laid her head on his shoulder.

"I know, love," he said as he laid his lips on her hair. "We could have done so much more. Mrs. Jenkins is another case in point. She's another lonely person. I can see we will have to start a group or meeting where people who are alone can join and meet others. Some sort of friendship group. The ladies could meet and sew, and the men could... let me think." He laid his head on the top of hers. "I know. We could make toys for the orphans while you sew clothes for them. Eh? We'd have to hire a room somewhere, and it would have to be somewhere nice. What do you think?" He held her away from him at arm's length and looked in the face.

She nodded; tears had pooled in her eyes. "That's perfect, Charles. Thank you." She lifted her face for a kiss, and he lowered his lips to hers; he first kissed away her tears.

"Have I told you how much I love you?" He cupped her face, then gently traced her lips with his. He enfolded her in his arms; his kiss was not gentle but full of passion and desire. "I'll never tire of this," he said against her lips.

Running footsteps and laughter broke them apart. Their boys were back. The boys had been fishing and hopefully had some fish for the midday meal.

Sal rubbed her salty cheeks, and Charles straightened himself, heading out the door as they came in. He ruffled their heads, giving a backward look at Sal and blowing her a kiss. He mouthed the word 'later' and left.

Sal nodded, then turned her attention to her two babies. At thirteen and fifteen, they dwarfed her. "What have you two brought us for luncheon?"

They slapped down a bag on the bench. "We had a great morning, Mama. Ten of the best," said Luke.

They tipped out the fish, and there were eight lovely big bream and two huge flatheads. "We've already scaled and gutted them, Mama," they grinned. "How about that, Mama? We could have kept more, but Dar says only to keep what we need. We threw lots of little ones back." Wills said proudly.

"We'll have a feast, boys. Thank you so much. Go and see if Ed is still awake and tell him." She could hear voices coming from their room, so she presumed Eddie was still awake. He'd keep them occupied for a while. Anna would soon be home after her visit to the Miller's. Best friends already, Gracie and Anna had grown even closer since they both became engaged to each other's brothers. Despite a three-year gap between them, the boys, Tim and Charlie, grew closer. Eddie, Jenna and the two Miller-Lockley couples were seen out walking together. Often, other siblings joined the group. They had rarely fought or disagreed in all the years they had known each other. The younger boys, without them, were not so peaceful. Wills, Luke, Sam, and sometimes Robbie Ellis were continually scrapping, and ten-year-old Ellen Miller was as much a problem as they were. She idolised Luke and would much rather do what her brother Sammy and Luke were doing than stay around with the girls. She wasn't interested in sewing but mentioned fishing and was off like a shot. Her mother, Molly and Sal often discussed her and wondered about her life and what she'd eventually do.

Her mind kept wandering back to that morning's conversations. First, the discovery that the Major was a Duke, then that he'd been courting Mrs. Meadows, and to hear that they would get married. Then, finally, to find that Mrs. Meadows is actually an Earl's daughter. Sal just shook her head. It was almost too much to take in.

The day progressed with no more surprises.

The doctor came mid-afternoon to check on Eddie, who was feeling much better. He was no longer dizzy, and even the pain had almost gone away. He was up and walking around when the doctor arrived. To keep him inside, Sal had refused to allow him to change from his nightshirt.

Hands Upon The Anvil

"My boy, if you were any tougher, you'd rust," said the doctor admiringly. "Other than a sore head with a hole in it, well, you're amazing. You can get up tomorrow, and if you feel up to it, you can return to work on light duties. So, only the work on the bellows, no hammering," the doctor said. "I'll go see your mother."

He went to find Sal in the kitchen. She welcomed him, listened to his prognosis of Eddie and cheered up when he said he'd given him the all-clear. He warned her that Ned and Christina would return later that evening as they wished to talk to them. He asked if there was some way she could send all the children except Eddie somewhere as they needed to speak.

As they often went to the Miller's in the evenings, she would send them all up there. They wouldn't expect Ed to go as he was unwell.

Sal asked the doctor to stay for luncheon as they had plenty of fresh fish.

"If you're sure, Mrs. Lockley, I'd love to stay. I'm a little *de trop* at the moment, so I am at a loose end." He helped set the dinner table and even assisted in preparing vegetables.

"Please, doctor, I am just Sal or Sally if you wish," she said.

"I've been living alone for many years. I married a long time ago, and sadly, my wife died in childbirth only a year after we married, as did our child. She lived long enough to hold our stillborn daughter, Charlotte, and then she passed away in my arms. We were unable to halt her bleeding. We did everything we could, but it was not enough." His grief was still raw after all these years. "Charlotte would have been Eddie's age if she'd lived." He paused to wipe his eyes. "Since then, I have made it my work to study childbirth and its complications. I threw my life into it. I had nothing else. You could say it consumed me for years. I've never looked for anyone else." He paused, thinking, "I've been here only a few months, but if I don't cook for myself, I don't eat. However, my cooking is very basic."

They chatted over the food preparation, and she learnt much about the childhood of the Major and the life he lived in England, nothing personal, just life about his life in general and his friends.

He said, "Thank you, dear Sally, for letting me air my grief. It's the first time I have been able to talk about her in many a year."

"Sometimes sharing is the beginning of healing, doctor," she said. Sal told him of her conviction. "My employer had lent me £1, and on the day I was due to pay it back, I was run down by a carriage. The money was stolen from me while I was unconscious. I was taken to a hospice, and it was there that my employer had me arrested for theft. No matter what I said, the obvious fact that I'd been run down made no difference. I was convicted of theft and given a sentence of seven years. I had served one year in the hulks, nearly a year with the Major; by then, I had been allowed to marry Charles and serve the remainder working with him in the Government Stores."

The Major had already filled in the rest of her story about how he had claimed her as his housekeeper. The doctor stood looking at this woman and how life had dealt her a rotten deal. He had also heard Charles's story from the Major and how they became friends when Jack Turner and Charles had reported, then helped, put down a mutiny on the convict ship on the way out to the Colony. They were both given a 'Ticket of Leave' and, over the years, proved their trust. Charles and the Major had become friends. It was an improbable relationship. Gerry thought they were very much similar sort of men both in nature and stature. His first impression is that Ned must have found some distant relationship, but he was just a friend.

Luncheon over, the doctor said, "I'll go and sit outside with my tea. It might be a little cooler." He and Charles sat on the verandah, talked over the problems of the Colony, and then Charles excused himself to attend to the Taproom.

Old Tom walked along the riverbank toward the taproom and greeted the doctor, doffing his grubby hat.

Others came and went, and the doctor watched, fascinated by the passing people from other walks of life. He'd seen the seamier side of life via his medical work. He was impressed by how these two people, whose lives had turned sour, had completely turned their lives around and made good. All their children were educated, well-mannered, well-dressed, and well-spoken. Opportunities were never passed up, and Charles obviously was a hard worker. Their children were a credit to them both.

Sal brought him out a large padded cushion and a few smaller ones. She explained there was a section of the verandah where you could lie in the heat of the day and rest. It picked up any cool breezes off the water; the doctor decided to do just this. He lay down and, within minutes, was asleep.

Old Tom was the only patron at the counter. Charles handed him a cider and suggested he, too, sit on the verandah to drink it.

Tom said he'd rather find a shady spot on the grass, and Charles later found him asleep, leaning against the trunk of a large gum tree. Ants were crawling on him, but he had not a care in the world.

The hot afternoon passed quietly. It seemed the world was asleep. Eddie certainly was. It was a deep, healing sleep. Eddie slept most of the afternoon, waking because of hunger. He sat on the edge of the bed to see if he was dizzy. He got off the bed and walked into the kitchen to find something to eat or drink. On discovering he was awake, Sal was in there and handed him a ginger beer and a slice of bread with thick butter and honey. "Hmm, delicious, Mama. That hit the spot. I could drink a dam dry, I think."

She handed him a jug of barley water and a mug. She said, "Get into this, my boy. I put some honey in this too."

He drank a mug full, then poured himself another one. He half-downed that too. "Ahh, that's a bit better." Then he finished off the second mug as well. "I was so thirsty. I didn't get much to drink at all yesterday and have been asleep most of today. I'll finish this outside. Thanks, Mama." He walked outside, carrying the jug and drinking a third mug full. He put the pitcher on the verandah's edge, sat, and stretched. He moved his head from side to side and checked if it hurt. He was pleased to find it was feeling much better.

The doctor had woken as he heard the bang when Eddie came outside. He called, and Eddie walked over to him. He poured the fourth mug full but, this time, offered it to the doctor, who took it and drank deeply.

"Delicious," he said while handing the empty mug back. "Better than a glass of rich red wine. Hard to believe, but sometimes you just need to wet your whistle."

Sal arrived with a few more mugs; she called Old Tom up and handed him a cool drink. She introduced him to the newcomer.

Tom looked hard at him and just shrugged. He brushed off a few ants and smiled at Gerry.

Sal laughed and said, "Oh, Tom," she knew that Tom had accepted him as a friend.

The doctor looked inquiringly at Sal, but she didn't elaborate. He asked Eddie how he was feeling.

Eddie said, "Good, sir. The head is a little tender, but I feel like myself again. I had a huge thirst, but Mama's barley water did the trick."

Tom entered the small taproom for a 'real drink.' He left the doctor and Eddie on the verandah. The doctor suggested that Sal wash the remaining blood from his hair and then check the wound. Ed was used to washing his own hair, but the doctor wanted Sal to do it so the wound would not get too wet. He showed her how to sponge the hair over a basin, with Ed turning his head to avoid the cut.

Soon, Eddie was sitting outside in the sun. He'd taken off his nightshirt and was shirtless, dressed only in his trousers, sitting in the sun drying his golden locks. "Oh, that feels nice." He said to his Mama as she sat fluffing out his hair. Once it was nearly dry, the doctor appeared with a bottle of spirits and a few more bandages.

"I'd like to dry this in the sun, then put more spirits on it and see if I can bandage it so that tonight the bandage stays in place. Tomorrow, you will need to wear a hat or some sort of thing at work to keep the dust out of it."

Eddie nodded, "Hey, I can even do that now." He smiled and punched the air. "Yeah!"

The doctor smiled and headed back to the Major's house for dinner. As he left, he told Eddie, "I'll see you in an hour or so."

He ambled back to the Major's place. He was greeted with, "Hey,

Gerry, you've just got time to change. Christina has arranged for the Bobarts to come for dinner. They have an appointment afterwards, so they can't stay long, so we can't be late. Shake a leg," said Ned. "How's the patient?"

Gerry answered, "He'll be right as rain but must nurse the head for a day or so. He's already up and dressed, well, sort of. I told Sal I'd come for dinner, so I will tell her we'll come later."

Gerry went and told Sal, then on arrival back, headed into the guest room, washed up, and shaved again before changing into a clean shirt. The Major offered him evening clothes, but he refused, replying, "Here, they have to take me as I am. I had no intention of staying, remember? I'll have enough of dressing up when we get home." He hummed happily as he shaved and was soon ready.

They walked the two doors to Mrs. Meadows' cottage and knocked. The new maid, Maryanne Connor, opened the door, and they were shown inside. She had come recommended by the Tindales. Ned insisted that Christina have a chaperone.

The Bobarts were already there and were warmly greeted. They had not yet been let into the full secret of who they would actually be marrying. There were too many ears around at the church to do so that morning, hence the dinner invite.

Major Grace had hired the maid-come-cook to stay with her, stocked up Christina's pantry before her arrival, and brought over crockery and cutlery for the evening. She, too, was the daughter of a convict. Her Irish family were known to the Major as honest and reliable, for she had occasionally worked with the Tindales before being employed by the Major. He'd purchased a large cut of hogget for dinner, and they had each raided their gardens for vegetables. Dinner would be a feast.

The maid brought in drinks, also supplied by the Major, although only he and Christina knew how little she had previously had in the house.

The five sat for dinner, and conversation flowed, pausing only when Maryanne entered and starting on her departure. It was mostly about Ed's wedding on Saturday. The cider, supplied by the Bobarts, was served after the main meal, and the maid finally retired to the kitchen. She shut the door to avoid disturbing the guests while cleaning up.

"Finally," the Major said. "We have a few things more to add to this morning's conversation. Everything is now sorted for our wedding on Christmas Day; we'll have it after everyone else has left the church. No one will then notice the few people who have stayed back after the service. This we couldn't say this morning with so many around." He took Christina's hand in his. "You see, you will not be marrying Mrs. Christina Meadows to Major Edward Grace."

Reverend Mr. Bobart said, "Eh, what's this? But I thought you said you wanted to get married? What have I missed? Do you now wish to cancel the service?" Elizabeth tapped his hand to be quiet.

The doctor leant back in his chair and laughed. "I'm going to love this," he said as he folded his arms.

Mrs. Bobart looked from one to the other. "Please explain..." She, too, reached out and touched Christina's hand. "Is everything all right, dear?"

The Major turned to check the kitchen door was still closed. He then said, "Oh, perfectly all right, but there is a little explaining to do before I fully enlighten you." He told his story and then said, "It's only because Eddie got attacked and hit on the head that Gerry helped him that we met at Charles' Inn. He told me my family were looking for me. You see..." he paused looking at each of their faces "...apparently, now I'm Edward, Tenth Duke of Gracemere. I had no idea until Gerry turned up yesterday."

There were gasps and astonishment from both the Bobarts.

Gerry chipped in. "Oh, it gets better...."

Christina said, smiling, "I'm not exactly just Mrs. Meadows either. I'm Lady Christina Catherine Meadows née Hunt, daughter of Earl of Riverdell."

"Well, I'll be blowed," said Reverend Mr. Bobart. "Gentry, eh? And you both never said a thing. I'm sorry, Your Grace," he said, embarrassed.

"Oh, Reverend, don't be silly, Henry. I'm to still be 'The Major' until after we sail. You are not to tell a single soul, *not one*, until after our wedding. Gerry knows, as do the Lockleys, and they have all been sworn to secrecy. Gerry and Charles will be our witnesses. Only the family will stay for the service. We won't have a hymn, as we don't want anyone to wonder why there is music when everyone should be celebrating Christmas in our homes."

Reverend Mr. Bobart looked somewhat flustered. "Are you sure, sir, my lady?" looking from one to the other.

"Now, if you start that sort of rubbish, you will give us away instantly. We shall be Edward, or Major, and Mrs. Meadows as usual. Is that understood?"

Both Bobarts nodded, too stunned to speak.

There was silence at the table, and Maryanne chose that moment to bring in a tea tray. There was a mishmash of cups, saucers, and two mugs, but enough to go around.

Christina poured.

Maryanne retreated again.

Christina handed Mrs. Bobart a cup and saucer, and her hand shook as she took it from her. "Oh, my dear girl, how I wish I had known. Oh, I should have done so much more for you if I'd realised how alone you were."

Christina merely said, "But for you and your friendship, Elizabeth, I would have given up long ago. My pride tripped me up more than once in my life. It's my own fault. I could have written to my father, but I didn't. I could have done more myself, but I was too proud. I did not wish to be proved wrong. I was humiliated." She fell silent.

They finished their tea, and the Bobarts made the excuses of another appointment and departed with further warnings ringing in their ears.

Maryanne was left to clean up while the others departed for the short walk to the inn.

Although it was dark when they left, the Major took her hand as they walked, not worrying if anyone saw him. The doctor walked on her other side and took her arm. They laughed as they walked. Weddings were the topic of conversation, but nothing specific was discussed, which was just as well as they were surreptitiously watched.

They arrived at the inn at closing time, just as planned. They were made welcome, entered the dining room, and were seated.

Eddie was already at the table, and the others quickly took a seat. Sal was hovering and offered them drinks. They all refused but said thanks, and she took her place.

The Major stood to make an announcement. "Dear friends, as you know, I was shocked yesterday to discover I was a Duke, no, 'The Duke'. However, this news was in itself good news as I opened doors that would have otherwise stayed closed." He paused and looked at Christina with a nod. "I would like you all to wish us well as my dear Mrs. Meadows has accepted my hand in marriage, and we're being married on Christmas Day after the morning service. Charles, Sally and Eddie, yes, you already know, but I asked to be the person to tell you four the next bit of the story ourselves. Over to you, my love." He sat down.

She blushed and spoke from her seat. "You see, I am not actually just Mrs. Meadows. I'm Lady Christina Catherine Meadows, only daughter of Earl of Riverdell."

Gerry laughed when he saw the faces of the boys.

Wills sat mute, unable to say a word.

Luke broke the ice, "Cor, a real live Juke and now a Lady too...an' an Honourabubble, is that how you say it?" He looked around at the three visitors.

Charles laughed. "Out of the mouths of babes." He turned to Luke. "Just mind your manners, my boy."

Luke looked suitably chastened.

The doctor and Major, on the other hand, roared with laughter.

Wedding plans were discussed, but the Major asked if the children could be excused when they had some other things to discuss.

Charles dismissed the five young people who left to sit on the verandah. They were charged not even to discuss it outside. Not a word.

After they had gone, the Major said, "Now, for the real reason, we've come. As you now realise, I must return home. Christina will accompany me, of course, as my wife and new Duchess. Gerry, too will return with us. This leaves two items of business we must dispose of." He took a mouthful of cider. "As you know, I own my cottage, as does Christina, and we have decided to sign them over to you as a gift from us."

Charles and Sal gasped in unison.

"This will give you somewhere to live when Charlie takes over the Inn, but still be close enough to walk down when required. The other cottage you may use as you wish. They are very similar in size, both with two rooms. We will have no need for the money, and it's the least we can do as a thank you for all you have done for me over the years."

Charles attempted to speak but was silenced by the Major, who was holding his hand up. "I brook no discussion. This has already been decided. For the first time, I'm throwing my considerable weight around as Duke." He laughed, as did the others. He was a big man, as was Charles; they stood eye to eye. He was certainly not overweight.

"Ned, you can't be serious? It's beyond our dreams," said Sal. "Thank you so much; thank you."

She stood up and walked around the table to unceremoniously hug both the Major and Mrs. Meadows. "Oh, I shouldn't have done that; I'm sorry. Just overwhelmed."

"I'm still your friend, Sally." Ned was still holding her hand. He looked down at her, "I started as your boss, became a friend and feel you are all family. It's the least I can do. Christina feels the same. When others in the community were sniggering behind their hands, you always have a nice word for her, as well as for others. A smile, a curtsy, a little respect can make a world of difference, you know. I have watched how gracious you have always been, not just to her. Trust me; I have watched, but too many others are in need. You never turned them away."

Sal's eyes were full of unshed tears.

"There's Bill Miller's friend, old Tom and his mates. Whenever they are hungry, they know where to come for a feed and know they will never be turned away hungry. You share whatever you have; I have seen you stretch food when you are hungry yourselves. I've often heard people being sent here for a safe place to sleep with no money to pay them. You have both gone above and beyond what any person normally would do. I have watched Charles, and you live as faithful believers and doers of Christ's word. You don't preach; you live it, and we can see this in your family, too. This is a token of our appreciation."

The doctor felt it was getting a little too serious, so laughingly inserted, "Not to mention that it saves you a lot of paperwork selling both places, Ned."

The Major sat down again, as did Sally.

Charles just shook his hand. "I'm overwhelmed, sir. Thank you."

"None of this 'sir' stuff, please. I'm Ned, as I always have been. I'll have to be kowtowed to at home. Please, Charles, just be my friend. I have few enough true ones." He said, nodding to Gerry. "I'm sad that I cannot take you back with me, Charles, and make you my Chief Steward. But you'd hate the life of rank and servitude. I'd rather know that you will always be here and be my true friend. You will have a much better life here. Thankfully, England's class society doesn't exist here to the same degree. Here, you can be your own man. You will now have some property, too, even though they are small. Call it your retirement abode." Ned continued, "You have proven your worth as keeper of the Government Stores. I recommended you because I knew you were trustworthy. You have run them for nigh on twenty-three years now, and I have never had a single complaint through the turmoil of Governmental changes. You did not take sides; you just did your job. You even assisted with the Gaol riots over lack of food. You stepped in and supported me when I needed you. You became friends with my friends just because I said you could trust them. Amelia, Jack, Hugh, and, of course, Perry and Katy White, to whom you were both first assigned. Then you built up this Inn from nothing but a barn and a wooden shack. But you were not content with that; you gave refuge to women who were mistreated. Charles, many live in your shadow, and it is far-reaching. Your faith is obvious by how you live. I may have shown you the path, but you lit that path with a thousand lights. Your children follow your example and live a Godly life. Look at how you have made the inn grow. Charles, you deserve far more than just my friendship."

Charles sat looking at his friend but said nothing, almost winded by the accolade.

The doctor said, "If I had known about you, Charles, I would have stayed here, but I normally stayed at the Rear Admiral Duncan Inn. If I had, I probably would have run into Ned sooner. However, I don't travel by ferry but by road, so I had not passed this way."

The Major put his hands flat on the table and stood up. "It's time we were going. You have an early start in the morning and things to do. Don't stay up too late talking; we won't change our minds, will we, dear?" He turned to look at his Christina.

"No, Edward," she said. "There will be no mind-changing anywhere, my dear man." She put her hand on his arm. "I still find it hard to believe that no one realised we had been courting for over a year and got away with it." She chuckled with delight.

Sal's mouth dropped open in surprise.

They all moved from the table onto the verandah, and Ned tucked Christina's hand in his arm, and the three guests ambled off into the dark.

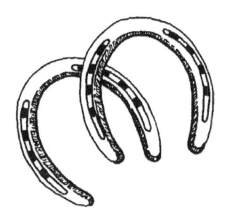

Chapter 15   The Day Arrives

*T*he next morning, Eddie woke with a clear head. It was his last workday, but he didn't have to appear until late and would be home for a midday meal. It was still sore to touch but was certainly on the mend. The doctor came early for a visit before he allowed Ed to go off to work.

"You'll do, son. Take some bits of rag to stuff in your ears and a hat of some sort. The noise will hit you hard, but you're fit to work," said the doctor. "Take care, and don't overdo it."

They walked out of the house and took different paths.

Mr. Tindale greeted Eddie as he arrived at work. Charlie had ducked up and told him he'd be along soon before disappearing again to go about his chores.

"How are you going, boy?" he inquired. "Feeling well enough to pump the bellows for me?"

Eddie said, "Yes, of course, sir. Probably no heavy hammering, but I can manage the small stuff just fine. The doctor told me to stuff my ears with some rag and keep a hat on to cover the cut. So I'll look a bit funny and won't hear if you speak to me, but otherwise, ready to get on with the job." He picked up the broom to sweep the floor and remembered his hat, which he picked up and jammed tightly onto his head. He cleaned the entire area and watched until the fire was ready for the bellows.

He worked steadily until noon when Mr. Tindale said, "That's enough for today, lad. Nothing urgent to do this afternoon." He surveyed the orders' board. "Most of the big jobs can wait until you get back from your honeymoon, and we'll have a few days before we leave." He crossed out two jobs with the chalk and wrote one more at the bottom of the list. "See, only the stock to build up again from the last order. Charlie and I got through quite a bit during the week. What we'll do tomorrow is do an inventory of what's here. I'll keep it up to date until I go." He put the chalk away and dusted his hands. "See you tomorrow, lad. Take care."

Eddie walked home in the heat of the summer day, glad to have a hat on as the sun beat down hard. Thankfully, most of the trip was downhill, so not a difficult one.

He kept on the hat as the wound still needed to stay clean. It had scabbed over and was well on the way to healing. Mr. Tindale had arranged for only a half-day today as he would be scrubbed up for his wedding.

His stomach was churning with nerves; he was pleased to have something to think about besides a huge wedding with a church full of people looking at him. It wasn't marrying Jenna that was the problem. He just wished they could have done it the same way the Major had planned, as a quiet, private affair. No, his concern was he hated being the centre of attention. He hated a fuss of any kind, hated even standing out in a crowd. His physique was in itself an issue, as he stood head and shoulders above the average man. His fair, wavy hair increased his inability to hide in a crowd. People would turn and look at this giant of a handsome man, women especially, and it embarrassed him. He was dreading the day, but yet anxiously awaiting it.

Sal stood, expecting his arrival. "First, my boy, I'm going to wash your hair. Doctor Winslow-Smythe said I must wash it to dry the wound immediately. He doesn't want the scab coming off too early."

"Oh, Mama, I'm a grown man; surely I can wash my own hair. I'll be careful, and I know where it hurts."

"So it does still hurt, does it? You said it was nearly better," she said accusingly but lovingly.

"I didn't want you to fuss any more than you are. I knew it would bother you," he said as he laid his arm along her shoulder. "I'll make you a deal. I'll wash it quickly, and you can dry it. How about that?"

"Hmm, all right," she said. "I'll towel it dry, and you can sit in the sun to finish it off." She walked off to get a basin and some soap. "I'll watch you do it, but there is actually still some blood at the back. I'll have to scrub that to remove it. I'm your mother. That isn't going to change just because you're getting married." She stood watching him, hands on hips and dropping bits of advice.

"Oh Mama, don't make me laugh while I'm upside down," he chortled.

She looked around. "Ed, as we're alone, there were bits of personal advice too from a woman to a man that I want to say... When your desire is high, and hers is not, never, and Ed, I mean *never* force her. It does the marriage no good in the long run. Get into the habit of never going to sleep without making up; hug her every morning and tell her you love her often; Bring her a flower, just to let her know you remember her. Be loving and tender; hold her often. Be yourself; she knows you better than you know yourself, so never try to deceive her...she'll know. I say these things with love. If in doubt, think, what would your father do?" She swallowed from her nerves. "Phew," thought Sal.

Ed spluttered with embarrassment while upside-down in the water but took the information on board. "Yes, Mama, this is all new, but I'll learn. I love her, so I don't wish to hurt her in any way."

Soon, she had him laughing as she scrubbed the back of his neck. "It's so long since I've had a chance to scrub the back of any of your necks. I haven't even been able to reach them for years. I'm not going to miss this opportunity."

Sal scrubbed his neck and ears and started on a remaining patch of congealed blood. He was laughing so hard by the time she finished that Charlie came to see what was happening. She grabbed him, too and said, "Your turn now, Chippy, my boy."

"Don't call me that, Mama. I'm not a little boy any more." He wasn't fast enough; she grabbed his arm and laughed. Soon, he too was in the basin and having his hair washed, and then his neck and ears were scrubbed, too. He complained as she scrubbed hard; Eddie enjoyed teasing and ribbing him.

"Big brother, payback," Ed said as he sat towelling his long hair dry. He turned so the wound was in the sun drying.

Wills and Luke also arrived and were told to sit by Sal. When she spoke like that, they dared not argue and sat. They watched Charlie knowing what to expect themselves. "Lukie, go fetch your towels. Scamper." He ducked off and was back as Charlie was standing up.

"Here, Mama," She took one and shoved it at Charlie. "Next," she said. She straightened her back and waited. "Come on. Be quick."

Wills shuffled up for his turn, then Luke.

Soon, all four boys were sitting in the sun drying their damp blonde locks; each had fair hair of varying shades. Although each wore it shoulder-length so it could be pulled back, Ed's hair was the longest as he had to have it completely tied back in a work queue.

Sal stood, looking at them. She thought, "All the boys were so handsome. Wills and Luke were destined to be as handsome as their elder brothers. They are four younger versions of her beloved Charles." Her heart stirred. Sal nodded; she was content that at least they would each present cleanly.

Anna had washed her hair after Sal had done hers earlier that morning. Satisfied her family were as clean as they could be, barring bathing them fully, she went indoors to continue food preparation for tomorrow.

In the hot sun, their hair did not take long to dry. Sal had Eddie's best Sunday clothes hanging and pressed neatly. He couldn't afford a new outfit, but she had made him a new shirt, and everything else was spick and span, likewise, the other boys.

Neither family would allow the couple to see each other the day before, so Marc said he'd come down and tell them when they arrived. They were staying with the Millers. The Major and doctor said they'd call by, which probably meant Mrs. Meadows would come too.

Eddie thought that the more he saw of her, the more he liked her. He was happy for the Major, as he still thought him. It was hard to think of him as a Duke.

Liza came over to help her Mama and Anna. Molly, Gracie, and Milly were all to arrive later.

Bertie came with Liza, and he caressed her cheek as she bent to kiss him a brief farewell. His eyes followed her until she was out of view in the house. He looked moonstruck. He walked over to the boys who were still sitting in the sun.

"Hi, chaps, what's up?" He laughed. "All scrubbed up for tomorrow? Did Mrs. L do it? My Ma did the same to me the morning of our wedding. 'There's no way any child of mine is getting married without them being scrubbed clean', he mimicked."

The boys chuckled and said, all agreed mournfully.

"At least you don't have a sore head," said Eddie.

Bertie had not heard what had happened to Ed. He gave Bertie an abbreviated version, mentioning that highwaymen had attacked him and then rescued by a doctor. Bertie would eventually find out the full story, but it was not for them to tell him. They all fell silent.

Bertie said, "Cor, just don't tell Jenna before the wedding. She'll have a fit."

With that, they all agreed. They would stay mum on that subject.

Soon it was too hot to stay in the sun; their hair was dry anyway, so they all headed around to the barn to assist in the final preparations of the barn and stable. They threw themselves into the work, favouring Eddie a little; he put it down to his being the groom. He didn't argue; his head still ached a bit. He wouldn't let on.

Charlie kept his eye on his little brother, noticing that occasionally, he put his hand to his head or covered his eyes. When he first saw him covered in blood, his heart flipped. He had not been there to protect him. So often, he had stood between danger and Eddie. Ed had never known either. Simmons! No, he'd never think of him again. That was the past. Ed protected him as much as he had been able to as well. It drew them close. He shook his head as if to make the memories leave. Ed had told him that sometimes Charlie would say, "No, no, leave me alone" in his sleep. He'd told Gracie everything; he felt that was only fair before he proposed. And Dar knew what had happened. Eddie only had ever guessed. Charlie shook his head to make those thoughts leave him.

They set the fire pit for tomorrow night and stacked the spare timber well away in case of flying sparks. They set out as much seating as they could and swept the floors clean. The stock was now out in the field next door, so they did not have to muck the stable out. All the movable items, like brushes, harnesses and the like, were all stored away. Many from the town would pass through and didn't want these things going for a walk. Empty kegs were brought around as extra seating or small tables. There were full kegs to put in the cellar to cool, mugs and other drinking cups to place out upside-down, then cover.

The place was ready by dusk, and Charles passed his eyes over everything and nodded approval. "All right, lads, time for tucker. Would you like to stay, Bert? Liza said it was your call; she hasn't had time to prepare anything for your meal, so you may as well."

Bertie said, "I'd love to if that's all right. Liza misses you all. Seems I'm not enough." He looked mournful but had a beaming smile on his face. They knew he was joking.

"Done," said Charles. "Wills, go tell Mama two more for dinner." He looked up to see the Major and Doctor coming down the street. "Luke, race in and tell Mama there could be four more."

Although the day's heat was passing, both men had been walking for some time and were hot. Charles greeted them both with a question. "Cool drink, cider or ale?"

The Major answered, "Cool drink for me, Charles."

The doctor replied, "Any chance of a cup of tea?"

Charles looked at him, said, "Yes," and shook his head. "It's so blooming hot. How can you drink tea?"

"I'm English." The doctor laughed but otherwise ignored the comment. "How's my patient?" he asked instead. He went off to find him and ask Sal for a cup of tea if it were possible.

Charles and the Major walked down into the cellar to check out the drink situation for the wedding. The Major perched himself on a keg as Charles poured a glass of lemonade and sorted how much they would need and how to make them accessible.

The Major admired this quiet man.

He had faced adversity and rose above it. His entire family were all good, upstanding citizens, admired by those who knew them. He'd done what he could to ease their way, but they didn't really need him. He, however, needed them. None were scared of hard work. And work, they all could. He had a soft spot for Eddie, though. Not just because of his name, but he'd always looked out for the lad as a child. He faced life straight on. Life's challenges never worried him; he'd survey the problem and work out a way to achieve the greatest success. He'd been like this since he was a lad. When he realised Charlie would probably inherit the Inn; he applied for an apprenticeship with Mr. Tindale without saying anything to his parents. It's the sort of lad he was. He was only six.

Ned would protect this family with his life; he loved them so much. One soldier, who was disliked and distrusted by most, he had tried to keep away from the boys. Ned avoided him where possible and allocated him the jobs where he could do the least harm. Chain gang supervision was where he used to be, but he was removed from that, too, as he took evil glee in whipping a man for little reason. He was supposed to be supervising a convict and let him escape. The convict had then attacked a friend's wife. More than one convict died or was hospitalised under Simmons's supervision. No one deserved that sort of treatment. That's not how to encourage them to work. The Major usually had him on guard duty, often outside the Barracks, as the Major knew precisely where he was. Standing nearly still for nigh on twelve hours was also a punishment. He smiled, thinking back. The stupid man thought it was a reward.

The boys were clearly scared of this scoundrel, Charlie especially. The look on their faces when they saw him confirmed their fear and loathing of the man. He'd never been more pleased when he heard Simmons died during a storm. Divine Justice. Thankful that the episode is now well over. Hard to believe that it was eleven years ago. The emotional scars in Charlie's life were profound. He trusted less, was quieter, and never pushed himself forward. Eddie protected him in any way he could. Hopefully, the lad will have a peaceful life; at least Ed will, with Jenna beside him. She was a strong and compassionate lady.

He had spoken to Tindale when the lad was young, and together, they had worked out a way for Eddie to have an education and Charlie to get some smithing experience. Something he would need when running the Inn. The deal between the men as the Major had paid for his tuition and Tindale for his accommodation. Tim had won a scholarship but could not accept it because he had nowhere to live. The Major's name was to be kept out of it, though.

Timothy's father supplied the money for most of the extra costs mentioned, but they helped him too by telling him it was less than it really was, but they had never told Charles that Tim had won a scholarship for tuition. They'd managed to cover up that bit of information, too, but that would get out one day. The Major thought, sitting up straight, "Oh my! I'll be gone soon. I think I have to tell Ed, but Charles has to know first." He sat up straight and said, "Charles, I have to tell you something. Eddie, too, but I'll tell you first." He took a breath, calm down, he thought. "Charles, it's about when Eddie went to school; there's something I want to know. There's way more to the story." He paused and took a deep breath.

"Tindale and I had heard that young Tim sat an exam and had won a scholarship for tuition at Mr. Cape's Academy but had no way of him taking it up without somewhere to live. We told Bill to keep that quiet. Well,

Tindale and I got talking about young Ed. I know I shouldn't play favourites, but he always has been special to me. Born on my birthday and named after me. He's the son I never had. You know that."

"Yes," said Charles, "I know, and it never mattered. He would have had a rough life but for the care from you. But I won't go into that."

"Simmons, you mean?" asked the Major.

Charles nodded. "Charlie, too, only he got it worse. He protected Ed from the worst of it. Ed still doesn't know that." Charles, too, was now perched on a keg. "I did all I could to keep them safe, but I couldn't always be with them."

"Well, we hit upon a scheme, Tindale and I, to get all three boys safe. We could have sent them to the new King's School, but Tim didn't have a scholarship for that, and it would not have removed them from Simmons. This way, Eddie would be safely in Sydney, with me paying tuition and Tindale taking care of the board with his sister, and he'd be with his friend Tim. Then Charlie would be working with Tindale and not available for Simmons. It was the only way we could try to keep all three out of his way. Bill could afford to pay the pittance Caroline Evans asked from him. We made sure she was never out of pocket for either boy."

They turned when they heard a noise on the steps.

Eddie had been sent to find them and had overheard the last part of the conversation. He stood in the doorway, mouth agape. "You did that for me, sir? Seriously? And for Charlie too and Tim as well. Have you any idea what this means?" Eddie wiped his eyes; he had a lump in his throat. "That first weekend I was there, and I saw *him* outside under the tree watching me, I was fearful, very fearful. I knew what was going on. Charlie still wakes up saying, 'No, don't touch me.' Simmons was getting sick of Charlie and beginning to follow me, but to Sydney, too? I would watch him looking at both Tim and me. I did all I could to keep Timmy out of his way. All I could think of was…well, I wished him dead. I thought, here we were, safe in Sydney."

Ed's memories of that night flashed back to him. He walked to a keg and sat. The Major could see him, head down, remembering. "Then the storm hit. It's how I saw him, the lightning, you know. Well, the storm was nearly overhead, and we were watching it through the upstairs window. Phil and I were kids and loved storms. So we kept watching it. The lightning hit the tree, and it exploded. John slept through it all."

Eddie stood up with his hands pressed onto a barrel. Deep in thought with the memories.

The two older men waited, giving him time to process the recollections.

Ed continued. "The emotions that went through me were very confusing. I was just a kid. I wanted him dead so much for hurting Charlie, but no way would I have killed him. That night I fled to Mr. Tindale, and I knew I could leave everything to him. I managed to say, 'Simmons,' but nothing more. He had protected me from him before. I only had to tell him, but I couldn't; I stood with my back to the door frame, unable to move. I couldn't open my mouth, but Phil did. He told him what happened. I just couldn't. I froze, I suppose. Looking back, I was in shock. Mr. Tindale understood, for as he walked past, he put his hand on my shoulder and just said quietly so only I could hear, "It's over, lad. Finished." I'll never forget that night. It's seared in my memory. I had to walk past the stump for the next five years. It never grew back, you know? The memory of him has not faded, but I was no longer afraid. What Charlie went through is too horrible to think about. I knew he was protecting me. I didn't know what to do but be there for him." His eyes swam. "I'll always be there for him."

Ed paused, remembering again.

Still, the other men stayed silent.

Ed lifted his head with confidence. "That night, I got on my knees and thanked God. I thanked Him then with childish prayers, but I've prayed every night since, not just over that, but over many things. Even leading me to Jenna. I have even thanked Him for the goats." He laughed. "I know many of the girls here. Most I wouldn't even look twice at. I had no special feelings for any of them, and then I met Jenna." He gave a gentle shake of his head, then lifted it and looked his father in the eye. "My Faith in Him, God, has grown too, but that night was the start. If God could see me through that, I knew He'd be with me always. I don't talk much about it. I try to live it. Hopefully, people can see it in my life and how I live. I try to be different from the other boys. It's why I don't hang around with them at the bars or around girls. Charlie believes too, you know." He turned his face, his eyes misting, a tear escaped, and he wiped it away. He looked back at his father, who walked over to him and just enfolded him in a bear hug.

Eddie hugged him back but looked at the Major over his father's shoulder. How could he ever thank him for what he had done for him? Eddie released his father and walked over to the Major, who had stood up. He looked him in the eye and also enfolded him in a hug. Mumbling, "Thank you, thank you so much."

The Major stood eye to eye with the young man, held him at arm's length, and said, "It's an honour, lad. It's all I could do not to deck that man. I do wish I had."

Ed gave a weak laugh. "Sir, you were always high in my estimation, but now you've topped it." He turned to his father, "Sorry, Dar."

Charles laughed. "Totally understood, boy." He walked over to him and placed his hands on his shoulders, "Now, deep breathe. We have to face the others. I'll let Charlie know his bit of the story sometime later. He poured it all out to me when he found out. So I know it all, probably more than both of you. Maybe next week I'll chat with him. Bill, too, but that can wait. Mr. Tindale told him some of it on the day after Simmons's death.

Let's go face the others."

Charles turned to the Major, "Once again, sir, I am in your debt."

The Major laughed and replied, "Let's call it one debt paid. You have given me much more." The Major patted Ed on his back. "Ed, I'm very proud of you."

Eddie just grinned.

Almost like he had three fathers, Dar, the Major and Mr. Tindale, he certainly had three guardian angels.

As Charles walked past Ed, he whispered, "I want to have another chat later. Back down here."

Eddie nodded. He picked up the lantern and followed the Major and his father up the steps.

The Major left for his home.

Charles walked inside.

Everyone was waiting for them as they entered the dining room. While they were downstairs, Marc had popped in to say that the family had arrived safely and were having dinner with the Millers. He didn't stay and headed straight back there.

Eddie had washed his face as he passed the water barrel. His mind is awhirl. He took a deep breath and followed his father inside.

They sat at the dinner table and were served by Liza, Anna, and Sal. Sal dished up in the kitchen and brought out the laden plates. She knew how hungry all the men were. She'd cooked a double-sized meal, knowing there would be extras. She would have leftovers tomorrow as only Bertie and Liza stayed to eat after all. At least no one would go hungry. Sal shrugged and smiled to herself.

The conversation was jovial. Charlie offered to take Eddie out on an Inn walk around town, but Eddie wasn't much of a drinker, and his head still made him feel a bit woozy. It was already buzzing after the conversation downstairs.

He declined politely, offering to postpone the evil deed until his wedding.

Charlie laughed and turned to Bertie. "Do you think he'll need any Dutch courage? Did you?"

"No way," said Bertie, "I wanted a clear head to remember every detail. And I don't regret that at all. I had a wonderful time at our wedding." He put his hand on Liza's. "Nope, I don't regret that at all."

"No 'Dutch Courage' for me either, thanks, Chip," said Eddie, knowing he hated being called Chip. It had the desired effect; he stopped teasing. "The doctor wouldn't let me go anyway. I'm still under strict orders to limit the alcohol to none."

They all sat at the table, talking over the arrangements for the next day. Sal handed out a list of jobs for each one and what needed to be done.

Charles added a few, then said, "All right, everyone, big day tomorrow. I'm going to show you two home, and we'll all head to bed. See you bright and early. We'll all walk to the church together. Bert, Liza, I'll see you out. Ed, bring the lantern."

Thus disposed of, everyone headed to bed. Sal and Anna did the dishes while the younger boys and Charlie washed and went to bed.

Charles and Eddie walked outside with Liza and Bertie. They stood waving until they disappeared into the gloom.

Charles said, "Well, lad, this is your last night as a single man. I think we need to have a father-son talk. Come." He walked back down towards the cool, dark cellar. They would not be disturbed down there, and more than that, their voices would also not carry.

Ed sat the lantern on a keg and perched himself on another.

Charles turned it down as low as it would go. "Some things are better discussed in the dark, son. There are some conversations parents dread to have to have with their children, no matter at what age, this would top them." He perched himself on a keg as he had been only a short time before. Both were just out of the reach of the now dim light.

Eddie sat, wondering what else would be revealed tonight.

Charles swallowed, "Where the heck do I start," he wondered. "Well, son, I know that you are wise beyond your years over many things, but some things have not crossed your path too much, and one of those things is girls."

"Oh, sheesh," thought Charles. "Son, I need to give you a few Father-Son tips about, well, the loving side, the physical stuff. The joy of marriage side. Some men sow their oats, as they say, and some don't. I'm not talking the horrible Simmons stuff, but the beautiful side of marriage." Charles swallowed and loosened his collar. "I know you haven't been a wild one. There are some things about girls you need to know. Especially for her and your first time together." Charles swallowed but continued, "For them, it will hurt, so go gently. Do not force yourself on her; make sure you are both relaxed, and things will come naturally. But be aware of her pain and give her time and love. Let her, shall I say, lead. The next time for her will generally be fine."

"Next time?" Ed exclaimed… His eyes grew wide with the information. How many times could he expect? His mind was a whirl.

Charles swallowed again and continued. "Also, be aware do not, and I mean never, use soap on yourself, on your, um, private parts. The lye, or carbolic or something in the cheap soaps that we have burns them. If you get it in your eyes, you'll know what I mean. They won't tell you; they will suffer in silence. Make sure you are always clean but only use plenty of hot water, but no soap on… well down there." Charles paused. "Ask any questions you need to. It's easier in the dark," he continued. "Another thing you should know is you must never force her. It's about love. If you force her, it becomes about power, and you can easily lose her trust. Remember, even in Genesis chapter 2 v 25, the Bible states, *"God made us for each other, for pleasure, and nakedness between husband and wife is natural."* And also, *"And they were both naked, the man and his wife, and were not ashamed'."*

Charles paused again. "Remember also how embarrassing the passages in Song of Solomon are, especially in chapter 7. Solomon's physical desire for his wife is, well, blatant. But there is a clear difference between lust and love. Eddie, you must never confuse them. The love and physical relations between a husband and wife are good and pure, and trust me, fun too. You must endeavour to keep it that way. Having said that, it need not be boring for either of you. It's sensual, and you must bring her pleasure by holding back as long as you can; when you do, trust me, your pleasure will be multiplied, as will hers. It should also be fun, great fun, it's relaxing, and it bonds you strongly. Making babies is only one outcome from this; I heard someone say it's relaxation, recreation, and procreation."

Charles took a deep breath, "Son, Jenna will have a power over you that will make you feel like jelly by just looking at her, and if you think she does now, wait until after the wedding. A simple glance from her will have you quaking with expectation and anticipation. She can awaken your desire with a wink. Keep this side of your marriage good and pure, and this will last all your married life. Defile that trust, and she can, and will, make your life hell."

The darkness hid Eddie's flushed cheeks, but it also hid Charles' cheeks. Eddie thought, "Yes, it was easier to say these things in the dark."

Eddie had one question but was too scared to ask. Was he too big? He stood head and shoulders over Jenna and did not want to hurt her. He knew he was well endowed. Even though they are the same height as Charlie, boys notice things. Hell, he had three brothers. Ed asked a few things, skirting around his thoughts, but just could not broach this topic. Finally, he said, "Dar, I'm so much taller than her and… well, she's not."

Charles seemed to work out what was disturbing him and put his mind to rest. "Be gentle and take things easy; give her time and do not rush or force things; be led by her, especially initially. She will be very tight the first time, and as I said, it will hurt her. Once in, stay still for a bit and be led by her. Be gentle; I can't emphasise that enough. Follow her lead, be guided by her. If she's half the girl your Mama is…well, let me just say, follow her lead." Charles added, "Do not be surprised to be, um, called upon more than once a night, especially on the honeymoon. And it does not always have to be either at night or in bed. Marriage has many benefits, Ed. Often!" Charles chuckled.

"Often?" Ed said softly. Just as well, his father could not see Eddie's jaw drop. But they did have six children. The thought had never occurred to him before. He wasn't quite sure how he felt about that. He'd rather not think about that at all.

Charles also brought up a few more difficult topics before they returned upstairs to bed. He flushed, then blanched, then blushed again. "Ohh!" was all he could manage, still thankful for the darkness.

Eddie was glad that he'd been brave enough to voice these subjects with his Dar. He didn't want to hurt Jenna in any way. He knew that neither Jenna nor he had any experience in this area. They had discussed it, and although tempted, they had saved themselves as a sign of trust and love for each other. They had decided early on not to put the other in a difficult situation.

Ed blushed numerous times during this conversation, as he thought his father probably had, too. As Dar said more than once, some topics are best discussed in the dark.

Ed said, "Thanks, Dar," as Charles turned up the lamp, and then they left the cellar.

Charles mopped his brow, thankful that *that* conversation was over.

"What a week it's been, my boy," he said as he followed Ed up onto the verandah with his arm along his son's shoulder. "A big day tomorrow, so off to bed. Sleep well tonight, as you may not get much tomorrow." He gently slapped him on his back and laughed. "Trust me in this."

Eddie's mouth dropped open. "Dar," he said, horrified. Then he thought, then murmured, "More than once a night?" He headed to bed with a smile.

"Yes, often," Charles chuckled.

The next morning dawned bright and sunny, as had the previous few days. It would be another hot one. The boys snuck out of their room and got on with their chores.

Eddie slept on. Occasionally, he'd jump or startle, but he slept on. Sal kept a motherly eye on him. She knew his head still pained him somewhat, but not enough to hinder him. She let him sleep as she knew too that he'd need it. She smiled to herself, remembering her wedding night.

The wedding was to be at 11 a.m. All the chores had to be completed by 10 a.m., and the rest of the food was prepared and placed in the cellar. That gave them an hour to get changed and get to the church. Sal went and woke Eddie at half-nine so that he could have a little extra time getting ready.

By quarter to eleven, everyone was ready; Marc appeared with the gig for Eddie and Charlie. James was brushed and glistening. The others were to walk up. The three tall men squashed themselves onto the seat and headed off with James at a walk. They arrived at the church in good time, and all waited in the shade for the bride's family to arrive, as well as all the rest of the guests.

Eddie sat on the gig step with his back to everyone. His nerves were getting to him. Ed was very pale and feeling woozy.

Charles appeared with his hip flask and said, "Swig this."

Eddie did, but just a small amount. "Ugh, Brandy."

"Again," Charles said.

Eddie did again. He looked up at his father.

Charles said, "As you know, I don't like spirits much, but at times like this, sometimes a little bit is good." Charles remembered how he'd felt on his wedding day. He knew Eddie hated crowds and especially hated being singled out, and his wedding was nowhere near as big as this one. Everyone knew him. Charles slipped his hip flask back into his pocket. "All right, lad?"

Eddie nodded, feeling a little better. "Head is still woozy."

Marc appeared, "They're coming. Come on, into the church with you." Charles and Charlie each grabbed an arm and jokingly dragged him towards the church, going in through the Vestry door. Ed had recovered. All were laughing.

As they went in, everyone else who'd been milling about outside filed into the church through the main door. Eddie stood in the front with Charlie and Marc beside him as the seats filled. It was hot. The music started playing something, but Eddie wasn't really listening. The music stopped.

The voices were hushed.

Eddie turned to see Jenna standing with Jack at the church door. His heart swelled with pride.

All he could see was her outline. He gasped. The light behind her gave her an aura.

She was about to start down the aisle when Mrs. Jenkins appeared beside her and presented her with a massive bouquet of exquisite roses from her garden. Jenna bent and kissed her and said, "Thank you." Beaming, she started walking towards Ed on her father's arm.

Her dress was royal blue, and a small veil covered her hair that trailed down her back to her waist. All he saw was her face. She looked beautiful. Her face radiated joy. She was to become his. His heart skipped a beat, wiping a wayward tear from his cheek.

She arrived at the sanctuary steps.

Jack stood between them. The service started, and at the appropriate time, he handed Jenna over to Ed, and Jack whispered to him. "Take good care of her."

Eddie merely nodded but with a huge grin plastered on his face. He just wanted to stand, looking at her.

Reverend Mr. Bobart's words interrupted his daydream.

"Dearly beloved, we have gathered here today to join..." the words droned on. Eddie stood holding Jenna on his arm, his hand on hers.

Soon, the Minister said, "Is there any reason why these two should not be joined in Holy Matrimony? Speak now or forever hold your peace."

Ed and Jenna held their breath...

There was a hush, then a rustle. "Yes," a voice called out from the rear of the church. "That man is a horse thief. I have the bill of sale to prove it." There was a gasp from many, including Eddie.

"What? I did no such thing," pleaded Eddie to the Minister and turned to Mr. Tindale.

The congregation broke out in a babble of murmuring.

"Silence!" yelled Reverend Mr. Bobart. The noisy confusion that rippled through the building soon quietened. "Although this matter should be discussed, now is not the time. This is no reason to halt the marriage service. Major, send someone to escort this man to the Magistrate's office and await him there."

Major Grace, although retired, signalled two soldiers to attend to the interrupter and escort him out.

Reverend Mr. Bobart turned to Mr. Moffatt, Justice of the Peace, who was sitting next to his wife in his family pew directly behind the groom's family. "Is this all right, sir? May we deal with this later?"

"Absolutely! Continue with the service," he ordered.

The congregation hushed, and the service continued. Soon, Reverend Bobart pronounced them husband and wife. He said to Eddie, "You may now kiss the bride."

Eddie willingly did as he was bid, and drawing the small veil from her face, he put his hand to her cheek and bent to kiss her lips quickly. However, Jenna pulled his head down and drew him into a passionate embrace.

Reverend Mr. Bobart coughed and whispered, "Enough!"

They drew apart, smiling.

Eddie was grinning.

They signed the register with Charlie and Marc standing ready to sign when Charlie leaned over and whispered something to Eddie, who nodded. Charlie walked down to the Major and whispered something to him, too. It flashed through Eddie's mind that they must have spoken.

The Major stood and said quietly, "Are you sure?" Charlie and Eddie both nodded, and he walked up the front to sign as a witness instead of Charlie.

Reverend Mr. Bobart signed the register, followed by Eddie in his neat script, then Jenna, Marc, and finally the Major. He looked at Eddie, winked, smiled, then signed it as "Gracemere" in his elegant flowing calligraphy. Reverend Bobart had left the section blank; he'd fill it in accurately later. The register was returned to Reverend Mr. Bobart, who merely looked at the signatures, smiled and quickly closed the book. He had a feeling this might happen. He smiled. Time for that small revelation later. He turned to the congregation, "Ladies and Gentlemen, please be upstanding. Let me present to you, Mister and Missus Edward John Lockley."

The congregation applauded, and Eddie and Jenna walked down the aisle towards the open rear door.

They were greeted by friends showering them with flower petals, but past them, Mr. Moffatt waited near the man in the dark trousers and two soldiers. He had refused to leave without the accused.

Eddie stood with Jenna until his family joined them and then whispered to Jenna, "I have to get this sorted."

She nodded and quickly reached up to kiss his cheek. "Let's just hope and pray that this is the 'worse' in the 'better or worse' of our marriage." She stroked his cheek. "I'll be fine with your folks. I love you. My husband, go and get this sorted," she said.

He called his parents over and the Turners too and explained that he must go with the Clerk of the Court and Mr. Moffatt. He would return as soon as he could.

Charles called Charlie over, saying, "Take Jenna and your Mama in the gig, start the party and not wait for us."

Charlie nodded.

Charles would go with Eddie. He thought, "What a day?"

Mr. Tindale, the Major, and the Doctor joined Charles and walked down to the Courthouse after Eddie and the others.

Mr. Moffatt opened the courtroom door, walked over to his imposing desk, and sat with his arms folded. He waited until everyone was settled.

Then he turned to the man with the dark trousers. "You! Name?" he boomed.

"Mr. Erastus Black, your honour," he replied, trying to sound confident.

Mr. Moffatt said to him, "Your timing was abysmal, you realise. I should lock you up for that alone, but let me hear your complaint." He paused. "This is not how it's normally done, Black, but this is not a normal case."

He looked at Eddie with the Major, Charles, and Mr. Tindale standing beside him. "I will hear this now, and my decision will be final. Do you all understand?"

All present, including Mr. Black, nodded and agreed with a resounding, "Yes, sir."

"Good, then. Sit!" said Mr. Moffatt. He motioned for everyone to sit down. They all sat, Mr. Black, with the two soldiers still at his sides, the others in the seats on the other side of the room. "Black, tell me again of your grievance against this young man?"

Mr. Black stood and proceeded to elaborate on the truth. He said, "The blacksmith's apprentice has stolen my hoss, and I wants me hoss back; the hoss is now known as James. I want it returned to me forthwith."

Mr. Moffatt listened intently to his long-winded story and accusations. He rested back in his chair, interlocking his fingers and tapping his thumbs.

"Hmm," he said. "Interesting take on the issue."

Mr. Moffatt waggled his finger, motioning for Mr. Black to sit. He looked at Eddie and was just about to ask him a question when Mr. Tindale motioned that he wished to speak. Mr. Moffatt nodded his head toward him and said, "There's obviously far more to this story. Care to elaborate, Tindale?"

Mr. Tindale stood and said, "Sir, if anyone is responsible for Eddie having that horse, it's me. May I please explain how?"

Mr. Moffatt merely said, "Please do."

Mr. Tindale continued, "This person, now calling himself Mr. Black, attended my smithy's shop some fourteen months ago with a very lame horse. He'd ridden it with one loose horseshoe and another missing. There were also other broken items on the harnesses he had me repair and some stock he required immediately, which I let him have as I still had his horse. When the time came for payment of the said work, he arrived to remove the horse, and the horse refused to go. As soon as it saw him, it started bucking and propping, ears back on its head and trying to bite him. After some stressful minutes, this man threw up his hands and walked off after saying, "I'm not paying for that. He's a foul-tempered brute, that one. You can have him. He's thrown me twice this trip. Tell me where I can get a hoss I can ride. I'm orf…" and he walked away leaving the horse and also leaving his account unpaid. I said, "What about my account." He replied, 'You got the bloody hoss, didn't you?' then he left."

"Now, the amount was not minor as there was other work I had done for him. As was the law, I could take goods in kind. So I, accompanied by my young apprentice, as he was then, went down to Major Grace's office and reported the problem. This was shortly before his retirement. The Major informed your office, who awarded me ownership of the horse now known as 'James'. I gave him to Eddie, my then apprentice, as wages, as I had no use for it." He stepped back and sat down.

Mr. Moffatt leaned forward, still listening intently.

"Hmm," he said again, "and you, sir, whom exactly might you be?" pointing to Charles.

"I, sir, am Eddie's father, Charles John Lockley; I am Keeper of Stores for the Government and have done for nigh on twenty-five years. I run the Jolly Sailor Inn down at the Queen's Wharf," said Charles confidently.

"Hmm, a Government Employee then, interesting! You must be trusted," he mused aloud. "Otherwise, you would have been booted."

Then Mr. Moffatt pointed to the Major. "Please explain how you are involved in all this, sir."

"I object to these people being involved," interjected Mr. Black, standing up.

"Silence that man," said Mr. Moffatt to the soldiers.

Mr. Black was forced back into his seat.

The Major stood, "On the day of the incident, I am the person to whom Mr. Tindale brought the horse. I am Major Edward Grace, recently retired. Until then, I was the Commanding Officer to whom all these issues were brought, as I was the Military commander in the area. I decided that as the said horse, at the time, was much in need of training, it was, as such, of not much value. He was barely worth the price of the goods taken by the plaintiff, Mr. Black. The re-shoeing of the horse remains outstanding, as does the cost of the broken stirrup, I believe." He looked to Mr. Tindale, who nodded. "In the intervening months, young Eddie Lockley trained and educated this same dangerous horse, and he has become the magnificent animal he is today. There is a strong bond between the two." The Major sat.

Mr. Black was looking decidedly uncomfortable. He was alternately red with anger and white with fear; two soldier's hands were still on his shoulder.

Mr. Moffatt once again leant back in his great chair. "Now, lad, if nothing else, you will have a wedding day you will never forget. Tell me your part in the story."

Eddie stood and gave a bow. He gave his version. "This man had come to the blacksmith's shop to purchase some goods and to have a lame horse re-shod. When he returned empty-handed to collect his horse, the horse shied, bucked and propped and would not go with the man. Until this stage, I had not been involved in the discussions; however, when the horse became upset, I took his reins and attempted to quieten him down. I was unable to do this until Mr. Black departed. I was not a party to the financial discussions about payment; however, I do know that this man left without paying for the goods he had previously taken or for paying for the work done on both the horse and the broken stirrup. The horse bucked at him, and he then refused to take the horse due to its temper and behaviour." He paused and looked at Mr. Moffatt.

"Is there more?" he asked.

"Yes, sir, there's more. I accompanied Mr. Tindale to the Major's office. We tethered him outside the office. He stood quietly enough. We reported the theft of the items and the man's refusal to pay, also for the abandonment of the said horse."

"Go on."

"Well, sir, the Major awarded the horse to Mr. Tindale to cover the costs of the goods. It was all done legally. I saw the Major, and he had Mr. Tindale report the payment default to the Courthouse, here, sir, in this office, then sign an incident report and officially register the payment default," said Eddie.

"So you can read, can you, boy?" Mr. Moffatt asked.

"Oh yes, sir, I can not only read and write in English but in French, German and Latin. My Greek is not too good, but I can speak it well enough. Sir, I attended Mr. Cape's Academy for five years," said Eddie modestly.

Mr. Moffatt Turned and addressed the accuser.

"So let me get this right, Black, you are a thief and a scoundrel, and yet you accuse this lad on his wedding day, in the middle of his wedding service, that he's the thief? Am I to understand this correctly?" Mr. Moffatt did not look impressed. All nodded.

Eddie, still standing although he had been motioned to sit, appealed to speak again.

Mr. Moffatt looked to Eddie and gave approval for him to speak again.

"Sir, I would like to tell you of another incident pertaining to this case, I think, possibly even leading up to today. On Friday last, I was making a large delivery of goods to Orchard Hills. On the return trip, I stayed with my now-wife's family for two days. I was about halfway home from Emu Plains on Sunday afternoon last week when three masked highwaymen set upon me. While on his horse, this man hit my head with the stock of his rifle. Well, sir, I am no small man, and it floored me. I was knocked to the ground." Eddie paused, letting this sink in. "He and the two other men were masked with only eyes showing. Only the other two had spoken at this stage. The third man only replied by pointing to what he wanted to be done. Eventually, rather than motioning to the other two, he spoke. As soon as he did, James, the said horse, started bucking and propping in his traces. His ears were already set back on his head, and this behaviour was unlike him. I could not work out what was wrong; he kept throwing his head, misbehaving and pawing the ground. The only time I had seen him do this was when his previous owner abandoned him." He paused, looking at Mr. Black. "The man repeated the exact words on Sunday last, as he had that day, with the same intonations. It was then that I identified him. I knew the voice, as did James." Ed paused again, letting that information sink in. He then turned to Mr. Black. "Moments later, the three highwaymen realised they were to be interrupted by another traveller. As one commented, the dust from a galloping rider came towards us. He repeated his comment of "I'm orf…" again, and it occurred to me where I'd heard it before. I knew it to be the previous owner of the horse. James had recognised him, possibly even his smell, before he spoke, hence his behaviour. The three masked riders rode off. Also, sir, I recognised this man's clothing. An unusual outfit, if I may say, is dark trousers and a tan brown jacket. Not the usual outfit for a person around here. His outfit had been commented on by my other as I had left. Because of his odd attire, he stood out."

"It was after they had gone that the good doctor here," pointing to where Doctor Winslow-Smythe sat, "… rode up and came to my aide. He is the brother of the person to whom I delivered the goods at Orchard Hills Farm. He will verify the state I was in." He paused, then continued, "Even though they stole a handful of coins and took my food, I believe that if the doctor had not arrived when he had, they would have stolen the horse. I cannot be sure of this, but I gather that was his intent as he said, 'Leave the hoss for now,' just before they departed." Eddie sat down.

The doctor had been sitting hidden by the others with his head down.

Mr. Moffatt wrote notes and then asked, "So, doctor, is all this lad said correct?" He drew in a sharp breath as the doctor stood.

"Yes, sir," Gerry stood, replied, and then sat down again.

"Well, the case is clear to me. Erastus Black, you are a liar, a cheat, a thief and now a highwayman. You are to be arrested this day and be sent to Van Diemen's Land for a term of fourteen years. However, I doubt you will last that long, as few do. Attempted theft is bad enough, but Highway Robbery is a capital offence. Remove this scum from my presence."

Mr. Black opened his mouth to speak.

Mr. Moffatt raised his hand. "I do not wish to hear a word from you, or I shall make it either Life or Hanging? Your choice!"

Mr. Black shut his mouth.

Mr. Moffatt waited until the soldiers removed the felon, dragging him out to cells below. He cleared the room, leaving only the principal characters of the account and himself, less the criminal. He stood watching until the door shut behind the last soldier. As the door closed, Mr. Moffatt turned to the doctor. "Gerry, what the blooming heck are you doing out here? You're supposed to be at home in good old England, doctoring in the maternity hospital." Harry Moffatt walked down from his chair and over to the doctor. He greeted him as a long-lost friend.

Eddie was standing somewhat agog at the proceeding that had just occurred, and now this? His head thumped. Charles came and stood beside his son and put a steadying hand on his son's shoulder.

The doctor said, "Hi Harry. I came looking for Ned here," nodding towards the Major. "Let's just say he's an old friend from school days at home."

Mr. Moffatt said, "Pull the other one, Gerry. We were at school together; he wasn't."

"No, we were at University together, Harry!" The doctor grinned and looked to the Major, waving the conversation over to the Major.

The Major stepped up. "Sir, now I can introduce myself officially. Oh, I am, or at least was, as you know, Major Edward Grace, but thanks to Gerry's arrival, I now find myself with a different title. I, sir, am now Edward, Tenth Duke of Gracemere." He bowed courteously and smiled sheepishly. "It seems my elder brother had died without issue, and I'm now the Duke. Dash it, Harry, you're not to say a word. Is that clear? Only my friends here know about this."

Mr. Moffatt and the Major had not only known each other but

worked together numerous times in their official capacities; it was not all that unexpected when Mr. Moffatt plonked himself down on his desk and roared with laughter. "Well, this takes the cake, Ned," he laughed again. "Eddie lad, lead us all back to the wedding party your wonderful father has planned. I'll make an announcement about that snivelling cheat and clear all this up. He's the last of the nasty brothers, Ned. His eldest brother, Cyrus, married your friend Amelia. The world is a better place without both of them. Please leave the announcements to me. And no, Ned, I will not mention you nor my friendship with Gerry. However, our wives await gentlemen." He looked to the Major and Gerry. "Well, some of them do."

The six men departed the office laughing. They headed down to the source of the music floating across the air from near the river's edge.

Charles and Eddie were bringing up the rear. They had managed to give their thanks as he passed them by.

Eddie knew he had made a valuable friend that day.

Chapter 16 Party Time

A hush fell as the men walked into the courtyard. As Harry Moffatt threw his arm around Eddie's shoulder, everyone sighed with relief. "I'll explain later; now, let this party get started. The groom has arrived." Harry said in his sonorous, booming voice.

Eddie noticed Jenna standing waiting for him next to the fiddlers on the cart in her beautiful blue gown. His heart swelled as he saw Mrs. Jenkins' roses placed in a bucket of water in the centre of the cart, pride of place. Even she was invited. She was sitting next to Mrs. Meadows, who had said she would keep an eye on her.

The Major was unable to show too much affection in public as their friendship, let alone their relationship, was still a secret.

The fiddlers started up again, and the chatter continued. Eddie left the group and went to Jenna. "I need to have a word with you…" They walked around to the side of the stable.

She was afraid of what he was about to say. A tear rolled down her cheek, but she stood mute, looking at him lovingly.

"Oh, sweetie, no, it's nothing like that," said Ed. "Jen, on the way back on Sunday, I was attacked by some highwaymen. I was hit and nearly knocked out. They searched for any valuables."

She gasped, remembering the vast amount of money he had on him. "Oh no! Are you all right?" She ran her hands over his arms. "What about the money?" she appealed.

"It's all right, sweetness; both survived. I'll tell you the entire story with all the details tonight, but I wanted you to know I'm all right. Mr. Moffatt will outline what occurred and the outcome of today. I didn't want you worried. I have a few days this week with a very sore head, and it's still a bit tender." He bent and showed her the scabbed wound.

She gingerly touched his head and exclaimed, "Oh, my poor Ed. But how did you save the money?"

He told her. "Because James was skittish, I had forgotten to put it in the strongbox. It was still in my pocket. As I got off the cart, I could drop the money pouch in the long grass. When I was hit, I fell onto it, and it was hidden. All they got was the food that your Maa gave me and my bag, as well as a few coins I had in my pocket." He proceeded to tell how the doctor had arrived and scared them off. This was the much-abridged version, and he'd get time later to fill in the gaps after her family had left. He enfolded her into his arms. "I'm fine, really, I am. The creep is now in gaol awaiting transportation to Van Diemen's Land. Let's get back to our party. I love you, Missus Lockley."

She reached up to pull his head down for a kiss. "And I love you too, my husband."

They stood in this embrace for some time until Marc stuck his head around the side of the shed. "Come back, you two. The main guests are missing."

Eddie released her, lovingly kissed the top of her head and said, "Let's go face the crowd." They walked back holding hands and were greeted with "Ooohs" and "Ahhhs" by everyone and much laughter.

On their arrival back, the Major bade them come; they walked over to him, still hand in hand.

Mr. Tindale, the Major, Doctor and Mr. Moffatt were in a huddle.

Mr. Moffatt said, "I'm just about to tell this rowdy mob the proceedings of today. Are you ready to become the town hero boy?" he said to Eddie.

"Gosh, no. Oh, please don't, sir," said Eddie; he blanched. "Anything but that."

"Too late, you already are," said the Major. "On my arrival at the party, I was approached by no less than five different groups. This same man had stolen, swindled or defrauded them; a few more swore that he was up to no good. Even Charlie reported that things had gone missing from the stables. Our Major, being known as a kind man but having retired, no one thought of reporting these things to him. The new Major had very little information to go on and was busy enough with the convicts and soldiers under his control. Because of the odd attire of this man, he was noticed."

The Major had included Mr. Moffatt in these various conversations, and he said, "What a dirty, rotten stinker. Now, I wish I had given him life. I doubt he'll last long in Hobart anyway."

She laughed.

Mr. Moffatt walked over to the cart and was assisted up onto it by some young lads. He clapped his hands but didn't manage to calm the masses.

Charlie saw how useless this attempt was and gave a long, loud whistle with his fingers in his mouth. This worked.

Eddie sat on an upturned half-barrel that the Major had placed next to the cart being used as the stage. Ed tried to look small. He had pulled Jenna onto his lap to hide behind her. "Oh, how I hate the limelight," he said into her back, then groaned.

Soon, silence reined, and Mr. Moffatt began to speak. "As this began so publicly, I thought I may as well finish the saga publicly." He looked around at the crowd of people. Nearly one hundred of the townsfolk were gathered; some he had tried, some he socialised with, and most he knew from one or another walk of life. He began, speaking loudly so all could hear. "As you know, Mr. Erastus Black interrupted the service of our dear friends here. I've known young Eddie since he was a young lad. Many of you have also seen him on his magnificent horse, James."

All nodded, and most said, "Yes."

"Well, it seems Mr. Black wanted his horse returned, but long story short. Black has been charged with various crimes already. However, he may yet have more charges brought against him. I have since heard more stories since my arrival here today. If any have further grievances, please come to my office before noon tomorrow, but that's getting off track." He turned to look down at Eddie, who, by now, had his forehead lying against the middle of Jenna's back, hoping he wasn't visible. "On Friday last week, Eddie was to make a large delivery out to Orchard Hills. As you all know, it's not unusual as we see him making deliveries everywhere. However, on this occasion, he was to stay two days with the Turners before returning home. You only have to look to my right here to see why he might be tempted to be waylaid so." He waved to Jenna.

A roar of laughter went around the listening crowd.

"On Sunday, he harnessed James and his cart and headed home. He made it to nearly halfway when three masked horsemen appeared. One of whom was dressed in dark trousers and a tan jacket. This same criminal then whacked our Eddie with his rifle stock."

Another gasp emanated from the crowd. "Nooo," many said.

Eddie pressed his head harder onto Jenna's back. He groaned again. "Sheesh," he muttered.

She chuckled.

"Well," continued Mr. Moffatt, "Young Eddie here noticed his horse playing up and, in his bloodied stupor, identified the said villain."

"Yeah," shouted one young man.

Mr. Moffatt cleared his throat. "Into this story comes another unknowing hero. Doctor Gerald Winslow-Smythe here." He motioned to the doctor standing next to the Major, "came upon the lad, all bloodied and gore, leaning on his cart and the waylaid steed. The lad, unable to stand alone in his stupor, could still give details of what had occurred. Our good doctor patched up our young friend and brought him home."

The crowd burst out in applause for the doctor. He turned to the crowd and bowed thanks for the acknowledgement but kept silent. A few yelled, "Woo Hoo," to Eddie.

Mr. Moffatt continued. "It turns out said doctor was visiting his good sister at her Orchard Hills Farm near Mulgoa. Suffice to say, our Eddie was in safe hands." Now, motioning to Charles, "His father said he was a sorry sight on arrival home, giving his parents much anxiety."

The large invited group gave a mournful sigh.

"Thankfully, our young blacksmith here is a strong young Adonis. He has bounced back and stands...." He looked down at him, "Err... no sits here today, trying hard to be overlooked. A reluctant hero, but were it not for this young man's strength and ability, the story may well have had a different ending. It may have been one of us attacked by these evildoers. We still have the other two rascals to apprehend. So, dear friends, be on your guard."

Gasps and words of acknowledgement emanated from the watching multitude.

"Now, I'm sure you'd all like to know the verdict."

The crowd all nodded.

"This evildoer appeared before me in my office this very afternoon, as you may all gather. I interviewed some witnesses to the charges against our tall blonde Samson here, and it was...." He paused for effect, "The decision is thus: that Mister Erastus Black, and not Edward Lockley, be convicted of theft, highway robbery, defaulting on a debt, abandoning his horse, and also for attempted horse theft. He officially forfeited the horse for non-payment of goods and services and has no further claim on it."

A cheer erupted from the crowd.

"Further to the conviction, I have sentenced him to a term of fourteen years in Van Diemen's Land. However, since my arrival this evening, I have since heard more complaints against this felon. I will hear those complaints tomorrow. His sentence may yet be increased to hard labour. For those with further information, please be at the Courthouse at ten o'clock tomorrow."

The crowd cheered and whooped for joy.

Jenna stood up from Eddie's lap as Mr. Moffatt had called Eddie, the doctor, the Major, and Mr. Tindale to the cart. "Please show your appreciation to these men who have cleared society of one rotten scoundrel."

They stood in front of the cart, and each bowed.

"So, James and his extraordinary owner will remain one of the sights of Parramatta," said Mr. Moffatt.

Eddie blushed, but he joined the men and bowed thanks to the watching friends who surrounded them.

"I'm sure, like me, many of you will continue to admire the carriage man and beast in this pair: Ebony and Ivory. A joy to behold." Mr. Moffatt was quite pleased with his oratory performance.

More applause ensued from the guests.

Mr. Moffatt was carefully lifted down from his elevated height. He stood back and watched Eddie, smiling.

Mr. Tindale walked over to Eddie and shook his hand, followed by the Major, then the Doctor. Many others queued and did likewise.

Jenna stood beside him, so proud of her hero husband. Also, so pleased that he was not more injured.

Soon, another keg was tapped, and more ale and cider flowed. The voices rose louder and louder. The laughter increased, and the fiddlers played. Most of the town of Parramatta turned out to see their favourite young blacksmith marry his lady. Most had known Eddie since birth. All knew the Lockley family as a whole and liked them all.

Old Tom took it upon himself to be a butler of sorts for the afternoon and walked around refilling glasses with a beaten-up old jug. Bill and Molly Miller had made him bathe and gave him a set of clean clothing for the event. Now scrubbed clean, as he walked past Mrs. Jenkins, he bowed before her and took and kissed her hand. She was shocked but delighted at his action.

As the hours passed, people came and went. The gift table was overwhelmed with homemade, gourmet items for the pantry and household items. The food was never-ending, as was the grog. After dark, rum barrels were brought out and opened after the fire was lit and the meal was eaten. Toasts to the happy couple were made from the cart.

Mr. Moffatt stayed for the proceedings and became the Master of Ceremony, as everyone could hear his booming voice over the commotion.

Eddie stayed off the rum as his head was still somewhat tender. The noise of the cheering made his ears ring. The ale was strong enough; he poured out the glass of rum he had been handed and headed for the fresh ginger beer. He wanted to remember this night forever. He never wished to let go of Jenna. She was his anchor, his Jenna, now and forever. She was not what you'd consider a small person, but compared to him, she was petite though tough as nails. She only came up to his shoulder but could put an argumentative person in their place with a few words or even a look. Yet she oozed compassion and care. She had cried at an injured animal and would reach out to the unloved and hurt people without blinking an eye. She didn't care what society thought of her actions. She knew she was doing something right, no matter what people thought. She would be there before anyone else moved if something needed to be done and no one else was stepping up. Mrs. Jenkins was a point in case. She was a changed woman. The gossiping and cattiness had stopped, and she'd started finding ways to help other lonely people. Jenna's care had won the day.

Jenna's laughing, liquid, honey-gold eyes often danced with emotion. Her long, light brown hair curled at the ends into ringlets and twisted around his heart. He'd often sit just spinning his fingers around her curls. They were so soft. Her skin, although suntanned, was like honeyed velvet. Her touch was gentle and loving. His heart would melt when she stroked his cheek, as she often was wont to do. She was beautiful. However, her beauty was not ostentatious nor pretentious. Her loveliness was from deep within; her 'joy of life' bubbled into her life. Tonight, her honey-gold locks encircled her heart-shaped face and generous smile. She was loved, and she was loving. Now, she was his. He looked at her in awe, unaware his devoted mother was also watching him.

Sal had sat on a log with a tankard of cider, watching her second son. The emotions of love and passion were clearly visible as he eyed his new wife. It was a sight a mother always wanted to see in her child's face. Finding a life partner was wonderful. They would be blessed if they could be as happy as she was with Charles. Her eyes drifted over to Charles; she met his across the barn.

He smiled and blew her a kiss.

Their bond was as tight today as it had been when they first got to know each other so many years ago.

Charles started making his way through the tangle of guests. He had not seen her for some time as she had been busy in the kitchen. The food was now served and eaten; she was resting. As he threaded his way across to her, he grabbed a tankard of cider and another of ale from Anna's drink tray as she passed him. Holding the drinks above his head, he struggled through the crush of people to Sal's side. He sank beside her and said, "Hello, love, what a fabulous day."

Sal laid her head on his shoulder and thought back through the years. "Oh Charles, now two of our children are married. I do hope they will both be as happy as we have been. With Anna marrying Tim next year, that will be three. Each has chosen well. I love Bertie and Jenna like they are our own. I feel Tim already is one of our brood. Charlie, too, is sorted, as Gracie has him well in hand. We have to keep praying for Wills and Luke. I'm sure God is already working in the lives of their future partners." She turned and looked lovingly into Charles's face.

He bent and softly touched his lips with hers. "My darling Sal, how could our children not desire the love that we have? They have seen other parents fighting and drinking." He paused, letting thoughts drift through his mind. "Our life has not been easy. We don't have expensive things, just the basics, but we have enough. Our family is loving and caring. They have seen this lived out in our lives and have learnt from it."

Charles looked down at her. Her eyes were misting. "Sal, you have been, and still are, a fabulous mother. I could never have asked for better. If we were still over there, we could have both been living on the streets with no hope or home. Here…" His hand swept the sky. "…here is a land of opportunity for anyone. Here, you don't have to be born into a good family; you must be prepared to work hard. This colony may have started with people being brought here against their will, stolen from their families and loved ones, never to see them or even hear from them again. Our children will have opportunities beyond the imagination of our families still at home." Charles stopped. He looked down at her again and lifted her chin, "Sal. This is home. It has been home for years, and I've never really thought about this before. I no longer yearn to return; I no longer regret being sent here. England is no longer home; from now on, it's just England, but never home again." Again, he bent, and their lips touched in first a gentle kiss, but his arm tightened about her as his kiss deepened. "Oh, Sal, I do love you so," he murmured.

She drew back and stroked her hand along his cheek, now bristling with whiskers. She rested her head again on his chest. "Yes, Charles, this is home."

The fiddlers had stopped playing some time before Charles had come over to Sal.

The chatter surrounding them was dying down.

Charlie and Marc elbowed through the packed crowd toward Eddie and Jenna, who were again sitting on the upturned barrel.

"Oh," exclaimed Eddie as his eyes widened. He then grinned.

Jenna hadn't seen anything as she stared at Eddie's face. She had one arm around his neck, stroking his face lovingly with her thumb. She whispered, "What, Ed?" She looked around and saw Marc approaching with a determined look. She giggled. "Ed, are they coming for us? I think it must be time to leave. Are you sure it's all right to stay tonight at the Tindale's place?" she said just as the boys arrived at where they were seated.

"Yes, sweetie," he said quickly.

"Ready?" said Charlie.

Eddie nodded. "Where is he?"

Marc said, "I've tied him at the back of the shed."

"Huh?" said Jenna.

Eddie laughed, "You don't think we're going to walk up there, do you, my queen?"

Bertie walked around the corner of the shed with James saddled and ready for them.

Sal and Martha had already taken their clothes to Tindale's guest room. All they now had to do was get there.

Ed stood up, placing her on the ground in front of him. "Come on, my love; we're going home."

As Bertie brought James around to them, the guests parted as the magnificent black steed appeared. James seemed to know that whatever was happening was necessary as he high-stepped his way into the yard with his neck bent high. He was a sight to behold.

Even when the guests started shouting and clapping, he stood unfazed. Charlie and the boys had plaited his mane and tail, and the girls had poked in flowers. His reins shone with polish, and his coat brushed to gleaming.

Eddie and Jenna walked over to him. "Hello, boy," said Eddie, "You've caused us a memorable day today." He pawed the ground in acknowledgement, but his ears were forward.

Jenna was standing at his head, and he started nuzzling her. "Yes, I love you too, dear James."

Both sets of parents came to the couple. Jenna hugged her parents, Martha, with tears in her eyes. Jack enveloped her in a bear hug. "Don't be a stranger, love. Come with Ed when he does deliveries."

"I will," she said, wiping away a few tears of mixed sadness and joy.

Ed shook hands with his father, then hugged him. "Thanks for everything, Dar. I'll remember," he whispered. He was looking over to Jenna and smiling. For his mother, he wiped away a tear from her cheek with his thumb. "Mama, I'm going to be living just up the hill. You'll get sick of seeing us," he said.

"That's not it, Eddie Bear. I'm just thinking about when you were a baby, and now you're married. That time has gone too fast. I teared up just scrubbing your neck again yesterday. Knowing it would be for the last time." She sniffed. "Just know I love you, and we, your father and I, are so proud of you; so very proud." She reached up and stroked his cheek. "You'll always be a baby to me. No matter how big you grow."

Eddie gently laid his arm around her shoulders and drew her to him. "Mama, you are the best mother a boy could have ever wished for." He bent and kissed her cheek, wiped away another tear, and then turned to Jenna.

"Ready, love?" He asked.

Jenna nodded. He lifted her lightly up and placed her sideways onto the saddle. She settled herself and leaned forward on James' neck. Eddie hopped up behind her and drew her gently back onto his lap. With her in his arms, he said, "Home, James!"

The crowd parted, cheered as they left, then closed again as they stood, waving goodbye.

James walked steadily up the hill to the forge.

They would stay in their new room at the back of the Tindale's place for their first night, which would become their home. James knew the way, and it was just as well; his riders were otherwise occupied.

They arrived at the forge, and Eddie dismounted; he flicked James's reins over the hitching rail. Then he turned back to Jenna and lifted her down. Rather than putting her down, he lifted her effortlessly from James' back. He carried her to the rear of the house to the flat where they were to live. Her arms wrapped around his neck, and the short trip took much longer than it normally would as Jenna waylaid him with kisses, pulling his head to hers as they walked.

He gently kicked the door open and carried her inside. "Welcome home, Missus Lockley," he said as he put her down. "I'll just light the lamp. Stand still until I get it sorted."

She heard the scratch of the tinderbox, and a flame flickered. Soon, the room was bathed in a soft, warm glow. She looked around. Although she had been here before, she saw that her mother had added some of the gifts they had been given last week at the Emu Plains party. The new tablecloth and some other things had been placed on the shelf. On the bed against the far wall was the beautiful blanket they had been given, along with the large blue jug and washbasin set, some mugs and other nick-nacks. She sighed, home, our new place." Mrs. Tindale had added some water and glasses and some fruit. There was a large hessian bag containing the potatoes from the Murphy's.

Eddie turned to her after he put the lamp on its hook on a chain. He pulled a cord, and the lamp lifted.

"Oh," she said, "That's clever. Look, it lights the whole room," she said.

They each needed to use the outside privy, and she went first, taking a small lantern with her, then on her return, took the opportunity of Eddie's absence to divest herself of some of the petticoats she wore. She laid them on a chair and turned down the coverings of the bed. She was about to tackle the buttons on her dress when Ed returned.

He came in freshly washed. "Hmm, you're right. I like the light; it highlights the entire room, doesn't it?… and I like what it shows me."

He gently took her in his arms, bent his head and kissed her. She wrapped her arms around his neck and responded accordingly.

Ed pulled the pins from her hair; it tumbled down. Then Jenna felt him fiddling with the buttons on her dress. He signed in frustration.

She giggled and murmured, "Ed, only every third button is real. The rest are false, which makes it easier to do up."

He chuckled, "Makes this easier to undo too," knowing the trick, as he flicked them open quickly. Her gown fell to the floor, and she stepped out of it. He picked her up and carried her to the bed, laying her on it and quickly divesting himself of his own clothing while she watched in awe. She had seen him shirtless while working. He removed the rest of her attire, kissing her gently as he did so. Then he joined her on the bed. She reached for him as he lay beside her. "Ed, I just want to say Maa told me that it hurts the first time, and I know about that, but I don't want you to worry; we'll learn together." She stroked back his fair hair before pulling his head down to meet her lips.

Ed looked down at the lovely lady in his arms. He would hurt her as little as possible. "Just take it easy," said Dar had said. "Cor, that's going to be hard."

She pulled him on top of her. He did not want to crush her. She wrapped her legs around his waist and pulled him close. He heard a gasp, so he lay still, and then she moved. Oh, how she moved.

The crickets were singing outside, and the soft crooning of love was the only sound to be heard inside, but the young couple inside had fallen asleep in an exhausted tangle of arms. All was well. Around midnight, Jenna awoke and lay looking down at her love in the lamplight. They had forgotten to turn it off. She was about to get out to do so when an arm reached out to draw her to him.

"Leave it; I like looking at you," he said huskily.

She abandoned the idea and turned to him with equal passion. Watching his face was beautiful. She blushed at the thought but wiggled so that he moved over her.

They fell asleep again, still entwined. They woke with the song of the first birds. The lamp had long ago burnt itself out, but the soft dawn light was enough to see.

Eddie woke first; her breath was soft on his cheek. His arm was around her, and her face turned to him. He turned gently to watch her sleep. He remembered the first time she had slept in his arms. It was only the day after they had met. His desire for this woman was astounding. He could not resist moving a strand of hair from her face. He gently touched her cheek as he did so, and she opened her eyes.

"Hello, lover," she said sleepily. "Aren't you glad we don't need to get up yet?"

Eddie nodded, too stunned to move. Eddie's eyes widened as she settled herself on him. "Dar said nothing about this," he said.

She chuckled.

He said, "And I thought last night was magic." This girl, his girl, was amazing.

Sated, they rolled over, exhausted once more and slept again in each other's arms. Dar's phrase 'more than once' came to his mind, and he smiled again. No one told him marriage was this good; no wonder Mama called it the 'joys of marriage' and, oh so worth waiting for. He smiled as he fell asleep with her in his arms once more.

The next time they woke, the sun was well up.

Eddie was hungry, and he tried to sneak out of bed. He had been awakened by a noise outside. Still naked, he padded to the door and peeked outside. A covered basket sat at the door, and he reached out carefully and brought it inside. He peaked inside, "Yum. Sweet porridge and bread." His mouth watered until he turned, and a shaft of sunlight fell across the bed.

Jenna stirred in the bed. Her arms were thrown above her head, her naked body lying in the sunlight. He looked and could not look away. Hunger for food forgotten, he climbed not so quietly back into bed. They really should leave soon, but why hurry?

She stirred and reached for him in her slumber. As she pulled his head down to her, she mumbled, "Again, please, I can't get enough of you." He willingly obliged.

Food could wait, and so could travel. This time, they did not fall back asleep; Jenna was also hungry by now and could smell the freshly cooked bread. Finally, they got out of bed, making it together, both still naked.

Ed turned to Jenna. "Jen, Dar told me when I wash my privates, not to use soap as it burns you, so you wash first. I won't use soap on those bits. Something to do with lye or caustic soda or something."

She nodded and said, "I know. It really hurts. Yes, it truly burns, and sometimes it's hard for girls to talk that sort of thing to men."

He nodded in reply. "Tell me if there's anything else I need to know, love."

"Okay, I will, but nothing comes to mind," Jenna said.

"Mrs. Tindale has left a kettle of hot water for us too. The jug and bowl are over on the sideboard." He left her to wash as he pulled on some trousers and went to use the privy outside.

By the time he returned, she had washed and was nearly dressed. "Can you do me up, please, husband?" She turned her back to him.

He slid his hands under her dress to cup her breasts. "Like this?" he said.

She giggled. "No, but I like it." She did not wear corsets, just a camisole.

He removed his hands and did up her dress. Then spun her around and lowered his head to her lips. "My turn to wash. Out you go. Before I change my mind."

She quickly kissed him before she ducked outside to the privy herself.

He washed while she was out, threw the water onto the flowers outside and cleaned up. He then prepared the food, ready to eat, from the tiny table in their room. By the time she returned, he was dressed and sitting at the table, ready for their breakfast. They sat shoulder to shoulder, eating the tepid porridge. They had no idea what time it was and didn't care. Occasionally, they fell into a comfortable silence, each remembering the uninhibited passion of the night just passed, a glance, a smile or a touch lovingly for the other. Eddie said, "Do you still wish to camp for the rest of the week? We could stay here if you want to."

Jenna smiled, "How about one more night here before we leave? I look forward to returning, but I do want to be with you. It's almost too late to leave today, anyway. It would be early afternoon before we left." She stood to take their plates to wash them. As she passed him, he reached out and took her around the waist. "We might have to occupy ourselves somehow then. Any ideas?"

"Oh," was all he could muster. He buried his head in her neck. This is so good, he thought.

She looked sleepily at him. "Let's go back to bed," she murmured on his neck.

"But…" he smiled, "Oh, who cares?"

He lifted her off him and carried her back to the bed. Without disrobing, he lay beside her, drawing her close, and they slept. If this is marriage, he thought before drifting off, he wouldn't have much time for work. But Dar was right; they didn't get much sleep last night.

A slight breeze blew the curtains of their window. They slept on, oblivious to the heat outside. The exhaustion and utter contentment gave them the deep slumber they both needed.

Late afternoon, they stirred again. Eddie looked at Jenna again as she was waking. He raised one eyebrow questioningly, and she nodded. He reached for her and pulled her on top of him again. She giggled. Although they were still dressed, it was almost more sensual than being naked. The touch was different, but the pleasure was the same.

"How about we go for a walk he said. I need to do something other than just lay around. Not that lying around with you isn't nice. If we go down the riverbank, there are some nice spots where we can be alone. That's if you want to be." Ed said. "But don't think you have to."

She walked to him, running her fingers through his unruly blonde hair. Her fingers stopped when they touched his wound. "Whither thou goest dear… I go' from now on, my love. I might need you again." She chuckled and reached down to close the flap on his trousers. He had forgotten about that. "You'd better cover yourself, though."

He looked down. "Whoops," he chuckled. Her drawers still lay on the back of the chair. "Stay as you are, just in case, then." Knowing she still had not reached for her wagon.

"Oh, I intend to," she said saucily.

He reached for some cider; it was warm, but he didn't care. It had been in the basket; his thirst was great, and he poured two tankards.

Jenna, too, also downed hers quickly. Handing it back to him, he refilled and swallowed the next one as well. He did the same.

"Ahh," he said. "Ready to go?" Eddie collected two towels, which he threw over his shoulder.

They snuck out the door, ensuring no one was at the forge or in sight. They walked down the back path towards the river edge.

James whinnied in his stable that he had heard them. He wasn't impressed they were going without him. Mr. Tindale said he would deal with him when he returned last night.

Mr. Tindale looked up when James whinnied from under the tree outside the forge. He saw the young couple disappearing down his secret track to the river. He often took this track to go fishing and occasionally took Eddie and Charlie down there. At the end of the path, there was a nice mossy area that he'd cleared and set up as a comfortable spot for him to while away relaxing hours fishing over the years. Margaret liked fresh fish; he'd gone often, sometimes alone, but more often with her. There was a small sandy area, and on a hot day, he and Margaret would go down and have a private dip in the water. Well, that idea was out for today.

Jenna followed Ed down the track. It was wide enough, but the scrub was thick on both sides and was well hidden. "Ed, who built this? Where does it go?"

Ed explained that Mr. Tindale had occasionally taken him fishing down here. It was his secret spot and very private. Even the ferry did not come up this far. Only the occasional canoe passed by, and the friendly natives often waved a hello. As a child, Ed and Charlie had made friends with many of the local aboriginal children. Although he didn't see them often, they would still wave.

It was the perfect place for a summer assignation. They arrived after about twenty minutes gentle stroll, and Ed threw the towels on the big log on the riverbank. It had washed down in a flood many years ago, and the boys had pulled up to its current position while the floodwater was still high. It formed a fabulous seat, but as it was over knee high and about ten foot long, it gave exceptional privacy behind it, but where it had settled meant you could walk around it and access the beach.

By the time they had reached the spot, both were hot and sweaty. Ed started peeling off his shirt and trousers. "Feel like a dip?" he said.

She nodded but said, "I can't. I have nothing to wear."

"Oh, don't worry about that; just leave your chemise and petticoat on." He helped undo the buttons on her dress, and it dropped to the ground. She grabbed it and threw it on the log. He put out his hand and led her into the water. Once there, he removed his trousers and threw them onto the shore.

"Oooh," she said and followed him into the water. She could swim like a fish from her days on the Nepean River.

"Come for a swim," said Eddie, "You can stand over here." She swam out to where he was. She went straight to Eddie and wrapped her legs around his waist, her arms around his neck. Her petticoat, of course, not only had hindered her swimming but had floated up, and he undid the strings, and it too was thrown onto the beach, her chemise he left on just in case someone did appear.

"Eddie, I had no idea married life was like this. It's soooo good," she said with a grin.

The coolness of the water surrounding them was a delight on their heated skins. The water washed over them as they laughed and played like young children. They had arrived back at the sandy bank. There was a splash in the water not far behind them, and they could see a school of fish jumping.

Eddie got out and grabbed the towels. "Quick, Jenna! Come out."

She, too, ran out, and he wrapped her in the other towel. As they walked to the back of the log, a large fin surfaced just where they had been only moments before.

She squealed as she hid behind the log. "Eddie, did you see that? It's a blooming shark."

Eddie grinned. "Yep, saw that, it's why I said, quick. As soon as I saw the fish jump in different directions as they did, I knew something was under them." He had wrapped the towel around his waist. The blonde curls on his chest glistened in the sunlight. He bent to pick up Jenna's petticoat and his pants and spread them over the log. "These should be dry in about half an hour."

She beckoned him with her finger and pointed to the mossy area behind the log. "We could have a rest if you're tired." She looked at him coyly.

"Again?" he said. "You're insatiable."

"You're very desirable, and I've waited a year for this. I could eat you all day, and I intend to try to wear you out." She lay on her towel most provocatively. "You could always just sleep, of course," she said, patting the towel beside her. "I don't take up much room."

He, of course, joined her on the towel, and she snuggled him for a while until she started playing with his chest hair. For a while, they dozed in the summer heat. She woke with a fly buzzing her ear. "Eddie, I'm so glad we waited. I feel that... well, that I'm bonded to you now." She traced around the outside of his nipple. It sent tingles through him.

He was trying to concentrate on her comments. It was hard as he was sleepy. "I'm glad too, sweeting. I certainly never believed marriage to be anything like this. I thought that if we could do it about once a week, that would be great. When Dar said fun, it never occurred to me that it was anything like this. But I had no idea."

Her hand crept lower, tracing patterns down his abdomen. His stomach doing summersaults, he groaned with desire. He couldn't take her again; she was delicious. Oh, he so wanted her. Dar had said not to demand...but she was doing this to him. "Oh, Jen, if you don't stop soon, I won't be answerable for what happens next."

Her hand moved lower. "Who said I'll stop you?" With that, her hand moved up the inside of his leg.

Heat raced through him. He rolled on top of her, "I warned you."

She giggled. "See, I got what I wanted after all." She drew his head down and nibbled his lips before kissing him.

Half an hour later, Eddie was now lying beside her and nearly asleep again. He was instantly alert. He said quietly, "I hear voices, Jen. Maybe this spot is known by others. Quick, let's get dressed." They scrambled for their clothing. He had finished doing up her dress, and they were innocently sitting on the log on their towels as Charlie and the boys emerged from the path.

"Ohh! Hi Ed and Jenna, sorry; I didn't know anyone else knew about this spot, but I forgot you would. I thought you were going heading away for the week anyway?" Charlie asked, somewhat embarrassed.

"Oh, we are," said Jenna, "But we slept in, and by the time we awoke, it was too hot to leave. We're leaving tomorrow."

Eddie nodded. He looked at Luke and Wills. "You're planning a swim, eh? I'd skip this spot today. There's a shark chasing fish out just there. We've just been here for a few hours." Pointing to a spot not far off the beach. "Jen and I had been watching the fish jump when a great swirl and a huge fin appeared. I wouldn't go in today."

Wills and Luke stood off to the side silently. Both had towels around their necks.

Luke cursed.

Charlie said, "Luke, don't swear, especially in front of ladies."

Luke blushed, "Sorry, Jenna. But I'm so hot."

Jenna merely laughed. "Don't growl so, Charlie. I have two little brothers, too." She turned to the boys, "We'll go, and you can have a quick dip. I would not stay in long, but the fish went a while ago, and although the shark may still be around, I think you could all at least get a dunking and hop out." She ruffled Luke's hair as she spoke. He was going to be a clone of Charlie, tall and blonde. Wills was more similar to Eddie. What a family! All were so handsome. She turned to Eddie, "Ed, let's leave our secret spot in your brothers' hands. We'd better head back and pack up for an early start tomorrow. You haven't told me where we are going yet, only that we shall be camping," she said.

"All I'm saying is it's out Windsor way. The rest is a surprise." He grinned. "Go to it, lads. We've been here a while anyway."

He put out his arm to Jenna. "Come on, love, you're right; we had better go and pack for tomorrow." She walked into his outstretched arm, and he wrapped it around her shoulder. He had their towels in his hand, and they waved as they left.

"Be careful, boys," Jenna said. "See you next week."

They walked back up the path until Ed had to drop his arm from her shoulder as the path narrowed, but he kept hold of her hand as they walked.

After they left, Wills found his voice. "Coo, did you see Eddie's face? He looks so different. Sort of content, but embarrassed too. I bet they'd been for a swim, too."

Luke chuckled. "But they only had towels."

Wills turned and gave him a dirty look, then raised an eyebrow. "That's all we have."

"Ohhhh," said Luke. "Oh yuck!" He put his fingers in his ears. "Don't say nuffin' more. La la la. Don't wanna hear."

Charlie laughed as he discarded his clothing on the log. It is evident that they hadn't brought anything to swim in either. The boys followed his example. Before they went in, they surveyed the water. No ripples, fish or swirls. "The last one in is…" said Charlie as he dived in and then underwater.

Both followed, but none went far from the beach. Knowing a shark was nearby, the planned afternoon of lazing by the water lost its gloss. Sharks were not something any of them liked. After lounging on the beach for a while, they all went in for a second dip, dressed, and headed home.

Chapter 17   The Honeymoon

On arrival back at the room, Jenna had changed out of her salty clothing and washed the still-damp undergarments. She packed what they thought they would need for a few days camping. Eddie mentioned it was near a river, so she packed a smock she had previously worn swimming at home. There was not much in their little room yet, but not much was required. Food and a bed, and they were content. Eddie was borrowing the wagon from the Inn, and James would take them. He'd arranged to collect it the morning after the wedding, but he knew his father would not worry if they didn't turn up. Charlie would let him know they would come tomorrow instead. Ed only had to take James down and harness him up. Dar and Mama had added bedding, cooking implements, and food. All they needed was their clothing.

Jenna chuckled, "They wouldn't need much of that either."

By the time evening came, they were both hungry. There was enough bread left for a snack, but Eddie and Jenna were now really hungry. They discussed what they would do for food when there was a knock on the door. Mrs. Tindale stood there with a pot of stew and a berry pie. Behind her was Mr. Tindale with a large jug of cider. "We were once a young married couple, too. We thought you'd need some more sustenance." He grinned as he handed over the jug to Eddie. Jenna took the stew and pie from Mrs. Tindale, thanking her immensely. As Mr. Tindale turned to go back to the main house, his arm slid along Margaret's shoulder. "Oh, to be young again," he said to her. Margaret raised her face to him, and he quickly kissed her as they walked back to the house. Both were only in their forties and were sad they had never been blessed with children.

It was such a beautiful evening that Ed and Jen sat outside and ate the stew on the bread left over from lunch. They followed that with the berry pie. Jenna took in the remains of the meal inside and brought out tankards of cider. They sat in the moonlight, listening to the slithering, burring and chirping of the night insects and animals. Owls swooshed low overhead, chasing some poor critter. They were on the large rocky outcrop overlooking the river. They could see some dim lights from the town. They watched as myriads of flying foxes took off from their roost and flew to their new feeding grounds. A shooting star streaked across the sky.

Jenna was sitting between Eddie's legs, her back leaning against his chest, his arms around her, resting on her stomach. He was relishing their closeness. How could he be so blessed? They discussed God and their beliefs about him. "Ed, could there be other beings on those distant stars?" They decided probably not. "How could our prayers be listened to by one being so big and so far away and still listen to every prayer?" But listened to, they were. Jenna mused, "You know, Ed, we are trying to put God in a box that we've made too small for Him. If God made the world, then surely He's taken our prayers into account. We both know He listens." They would leave the how-to Him. Their Faith and Trust in Him were complete. They did not need to understand, just trust. It was enough.

They discussed children, as they had before, how many, and what names they liked. She laughed jokingly that she could already be carrying one. Eddie told Jenna of his dream for the future. "One day, Jen, I want to have a factory, a foundry and maybe a shop for them both, one that makes iron things that can be poured in bulk, not all handmade. I want to be able to use the minerals found in this raw country and make these tools from its own ground." He paused, still thinking. "We have a start in this country that if we had been born in England, we could never even dream about. I do not want to be rich, although that would be nice. I want us to grow with this country. Our parents have used the adversity thrust upon them; they have turned it to their advantage. I would like to continue that. To grow, to bring our children into this new world and be strong." After some time, he continued, "The foundry will have to wait until they find more coal and some minerals in this fine country. So I was thinking about a proper store for the smithy shop. Instead of having the stock at the forge? What do you think?"

Jenna turned to look at him as he stopped speaking. "If that is what you want, my husband, then that is what we'll aim for. I'll work my hardest to help as long as I am alive. Mr. Tindale is amazing that he's brought you into partnership with him; it's an incredible start. You could start by bringing in more help, like Wills, Luke, Sammy or one of my brothers, maybe even them all. Robbie, Bertie's brother, has been working a bit in the saddlery, but he's really skilled with making fancy bits and bobs for the harnesses. He might also be interested in doing a few days a week at the forge. Liza said that every time he sees some fancy harness, he hangs around to offer to hold the horse; he can copy the designs. She said he's also designing things himself. Working at the forge could help him, too."

Eddie said, "Jen, how do you know all this? You've hardly met Robbie."

"Oh, I listen, Ed. I look and listen a lot," she continued, snuggling back against his chest. "Liza talks about him often. He's quiet, but he doesn't let much past him. I'm a bit like that, so I noticed him. You know, Wills is a bit like this, too. He's in Luke's shadow. He may be older, but he's bright and quiet. I'd like to work out some way to send him to school like you were, both of them. Do you think we could manage it?"

Ed sat upright, nearly knocking her off the log. "Cripes, I know what I have to tell you. I can now that we're married. I was sworn to secrecy until then. But I only found out some of the details two nights ago."

She turned to look at him. "What do you mean? About your accident, well, attack? Yes, I want to know." She settled back against his chest again as he began the entire story, with nothing left out this time.

When Ed got to the bit about who the Major actually was, he stopped and turned her head to his. "Jen, you have to promise that you will not say anything until he gives you leave to do so. This is vitally important, do you understand?"

She nodded, saying, "Of course, but what do you mean?"

"Jen, when the doctor arrived, it was no accident that he was here in the colony. He came from England to look for the Major. Only that's not who he knew him as. They were, are, actually, friends from childhood. Doctor Winslow-Smythe brought news that the Major's father died five years ago and oldest brother died two years ago."

"Oh, the poor Major," she said.

"Well, it goes a little deeper than that. Do you know that in England, the oldest son of the Toffs gets everything? The rest of the sons only get an allowance and a bit of a title called a courtesy title. The Major didn't want that, so he didn't use his real name when he enlisted. He also argued with his older brother. His family only knew he had come here; that's all he'd told them. But there was no one registered under his real name. They couldn't send his allowance; he wanted nothing from them. He has his pay, but that was all. When he wrote to his mother when friends went home, he only wrote as 'Ned' with no return address. He apparently left a sealed letter in his file in case something happened to him. It was for his mother. As he's still alive, it was not opened." He paused. "I'm getting a bit long-winded, but there is a point. When the doctor recognised him, he explained all this but then dropped a bombshell. The Major had figured that his father would have died by now. He thought his brother would have had children well before this. Remember, he'd been out of contact for two decades. The Major's brother had been married for nigh on twenty-five years. The brother never had a child. So..." he took a breath "...so the Major is now the Duke. His real title is Edward, Tenth Duke of Gracemere. I'm unsure how to address him officially, but he just wants us to still call him Major."

Jenna spun around. "He's what? A Duke? You're kidding, aren't you? A real live English Duke." She could hardly see his face now but knew from his tone that what he'd told her was true.

"Let me finish; there's more," Eddie said.

"More than that? Seriously?" said Jenna, sitting and gazing at his face.

"Oh yes, there's more; we're getting to some good bits." He kissed her before continuing. She drew away and again looked at him intently. Eddie continued the story. "Well, apparently, the Major moved to his current house after retirement because of the lovely blonde widow we both know, Mrs. Meadows. Well, unbeknownst to any of us, things had developed somewhat between them. They kept it secret, even from us, but they have been courting since she came out of mourning. Because he was only a Major and already retired, he had little money and no prospects. He would not progress their relationship. Obviously, both wanted more. All this happened on Monday night when I was asleep after being hit. I missed the telling of this, but because I'm involved a bit, the Major, doctor, and Mrs. Meadows arrived on Tuesday with part two. Only Mama, Dar and I were there."

Jenna was intrigued. "And…?"

"And, this is where it gets good," he continued. "After the Major had found out who he now was, he hot-footed it to Mrs. Meadows and proposed that very night. She accepted him, but he intentionally didn't tell her who he was. So she accepted him, thinking him still a retired soldier. He waited until they were at our place on Tuesday and told her in front of us all." He stopped rethinking the entire episode. "We didn't know what to expect, but rather than stress, she merely chuckled. She said, 'Oh, Edward, it seems neither of us has been fully honest with each other'."

"Huh?" said Jenna.

Ed looked down at Jenna, "Jen, she's Lady Christina Meadows, daughter of an Earl, Rivendale, no Riverdell, I think. Well, something like that. My head was spinning anyway. After that, things got a bit complicated, but the long and short of it is they are getting married on Christmas Day after the service. It's to be secret, but we're all to be there."

He felt Jen nod. "Okay, but how do you fit in?" she asked.

"Well, this is the bit I only found out on Friday night. It wasn't just Mr. Tindale who sent me to school, but the Major, too. He paid my tuition, and Mr. Tindale arranged my board with his sister and covered my costs. You see, I was named after the Major and Mama's grandfather Eamon (that's Edward in Irish), and because of him, Dar got his 'Ticket of Leave' your Pa, too. He always was very good to me as we share a birthday. He figured he'd never have children himself and wanted to do something for me. Looking back, I should have realised he singled me out, but he was subtle. I never guessed it. I haven't spoken to Mr. Tindale yet as all this happened the night before the wedding. Then there was the fuss over James. Believe it or not, it nearly slipped my mind. Jen, this is why Charlie got him to witness our wedding. We have a Duke officially sponsor us with his approval. It was the least we could do. Did you see how he signed? It just says, 'Gracemere'." Ed smiled. "It's why he looked at me and grinned. It was the very first time he signed his title."

She was like Eddie was when he first heard the story; she, too, was silent. Words seemed to have been sucked out of her. "Eddie, Oh, Ed. Really? Is this all true? Our first son will be named after you both, then." She said excitedly, "Oh, Ed, Mrs. Meadows is young. Young enough to have children. She's only about ten years older than me, maybe a bit more. Oh, I hope they have children. Wouldn't that be so wonderful?" She stopped talking, thinking. "Oh, Ed, they would be the same age as our children. Isn't that funny?" It had grown late, and by the time the story had finished, they had been sitting outside for a few hours. All the lights had been turned out, bar their own. The stars were out, and they saw a couple of small shooting starts.

Eddie thanked God for blessing him with such a wonderful wife. They sat outside with his arms again wrapped around her waist. She was leaning back against his chest, her head against his neck. "Oh, Ed, I love being married to you. I just wanted to say that. I look forward to having your babies and, well, everything."

"Talking of children, Jenna... it's time for bed again, isn't it?" He stood, pulled her up and carried her inside. He didn't bother lighting the lamp; there was enough light from the moon. He laughingly threw her on the bed; she squealed and slapped her hand over her mouth. She was giggling loudly. Both divested themselves from their clothing; he climbed in beside her. "We have an early morning, but I must say good night properly, wife." He took her in his arms and took possession of her lips.

She sighed delightedly. "Yes, husband, mine," she voiced in mock obedience. She reached up for him. Sometime later, they snuggled down to sleep in utter exhaustion, still entwined in each other's arms. The night passed peacefully.

The screech of cockatoos in the tree outside their room awoke them in the pre-dawn gloom. Ed looked at his slumbering wife, again lifting a wisp of hair from her face. "Hmmm," she said, "Morning, husband mine." She reached across to his face and stroked his bristly chin. "I'd say kiss me, but I'd end up with a rash again. Oh, who cares?" She leaned across him and greeted him passionately. They started their day with a little more than the loving embrace she had promised. "Sweeting, I'd love to stay here all day doing this again, but if we're going, we'd better get moving." He mumbled against her neck.

She reached over to nibble his lip and kiss him, then rolled off him and crawled out of bed. "Meanie," she said.

He pulled on his shirt and trousers and plodded out to the privy. Jenna donned her now dry camisole, petticoat and dress, leaving off her corset as it would be too hot to wear such constricting clothing. She stuffed her remaining things into their duffle bag. She noticed Ed had packed a nightshirt and laughed. He had also added some tattered shorts. She added a hairbrush and a few other items she needed, including a drawstring bag that she shoved at the bottom. Her monthly menses were due at the end of the week, but she was hoping she would get through this week without them. For once, she hoped they would be late. She was as yet too embarrassed to mention this to Ed; however, as he had sisters, he was sure he knew what it was about. He walked in just as she pushed this to the bottom of the bag.

"Packed then, love? Can you put this in, too? It's my razor." He rubbed his chin. "See all nice and smooth." He grabbed and kissed her.

"Yes, Ed," she drew a deep breath. She pushed him into the chair. "Ed, now we're married, we need to talk about personal things. As you have sisters, I presume you know about menses? I'm due for mine at the end of the week, but I thought you should know. I'm normally like clockwork, so that's what I was shoving to the bottom of the bag." She blushed.

"Sure, sweets, I know about that, and I understand. We'll just have to make the most of the time before that, won't we?" He stood and took her in his arms. "Don't worry, sweetheart; I went without for over twenty years; I can manage a week."

She hid her head on his shoulder. "I just wanted you to know," she mumbled.

He laughed. "We could both probably do with a rest anyway."

"Well, you might," she threw over her shoulder as she ducked out to the privy. She had her morning wash.

Eddie made the bed and tidied the room. Ed grabbed the bag on her return, and Jenna picked up the basket of clean dishes for the Tindales. She would leave it on their doorstep with a flower on it. They crept out quietly; Ed closed the door gently. Jenna placed the basket and tray on the doorstep. Ed went to the smithy holding yard and opened the gate for James. He quickly slipped on his bridle, and they walked swiftly down the hill to the Inn. The family was already stirring when they arrived.

Sal greeted them warmly. Hugging Jenna and whispering, "Is everything okay?"

"That's an absolute yes, Absolutely!" She looked lovingly towards Ed. "He's wonderful," she said dreamily. Jenna nodded again. "Oh, yes, everything is perfectly, wonderfully fine. We were… let's say, enjoying ourselves so much that we decided to delay a day. I presume the boys told you we met them on the riverbank yesterday?"

Sal laughed. "Yes, they did, as long as you're happy. I have hidden a small packet under the mattress for you. Something fun and wifey," She winked. Jenna's eyes widened, and she mouthed thank you.

Sal said, "There will be things you need to ask; just know that we can talk when you need to. I'm not your mother, but I know you'd ask her things if she were closer; please don't be afraid to ask."

Jenna nodded and said, "Thanks, Mama Lockley; I will if necessary." She kissed Sal's cheek.

While they were talking, Charlie helped Ed harness James and attach him to the wagon. Charles had built on a cover like he'd seen Jack do with his wagon. It allowed the wagon to be almost weatherproof and turned it into somewhere they could sleep safely. Summer brought out snakes, spiders, and the occasional rain shower. Jenna's fears of snakes led to adding the new wagon cover for this trip.

"Jen will love this; thanks, Dar," Ed said as he stood looking at it. "And thanks for the talk, too." Ed grinned at his father.

Charles led James and the wagon to the verandah. Ed placed their bag on the wagon as Sal brought out two baskets of food, a camp oven, mugs, some utensils, flour, tea, sugar, and honey. "Thanks, Mama," he said as he bent and kissed her cheek.

She stroked her hand along his cheek, looking him in the eyes. "Happy boy?" she simply asked.

He nodded, "Very. She's wonderful." He grinned, looking at Jenna. He put out his hand, and Jenna took it. She walked down the step of the verandah, and he lifted her onto the wagon's seat. Ed walked around the other side and climbed up, too. Charles handed him the reins as he sat down. "See you two on Sunday. Take care. Don't camp too close to the river if that's where you're heading. We could get a sharp shower of rain. I've added an extra canvas just in case."

"Thanks, Dar," said Eddie, and Jenna waved to Eddie's parents as they drove off. The dawn morning was chilly. She slid over a bit closer and laid her head on his arm. "Where are we going, Ed? Not that it matters as long as I'm with you." He handed the reins to his left arm and slid his right around her, drawing her to him.

"Do you remember when your Par sent us to Mrs. Walker's to collect her produce?" he asked.

She nodded. "Sure do," she said.

"Well, I noticed the flat along the river and behind a hidden knoll was the perfect place for a camp. I asked her if we could stay there for our honeymoon, and she was delighted but told us not to be on the water edge." He looked down at her, smiling. "So we only have to go as far as Richmond, then back a bit. I don't think you have been along the road from the north, so it will be a new trip for you."

"Sounds nice, but anywhere is nice if I can be with you."

"We can swim there too, no sharks. Dar has filled the wagon with so much stuff you'd think we're going for a month rather than just five days."

"Your Mama has done the same with the food." She looked at the pile of produce Sal had included. "As long as we can reach the bed, I don't care." She looked up at him saucily. "How long until lunchtime?" She was looking at the sun as it peeped over the horizon. Although dawn had just passed, it boded to be another hot day. She sighed. "So long."

Ed laughed. "You're incorrigible. We've only just got up."

"So," she said suggestively.

Ed laughed. "We'll stop at Vineyard at about noon. But there are a few other spots we could always pull off. There's a place where we can rest awhile and even paddle in the creek. It's about halfway. Will that satisfy your majesty?"

"I suppose so," she sighed contentedly. They had left the outskirts of the town.

"Tell me more about your dream of a foundry. Have you thought about where you want it… or anything more about it," she said inquiringly.

Eddie looked at her. "Seriously? Okay…I don't think it can happen for some years, as we'd have to have a steady source of coal, not to mention somehow get the raw mineral here. There's enough coal for the one in Sydney, but more must be found. When that happens, and we work out a way to get it here, we can start working on it. In the meantime, I'd love to enlarge our forge, but I would like to give it a year working it myself to get the hang of management."

"Okay, then what?"

"Well, as you said, why don't we bring in the boys over the next year and see if they'd like the work? Wills first, as he's already spent a few sessions up there over the few school breaks and when we get really busy. Then, as we get more business, bring in more workers."

"I could build on the existing smithy shop and make that bigger. It would also get the stock out from underfoot. We could make all sorts of things that we're currently bringing in from England. Oh, there's so much that we can make here. We just need skilled people to do it. Oh, and we need the minerals, especially the coal." He looked down at her, snuggled under his arm in the cool of the morning. He kissed the top of her head. "I dream big, sweetheart. But I believe this country will boom and have wealth and resources beyond belief one day." He paused, dreaming of what this vast brown land would look like in the years ahead. "Look at what Mrs. Macarthur has done with her sheep. In just forty years, we have hundreds of them. And there are now huge herds of other stock. Remember the goats?"

They laughed whenever they thought back to that day, only last year when he'd rescued her from being stampeded by a marauding herd of goats running amok down the main street in Parramatta. "Look at the farms and prosperity of those prepared to work. Freed convicts now run many or those who have earned their tickets. Look at our own fathers. Yes, this country had huge possibilities." He fell silent, musing over other thoughts.

He looked down at her and saw she was asleep. He smiled to himself. "Ah, well, I can dream big."

She stirred at the Castle Hill turn-off. "Oh, I'm so sorry, Ed. You've worn me out. Where are we?" She sat up, rubbing her eyes.

"I was just about to wake you. I need two arms to drive this section. We're passing the Castle Hill Road. It's out there that the uprising happened about thirty years ago. It's a bit hilly here, so I'll need two hands on the reins." He slowed James to a walk and held him back as they descended the steep hill. James took it in his stride. "We're a bit away from Rouse Hill, but I thought you might like a rest here. This place is named after Mary Rouse, Governor Macquarie's governess for his son. She had a farm here after her marriage. There's a nice shady place we can stop for a bite, a drink and a wee tree if you'd like."

"Oh, yes, please; how's your arm? Is it asleep?" she asked sheepishly. "I could do with a wee stop."

He pulled James off the road at the bottom of the hill and under the shade of some scrubby trees. "I'll get him a drink while you find a tree."

She slipped off the seat and walked to a large gum tree. She checked the area for snakes this time. When she finished, she headed back. She'd just arrived back at the wagon when they heard a *craaaack*. They looked back to see a huge branch fall from the tree she'd just been squatting under. "Oh, you're kidding. Ed, I was just there." She threw herself into his arms, shaking.

"You do choose dangerous spots, don't you?" He laughed. "God was protecting you… again. You're giving your guardian angel a good workout." He comforted her for a while. She was still shaking. "Can you watch James while I find my own tree?" He walked over to the same tree to check out the fallen branch. While he was gone, she crawled into the wagon and raided one of the baskets that Sal had given them. There was a bottle of ginger beer and some cake. She placed them on the seat and stowed the remaining food into the basket. Next, she hunted through the other goods for some mugs and found some hobbles for James.

She was just putting everything back when Eddie said, "Is it comfortable? Do you think we should test it out?"

The same thought had entered her mind, and she just nodded with a big grin. "I'm already ready." Lifting her skirts. "I left them off this morning." She giggled.

"Well, I'd better check out the bed myself." He said, climbing up into the bed under the canopy.

Anyone nearby would have heard lots of oohs and aahs before they eventually emerged somewhat mussed up but contented. They decided that the mattress would do. Jenna reached for the ginger beer, but Eddie said, "If that's Dar's, do not open it here."

She passed it to him as he crawled out of the front of the wagon and put his foot on the reins. He popped the top as she held the mugs. *Bang.* Sure enough, the top blew off, and he aimed it away from James. James started. Thankfully, Ed had his foot on the reins. "Steady boy. No need to stress." He settled him down.

Jenna caught the overflowing drink in the mugs. "Glad you warned me. That could have been messy."

Ed filled the mugs, and they drank deeply. They ate their cake and were soon back on the road.

After a late but quick stop for lunch, they arrived at Mrs. Walker's farm. She greeted them warmly and directed them to the camping spot near a fenced paddock where James could roam at will. She laughed. "It's where I keep my mares, so he'll be happy as well. Hope you don't mind; I could do with some nice foals." She said that if they needed honey, eggs, butter, cream, or some milk, to come up and get some.

Mrs. Walker had several convict girls who milked her cows and wove baskets for sale. They and their partners worked on the farm. They knew her first husband had died in a flood some years before, and she remarried, but there was no sign of this elusive man. Jenna vaguely remembered him from her childhood. She knew that her husband was often out with their sons on one of the family farms at Bathurst. Her eldest son and his wife carried on at the farm when they were out there.

Martha had questioned her when her first husband died. Hetty Walker said, "If Elizabeth Macarthur can run her farm alone, then so can I." And wow, what a farm.

After their incident on their first stop with the tree branch, they stayed well away from any trees. Eddie set camp up well away from the river's edge. It was swelteringly hot, but as they knew, summer storms can hit overnight. And on the river, the storm may not even be local but miles away upstream or in the hills. Because of one of these, Mrs. Walker's husband, Joel, had died. She had gone to live with the Turners for six months after that tragedy.

They chose a spot just a short distance from the fence where James was to be. It was on the far side of a level area where the original farmhouse had once stood. Jenna collected flood wood for their fire, and Eddie set up camp. He discovered that Dar had even put in an axe. He didn't think he would need that. Jenna had done various loads of wood. She had a pile of kindling, another pile of medium dead wood and now she'd brought a branch. She dumped it near the camp and headed off again.

"Looks like I'll need to use the axe after all." He laughed. He made a few trips to the river, collected some large river rocks, and made a campfire in their chosen area. After setting up the iron tripod for the camp oven and billy, he set the fire.

Jenna returned with her next load and said, "Ed, there's a lovely spot down there for a swim. It looks like a pool of crystal clear water just under a little rocky waterfall. I hope it stays hot, as the water is icy. Hard to believe, isn't it?" She was so excited. "Talking about hot, why don't we test it out? Let me change first." She didn't wait for Ed to answer but hopped up into the wagon and dug into the duffle bag. She pulled out her clothing and other bits and tucked them on her side of the bed. She found her smock and quickly changed, and she discovered that Sal had also included a couple of towels and grabbed those as she jumped off the wagon. "I'm done. Are you ready?"

He said, "Nearly," and reached for the bag too. He pulled off his shirt and dropped his work pants.

She stood watching. "Mmm," was all she said as he stood naked.

He pulled on the tattered cut-off pants. "Yep, ready."

They walked down to the river hand in hand. Ed had the towel over his head, covering his back and shoulders. The heat of the afternoon had been intense. Just walking down to the river in the sun was hot work. Both were drenched with perspiration by the time they got there. They threw down the towels and raced into the cold water.

Eddie waded into the pool and said, "It's only waist deep, so don't dive in." He sat down and went under the water. "Brr, it is cold."

Jenna waded in, too and intentionally fell into his arms. "I can warm you up."

He ducked her. She came up spluttering, "Oh, you." And splashed him. They played in the water for a while, as they had now acclimatised to the temperature. She swam across the pool, as although it was shallow, it was quite wide. She didn't see Ed duck under the water and sneak up beside her. She squealed as she felt his hands under her smock. They crept up further until he was cupping her breasts. "Oh nice," they said in unison.

He twisted her around and drew her to him. "I like your swimming hole." And be bent to take her lips. "That's not all I like about you."

"Oh," she exclaimed. "Oh, nice and nice," as she settled on him. "I'm going to enjoy our honeymoon if this is what we do."

They occupied themselves pleasantly for some time before noticing that cattle were heading for the creek for a drink. They decided to head back to camp and get the rest of the site set up before dark. Eddie put on his wet shorts and then wrapped Jenna in a towel, bending to kiss her as he did. "I'm certainly enjoying myself. Dar did say it was fun practising making babies. I agree," he said as they walked back.

"It is, isn't it? Who knows, I could already be carrying one," said Jenna, touching her stomach. She laughed. "We've certainly given nature enough chances."

Eddie looked at her, stunned. "Gosh, I never thought of that. Maybe we had really better talk, babies. We knew we wanted them, but it never occurred to me that it could be that fast."

She laughed. "Even if I am, it won't arrive until spring."

Eddie started counting on his fingers… "That long? I know very little about that sort of thing. Oh well, that gives us time to practise some more." He grabbed her and swung her around, then put her down and ran from her, twisting and begging her to chase him.

She did. Both arrived back as camp nearly dry and just about as hot as when they left.

While she changed her damp smock, Ed took the buckets and went to the creek's closest section to fill them. She put her mind to what they'd eat for dinner. There were eggs, butter, a loaf of bread, some vegetables, and some pickled meat in a brine tub. "Mmm, nice," she thought, "Tonight we eat like kings."

She lit the campfire and set the camp oven onto the tripod to get hot.

She saw Eddie coming back with the water. He was still shirtless. She stood watching him, thinking, "Oh, he's so delicious." His physique was incredible. She sat watching how he handled those heavy water buckets like they were empty. They weren't; she could see water slopping out of them. Oh, she was so enjoying being married to him.

Maa had taken her aside a few days before they left home, and they had a long talk about All sorts of intimate things. Very intimate things. Jenna's eyes were wide with awe during their talk. She had said, "Although the man had the drive for the physical closeness, the woman could make them so much fun. This was all part of the union of marriage, or Joy of Marriage, each bringing different things to it and making it good. It built up trust, openness and honesty." Ma had also said, "The marriage bed was never to be defiled. There would eventually come a time, hopefully years from now, when the physical side may become less important, but the first flush of marriage is a delight. Enjoy it, relax, enjoy, and practice making beautiful babies." She then said, "Try different positions, places and times. Don't always plan; use the moment, enjoy the day." She was also correct about making a glutton of themselves on the honeymoon. "Oh, she was so right." She shook her head as if to keep her mind on track. Food: she had to cook food.

Jenna brought the ingredients to the fire, cut off some meat, and mixed it with some vegetables to make a stew. She had the meat sizzling and the vegetables chopped, ready to add. The eggs she'd leave for breakfast.

As Eddie returned, the smell of cooking onions and meat met his nose. She was stirring the sizzling meat. "Oh, yum, that smells delicious." He dumped the buckets down and bent to kiss her. "What's wrong, sweetie?" he asked as he noticed tears running down her cheeks. He dropped to his knees beside her and embraced her. "Are you all right?"

She giggled, "Of course, silly. It's the onions."

He plonked back on his butt. "Oh, phew, I thought something had happened." They laughed. Ed collected plates and cutlery from the wagon.

Jenna finished adding things to the pot and added a mug of ale. She put the lid on and left it to cook, "Dinner in thirty minutes, sweetie. How about we set up the rest of the camp while it cooks? They dug out everything else from under the mattress, surprised at what Sal and Charles had included. Jenna was thrilled to find two large bowls. She could make some soda bread and wash up in one, too. She asked Ed to check on the stew, and she felt around under the head of the mattress and found a small wrapped parcel tucked under it. It was tied with a ribbon, so she knew this was from Sal. She wondered what was in it. She moved into the light and carefully unwrapped the package. Into her lap dropped a very lacy item of ladies' underwear. There wasn't much of it. "Ohh," it was all lace and very see-through at that. "Ohh," she said again and giggled. She peeked out to ensure Eddie was busy, quickly removing her dress and slipping it on. "Nice, it does up at the front. Even nicer!" She laced herself into it and slipped her dress back on.

Eddie appeared at the back of the wagon with a stick alight. "I thought I'd light the lamp. Are you all right?"

"Yes, fine, I'm just sorting out everything. I'll be down in a moment."

He lit the lamp and hooked it onto the metal pole Dar had shoved down the wagon's side. "There's some light for you, sweetie."

"Thanks, Ed; I'm coming now." She waited until his back was turned, grabbed the ribbon, and hid it. She hopped out of the wagon and followed him back to the fire.

"See, all done," she said breezily. She was intensely aware of her new undergarment and the response it would bring later that evening. She smiled to herself.

Ed had the billy ready to put on the fire hook when the stew was cooked. They continued their conversation about children and got to discussing names. Both agreed with Edward for a boy to be known as Ned, but they debated middle names, finally deciding on Edward John Charles not to leave anyone out. Jenna's father was John, but it was also Charles and Eddie's middle name, named after Charles' father. "Funny thing is, they are the same as the Major's names. And what about a girl?" said Ed. They brought up a few names and decided on Christina Sarah Martha. "Martha is my middle name, remember." Jenna checked on the stew a few times and eventually said. "It's finally cooked." Eddie passed the plates, and she filled his plate to the brim; hers was just one scoop. She knew how much her brothers ate and was sure Ed ate more. She watched him eat and offered more.

"What have you put in this? Mama makes a stew from the same things, and it doesn't taste like this." He took another mouthful. "It's blooming delicious."

"It's not what you put in it. It's how and when you put them in. First, I fried the meat in butter, let it dark brown, and then added the onion. It goes sweet, brown and sticky. Only then can you add some water to get the juices off the pan? You add the vegetables and then finally the water. Then, put it back on to cook. It's nice, isn't it? Maa taught me," she said, digging into another spoonful of stew.

"I'm going to get so fat being married to you if you cook this well." He spooned in another mouthful, waving the spoon in the air. "Absolutely delicious, mmm!"

She laughed again. "Just wait until you see what I do with the eggs tomorrow."

While Eddie was eating his second helping, she mixed up the ingredients for a loaf of soda bread. As she had no milk and didn't want to waste the ale, she used half a bottle of ginger beer from this morning and half a mug of water. She put it in the now emptied, wiped-out stew pot and sat it aside for a while. Eddie watched her, intrigued. Mama had only ever made it with milk. He wasn't sure he'd like the ginger beer bread. She seemed like she knew what she was doing; he shrugged. He wouldn't go hungry anyway.

He was puzzled that she hadn't come and sat beside him after putting the bread onto cook. She sat poking the coals with a stick but kept glancing towards him, but not talking. It was a companionable silence with occasional comments about fires and peace. Her face was illuminated in the remaining flames from the fire. He was content to lay back and watch her. Emotions flicked across her face as thoughts wandered through her mind. He was in awe of this micro-packed woman. She'd blown him away with her willingness to satisfy him and enjoy herself, too. He'd discovered that Dar was so right that the fulfilment was multiplied four-fold or more by holding back. As a virile, healthy male, his appetite was large; hers equalled his. In no way did her size, or lack of it, hinder his well-endowed body in any way. Dar was right about that, too. The thought made him say, "Jenna, think you might be ready for bed soon?"

"Yes," she said. "The bread will take an hour or so to cook. I've scraped out the coals so it won't burn. I'll go for a wee walk then join you. As we've swum, I won't need a wash tonight." She hopped up, "Join you in a minute." She ducked around to the other side of the wagon and up the hill a little. No need to look for a tree as it was dark.

Eddie took the opportunity to do likewise, and they arrived back at the campsite simultaneously. She walked over to the wash-up basin and sloshed in some water. "I just want to wash my face." She did and walked to the back of the wagon.

Eddie was waiting for her. He put her hands around her waist to lift her onto the wagon. "Oh, what's this?" he said as he felt something under her gown.

She giggled and turned up the lamp. She started to undo her buttons provocatively.

He quickly divested himself of his clothing before he hopped up and joined her. He reached over and helped with the buttons on her dress only to discover that tonight, there was another layer. "Oh, this is interesting. Show me more." He lay back, obviously impressed with what was beginning to show.

She pulled the gown over her head, and when it was gone, she was covered only with a see-through lace creation.

"Oh, cripes, that's incredible! Where did *that* come from?" He so wanted to touch her, but he wanted to look too. But, oh, did he want to look.

"Believe it or not, this was a gift from your Mama. She tucked it under the mattress and whispered that it was there." Jenna giggled. She was embarrassed but enjoying the effect it had on him.

"What?" he said, stunned. Alternately blushing, thinking of his parents enjoying their physical union, and almost wanting to devour her himself. He pushed the thoughts from his mind and set to enjoy himself and pleasure her, too. She was enjoying the effect this was having on his body. She was on her knees, stretching and twisting in front of him. He could wait no longer and reached out and held her before passionately kissing her and turning around to put her under him.

They were even less inhibited here than at home. This was only day three of their marriage. His mind was fogged with lust for his wife, and she was willing to oblige his need for her. Hers, for him, seemed to be even lustier. She was just as happy with a quick coupling fully clothed, a romp in the water, or comfortable in a soft bed. She lay in his arms, totally spent... or so he thought.

They both got up to remove the bread from the fire and tend to the coals. They returned to the bed. She reached out for him again. As she lay in his arms, he slowly unlaced the front of this lace creation and finally removed it from her. He reached up and turned out the lamp.

Eventually, they fell asleep in each other's arms, with legs again entangled.

They were awoken by the moo of cows coming to drink. One big brown cow with big horns decided to check out the strange thing in her field. She stuck her head under the canopy and mooed. Jenna sat up and yelled. Ed woke to a bare butt in his view of the outside world. "What a nice view to wake to," he said. He gently gave her a small tap on her butt.

She giggled. "I didn't want her eating our food."

He said, "We can get more food. Just do *not* go out there with no clothes on. There could be a stockman with them. But while you are divested of them...."

They finally emerged, dressed from their bed, and she said, "If you can fix the fire again, I'll go and wash. Then I'll cook you some breakfast. The water is still hot in the kettle from last night's fire; I won't be long. You can use the rest to shave, or I'll get a rash."

They were ready in about fifteen minutes. Jenna was already doing something with the eggs. She cut off a small chunk of the meat and diced it very finely; it went into the pan with a bit of butter. It spat and sizzled. She added a slice of onion. She took a cloth and poured the mixture onto a plate. Eddie had not been watching too closely, but she had something white and fluffy and mixed this cooked stuff into it and poured it all back into the camp oven. She spread out the fire until it was mostly coals. When it died down a bit, she put the pan back on the hook. She cut some of her bread and held it on a stick close to the coals until it was toasted. She cooked four of these and buttered them as they were each done, three for Eddie and one for her. She checked the eggs and put the lid on the pan. Eddie was lying, watching her, not what she was doing, but just watching her. He was besotted. He doubted that he deserved such an angel, yet he thanked God again as he watched her.

"What are you thinking, sweetie? Your face just relaxed. Are you worried about something?"

He didn't even realise she'd been watching him too. "I'm just thanking God for you, Jen." He kept talking, "Dar read me some of the Song of Solomon the night before the wedding. I have never understood that book in the Bible before. He explained that humans were made not just to make babies but to enjoy it and relax, too. We're ticking all those off the list. He said to make sure there was mutual pleasure. Dar reinforced the "mutual" pleasure to me. We sat in the cellar in the dark and talked. I'm so glad it was dark with the things we talked about. I'm sure he was blushing; I certainly was. I was worried that I was too big for you. I would not have hurt you for the world."

She laughed. "Maa had *the* talk with me, too, but it was a couple of days before we left for our wedding. I think she thought maybe we'd preempted the wedding on the day they got rid of us." She paused. "As I normally ride astride, I think I was a bit stretched, you know, down there. Maa told me it would hurt the first time. It was initially uncomfortable and painful, but it passed so fast. I just wanted you in me." She looked shy. "I love you, Ed; I love you so much, so very much. I want our marriage to be everything you have ever dreamed of and more. And if God made this side of marriage pleasurable, I'm not going to argue with Him." She checked the pot and said, "It's cooked."

Then she looked at him again. "I know we'll make a glutton of ourselves for the first weeks or longer, but it's okay; I'm enjoying it, and I think you are too."

He grinned and nodded. "Am I ever," he said.

She took the pot off the hook and set it on the ground. She hung the billy, pushed up the coals, added more wood to the fire, and then served the cooked concoction. Jenna placed three slices on Eddie's plate and handed it to him. He dug in his spoon and took a mouthful.

Expecting it to be chewy, it melted in his mouth and had a delicious flavour. "Hmmm, wow," he said again. "This is heavenly." He took another mouthful, then another.

"Told you," she simply said and dug into her share.

The rest of the week was spent playing, swimming, sleeping and generally gorging on the delights of each other's bodies. They'd go for long walks, occasionally heading to Mrs. Walkers to restock the perishable foods. They'd pay for her goods, but Eddie would chop some wood for her from her woodpile. Soon enough, the week was over, and they had to return home. The good thing was that they never had to part again.

James came when Eddie called and was harnessed to the wagon. It had lightly rained overnight, and some things were damp. They had slept so soundly that neither had heard it. There was some rainwater sitting on the lid of the camp oven. The fire was completely out the next morning, and the wood was wet, so they realised the skies had indeed opened. They decided not to re-light it. Eddie took the rocks back to the river, but the remaining wood they left next to the dead fire. They would return again someday. They'd had a wonderful time, but it was time to get on with life.

James stood placidly as he was harnessed and then tied into the traces. He had spent his week friskily with the mares in his paddock. He threw his head a few times when he heard the whinny of one of his mares but stood still. By the time they were ready to go, it was just before mid-morning, and they called in on Mrs. Walker to leave her with the rest of their dried goods. There were girls weaving on the verandah, but she came and accepted the much-appreciated goods.

Sal had put in a big bag of flour, salt, and a box of tea. Although they had used some, there was much left. She appreciated this and accepted them gracefully. She supplied them with a large clay jar of honey and filled a homemade basket with eggs. She stood on the verandah, waving until they were out of sight.

Ed admired the basket. "These are lovely, Mrs. Walker."

Jenna kept turning to wave. "Oh, Ed, she must be so lonely. It must be so hard for her." Jenna thought a child cried somewhere, but it must belong to one of the girls who worked weaving with her. She turned back to have another look, and At that moment, a tall, dark hair man appeared.

He said, "Hello and congratulations, Jenna."

Jenna gasped. She realised that this was Des Bolton. She had not seen him since she was young. She said, "Hello, Mr. Bolton; nice to see you again." She remembered that her parents had mentioned that Mrs. Walker had remarried but kept her first name, but she had not seen him for many years. She had all but forgotten.

James took the path he had come along a week ago. He needed little direction.

Eddie held the reins loosely as Jenna sat with his arm around her. He had to concentrate as he drove through Windsor, but they were back on the road to Parramatta. They had made good time as the weather had cooled. They stopped for lunch at a creek they'd passed on the way out. They knew they had to get home before nightfall, and although they would like to have postponed the inevitable, they returned to the wagon and continued.

They had travelled about an hour when Jenna sat bolt upright and gasped. Ed turned and looked at her, puzzled. "What's up, love?"

She looked at him. "Ed, I told you I was due for my menses. They didn't come. I'm never late." She touched her stomach. "I wonder?" She looked at him. "Do you think…?" she blanched. "It's only two days, but seriously, I have never ever been late. It's every twenty-eight days on the knocker."

Ed looked at her; his mouth dropped open. "Seriously? We talked about this, but I thought you were joking." He put his arm around her again and hugged her. "Oh, Jen, are you okay if this is so? I am. So don't get me wrong. I'm over the moon, but it's so soon."

"Ed, I was joking before. I'm stunned but thrilled if it's true." They fell quiet, each thinking of the change in their lives that this would mean. "I could just be late, you know." She alternately blushed and blanched as her mind flicked from thought to thought. "Your ma will know Ed. She's had six."

Eddie, too, fell silent, consumed with thoughts he hadn't expected to have for a long time. He kept looking down at this wonderful girl cuddled up next to him. He bent and laid his head on the top of her hair. "Gee, I love you so. If it is, that's great. If not, we can keep practising."

She lifted her face to his. "Are you sure you don't mind?" Her eyes were filled with unshed tears.

He wiped one away with his thumb. "Why would I mind love? I'm delighted. I'm just stunned." He put his arm around her and pulled her closer.

"Ed, I'm torn between laughing and crying. I wanted to have time with you before this. I knew it was possible, but…" She wiped away a tear but laughed. "Oh Ed, I'm excited but so scared, silly too." They talked and talked, sharing feelings and every emotion. "Ed, when we return, I want to talk to your Mama. Alone at first, as there are some things I need to ask her, then I want you to join us. We'll walk this path together every step of the way." Her voice shook on the last few words.

"That's fine, love. I'm here for you, whatever you want." Waves of love for her swept over him anew.

By mid-afternoon, they were on the outskirts of Parramatta. They'd be home earlier than expected, but that was time they'd need. "Oh, Jen, the family dinner is Sunday night. We'll be asked to stay," said Eddie

"That's great, Ed. I'll try to catch your mum as soon as we get back then." She wrapped both arms around him. "I still can't get close enough to you."

James lifted his head; he knew he was close to home. His pace picked up, and Eddie had to concentrate on negotiating the pedestrians, horses and vehicles. As they entered the town, Jenna had moved away from him, as was proper. They turned into the street leading to the inn. James showed he was happy to be home as he started prancing. Head bent and held high, and knees kicked high. They laughed. His ears flicked at the sound. Eddie reined him next to the verandah, and Charles appeared to hold James's head. They greeted him warmly. Eddie hopped down and turned to lift Jenna down, placing her gently on the ground. He gave her a quick kiss and motioned for her to seek his Mama. She went off, leaving the unpacking to the men.

Jenna entered the house to find Sal. Sal was in the kitchen and turned when she heard someone enter. "Hello, Love," she said. "Nice to have you back." She paused and looked questioningly at Jenna. She stopped what she was doing and turned to her. "What's wrong, love? Is everything all right?"

She opened her arms, and Jenna walked into them. "Everything is fine, Mama Lockley, but I need to talk to you. Woman stuff. I'm just emotional."

"Ahh," said Sal; she wiped her hands on her apron and took it off. "Let's go sit on the verandah in the shade."

She poured two mugs of tea and handed one to Jenna. She took Jenna's hand, and they walked outside.

Once seated, she said, "Now, love, what's up?"

"Oh, nothing is up precisely; I just need to ask some lady stuff questions." She blushed. "You see, I was due for my menses two days ago, and, well, they didn't come. Could 'it' happen that fast? Could I be... well, could I be, um, 'interesting' already? When do you know?"

Sal laughed, "Oh, sweetheart, is that all? I was so worried. So much can go wrong with a young couple when they first marry. That side of marriage can be a trial or a treat. By the looks of it, for you, it's the 'treat'."

Jenna nodded and grinned.

"As to the menses, I was spot on with mine, and like you, I knew a few days after I was late. Within a few days or even a week or a bit longer, you'll start feeling sick in the mornings, and then you'll know for sure."

Eddie stuck his head around the verandah; Jenna nodded and waved for him to join them. He sat close to Jenna, wrapping his arm around her and drawing her close. "Hi, Mama," he grinned.

"Mama, there's a question I wanted to ask you with Ed here." She blushed, "If I am with child, can we still... well, you know? Is it safe? It won't hurt the child, will it?"

She heard Ed take a quick breath. He had never thought of this before. Sal said, "Yes, dear ones, it's fine, and it's safe, but as the pregnancy progresses, you have to be more gentle. You will find ways to, shall I say, accommodate the bundle of joy. Towards the end..." she paused with a smile on her face. "Well, when you know it's about time, they say that you can sometimes hasten things," she paused, looking from face to face, "The way it got in, er, can hasten the way to get it out." She looked a shade darker. They all blushed, then laughed.

Sal turned to address Ed, "Son, you will find her more emotional; this is normal. She'll be in tears for no reason and laughing the next, and sometimes angry for no reason. This is her body settling into the changes happening inside. Hug her, love her and just be there for her. Be understanding and talk to me when you need to. It's her body undergoing an incredible change, and it's a huge change. She's growing as a person. Remember that and be accommodating. You will know for certain in a week or so when she feels sick in the mornings. Keep a basin next to the bed. Charles used to bring me a cup of black tea while I was in bed every morning, which helped tremendously. With you, I could only have sweet black tea, Eddie. Another trick is baking soda, fine sugar, and a bit of lemon. Yes, this sounds strange, but keep some with a lemon peel in a container and mix it with some fine sugar. When you're feeling sick, have a half teaspoon full, dry. Just sit it on your tongue. I have no idea why this works, but it does."

The two young people sat in silence. Still stunned that things could happen so fast. They had only been married for eight days. They were still getting used to each other. It may yet be a false alarm, but it was good to know if it wasn't. Sal gave them other useful information. She told them not to tell anyone until they were sure, not even Charles. When Charles joined them a little later, she left them talking. Jenna soon made her excuses and went to help Sal in the kitchen. Sal greeted her, handed her the knife, and pointed her to a pile of vegetables. They talked quietly until Jenna turned to Sal and said, "Mama Lockley, can I just call you Mama?"

"Of course, dear, you are now my daughter. I'd be delighted. Oh, and you are staying for dinner, aren't you? We have visitors coming. I can easily squeeze in two more places."

"We'd love to, thank you," said Jenna. They got stuck into the pile of vegetables. The smell of roasting meat was delicious. Once Sal opened the oven to check it, she turned to Jenna. "Another way you'll know is when the smell of meat cooking, or sometimes soft egg, turns your stomach. This happened with me for each of them."

As dusk approached, the family came from everywhere. The three boys had been swimming. Tim appeared with Anna; they had been visiting at his house. The Major, the Doctor and Mrs. Meadows all appeared. Each was handed a mug of cider or ginger beer on their arrival. Anna and Mrs. Meadows, who had finally persuaded Sal to call her Christina, joined Jenna and Sal in the kitchen to help. Liza and Bertie were the last to arrive. Bertie apologised, and Liza blushed. Sal just smiled.

Sal looked from one face to the other. "Hmm, she looks a bit peaky, I wonder." She bent and pulled the roast meat out of the oven, "This will do it if she is." She clattered it down on the bench, eyes on Liza. Sure enough, Liza excused herself and walked outside quickly. Bertie followed hard on her heels. Sal smiled to herself. "Two at once," she thought. They would tell her when they were ready. Funny how Jenna had sought her advice, but her own daughter had not. She wasn't worried; sometimes, it's easier to talk these things over with someone not so close as Jenna had. "I'll have to talk to Molly," she thought.

Dinner was a success. Charles asked Ned to carve, and he showed the boys how to carve a joint properly. At the request of Charles, who'd asked him to bestow a little table etiquette on them all, the three English friends took it in turns to show them how to hold their cutlery correctly; this was the least problem as Sal had watched the Major when she worked for him had taught the children and Charles. Then, there was how to set the table properly. Due to the lack of cutlery and courses, this had been difficult. Christina brought a canteen of cutlery over one day from the Major's house and gave them a lesson on this. In particular, Anna took great interest and would be the only one who would probably need to know how to do this. Tim could be in charge of his branch of the Law firm soon; she knew she'd have to entertain all sorts of guests. She listened hard.

Charles stood watching it all, with vague memories returning to him. Ned saw the look flash across his face, recollection, awareness.

The doctor and the Major instructed all the men on how to bow and shake hands properly. A loose hold was like shaking a dead fish, said the doctor. He laughed as he showed them what he meant. The doctor continued, "Also, to be careful of your strength. A strong, firm handshake for a young man is fine, but as you get older, hands can be painful, so learn to be firm but gentle to an older man, and never shake a woman's hand."

Ned used Christina's hand. "For a lady from any walk of life, you take her hand gently in yours and merely bow over it. You may kiss the hand if she's related or close to you; otherwise, do not touch your lips to her."

He looked at her and smiled, "For your lady love, turn it over and kiss the palm." He did so, and she blushed. His last comment was directed at the two young boys whose eyes were as large as saucers.

"Aww, why would you want to kiss a lady? Yuck," said thirteen-year-old Luke. Wills nodded in agreement, then wistfully thought of Cathy.

Charlie laughed. The Major had brought some cravats and neckties. After the meal and the table cleared, the three taught everyone how to tie a fancy cravat. Ned produced some gemstone stick pins and proceeded to tie some fancy styles. He had about ten starched cravats with him. Tim watched in awe, getting Ned to show him twice more how this look was achieved.

Mrs. Meadows and the Doctor showed the other men, using Charles as a model, to achieve a fancy look with a simple necktie or even just a neck-kerchief around the neck. The difference was striking.

Jenna asked Mrs. Meadows to show her again how one, in particular, was done. She showed her again and then got Jenna to do it twice herself. Eddie was so tall that he had to sit while they fiddled with his neck, all the while with a goofy, cheeky look on his dimpled face.

"When will you doll me up like this?" he pleaded plaintively. "Dar, you didn't tell me I'd have to play dress-ups when I got married." This sent everyone into whoops of laughter.

"Methinks you protesteth too much, lad," The Major said as he approached them. "With two beautiful women fawning over you, I would not complain too much." He slid his arm around Mrs. Meadows' shoulder and gently kissed her cheek. "Thank you for showing my protege how to smarten himself up." He bent lower and whispered to Eddie, "Wear it on Christmas Day, Ed." Eddie nodded.

While the men were occupied doing this, Liza sidled up to her mother. "Can we talk?" Sal nodded and walked out to the kitchen. Liza followed a minute or so later. Sal stood waiting and opened her arms when Liza entered.

Liza walked into them. "Oh, Mama, you know. How?"

Sal smiled. "It was the cooked meat, love. I've had six children myself, sweetheart. I knew that would tell me if what I suspected was true?"

Liza bemoaned her condition. "I'm so sick in the mornings, and when I smell meat, I can't cook it for Bertie, and I feel so ill sometimes."

Sal repeated the instructions she'd given Jenna mere hours before. She didn't let on and would let them share their news when they were ready. Sal made up some soda and sugar mix for Liza to take home. Liza tasted it and put it in her pocket. They returned to the dining room, arm in arm. The night closed in, and soon everyone was gathering to leave.

Liza and Bertie walked with the doctor, the Major, and Mrs. Meadows. They said goodnight at Mrs. Meadows's gate and continued to their place.

The doctor said, "Goodnight, Tina. Sleep well," and took the armload of neckties from the Major and went inside.

The Major waited until the street was empty and took Christina in his arms. They stood under a tree; the moonlight cast a shadow, and they moved deeper into the shadow. "I am so looking forward to not having to say goodnight like this. Only two weeks to go."

One of the problems of a secret wedding was the Banns.

Reverend Mr. Bobart had slightly twisted the rules for him by changing their names slightly. Ned Gracemere and Tina Hunt had not been connected with Major Edward Grace and Mrs. Christina Meadows.

No one said a thing. Both names were actually real and accurate, but only a few knew this. The Banns had washed over the majority of the congregation without a ruffle. Only the family knew, his adopted family. Christina reached up to pull his head down to hers. "Oh, Ned," she paused. "No, I'm not going to call you Ned; you're my Edward, for you are my protector."

"You can call me what you like, my love, as long as you keep calling me." He crushed her to him in a passionate embrace. "I have wanted to do this for such a long time." He spoke softly, his lips pressed against her hair. "I want you so close to me so I can care for you."

They stood together for some time, only pulling apart when footsteps were heard drawing closer. They stood apart but still in the shadow of the tree. Once the person had gone, Ned drew Christina to him again. "Darling, I've been meaning to talk to you. I know you are short of ready funds. I, however, am not. Especially now, I know it's not usually done, but here in the colony, rules are often bent, like us out here alone. You will need a dress for the wedding and more gowns for the trip home. While the ones you have are beautiful, I would give you, let's say, an advance on a dress allowance. You'll be a Duchess and have to dress the part. That, of course, can't be achieved here; we'll travel to Paris and fill our wardrobes. There's nothing like a new gown for a wedding. Would you be willing for you to do this for me?" He looked into her eyes, which he could see in a shaft of moonlight. Holding her face, he bent and kissed her swiftly.

She smiled. "Oh, Edward, I would love a new dress or two. Especially to be married in. Sally and I were going to make one as a surprise for you. I saw one in the window in one of the shops that is truly beautiful. I've learnt not to be proud of trivial things. I also need some other more intimate items of apparel. Some of that can wait until Paris, but some I really need now; mine are threadbare." She put her head on his chest in embarrassment.

"Oh, my love, I wish I had known how tough it was for you. Jack and Bea Barnes tried to tell me." With one arm around her, he reached into his pocket and took out the roll of notes he had in there. "I have some here ready, hoping you would say yes. £120 should buy you enough to be going on with, shouldn't it?"

"Oh, lawks. Yes, Edward. Here, I can buy a wardrobe full of gowns for that. Paris, on the other hand, might be a little more expensive." She took the money from him and said, "I'll put it away safely," and stuffed it down the front of her dress. "Now, no one can get it but you." She looked up saucily and kissed him. "Thank you, my love."

He laughed somewhat loudly, and she clapped her hand over his mouth. "We'll get caught by someone if we stay here."

He drew her to him again for a deep, passionate goodnight kiss. His emotions were getting the better of him. He pulled away breathlessly and groaned, "Those two weeks can't go fast enough as far as I'm concerned. I've waited so long to be able to approach you now. I don't want to let you go."

"Edward," she said softly, looking into his face, "I've been married before. I know a man's needs. We don't have to wait if you can't," she said quietly.

Ned pulled away from her. "No, my beloved! I intend this marriage to be all that is good and holy. We'll wait. The discipline of the last twenty-five years and more will put me in good stead." He smoothed her tousled hair and kissed her nose. "Two weeks, my love." He walked her to her door, opened it, and pulled it closed after she entered. Groaning with desire, he walked back to his cottage just two doors back. He straightened himself before he entered, expecting jibes from Gerry.

There were none. Gerry handed him a stiff drink. "You look as if you need this. Only two weeks to go. Did she take the money?"

The Major took the drink and nodded but said nothing. Ned tossed it back and handed his glass to Gerry for another.

"Good, she needs it." They sat sipping their drinks in silence.

Ned's gaze was fixed on the tawny liquid. "She asked me in. Oh, Gerry, I nearly went. But I would not do that to her. She means too much to me. I wish a Bishop were around so I could get a Special License. As it is, we just fit into the three-week window for Banns. Bobart tweaked the dates once I let on who I was." He sat, looking into his glass.

Gerry offered the bottle. Ned shook his head but held out his empty glass for a refill. Gerry refilled his glass. "Last one."

They drank the last ones slowly.

"Lucky Devil! She's worth waiting for," was all Gerry said. "Little Tina all grown up. Who would have thought she'd become such an astounding beauty. Maybe I should start looking around when we get home."

"Gerry, one thing I meant to mention, I would like you to stay on here after we get married as I'll move in with Christina. It will only be until we sail, but I don't want to start making passage enquiries until the deed is done. The word might escape. Is that all right? I need people to see the lights on here, so it would assist us if you stayed."

"That's fine, old chap. I'd like that," Gerry replied.

"We have to pack up both places, not that we'll take much, just the personal items. Before we leave, we've decided to give them to Charles and Sal as a thank you. Harry Moffatt is arranging that. Eventually, I hope they will move into one, but I'm not sure what they will do with the other in the long run, but Sal said something to Christina about having a place where lonely women can meet for companionship. I'm sure they will work it out," the Major said. They sat until their glasses were empty, and then both retired to their rooms.

Chapter 18   The Storm

*T*wo weeks flew by. Ned did not let the situation arise that he was alone with Christina like that again. He might be tempted again to go into her cottage with her. He knew how hard it was to say no.

Eddie and Jenna settled into the cabin at the back of the house. The Tindales had left on Monday to spend Christmas with the family in Sydney. They would return just before the New Year to complete their pack-up and move.

Jenna had woken up the last two mornings feeling ill but had not thrown up until this morning. Ed was looking after her like a man with a bubble. He had taken the advice of both the basin and cup of tea to heart, and she was not allowed to rise before he'd brought her some tea. Their nocturnal activities had not abated, but they had not been so energetic, just in case. It now seemed certain that she was with child.

Liza had told Jenna last Sunday evening when they both had run from the kitchen when the meat appeared. Both stood giggling and shared their joy. They were sure the rest of the family would work it out soon enough, but neither announced anything. Sal just smiled.

Bertie and Ed each raised an enquiring eyebrow to each when their girls whispered to their husbands. A smile and a nod was the reply to each other.

The weather was oppressively muggy. Sitting still was a challenge in itself. Sal, Jenna, Anna, and Christina were madly sewing clothing for her wedding. She had bought the lovely blue gown she had seen, but Christina wanted a cream gown for her wedding and knew she could not buy one without speculation. She and Sal chose the fabric together. Sally carried it, so the shop staff presumed it was for her. Sal and Christina cut it out on the big table at the Inn. The four ladies met daily, working on it together. She would have liked white, but the cream would have to do as she had previously been married. Liza joined them occasionally. It had been so hard keeping their secret, but so far, they had managed.

They each held their breath every Sunday when the Banns were read. Each week, nothing happened. The Banns would be read for the final time on Christmas morning, even though it was a Saturday. They would be married soon after that service ended.

The Sunday before, St John's church was full to almost overflowing. Everyone had come to Parramatta to celebrate the special week; many would stay on.

The weather was close and muggy. It was the Tuesday before Christmas, and a storm was brewing. You could feel it in the air. As the ladies sat sewing, their hands perspired. Sal suggested they seat themselves on the verandah in the shade and do the gown's finishing touches out there. They laid the sheet on the verandah and placed the gown on it to work on. Sal sat the hem on her lap and stitched. Christina was sewing some intricate stitches and some embroidered roses around the neckline, and Jenna and Anna each had a sleeve, and Christina taught them how to sew grub roses around the cuffs. They worked while chatting and were soon finished. The termites had just started to fly, so they went inside. It was a sure sign of rain.

Christina and Sal went inside to try it on to make sure no more alterations were needed. "It's perfect, Sally," Christina said as she twirled around. "However, I want your opinion on this." She unwrapped a small parcel and drew out a blue floral silk georgette organza overskirt. "I thought if I covered the skirt for the morning service and removed it for the wedding? No one would think this then looks bridal."

Sal looked at her. The cornflower blue made her eyes shine. "Oh, Christina, that looks fabulous. The Major will find it hard to keep his eyes off you."

"Shh," she whispered. "He already finds it hard to keep his hands off me, let alone his eyes." They laughed, giggling like school girls.

Sal left her alone to change back into her street gown. It was also new, as were her undergarments and petticoats. She threw her old undergarments in the fire, so threadbare were they that the last time she had pulled on the last pair of drawers, they shredded. She fingered the delicate lawn camisole and drawers and looked down at the new lacy corset. Her underweight body was slowly filling out. The good food Edward kept slipping her was delicious. At least she'd not be ashamed to undress in front of him now. She even had some fleshed-out curves again. She hastily pulled on the new gown and called Sal to help do it up at the back.

They wrapped up both the wedding gown and the overskirt and

carefully laid them in her basket. She had pressed them after Maryanne had left to visit her mama, Cara, for the weekend on Friday. Until then, they would stay hidden. While she was wrapping the dress, Sally sat on her bed, chatting. She invited her to stay for a bite to eat. She loved the informality of the invitation, and she accepted.

During lunch, they talked about life and how their paths had taken a very different direction from when they were each young. One started with everything and ended with nothing; the other started with nothing and finished with everything she could desire. As it was so hot, they wandered back inside.

Christina looked at Sal. "What changed, Sally?" She was puzzled about how she could be so content.

Sal told her, "I'm just glad to be alive. God made my heart peaceful soon after starting work with the Major. He has an aura of peace about him, Christina. Have you noticed? It took me a while to work out what it was, but finally, I understood. It was his faith. He has a strong faith in God. Everything he does is centred on that. His soldiers know him as both just and fair. He is a good man, and there are few of those." She looked at Christina, "It took Charles to spell it out for me, though. Have I told you how I met them both?"

Christina shook her head, her heart constricted. She wasn't sure she wanted to hear, but yet knew she had to know. Many soldiers took convict women as comfort women. She knew she had to know. She had to hear it straight from Sally. The ladies had grown close in the last month, both regretting their shyness hindering them from reaching out to the other. She laughed that her dearest friend in the world was an ex-convict. Her husband-to-be was a Duke, and one of his best friends was also an ex-convict. It just shows how little 'class' means; it's what's inside the person that counts. This country had shown her that. It had taken a nearly failed marriage and a trip halfway around the world for God to reach into her proud heart.

Sal continued, "I had just been marched out of the Female Factory. We were going up for assignment. I was in shackles, and although I was ashamed, I would not show it. I was so frightened. In the Women's Workhouse or Female Factory, we were told we would be used for whatever purpose our new owners desired. Charles caught my eye across the yard; I could not look away; I saw compassion on his face. Christina, our eyes locked; neither of us could break the stare. He was there with the Major, whom I saw first. To this day, I don't know why they were there; I just saw them together." Her mind flashed back to that day. "I was pushed and stumbled. I lost him in the crowd, and next thing I know, Private Reid had me pulled from the line-up, and brusquely, I'm told to follow him, pointing to the Major. I did. I had no choice anyway; I'd learnt that already. Jack and Charles followed some distance behind the Major. We all arrived at his office, and I was stunned when he held the door open for me. No one had ever done that for me before, at least not since London. The other man was Jack, Jenna's papa. He was handed a sheet of paper, and then he left. The Major sat at his desk in the office, and until Reid left, Charles was outside. So, I was left with these two men. I thought maybe they were going to rape me. I'd seen it happen often enough on the ship. I was scared." She caught her breath with a sob, remembering.

Christina put out her hand and held Sal's.

Sal continued, "Charles walked in quietly and shut the door. "Cripes, I'm in for it," I thought. I shrank back to the wall. I had never been with a man, but I saw what they did to other girls." She paused again. "Neither man approached me; all I could do was look from one to the other to see who would go first. I was scared, really scared, Christina. Instead, the Major goes to the stove and pours three mugs of tea. Who serves tea before a rape? I relaxed a bit. Maybe this wasn't what I expected. The Major motioned for me to take a seat. I did before my legs gave out. Charles did, too, but on the other side of the room. Only then the Major said I was to be his friend Perry White's housekeeper and that I also keep the Major's cottage clean and nothing more. Did I understand that I was safe? I just nodded." Tears were streaming down her face as Sal retold the story.

"He said, 'You are under my protection, and no one will hurt you?' I was so relieved that I burst into tears. It was then that Charles came over to comfort me. He knelt before me and took my hand. It was then I looked into his face that I saw love and compassion, not lust. He cared what happened to me. After all those fearful times, especially in the hulks, I was safe. I knew I could trust these two men. I did not know why they had chosen me, but I was mighty glad they had. For the first time in months, I was safe. I cried, oh Christina, how I cried. Charles was now on his knees, took me gently in his arms and let me howl like a baby. After that, I never had eyes for anyone else but Charles. I found out later that it was because Charles saw me in the line-up that the Major had applied for me to go to him. I don't think he needed a housekeeper, but it was an excuse to rescue me." Sal hiccuped.

She looked at Christina with tears still flooding her eyes. "Ned never looked at me that way, Christina. Not once, and neither did I. I just wanted you to know that. Never, not once, ever, and there was never anyone else for him until he met you." She sniffed. "Christina, I kept working for him after I married Charles only weeks later. I never really stopped as I still do his clothing repairs and washing. I got to know them both well. During that time, we three talked often. I could see something in these three men that was different. I wanted what they had. It took a while, but I found out it was their total trust in God. Neither said much, but they lived it. It hit home when one day. I said something to the Major about me being a convict; he just said, 'You know Sally, God has already wiped your slate clean. You just have to accept it. It's that simple."

By now, the ladies were sitting side by side on the bed. Christina was in awe that this woman could relate her horrific tale, and she put her arm around her.

Sal continued. "I was stunned into silence. I had not been to church as a child. We were very poor since my papa died, and if I didn't work, we didn't eat. I had not heard much about Jesus. I had no idea what church was all about, as I only went to learn to read and write. So I started listening on Sundays when we went. I had to sit at the back next to Charles in the convict section; we would hold hands secretly. We both listened hard, and soon, I knew I had to accept that only God could wipe my slate clean. The Major explained that when a person forgives, it's like wiping a chalkboard with a duster. You can still see the remnants of the words. Mankind forgives but not forgets. When God does it, he used a wet cloth, only that cloth was soaked in Jesus' blood. Our sins washed away thoroughly because it took for Him to die so that we can live as He wants us to."

She paused and swallowed, wiping her eyes. "I became a new, clean person that day, Christina. I didn't understand, but I did accept it. I felt new, but I also felt worthy. Yes, worthy. I'd never felt that way before. I could hold my head up again, but not in pride, in worthiness." She stopped to wipe more tears away. "Christina, that was twenty-four years ago. Charles and I married soon after that conversation, and together, we have striven to do the right thing. It hasn't made us rich or popular, but we know we're right with God, and for us, that's all that matters." She looked at Christina; she, too, had tears in her eyes. "I love Charles as much today as that first day."

They sat quietly for a few moments before Christina looked at Sal. She had tears pouring down her face. She said, "Sally, you've just shown me the way back to peace. I had stepped off that path. I was so alone; I should have turned to God. I could always see that love in you, but I didn't want to reach out to anyone because of my stupid pride. I had no idea you were a convict, nor Charles. That doesn't matter anymore, does it? I stepped off God's path for my life for a while. It has taken you, Sally, to lead me back. I feel I can breathe again."

They hugged each other before Sal sniffed and said, "Well, that'll make my eyes puffy."

Their laughter broke the tension. "I need a cup of tea. I'll tell you my story over the tea," Christina said. They made tea, sitting in the kitchen and drinking it. Charles stuck his head in behind her, and Sal waved him away.

Sitting in Sal's kitchen, Christina poured out her heart. "Life was hard after William died. I had so little money and knew no way to get any. I lost so much weight that my body didn't...well, work properly any more. I was underweight and too thin. I was falling into despair, too. Then Edward moved in two doors up. He would anonymously leave parcels or boxes at my door, but I knew it was him, but I needed it. With good food in me, I started looking forward to living again. Edward showed me some interest; I was certainly looking at him. A year ago, we started officially courting. I had been widowed for a year by then. But I was so, so very lonely. My pride got in the way." She heard footsteps approaching and hurriedly said, "You know that rest."

This time, Charles came in and mentioned that the Major and the doctor had arrived. Both ladies wiped their eyes and made tea for everyone. They all leaned on the verandah railing, sipping the hot, strong brew. Termites were flying, and the birds had fallen silent. After some time, they heard distant thunder and Charles, Sal, and the doctor walked around the side of the building to see if they could see the storm coming. They were horrified. A massive roll of dark clouds approached them with a green-tinged sky behind them.

"Cripes!" said Charles. "Sal, gather inside everything you can. This one is going to be big. Hail, too, by the looks of the sky." He called Charlie and the boys from their jobs in the shed and set them to work bringing in the stock and hens. Anna had gone back up to Tim's place when they had finished sewing. Hopefully, she'd stay with Molly and Bill until after the storm passed. Jenna had left some time ago to go home.

The doctor returned and told the others, "Sorry folks, we're in for a big blow. Ned, I'd like to get back if I can and prep my Med bag if needed." The week after he arrived, his luggage arrived on the ferry with Captain Roberts. Gerry now had with him his full medical bag and lots of equipment. He had set himself up as a travelling doctor so he could travel and work as he searched for Edward. He had only been in the colony for two months before they met. The doctor hurried up the driveway and out of sight.

The Major waited for Christina. She said, "I'll leave my parcels here if that's all right. I'll collect them tomorrow." Sal hugged her and just whispered, "Thanks for listening."

Christina whispered, "Thanks for lighting my path again, Sal." She reached for Ned's arm as they left.

The Major took her hand. They walked out of the yard and then up the hill to their homes. "What was that about?" he asked gently.

"Edward, I had lost my way for a while. It's taken Sally to show me the path to faith in God that you showed her all those years ago. I'm sorry I asked you in the other night. It was wrong of me. I'd forgotten everything I had learnt when I was young." She looked at him, her face aglow.

"Do you mean that, sweetheart? Truly?" He grabbed her and swung her around. "That makes me so happy. I was wondering how we were going to make it work. I've watched you at church over the years. The essence was there, but something was missing. Let's call it the difference between head knowledge and heart knowledge."

"Yes, I know… now," she said. "I had the words in my head, but somehow, they never reached the heart. I'd been taught *how* to behave, but I missed the meaning of *why*. Now I understand." She skipped with joy. "Edward, I feel like I'm washed clean. Does that make sense? I feel new. I'm nearly thirty-three years old and feel carefree like a child again."

"I'm forty-four, my love, and I feel refreshed every day I wake," he stopped. "When is your birthday? I don't even know."

She laughed lightheartedly. "I'll give you a hint. What's my name?"

"Christina," he replied

"And why do you think I was called that?" she asked. "Darling Edward, I was born on Christmas Day, Christ-mas Day, Christ-ina. Our wedding day, I turn thirty-three on Saturday."

He gasped.

They made it back to the row of cottages as the rain started. They went to Christina's cottage and asked Maryanne to accompany them next door. The roof leaked in her cottage, and it looked like it would be heavy rain.

By the time the girls arrived at the Major's door, the wind had hit with a vengeance and was blowing all sorts of debris around. As they entered, they heard a crack and looked back to see one of the large branches on the tree outside her place break off and crush her front fence. They hurriedly went inside and closed the door.

The doctor had all sorts of medical things spread on the table. He put everyone to work. "I have not needed these for some time, so I want them clean. Ned, can you put on a big pan of water to boil? Maryanne Christina, I want you to wash your hands with lots of foamy soap and fingernails, too. Then, dry them on a clean towel. Then you can both help me tear this sheet into bandages and roll them up." He set about his work with other instruments. "Sorry, Ned, but I chose one with a tear. I hope you don't mind. Is there anything else I can use?"

Christina laughed, "Gerry, I have few that don't have tears. I couldn't sell them as they were too old and worn."

Maryanne chipped in. "Ma'am, I jus' washed 'em all too. So they are clean. Will I shoot over an' get 'em?"

"Yes, please, Maryanne, I'll come with you," said the Major.

They left, and a gust blew the door out of the Major's hand as they exited. He managed to close it with a bang. He had to help Maryanne over the fallen branch and fence, but they made it inside. She quickly gathered up the sheets and some old towels that had just come off the line too. "Grab anything you can while you're at it. Bring some sleeping attire for you both. You're both staying at my house tonight."

Maryanne's eyes grew big, "Sir, No."

"Yes, you are. Dash it, girl. Hurry," he said impatiently.

She fled into both rooms and gathered an armload of clothing. She stuffed it into a basket and joined the Major.

He'd found a blanket, a sewing basket with scissors and a few other things and took them too. She took them from his arms as he collected the sheets and the towels.

Maryanne grabbed their cloaks as she left. The Major closed the door, and they sped quickly back to his house.

Christina met them at the door, opening it for them. She had to put her back to it to close it.

Ned dropped this pile of linen and took her in his arms. "Love, you're both staying here tonight." He bent his head and kissed her. They turned to see Maryanne, mouth open, looking from one to another. "I think we'd better let her into some of our secrets, don't you?"

She nodded.

With his arm still around her, he said, "Maryanne, I'd like you to meet my not-too-distant future wife. We're being married on Saturday."

"Oh, coo, Missus. I was so hoping he'd come up to scratch. It seems he's beaten me to it," she thought. "Saturday, but the Banns?" She stood looking at them. "You're Ned Gracemere, and you're Tina Hunt. I heard Dr Gerry here calls you that; I never twigged. Well, I'll be blowed! But them's not your real names; is that legal?"

"I told you she was quick," said Christina.

"Damn! Sorry, love." He apologised for swearing. "Looks like we have to spill the whole can of worms after all."

She stood looking at the pair of them. She was grinning from ear to ear. "There's more?"

"There's more. But first, before we tell you, this does not leave the building, all right. At least not until Sunday; we'll be safely wed by then."

Maryanne nodded, still smiling.

"May I introduce you to Lady Christina Meadows, née Hunt, and I am…" he was beginning to enjoy this revelation, "I am Edward, the Tenth Duke of Gracemere, at your service, ma'am." He gave a mock bow.

The doctor was standing beside Maryanne, and it was just as well as she fainted, and he caught her as she fell.

Christina laughed, "You might have overdone that a bit Edward."

The doctor laid her on the settee and lifted her feet. "She is out cold, poor dear," he said

After a few moments, she stirred to see three anxious faces peering down at her. "Ohhh! Did I flake? Silly me. You really shouldn't play tricks on a person like that." She put her hand to her head. She sat up slowly. "You were joking, weren't you?" All three shook their heads.

"An' I suppose you is some kinda fancy person too?" She said to the doctor.

He nodded. "Sort of, only I don't precisely have a title of that ilk.

Doctor Winslow-Smythe will do me nicely. My brother does, though." He wasn't game to say he was 'The Honourable.'

"Toffs! An' I never picked it. I knewed you was gentry, but Toffs. Humph! Well, I suppose I can keep your secret, but only if I can come to the wedding." She struggled to sit up, then grinned.

They all laughed.

"You have us over a barrel, lass," said the Major. "Yes, you can come. But not a word to anyone, mind."

She shook her head and grinned again. "Gotta love a weddin' and a secret one at that. I'll be there. You betcha." She turned to the doctor. "I'm good now. Wot ya want me doin'?"

Gerry made everyone rewash their hands with lots of soap, and then they had them cut and roll the sheets. One of the sheets he turned into slings. He also taught them how to tie on a bandage and how to put on a sling.

The Major had some basic knowledge, and Maryanne said, "I'se got little brovvers, I'se used to cuts and scrapes. I knows you gotta stop the bleedin' if there's a cut; an' to splint the arm if it waggles wrong. My littlest brovver had a bad one with the bone sticking out, we had to get him to the hospital for that one. Mos'ly we fix 'em up at home. Thankfully, they'se now grown. It's been a while, but I'se good wiv blood and stuff."

Christina admitted her sad lack of knowledge in this field, but the blood didn't worry her. "I've delivered babies and can attend to wounds." She had never had to attend to a broken bone. She had previously cleaned and bound bloody wounds; only she'd used brandy.

Gerry exclaimed, "Excellent. All right, now we have to wrap and prepare the instruments. I like to keep everything exceptionally clean. I find that the patient heals better. They should be well cleaned by now; they have been boiling for over half an hour."

They kept rolling the strips off the first sheet. One of Christina's sheets was too thin for bandages, but they tore it into smaller squares. "Excellent, excellent," he muttered. "Okay, folks, come with me." They all followed him into the kitchen. "Ned, where's some brandy or rum? I need to clean the table, oh, and a clean cloth."

The Major brought out a bottle of overproof locally brewed rum. "Here, this stuff is too potent to drink; it's probably illicit."

The doctor broke the seal and sniffed it, then pulled back quickly. "This will do nicely." Sloshing it liberally over the table, he then wiped it with a clean cloth.

He waited until it dried and placed the pile of squares of linen on the now-clean table. "I'm going to take these out of the boiling water one at a time. I'll place it on a square of cloth, and without touching it, I want you to wrap it up and tie it with that string." They saw a small bundle of strings he put on the bench next to the stovetop. Some twenty instruments were in the pan, one by one; they were dug out and wrapped. He had a bundle of oilskin pouches and sorted them by feel into different coloured pouches. Once repacked, he placed his *go* bag near the door.

They had no idea how much time had passed. They had been busy for what seemed like a long time.

Maryanne noticed it was getting really dark outside; her tummy was rumbling. "Cor, I'm hungry, Gov. Can I raid your cupboards and rustle us up somefin' to eat?"

The Major pointed to where he kept his food, and she nodded and then shooed them all from the kitchen. "I cun fix somefin' for us to eat from this lot."

They retired into the sitting room and continued to roll bandages by the lamplight. They had no idea what time it was, it felt late, but that may have been the storm. It was indeed very dark, black dark, outside.

The storm hit with a vengeance, the wind screamed, and the doors and windows rattled, but thankfully didn't break. Maryanne brought in dinner, and Christina insisted she stay and eat it with them. She wasn't going to until a crack of lightning hit close by. They all jumped. The air exploded in arcs of electricity. Rolls of thunder were almost instantly followed by rack after crack of lightning as they hit nearby. Maryanne was soon sitting on the settee with her head under a pillow. She was shaking. "I hate storms," she said.

Christina sat beside her and comforted her until she, too, jumped when one deafening bolt landed close to them.

Half-eaten food was forgotten; the wind was making the shingles flap. Then they heard a huge roar that grew and grew. It was followed by a sound like something exploding. Maryanne screamed.

Christina shuddered in the Major's arms, her head on his chest. The Major kept holding Christina and the doctor in the chair next to the settee with his hand on Maryanne's head, comforting her. Maryanne squealed with every crack and roar. It seemed to go on and on for ages, and then, as quickly as it came, the storm passed. The crickets and frogs started singing, and they knew the worst of the storm was over.

Gerry checked his watch, surprised to see it was not nearly as late as he thought, only seven o'clock. On a typical night, it would still be daylight.

Once the noise stopped, Maryanne recovered quickly and reheated the dish she'd made. They ate hastily, knowing the doctor could soon be called to help anyone injured. Woking on an empty stomach was not good.

They had finished eating, and Maryanne took the dishes into the kitchen when she noticed a red glow coming through the window. "Cor, Major, what's over there?"

He came into the kitchen and stood watching. "Gerry, look," he called.

The doctor came in. "I think we'd better head out. Looks like a fire somewhere, possibly near the church. I'll get our coats."

"Maryanne, stay with your mistress. Do not leave her side for an instant, do you understand?" She nodded.

He left the room and went to find Christina. "Love, we have to go. Maryanne has been instructed not to leave you. If you get frightened, go to the Lockleys. No. Actually, sweetheart, I want you to go there anyway. Straight away, love. Send the boys. Under no circumstances come looking for us. There will be looters and ruffians out looking for easy access to steal." He took her in his arms. "Oh, please, God, stay safe. I could not endure it if I lost you now. Yes, love, that's prayer." He kissed her forehead. "Pray for me too. We'll send the badly injured to the hospital, but you'd better set up somewhere down there to do bandaging."

She held on to him. "Oh, Edward, I will be praying too. Stay safe."

He caressed her cheek and then kissed her passionately. Before he could change his mind, he released her and walked to the door, shrugged on his oilskin coat, wrenched the door open, and walked out into the driving rain.

Maryanne came into the sitting room. "Ma'am, come look at this. It's what the Major saw."

Christina followed her into the kitchen and saw a red glow from a fire flick into the sky. "Oh, no, it's the church, Maryanne. Quick, get out, cloaks; we're going straight to the Lockleys. Now! Grab the rest of the bandages and my sewing box. I'll bring these blankets and a few of those pillows. Doing something is better than nothing. They might be able to send the men to help. Keep everything as dry as you can."

She bundled as much as she could and wrapped her lot in a blanket. Maryanne did the same, and they put their cloaks on and headed down the road to the Inn.

Sal greeted them on the verandah. She took Christina's bundle and handed it to Anna. She said nothing but opened her arms to Christina.

Maryanne followed Anna inside.

"Oh, Sally, I'm so frightened. Edward and Gerry have gone to the fire. Has Charles gone too?"

Sal nodded, "Yes, and he has taken the four boys. Jenna and Eddie arrived some minutes after the storm passed. We didn't know, but they look down on the church from their place. The glow lit up their room." They stood arm in arm, watching the sky.

Christina said, "Gerry knew this would happen. He's had us making bandages since we went home. I have the spare bandages here and some slings. He taught us how to use them too. Edward told me to come here. He didn't want me there alone."

Sal said, "I'm so glad he did. I feel better with you here too. Christina, they are in God's hands; we can only pray they stay safe. Let's go turn this place into a bandage station. First, I'll put lots of water on to boil."

They walked into the kitchen.

"Girls, we're going to prepare this place for any injuries. The hospital will be overwhelmed with the badly injured, and I'm sure Doctor Gerry will send some here," said Sal. She pulled a bottle of Heatherbrae Whisky from the cupboard. "This is my strongest spirit here, but it will do."

Christina nodded, "Yes, that's what Gerry said he'd do."

The next few hours were bedlam. The rain still pelted down; the darkness was enveloping. They could hear the river rising but couldn't see how close it was in the darkness. People kept arriving throughout the night with cuts, scrapes and broken arms. The girls kept dousing the wounds with rum and bandaging. Christina met each one and assessed them before sending them to be washed, cleaned up, and bound by Sal and Maryanne. Jenna was on bandage duty, and Anna kept up supplies of hot water.

Once treated, the patients were sent to the shed to occupy hammocks or the barn where ever they could find a place to rest. Both timber buildings had withstood the storm. The women each grabbed a few hours of sleep through the night. Sal had sent Jenna to lie down early in the evening.

At dawn, the last of the storm had passed. The sun rose on a shattered town. Anna was pouting until she saw Jenna the following day. She grabbed a basin and threw up.

"Ohh," said Anna. "Mama knows something, doesn't she?"

Jenna nodded. Head in hand, she groaned.

"You need a cup of tea, love," Sal said as she walked in. "Looks like the secret is out."

Jenna just nodded again.

Christina walked in as Jenna threw up again.

"Ohh," said Christina. "Poor love. Now I know why Sal wouldn't let you lift the water pots."

Sal handed her a mug of tea and a jar of white powder. "That first, then the tea." She tipped some in her hand and popped it in her mouth.

"Oh, it fizzes," Jenna said, giggling whilst foaming at the mouth. "It's nice, though. It's lemony."

"What's that?" asked Christina.

"Nothing more than baking powder and powdered sugar with lemon juice for flavour. Helps with morning sickness. Nothing in it to hurt, either. Trust me, it works. I've had six confinements." She pushed the tea closer to Jenna, "You'll be right now once that's in you."

All the girls had slept in their clothes. Christina took the boys' bed, Jenna curled up next to Anna, and Sal grabbed what sleep she could while keeping her eye on the others. They were all tired, but they kept in mind that none of the boys had slept at all.

An hour or so after dawn, the men arrived back at the Inn. All were exhausted and filthy. Gerry checked out the patients in the shed and barn while the rest of the boys ambled into the kitchen.

Charles took Sal in his arms, as did Ed with Jenna and the Major with Christina. They assured them they were all fine, just tired.

Sal made tea. There was nothing like a cup of hot tea to help when stressed. She handed it out and put a big spoonful of honey in each mug.

The Major took a deep drink. "The fire wasn't at the church, it was the hall next to it, but the church is nearly destroyed. The Rectory is the worst hit thought. There's a strip of devastation through the middle of town. Roofs are gone. It's torn right through the middle of the church. The roof is nearly gone." He sounded exhausted. "Looks like the town was hit by a tornado last night. That's what the roar was."

Gerry came in, dirty and tired too. "You did a wonderful job, ladies. I've sent most of the patients home, that's if they have a home to go to. There are three to be taken to the hospital for more treatment. The other wounded men are escorting them there. They are the ones with broken arms."

Sal took one look at him. He was smeared with blood and had a tear in his jacket. She handed him some sweet tea too.

Feeling that it was not too hot, he downed it.

Charles outlined more of the damage. They had come home for a few hours of sleep; then, they would head back and start the cleanup.

The Major stood and said to Christina, "Darling, you stay here if you don't mind. The rest of the tree has fallen, and you can't enter your door. Do you mind Sally?"

Sal shook his head. "Of course, Major."

He bent and gave Christina a quick kiss. "We'll be back in a few hours. We need to sleep." He and the doctor stood and left.

Charles said, "We're the same. We'll sleep for a few hours, then head back."

Charlie and Eddie headed for the girls' room and were asleep almost before their heads hit the pillows. Wills and Luke were already asleep; they hadn't even had tea.

The girls crept into the kitchen and talked about how they could help. Jenna decided to harness up the cart and dray with Bobbs and James. They added axes, spades, shovels, saws, hammers, and nails.

Jenna and Anna went to the smithy shop, filling some baskets with assorted nails. "If the shingles were off, they'd need repair." So, she added two extra boxes of roofing nails. Jenna had helped sort the stock, so she knew where everything was kept. They loaded some baskets and carried them back down to the Inn; Anna took the heaviest one and apologised for her earlier behaviour. Jenna had one basket and also held a pile of empty hessian bags.

They arrived back tired but laughing. They split their booty between both vehicles. They added a few small barrels of water, some mugs, and a basket of warm buttered, sliced soda bread onto each cart. Sal appeared with a basket of hard-boiled eggs, still warm. By the time they had assembled their loads, hours had passed.

Charles emerged heavy-eyed but feeling a bit better. Sal shuffled him into the kitchen and placed a large plateful of bacon, eggs and toast in front of him. More sounds were coming from the girl's room, and Eddie and Charlie both appeared. Both were rubbing their eyes. They, too, were handed tea and a plate of food. The Major and Doctor Gerry joined them shortly afterwards and were soon all eating.

Sal thought she'd let the young boys sleep; they would need their strength later when the men were flagging. They had other ideas. This was the most exciting thing that had happened in their short lives. Even more exciting than finding their Dar's best friend was a Duke.

Anna and Jenna were told to stay home and instructed on what to prepare for later. They needed to make lots of soda bread as that was quicker than yeast bread. They got busy.

Everyone else hopped on the two carts and headed to the church square.

What they saw on arrival stunned them. The church roof was shredded. There were many milling around in shock, the damage to not only the church but many nearby buildings as well. The Sanctuary was undamaged, as was the vestry, but, oh, the Rectory, there was virtually nothing left.

As the newspapers were later to report:-

"The Reverend Mr. Bobart has suffered more severely still. The whole north-west end of his house is uncovered, and masses of wood, shingles, rafters, beams, and even a coping stone, weighing nearly two hundredweight, were carried along with the whole extent of the roof, and thrown, without touching it, over the kitchen (an out-building) to the eastward. The ruins there are really astonishing; the ground for nearly sixty yards, more or less, is literally strewed with straw. One mass of stone fell, I believe, into one of the bedrooms through the ceiling. It is a great and providential mercy that this did not occur in the night, for the rooms both in the church and parsonage are inhabited, and so sudden was the mischief that life might have been lost."

No one spoke. All sat just looking. Shocked.

Christina noticed that the clock had stopped at six o'clock. It felt so much later than that when the storm hit. Maybe because it had been so dark, she hopped off the cart and crossed to where Mrs. Bobart stood, two small children clutching her skirt.

Christina stood looking at what remained of their house.

Tears were streaming down her face. "A twisting wind ripped it apart," was all Elizabeth could say to Christina. "It just exploded. We were hiding in the office. It's the only room undamaged. The good Lord protected us."

Christina enfolded Elizabeth in her arms and let her sob. "At least you're safe, Elizabeth," Christina whispered.

Her action spurred everyone to do something.

Repairs were out of the question. Cleaning up is what was needed to make things safe.

Wills and Luke started first.

Charles gave them a warning to watch for broken glass and nails. They took off, each carrying a bag. Other boys soon joined them.

It would take days to clean the yard. The boys had started piling up shingles; most could be reused. Broken glass was in another pile, branches in another. Some of which had already been piled for firewood. The boys and their friends worked out a plan of action; they cleared pathways first.

The men started at the Bobart's house. Christina said they could stay at her place as she had a spare room.

Elizabeth was still weeping as they entered what remained of their house. She and Christina finally made their way past the crumbled guest room and into their bedroom and were able to gather armloads of clothing. It took hours, but eventually, they had cleared the bedrooms of all their clothing. Then they collected books and other items from the untouched office. Other valuable items that the wind had spared were also packed.

Eddie had emptied one of the wagons, and they loaded everything they could onto it.

Charlie and the Major had gone back to remove the tree that had fallen on Christina's fence and door. They had just finished when the loaded vehicle arrived, driven by Eddie. The three men unloaded everything into Christina's sitting room. They could sort it out later. At least they had somewhere safe and dry to sleep, and the children would have to sleep on the floor. After an exhausting day of working hard, everyone arrived at the Inn for a meal.

Jenna, Anna, and Liza, who had come to help, had cooked up a massive pile of food for anyone who arrived. They had made a huge stew as it could stretch by adding potatoes and would keep hot no matter when it was eaten. They had made soda bread, which didn't take as long to cook.

The men were almost too tired to eat, and everyone went to bed with little conversation other than the bare necessities. Maryanne had cleaned out the room she had been sleeping in and set it up for the Bobarts. She would sleep on a truckle bed in the other bedroom with Christina.

Everyone was asleep by dark, knowing they would be needed again tomorrow.

Liza and Jenna had let on to the family that they were both in the family way.

Hands Upon The Anvil

No one felt like celebrating Christmas, but the church ground was cleared by Friday evening. The congregation was asked to bring blankets for an outdoor service of Thanksgiving, for there had been no deaths. The fire had been in an old building earmarked for removal and had not spread to any other building. The lightning strike on the church had hit and stopped the clock, it blew off the shingles nearby, leaving a massive hole in the roof, but it did not catch fire. Yes, a Thanksgiving service was in order.

Elizabeth sent the children to her sister, Martha, as they had little room in Christina's house but no room for the parents with her sister.

Christina and Elizabeth stood in the shattered church and discussed if the wedding could still occur, and they finally persuaded the men that it could.

They planned the ceremony after everyone left after the service; they would sneak into the Sanctuary through the vestry door and have the wedding as planned.

The service was a 'go.' The wedding ceremony was on.

The men removed all the debris before Maryanne took charge of 'doing' the church. She mobilised the girls to clean the Sanctuary. The ladies were to sort out the linens for the Altar.

Elizabeth and Christina had joined them. Many even came to help, not realising why this family had taken a special interest in its restoration.

On Friday, Mrs. Jenkins brought some of her roses that had survived and bloomed since the storm. She placed them on the Altar, bowed and left. She also did not know about the upcoming ceremony.

The Sanctuary had remained virtually unscathed by the ravages of wind. There were a few leaves and some dampness.

In the morning light, the damaged roof brought in shafts of sunlight that caught and flashed from the gilt cross.

Chapter 19   Christmas

*T*he day dawned bright and sunny. The overwhelming humidity of the last week passed, and the wind had dropped to the point of being breathless.

The service was to be earlier than usual, at 7 a.m., as it was now outdoors. This meant that everyone would be gone soon afterwards, and the family could sneak in to celebrate the wedding.

Sal arrived, and with Elizabeth's assistance, they helped Christina dress. They added the blue overskirt, and Elizabeth handed her a parasol, which matched the skirt. She looked amazing. The Bobart's town carriage survived the storm and had been taken to the Lockley's shed with their mare. It was now harnessed to their bay mare. The Bobarts and Christina drove their carriage to church and waited in the Sanctuary. They stayed out of sight of everyone, remaining hidden until everyone was singing. They managed to keep out of sight, even the family. Christina could see the Major sitting off to the side, but she was hidden from view by the tree trunk.

The Christmas Thanksgiving service finished, and everyone moved away quite quickly.

Elizabeth ushered Christina to the back of the remains of the Rectory to await the time. There was a small sitting room near the office that they waited in.

Sal said, "They have all gone; come on."

They stood to leave, and Elizabeth opened a drawer and grabbed something.

They walked back to the church and in through the vestry door. Sal helped remove the overskirt.

Elizabeth caught Christina's hand. "Wait, I have something for you to wear." She unrolled her own wedding veil. She placed it on Christina's head and put a large flower wreath on top to hold it in place. She looked beautiful.

Christina hugged her. "Thank you, dear friend."

Sal handed her some white roses taken carefully from Mrs. Jenkins's flowers on the Altar.

Sal walked into the shattered church and sat in one of the undamaged front pews with the family, and they waited.

Elizabeth nodded to her husband, who stood up and waved the couple together. They came together at the steps to the Sanctuary. Christina glowed, the cream gown reflecting the sunlight. The Major was awestruck.

The service started.

They were soon husband and wife. Only those present knew their secret identities; Elizabeth knew something else.

"You may now kiss your bride." Ned heard the words he'd waited for more than a year. He moved her veil aside; it wasn't covering her face but had slipped over her shoulders. He lifted her chin and kissed her, whispering, "I love you, my Duchess."

"I love you too, my Duke," she whispered back.

In that service, their new identities were accepted and declared. The Major was now happy to be known as His Grace. However, they wouldn't announce it yet. Christina was Her Grace, and she would one day wear that silver strawberry Coronet of a Duchess well.

During the signing of the register, Elizabeth moved to Christina and fiddled with the floral wreath. She removed half of the head wreath, leaving just a crown of strawberry leaves. It was not silver with diamonds; there were more than eight leaves, but she was now a Duchess and wore a ducal coronet. The Major gasped and smiled. He gave a big smile to Elizabeth. Christina lifted her hands and felt them and realised what they were too. She turned and thanked Elizabeth. They signed the register, and Gerry and Charles were called as witnesses. The marriage above theirs was Eddie and Jenna's, a mere three weeks before.

The Reverend had printed his title and left room for a signature underneath it. He signed Edward, Gracemere, and Christina signed her name for the last time. However, she noticed that Henry had written her full title as The Lady Christina Hunt Meadows. She lifted her eyes and smiled at Ned. Her Edward, now and forever.

Maryanne was in tears, as was Sally.

The service was over, and everyone gathered in the Vestry.

Maryanne threw some flower petals she had collected.

The number who had been admitted into their secret had grown. Eighteen crowded the room. Everyone had to meander back to the Inn without causing too much interest.

Eddie brought their town carriage for the married couple, as the veil and coronet would have given their secret away. Charles and Sal travelled with them. All the others would walk down leisurely. Elizabeth and Henry Bobart still had to lock up the Vestry before leaving.

Gerry, Maryanne and Jenna had decided that Gerry would move

into Christina's house with the Bobarts, leaving the newly married couple a place to themselves. Maryanne and Jenna packed up much of Christina's clothing. Gerry did the same, and they changed rooms. They would sort out their possessions later, but there was enough for a few nights. Maryanne would sleep in the sitting room of Christina's cottage on her truckle bed.

With everything that had happened that week, it would be nice for the newlyweds to have some time alone.

Amongst the devastation of the past week, Sal had managed to cook up a feast. A roast was cooking while they were at church, and only the finishing touches had to be added. All would be ready by the time everyone arrived.

Ned could barely take his eyes off Christina. Finally, they were married. She looked at him across the room and walked over to him. "I was thinking, Your Grace, maybe you would like to walk me home so I may change. I would not like to dirty this gown." She dropped her eyes and gave him a saucy look. "It should take me about an hour, don't you think?"

His eyebrow raised. "Oh, my love, I would not like you to walk alone; I shall happily accompany you. I shall explain to Charles."

They walked to Charles, who was deep in conversation with Gerry, and he explained Christina's desire to change her lovely cream gown.

Gerry grinned, "Ahh, Ned, Tina," addressing Christina, "Maryanne, Jenna and I have moved your clothing into Ned's house and mine into yours. Tina, Maryanne has hung your gowns in my old room. You may need to check that they are all there." He turned and winked at Ned.

Ned grinned and mouthed, "Thank you." He left with a spring in his step. They took their farewell from Sal, promising to return once they were changed. They would be back in time for the noon Christmas meal. They sauntered off slowly, wandering up the hill hand in hand, no longer caring who saw them.

He opened his door, bent to pick her up, carrying her over the threshold. He kicked the door shut, taking her directly to his bed, and gently lay her down.

She pulled him down beside her. "I'm never letting you go again," she whispered as he was about to kiss her.

Back at the Inn, the kitchen was crowded with many cooks. Sal turned and sent both Liza and Jenna out of the kitchen. "The table needs setting, you two," she said.

Maryanne was washing pots and pans as they were used. She was singing carols as she worked, it caught on, and soon all the ladies were singing carols at the top of their voices as they worked.

Gerry, Charles, and Reverend Mr. Bobart sat on the verandah, ales in hand. The rest of the boys were hanging around the barn, also tankards in hand.

Everyone had worked out that both Bertie and Eddie were to be fathers. Much back-slapping and congratulations ensued. Eddie said, "It's so early for us; please don't say anything to anyone else yet. If she weren't so ill, no one would know." He looked embarrassed.

Charles joined the boys to ask Eddie and Charlie to help him with a small job. They followed him as he led them down to the cellar. He led them to the back and pulled back a cloth. "Can you take that upstairs, please? I bought a box of French champagne for today's celebration. I do not know what it's like, but I noticed it's been going to Government House, so it must be drinkable. I have purchased a case for our celebration."

They decided to take two bottles each first and get the rest as needed, as it was cooler in the cellar.

They arrived upstairs as Christina and Ned came back. She was dressed in the cornflower blue gown she'd seen in the shop window. It had a lace trim around a neckline, and she looked fabulous. It outlined her tiny waist with a dropped-point full skirt.

Gerry was looking at their faces. For the first time in a long time, Ned's face was relaxed, and Tina's glowing even more. He met his friend's eyes across the room. Gerry raised an eyebrow, and Ned grinned back, his eyes twinkling with happiness, and gave a slight bow, smiling.

Charles walked in with a bottle of champagne. He handed it to Gerry and asked him to do the honours. There were no fancy glasses at the Inn, so Charles had raided the Government Store again and borrowed two boxes of the best champagne glasses destined for Government House in Parramatta.

Gerry popped the cork. Charles was holding a glass ready and caught the overflow. Gerry opened and poured two more bottles, filling each of the glasses.

Maryanne was brought in and joined the celebration.

After each person had a glass, Gerry said. "Let us drink a toast to the bride and groom."

Everyone cheered and toasted them. More toasts followed, and the ladies retired to the kitchen to bring out the food. Platter after platter was brought from the kitchen and placed on the sideboard until it was full. Christina and Ned sat at the head of the table, Charles and Sal to either side of them along the bench seats. Gerry was at the foot of the table but held court as the conversation included everyone. Maryanne was encouraged to join in and eventually was persuaded, but the only spare place was next to Gerry. She was overwhelmed as she had discovered him to be an Earl's son.

Soon rank and pomp were discarded as merriment ensued. Maryanne was waited on by Sal, Sal by Maryanne and so on. All attended to the needs of the bride and groom. After the first course had been cleared away, Jenna and Liza called in Maryanne, and the three girls disappeared into the kitchen. Maryanne stacked the dishes as Liza and Jenna bumped and banged. Maryanne appeared at the door smiling, holding a jug of custard.

"Please, Yer Grace, m'Lady," she nodded to them. "We'se wanted to do somethin' special for your'se, so we'se been cookin' up a storm."

Jenna appeared with a cake covered in whipped cream with the number 33 on top written in strawberries with eight leaves around as decoration, and Liza brought a Queen pudding with a bowl of cream.

"We couldn't find a Jook's puddin', so this is the nearest we could do," said Maryanne.

Everyone laughed. They had forgotten it was Christina's birthday today too. Maryanne had not.

Elizabeth Bobart caught Christina's eye. She wiped away a tear but smiled. "What a week," she said, "One I'll never forget. Thanks to darling Christina we have a roof over our heads and a dry bed to sleep in. I can never thank her enough. I would not have missed this luncheon for anything. But we must leave to join the family soon."

The meal continued. A second trip to the cellar was needed. Charles was just about to call the boys. Ned asked if he could come.

They entered the cool, darkened room and gathered the last six bottles of champagne. "Charles, how can I ever thank you for all this? We hoped to have a quiet wedding and slip away. The storm put paid to that."

Charles laughed. "Well, you've already, um, slipped away." He paused, swallowing. "Ned, I'm going to say something I told Eddie. It's personal, but it's needed. Christina is the love of your life, and I'm so pleased you have her. She knows about things, as I'm sure you do, but something I learnt early in my marriage was, let's say, I was too vigorous with my cleansing. I saw Sal was in great discomfort after we had been married a week. We discovered that the carbolic or lye in the soap I used in my private areas burned her. I had no idea. Hot water is all you need." Phew, he'd said it.

Ned chuckled. "Charles, only a true friend, could have said that. Thank you. I had no idea. I will remember. Not the sort of thing you hear about in a Soldiers Mess, I assure you. Just one of the few topics not discussed."

They laughed as they took the remaining bottles upstairs.

~

Christmas Day and the New Year came and went. The weather was still hot and muggy. Christina had fully moved into Ned's cottage, and Gerry settled into her old room. Word had crept out about the secret Christmas wedding. Bill and Molly found out from Gracie. However, It wasn't until January, when the church's next marriage occurred, that the newly married couple's identity was finally revealed. The church still had no roof, but they had cleaned it up enough for some partial use.

One of the soldiers in the Major's old brigade married his sweetheart. On signing the register, he noticed the signatures above his own as he was signing. He knew the Major had married Christina Meadows, but

Edward Grace was not the name next to hers. He read the printed name and gasped. He signed, then spun around and looked directly at him, mouth agape.

The Duke just smiled back sheepishly. He leaned towards Christina. "I think our secret is out. He read the register. Prepare yourself for an onslaught."

Sure enough, on leaving the church, the new bride and groom spread the word as people left. By the time they appeared, the churchyard was in almost pandemonium.

The Reverend Mr. Bobart stood beside his wife, her arm hooked onto his. "All is now revealed, my dear. About time too. I thought it would sneak out today. They have to get used to it sometime."

Elizabeth replied. "Henry, you are naughty." She smiled as she patted his hand.

They turned to walk back into the broken church. He stopped. "God is in his firmament, and all is well. Yes, I know it's a paraphrase, but it's true." They stood looking up at the blue, blue sky. "Sometimes I think it will be sad when the church is repaired. It's so beautiful. Since the storm, I have often thought of Psalm 19 as I have been in pottering around."

"The heavens declare the glory of God;
And the firmament shows His handiwork."

After the congregation returned home, the word spread throughout the small town quickly.

By Monday, when Ned and Christina walked by the riverbank in the cool of the morning, every person they passed greeted them with a bow and "Good Morning, Your Grace." Ned would bow and keep walking.

They would have to get used to this as the time for departure was drawing close. Ned had finally booked their passage on the *Sarah Botsford*, a barque under Captain Wallace's charge. It was due in port soon and would have a few weeks turnaround. This would give them until early March to pack what they intended to take and transport it to Sydney.

Thomas and Margaret Tindale had been let into the secret early. They had returned after Christmas to pack what items they would need to furnish their room at Caroline's place. She was there with her youngest son John, who worked as a Naturalist. He worked with Mr. Holmes at the new Australian Museum. He often had his head in the clouds but was always good company.

Thomas had booked a suite of rooms for them at The King's Arms, one of the better establishments in Sydney. The dates were somewhat flexible as there was no definite sailing date. He had put a hold on the entire month of March.

Most nights over summer, there had been a gathering of clouds, and it had rained either late afternoon or at night, more nights in January. The church did not fare so well in this inclement weather, open to the sky as it was. Services were held on the church lawns, and they were well attended by the town.

The Bobarts had finally moved in with her sister Martha and her husband. Their house had been hastily rearranged for them; their stay would be outdrawn until the Rectory could be repaired. Plans were already underway for this.

February came and went.

Liza and Jenna had both announced to the greater community that they were expecting, and by early March, Sal was watching Christina; Sal was sure she was showing signs too. Christina was pale and wan sometimes. "I'll find out for sure next Sunday. We'll have a roast again; that will do the trick."

Sure enough, she asked Christina into the kitchen to talk while preparing luncheon for the family. Sal pulled out the roasted meat tray and put it on the bench before Christina had perched herself on a stool. That did it. Christina departed quickly to the verandah, closely followed by Sally. "Ha, I thought so," she said.

"Thought what, Sal?" Christina asked.

"If you haven't yet worked it out, you will soon. Had your menses since you were married?" Sal asked blatantly.

"No! Oh, Sally, do you think I might be... um, interesting? So soon?" Her hands fell to her flat stomach. "After years of marriage, I never fell pregnant. I thought it was me." She stood in awe and wonderment.

"Really?" A smile slowly spread over her face. Her eyes were shining with overwhelming joy.

"Meat did it for me every time, and I've had six. I couldn't stand the smell of it being cooked. Doesn't work with everyone but more often than not. Soft egg yolks were another thing. It was always the first sign for me. Worked for both Liza and Jenna too, although it was early for her, very early actually." Sal paused. Thinking of the two girls, Liza would be a month further along than Jenna, but Jenna had already let out her dresses once, saying that they were tight. This was puzzling, as she was only just four months along. She had also been a lot sicker than Liza. Time will tell.

Christina stood in silence, thoughts running through her mind.

Sal said, "Does Edward know?"

Christina shook her head. "I didn't know until you told me."

At that moment, Edward appeared. "Know what love?" He had seen her hasty departure from the kitchen as he had been sitting so he could watch her.

Sal said, "Now seems as good a time as any," and walked back into the kitchen.

"Edward, no, Ned..." she started.

"Oh, now I know something is wrong. You never call me that." He put his hands on her waist and drew her to him. "It can't be that bad, love.

A problem shared is…."

She interrupted. "Edward, it's not exactly a problem, but it *is* shared, at least will be."

He looked very puzzled.

She took one of his hands and placed it on her stomach. She then looked him in the eye. "No, not a problem at all. It seems the problem was not mine after all."

Ned looked lovingly at her, and then it dawned. "Are you serious? Can it be? Oh my, how wonderful!" He swept her into his arms and passionately kissed her regardless of anyone watching. "Oh, my dear love," his voice caught; he had a lump in his throat. They stood in each other's arms, both deep in thought.

Charles walked into the kitchen in search of Ned.

Sal grabbed his arm. "Leave them," she said, nodding for him to look out the window instead.

Charles saw them embracing. "What's happened? Anything wrong?"

"No," said Sal. "They are all fine," she smiled, waiting for that to sink in.

It took nearly a minute. Charles swung around. "No," he said, "but you said Christina wondered if she could have children. She had not fallen during her last marriage," he exclaimed.

"Well, it seems the problem was never hers. She thought she had a tummy bug. She's been sick for the last month. So we have another honeymoon baby on the way." She placed the vegetables on a platter and handed it to Charles. "Just as well; they are heading off soon so the babe can be born in the Castle. I hope it's a smooth trip home." She stuck her head out the kitchen door, "Come on, you three. Lunch is served."

Ned bent and kissed the top of Christina's head as they walked back into the kitchen. He could not wipe the smile from his face. He made an announcement as soon as they walked in.

Jenna had been already wondering and guessed as soon as they came in. She raced over and hugged her. "I thought you may be. I'm so excited for you both too."

Ed was the first to shake his hand. "Who would have thought, sir, that we'd be fathers at nearly the same time? Congratulations!"

The Major beamed. He was still trying to get his head around it. But he was over the moon.

Later that afternoon, when most of the young family had gone, Charlie walked Anna to visit Gracie and Tim. The two young boys had gone to the river for a swim. Eddie sat on the verandah with his arms wrapped around Jenna, Ned with his arms around Christina, both still stunned, and Charles sitting next to Sal, holding her hand.

Gerry sat alone, watching them all, smiling to himself. "Do you know, I often wonder how God loves to twist and weave people's lives in strange ways? If Ed here had not been attacked and I would have still been looking for Ned under a different name, I could only presume he was using, as I knew he was not enlisted under his own. That was a fruitless search. One day there will be a term for this."

Christina lovingly looked at her husband. "Edward would never have asked me to marry him if you had not sprung your news on him."

Charles said, "Oh, it started long before that. It was on the ship out. I noticed you watching me, Jack and I knew I could trust you. You were not like the other soldiers. I knew you would believe Jack and me when I told you what the others had planned. But I had to do it on the down low. You understood and took me aside and questioned me in your cabin. I have often puzzled over that."

Ned simply said, "You reminded me of someone. I was intrigued. You know Charles, you never told me about your family. Neither of you have ever mentioned any family at all."

Sal said, "There was only my Mama and me. Par died when I was young. My Mama ensured I could read and write, so I got a good job, but she got sick. I told my story to Doctor Gerry, but I don't speak much about it. I borrowed £1 to take her to the doctor and worked hard to earn money to pay it back. I was on my way to do so when a carriage knocked me down. The money was stolen, and I got arrested. I never saw Mama again. I was considered Irish, so mistreated. I had never even been to Ireland."

"Charles? And you?" asked Gerry.

"Ned can vouch that I was accused of sheep theft. The butcher used to run his flock down the street to the knackery. We all knew to keep the yard gates closed. We were on the outskirts of town, but the one at the front of our place had a broken hinge and would not stay shut. We used to keep a rock behind it, but someone forgot to put it in place that day. I came home one afternoon to find a stray ram in my yard. I was shooing it out when the Constable came with the owner and arrested me. I wasn't hung because I could prove I had not been there when the flock went through. I got fourteen years and transportation. I blamed God; I blamed my mother and my little sister. I could not see how God could let this happen. I was so angry. I knew I was innocent but hung around with a rough group." He sat thinking. "After six months sitting in the stinking hulks, I was put on the Major's ship. I thought the hulks were bad, but the conditions on board the transport ship were even more cramped, and our boat had a rough trip. Thanks to Ned, we were only below decks for a short while. At least the hulks were still. So mix all those smells together with vomit and stench. Well, you get the picture." He had looked at both Christina and Jenna and saw them both blanch. "The only good thing is I got chained next to Jack Turner, Jenna's Pa. Even then, he was a man of faith. We talked a lot; we even prayed a bit. That was hard to do, but because we were quiet, we could hear others' whisperings, which is how we discovered their mutiny plans.

You know the rest, Ned. You know what life on board was like." Charles sat pondering the past.

Ned asked, "Where did this occur, Charles? Was it in London? I never looked, and the full records were not sent anyway."

"No! We lived in Kent in a village called Coxheath. It's near Maidstone. Pa died when I was young; I was about five. I don't remember him very much, but he was a soldier. We had the cottage and some income from somewhere. I never bothered to ask Ma. The last time I saw them was in the courtroom. Ma and my sister were both in tears," he said. "Their names were both Elizabeth. I called Liza after them both. It's hard to believe my sister would now be thirty-six. I still think of her as a kid."

Christina and Gerry looked at Ned.

Ned shook his head.

Charles said, "I feel guilty now; I never wrote to them again. I should have, I know. Maybe I will. I presume the cottage is still there. Maybe Lilabet is still living in it." Charles mused, "It was a pretty two-story cottage with a thatched roof called *Bramblemere*."

Ned gasped, then squeezed Christina's hand. His gasp went unnoticed by Charles. However, Gerry's eyes flew to Ned.

Ned blanched.

Chapter 20   Sailing Away

*C*aptain Roberts arrived with a note from the King's Arms Hotel manager. It read, "The *Sarah Botsford* will be leaving next week. Captain Wallace had a few passengers booked in, so he's allocated five cabins for you. He's not had a Duke and Duchess on board and offered to even give up his own cabin."

The tides were right; the weather looked calm. Ned, Christina and Gerry packed their belongings. They sent them by a carrier to town, but as it was a rough trip by dirt road, it would be better for Christina to travel by ferry in her delicate condition. Ed and Jenna decided to accompany them. Charlie would be on call at the forge if required.

The trip to Sydney was to occur the following Wednesday. All the family and many friends went to the wharf to see them off. Even Harry Moffatt came to bid Gerry goodbye. The Major's 48th battalion gave them a guard of honour onto the waterfront and farewelled the ducal couple with a fifteen-gun salute in recognition of his new status.

Sal handed Christina a wrapped ceramic jar with a cork lid with a ribbon tied around its top. "It's not so much a gift as medicine. Hopefully, your sickness will abate soon, but this will help; half a teaspoon as required. Get more made-up on board. It's easy to make. The recipe is written on the card."

Christina hugged and thanked her friend. There was so much more to say and no time left. She just hugged her again. Tears filled her eyes. Elizabeth Bobart had said her farewells in private earlier in the day. Charles had spent much time with his dear friend. He found the parting hard.

The ladies were handed aboard by Gerry. Eddie and Ned sorted the remaining luggage and their small bag too. The little steam paddlewheel ferry pulled out and headed off down the river. They stayed waving until it was out of sight. Then as they had done so many times before, they headed back to the Inn. Sal was teary. Charles was too, but he tried not to show it but wiped his eyes.

"Sal, how would you like a trip out to see Jenna's parents? I think we deserve a break. As soon as Eddie gets back, we'll go." He asked as they were walking back. He had his arm around her shoulders.

She merely nodded, too sad to speak. Tears started to flow, and Charles stopped and just embraced her. "I'm going to miss her so much. I'm so sad I wasted so much time when we could have been friends long before." She sobbed into his shoulder.

Charles said quietly into the hair. "You know, I don't think they will forget us." His heart hurt.

~

Eddie and Jenna had arranged to stay at The King's Arms with Ned and Christina.

Ned had booked rooms for them all. They would remain until they sailed on the Friday tide and return home on the evening ferry with Captain Roberts.

Mrs. Evans had invited everyone to dinner the night they arrived, and Eddie escorted them on the short walk to her house.

Eddie and the Major hung back as the doctor ushered the ladies inside. Eddie said, "Sir, this is where the tree was. I was in that upstairs room." He pointed to it. "He was standing right here and just looking at my window." He shivered, remembering back to that fateful night eleven years before. "The storm was overhead, and the lightning was one after the other. I saw the tree get hit and explode. I knew he had still been under it. He had no time to move."

He felt an arm on his shoulder. "Thanks for telling me, lad. I would never have sent him if I'd known you had already left. But God had other plans. I'm not saying He struck him down. But by you seeing what happened, it became real. You knew you were safe. It is over. Lay that ghost to rest, Ed."

Eddie nodded. "Yes, sir, it's funny, but now I've shown you. I think I can." They went inside and joined the others.

They walked back to The King's Arms after the evening meal.

Both ladies were tired and said they would head to bed. The men decided to head to the sitting room for a post-dinner drink. They discussed how sad it was that Mrs. Evans would likely never find out what happened to her husband. His ship was probably lost at sea. It was just so sad.

They covered various subjects until the conversation turned to the interesting condition of both ladies.

Gerry drank to the two prospective fathers. He lay back in the armchair and said, "I'm glad I have a chance to talk to you both. I'm putting on my doctor's hat here." He pretended to pull on a hat. "I have been observing both the ladies with my doctor's eye." He paused, eyeing them both, before continuing. "Firstly, Ned, I'm glad I shall be with you on this trip, as Tina's condition can make her one of two things. She will either be fighting fit, or she will be very sick. Hopefully, the former, but like Jenna, she has been surprisingly ill. I've seen this often occur in later age confinements," he paused, "But more often, where the mother is carrying twins."

Both prospective fathers had just taken a mouthful of their drinks. Both choked and said in unison, "What?"

"I thought I should warn you, both of you; it's a possibility. Ed, I noticed that Jenna is showing already. Although I have not examined her and won't, as I don't think she is further along than you say."

Eddie shook his head. "No! Absolutely not possible."

"Then, as she is showing already, complaining her clothing is tight, and Liza is not, and she is a month further along, this could, and I say could, be a possibility too. You don't have to say anything to her but keep it in the back of your mind."

He turned to his friend. "Now, Ned, in your situation, when the said mother is beyond the age of thirty summers, it is more likely that she too may, and I again say *may*, fall with twins. Her constant illness has worried me. When I considered it, it occurred to me the only solution in both cases." He let this sink in, intently watching their faces.

They each looked at each other and then back to the doctor.

Ned spoke first, "Gerry, damn you. How dare you pull my leg like that. You had me for a while."

Eddie nodded and exhaled slowly with relief.

"Ned, old boy, actually, I'm serious," said Gerry languidly, reclining in his chair and taking a swig of his drink. "You too, Ed; better to be prepared."

"Cor," was all Eddie could muster. Running his hand through his blonde tresses, he broke out in a cold sweat. "Twins." He looked over at the Major.

He, too, was mopping his brow. "Two! Well, I'll be blowed. We weren't expecting any. Christina said she had never fallen in her first marriage. So we knew that was a possibility that we would never have any. That didn't worry me as long as I had her. I still have two more brothers, and you told me they both have sons, Gerry?" He looked inquiringly at Gerry.

"Yes, they both have sons," confirmed Gerry. "Twins can run in the family, including one set of twins in yours, Ned."

Then Ned said, "Damn it, I forgot that Paul had been a twin." He looked aghast. Ned frowned at Gerry. "Well, the succession is safe. Now to keep Christina safe, and I go and do this to her." He mopped his brow again, then groaned. "Oh, my poor love."

The three sat in stunned silence for some time, holding their glasses but not imbibing. All three were deep in thought, but Ed made excuses and returned to his room.

Later that evening, as they walked up the stairs, they came upon an interesting site. Ned and Gerry saw Mr. Falconer-Meade heading down the stairs with one lad. A young man was walking up the stairs in front of them. He stopped and gazed at what he saw. Coming up the stairs was another young man about the same age accompanied by Mr. Falconer-Meade. The three stood looking at each other. The young men were the mirror image of each other. They had stopped, staring at each other.

Ned and Gerry nodded good evening to Falconer-Meade, but he did not notice them; he, too, was staring at the newcomer. They had to step around them to ascend to their rooms. The doctor looked back and shook his head. "Twins and their tricks," he thought to himself and laughed.

Eddie and Ned both had restless nights, thoughts flying through their minds. Both awoke to their wives being sick. Both now understood the possibility in front of each of them. They each had to tell their ladies. They each decided to let them know of the conversation the previous evening.

Ned had risen before dawn and gone for a walk, where he farewelled his friends at the barracks. After returning to his room, the four descended to a late breakfast. Gerry was awaiting them in the dining room.

"Ahh, you're here. Sleep, all right?" he asked benignly.

Ned said, "No. What do you think? You set the cat amongst the pigeons, didn't you."

Gerry was smirking. "Don't blame me. You each did this yourself." He was soon in stitches.

Jenna and Christina looked at each other as their respective husbands had not discussed the other couple. "You too?" said Jenna. "I knew I was bigger than Liza. Much bigger. I'm even feeling little flutters, but I'm so tired and so very hungry."

Christina echoed, "Oh, so am I. I eat a full meal and am ravenous again in minutes. I want the weirdest things. Cabbage, spinach and beans. I hate cabbage." She looked at Gerry, "You mean this really is possible? I didn't even think I could have children, and you throw this at me." Christina said in mock horror.

Gerry threw up his hands, "Again I say. I didn't do this. Blame them," pointing to Ned and Eddie.

Both men looked sheepishly at each other.

Gerry roared with laughter. "You really should see your faces. Don't you understand how wonderful this is? I think it's marvellous. Absolutely blooming marvellous!" His comment broke the ice. He turned to Christina. "I'll stay with you until the babe or babies are born. Feel free to get a specialist in London, but Tina, Ned, I'll be on hand if you need me. You will both need careful watching. Tina, as you're a little older than Jenna here, you will need to take more care." He turned to both ladies. "I want you both to eat carefully. Lots of fruit and vegetables, and not too much sweet cooking. And walk a lot, and I mean a lot, not too strenuous, but lots of it. A couple of miles a day if you can."

He turned and addressed all four friends. "Walking will help when the birth comes. I want you both to walk. It will be harder on the boat for us, but we will manage. Around and around the decks, the poop deck or whatever they call it, and steps too."

He then addressed Eddie. "Ed, while you are here or soon after, go to the hospital and see the staff. Introduce yourselves to the doctors and let them know your suspicions or my suspicion, I should say, and book her in…" he counted on his fingers, "…from August. You are then to stay here in Sydney until they are born. That could be up to a month, but often twins come early. I've seen the hospital in Parramatta; I do not want you there. Charlie must run the forge or get Tindale back for the month. You're to stay with her, do you understand?"

Eddie sat listening. He nodded vigorously, "Yes, sir." The reality of the impending birth was setting in for Ed.

"Ned, we'll set up your place and bring in some nurses. I shall train myself. I have had a great deal to do with birthing babies. It's my specialty. I turned to this after my own dear wife, Emily's death after her confinement, but recently I lost heart. I needed a break. Hence my trip here." Looking back at the girls, he said, "It's why I picked up your err symptoms, where other physicians may have missed them."

People were looking at them and the noise they were making. They decided to go for a carriage ride to Mrs. Macquarie's chair. They could talk more freely there without people listening in.

The carriage dropped them off close to the point. They walked out along the shady road. Gerry sent the two men off for a walk and saw them leaning on a wall, watching the harbour's activity. Gerry sat on the large stone seat with the two expectant mothers being pumped for information.

Some topics he brought up as he knew they would not ask as they were first-time mothers. Questions that only a doctor would know how to answer.

After half an hour, the ladies joined their husbands.

Garry sat alone on the recently vacated stone chair with his hands behind his head and watched the two ladies walk to the foreshore, arm in arm, to search for their men. His heart stirred in loneliness. "Maybe I am not too old to marry again. Look at Ned, and he's a year older than I. Dash it; I can't grieve for my lost love forever; she would never want that. Emily would want me happy, not alone and miserable. She made me promise that, and I failed her." For the first time in many years, the future did not look so bleak. He would keep his heart open to God's will. He watched the ships unload parcels, boxes, and loads of goods at the quay. One ship caught his eye. Hmm, that looked like a stretcher. He watched for a while as a patient was unloaded. Not my patient, he thought, but still shot the injured person a prayer. He walked down to join his friends with renewed spirit.

On their return to the hotel, they greeted Mr. Falconer-Meade again as they walked in. Ed recognised him from Liza's Wedding as the unexpected guest. Ned, from a meeting he'd had with him. Mr. Falconer-Meade was leaving with both boys. He quickly introduced them to both his grandsons, Joshua and Tad.

Eddie grinned. "Tad, I have not seen you since school. Do you remember me?"

Tad nodded. "I do, Ed, but I did not think you would remember me. I spent most of my time with Tony." They couldn't chat and hoped that they would catch up later.

Mr. Falconer-Meade told them he had finally found the lost child. They had only met the night before. Then, they departed for an appointment. Tad was taking them to meet his mentor, Ricky English.

Gerry, walking in behind the Major and Ed, noticed they too could have been related by how they stood, walked and even looked, thought the doctor. So similar were they, the Major being slightly taller, the lad more muscular. Even the shape of their heads was identical. Ned said Charles reminded him of his youngest brother. "I wonder? *Bramblemere*, eh?"

They had been gone for over an hour before they returned to the hotel. There was a note awaiting Eddie. He saw it was from Mr. Tindale.

EDDIE,

I AM WRITING QUICKLY TO LET YOU KNOW OF A MIRACLE. WE HAVE JUST HAD WORD THAT DOUGLAS WAS FOUND ADRIFT OFF THE COAST OF JAPAN. HE IS ALIVE. I'LL GIVE YOU THE DETAILS WHEN YOU COME, BUT HE'S JUST ARRIVED IN SYDNEY. COME AS SOON AS YOU CAN AND BRING YOUR FRIENDS.

THOMAS TINDALE

"Oh," uttered Eddie. "Major, read this." He handed him the letter. "He's alive. Mr. Tindale wants us all to come. Do you mind if we go along now?"

Gerry groaned to himself. I bet that was the stretcher patient, thinking back to the boat this morning. He prayed again.

They were greeted at the door by Mr. Tindale and a beaming smile.

Eddie was welcomed with a bear hug, as were all the rest.

Gerry looked concerned.

A tall gentleman with a handlebar moustache stood in the hall with a big smile. He, too, greeted Eddie with a bear hug, who hugged him in return. "Captain Evans, sir, you're alive," Ed said, shaking his hand.

"We would have been here earlier, but one of the sailors fell from the rigging this morning and broke a leg," the Captain explained.

Gerry breathed a deep sigh of relief. So, not the stretchered patient, after all.

Effy brought in tea for everyone. They settled in the sitting room and waited. The Captain began his story. "We were caught in a terrible storm. The seas were so rough that they broke over the tops of the masts until they all broke. We knew we were miles from any land and were doomed. We could see or do nothing but hold on and pray. We had lowered the sails and tried to ride it out. Then the masts broke. It blew for a week. We seemed to be taken with the storm as it moved. The wind screeched all around us. We nearly sank so often, but the lads kept the pumps going, and somehow we survived." He mopped his brow. "The storm finally passed, and we thought, 'How did the ship not break up?' So often, we were in danger. We had broken masts and so much damage, but we were afloat. We all fell on our knees and praised God. The rudder, too, had gone. We could not steer. So we sat, and we sat, now becalmed. We had replenished the barrels with the rainwater from the storm. We managed to catch fish. We had lots of stores on board. Lots of them, and worked out a way to light a fire. We had little fuel, so we eked out the wood to only cook the fish. One night, we caught a big tuna. It took a little longer to cook, and the ship's deck caught fire before we realised. We were in the galley eating when the alarm sounded. Too late, the deck of the vessel was well alight. Thankfully, the lifeboats were still serviceable, and we filled them with whatever food and barrels of water we could before the ship was fully involved." He took another swig of his tea. "The thought ran through my mind: God, how can you do this to us? What have we done? I should have trusted Him." Douglas paused. "When we finally abandoned ship, we had been in the water for less than three hours before some Chinese fishing junks descended upon our position. They had seen our 'signal' and came to help."

The listeners gasped.

"Oh, it gets better," he continued. "They were a fishing fleet from Peking, China, and were on a discovery voyage to look for more fishing grounds. They had never ventured this far offshore before, and only by chance were they in the area." He looked over at Caroline. Tears were streaming down her face. "Come here, love." He pulled her onto his knee and hugged her tightly. Her arms wrapped around his neck, and her body shook with sobs. "It's all right; I won't be going back. I promise. My sailing days are over."

She looked up. "Promise, my love. Promise me."

He nodded, then continued, "We were over two thousand miles off the coast of Japan. There were no islands near us. We would have died had the ship not caught fire." He laid his head against Caroline. "Caro, when I heard where we were, I knew God had *not* forgotten us. We were in his hands the entire time." He turned back to the rest of the listeners. "Now for the loss of time. It's been a year and a half since we set sail from here. We sailed up all the through the Spice Islands; we had been to China and loaded up with tea. We were on the homeward trip, just passing the southern tip of Japan, when we got caught in the storm. Some of the original crew had swapped in Guam on the northbound trip. The crew we picked up were mostly Spanish-speaking sailors. We had our communication issues, but we coped. I found one on board who could speak both languages, so he became my interpreter. I'm getting off the track. After the junks picked us up, we were separated. The Chinese boats divided us between their five smaller ships, and I, along with my first male and cook, were placed on the lead junk." He reached for his tea and took another deep drink. "We lost track of the smaller junks in another storm and hunted around for them for some eight weeks. Eventually, we headed back to port. If you've ever sailed in a junk, they are not the fastest boats on the water. Well, it took bloomin' months. I was so frustrated. I had already lost track of time and date." He looked at Caro. "I wanted to be home with you, sweetheart."

"By the time we rounded the southern tip of Japan, we were low on everything. Our Captain took the shortest route, and we ran aground. We were taken prisoner in Japan. I didn't even know that the two countries had issues with each other. We were accused of spying and thrown into prison." He kissed Caro, looking at her lovingly, drinking her in. "It took eight long months for us to be released. Eight long months. Then we headed straight back to China, and that took another month as the ship had been damaged while in Japanese possession."

He reached for his cup and took a gulp. "Finally, on return there, I had to wait for a ship home. I took the first one I could, which took six weeks, and I'm not leaving again. I have already notified the East India company that I have resigned. No more free tea or spices, but I'm home."

Caro burst into tears again. She was still sitting on his lap and holding him tightly with her arms wrapped around his neck, her head resting on his neck. He held her as she sobbed.

Mr. Tindale beckoned for everyone to file into the kitchen, and they silently filed out and gathered in the kitchen. "Well, folks, this has been wonderful news, but it throws a spanner in our plans, Ed." He looked at Eddie. "We'll have to move back home as Caro won't want us under her feet now. Sorry, lad."

Mrs. Tindale took Jenna's hand. "We want you to stay in the back room, though, dear girl. Don't think you can't; we'll return to the main house."

Ned interrupted her, "I think I have a solution that will work better for everyone, and I'm sure they will tell you why later. Christina and I have told your parents they are to have our cottages. Our way of saying thank you to them. Well, I suggest you move into my cottage as Christina's cottage still needs the roof properly repaired. Both cottages have two bedrooms."

Eddie said, "Thanks, sir," smiling, he nodded. He turned to Mr.

Tindale, "Mr. Tindale, we've all been talking to Dr Gerry here, and he's been watching our wives, unbeknownst to us. I'm not sure if you realise, but they both are... err, um... in an interesting condition," he mumbled "And he thinks both ladies may be carrying..." he swallowed then said, "twins." He tugged at his collar. "I haven't got my head around this yet; I don't know about you, Major, but it looks like we're possibly going to need more than just one room."

The Major chuckled. "Our new home at home has a few more than that."

Gerry smiled and rolled his eyes, thinking of the enormous crenellated walled and moated Gracemere Castle with over two hundred bedrooms. He just smiled, thinking it was comparable to the best royal palaces.

Mrs. Tindale was still holding Jenna's hand. She drew her close and exclaimed, "How exciting. This is wonderful news."

Mr. Tindale relaxed. "Well, this is good news, lad. It seems that we will have another, shall I say, um, *interesting* year ahead of us, and congratulations to you too, sir, ma'am."

"Oh, for goodness sake, Thomas, drop that. If you can't call me Ned as you have done for two decades, try Edward, or Major will suffice. It's how I still think of myself anyway," said Ned.

"And I'm to be Christina," she chuckled. "I'm still getting used to the idea of being with child, let alone the possibility of twins. Throw in a Duchess, and I'm... well, almost floundering. I'm going to hate getting back to the strict formality of home. I'd try to persuade him to stay if Edward weren't the Duke. The weather here is, on the whole, nicer, too," she said. "And on the whole, so are our friends."

Jenna reached over the stove and pushed the kettle back onto the heat. "I think it's time for another cuppa. And I could do with some cookies, maybe more than a few, actually."

"Me too," said Christina.

"Now, ladies. This is what I mean by watching what you eat. Less cake, more fruit," said Gerry.

Jenna laughed, "Yes, Father," she joked.

They were still in the kitchen, talking, when John arrived home. He had been sent a note earlier but had been out of the office and had just arrived home. His Uncle met John at the front door, who told him his father was home safe. He bolted back inside to see his parents still sitting wrapped in each other arms on the settee. His father reached out his arm to his son and drew him down to join them.

At nineteen, he was at that awkward age of nearly being a man, but not quite. He wept with joy.

Phil and Stevie followed later in the afternoon.

By the time they had arrived, the others had all left. They let them reunite in peace. They would rejoin them later.

The group walked back leisurely to The King's Arms, where Gerry had previously ordered luncheon for everyone. They were greeted by the butler with a note elegantly addressed to Ned. This was handed to Ned on a silver salver that shook slightly on the footman's hand.

"*His Grace, The Duke of Gracemere.*"

Ned groaned. "And so it starts," he muttered as he read it. "I have been summoned to Government House for afternoon tea." He looked up, "Sorry, friends, but I'm accepting for us all. Lieutenant-Colonel Sir George Gipps has been on my back for years. He was the reason I retired when I did. Well, one of them." He looked at Christina. "I'm going to enjoy this, and you're all joining me to watch. He's a stickler for paperwork, and mine was never up to scratch. 'Too wordy' was always his comment." Ned laughed. "You two," talking to Ed and Jenna, "… are going to have your eyes pop when you get inside his residence." He snapped his fingers, and a bell boy came running. He gave instructions for paper and ink to be brought. He quickly penned a curt reply stating:

The Duke and Duchess of Gracemere
Accept with pleasure your invitation. I am free at three o'clock.
We shall be accompanied by a party of five.
Gracemere.

He read it to the group, and as they laughed, he called for wax, sealed his letter with his EG seal ring, and called again for the bell boy. In his best ducal voice, Ned said, "Have this delivered to Government House immediately, my good man."

Jenna giggled once the lad had gone, "Oh, the poor boy."

They went up to change and rest after luncheon.

Ned engaged a sitting room downstairs for the Tindales for the afternoon. Eddie returned and sat with them, discussing his ideas about the forge. He thought, 'Now it was as good a time as any, as they will be coming back, I'd like to let them know what I'd love to happen.' He suggested employing some younger boys to join them and possibly enlarging the smithy shop rather than the forge. They could also hire someone to run the shop and thus empty the forge, leaving more room to work. They could easily add another anvil or two if they removed all the stock items. He and Jenna had sketched his plan, and he brought it with him, intending to find time to talk it over with Mr. Tindale.

He and Jenna had walked the area and tossed and juggled plans and ideas. They had settled on this design, which also gave them room to expand with possibly some saddlery items and make the shop a one-stop-shop for all things for leather goods and ironmongery.

He talked about his dream of a foundry but said, "That is not yet plausible due to lack of coal and coke. I want to think about how else we can grow." He looked inquiringly at Mr. Tindale. He then got up and walked around the room, stopping to look out a window.

Mr. Tindale sat holding the drawings and humming and hawing. He showed it to Margaret, and with heads together, they pointed and whispered. He called Eddie, "You know, lad, I think this would work. I've only been thinking about the ironwork, but why not mix it with the finished leather goods? No, I like this. We'll get on to this as soon as we return home." He slapped his hand on his leg. "Damn, yes. I like it."

Eddie sighed with relief. "Sir, I even have someone who could initially man the store, well, 'girl' the store." Eddie hoped he wasn't overstepping the mark. "Maryanne Connor, the maid the Major hired for Mrs. Meadows, is now looking for a job. She's a trustworthy and keen worker. She didn't want to leave or go to England with them as her family was here. I know she's honest, and that's half the battle."

"We know her, Ed; she first worked for us." Mrs. Tindale told Ed. "It's how the Major found her. Her parents are livers, but she's one of seven children of an Irish couple."

They sat discussing the future of the forge. If their plan worked, many new hands could be upon the anvils. They would employ some of the young men from their family plus friends. Mr. Tindale would remain the principal blacksmith and ultimately have full authority over all decisions. At the same time, Eddie would lift the weight from his shoulders with the heavy smithing and training of the younger apprentices. By the time Ned and Gerry joined them, they had decided where to start. The Tindales returned to the Evans' house to change into afternoon tea gowns and visiting clothing. Ned and Gerry took Eddie upstairs.

Ned said, "Do you remember that afternoon we taught you how to dress up? Well, you're being put to the test. Gerry is about your size, and you're wearing one of his outfits for this visit. Christina has taken Jenna in hand."

The two Gentlemen stripped him of all but his drawers. Then he got togged up, as Ed called it. His hair had been done, parted in the centre and brushed back, and his queue tied with a black velvet ribbon. Gerry then dressed him, finishing with a lace cravat. Ed didn't feel too uncomfortable until he put on the shoes. The Major's shoes pinched; he wasn't used to pointed-toe shoes. They walked out, knocking on Jenna's door. Christina had taken one of her new gowns, a yellow one, and dressed Jenna. They stood looking at each other. Neither believed what they saw.

Jenna looked enchanting. She was in a yellow, sprigged muslin gown with her honey-gold hair up-do with tiny braids. They were curling the ends around her neck, the full skirt of her gown accentuating her waist.

Ed was dressed in a fawn frock coat, pale champagne-coloured trousers, a brown damask vest, and an intricately tied cravat. Gerry carried his top hat.

Ed put his arm out for Jenna as he'd seen Ned do for Christina. She gently touched his arm, and they all walked downstairs. Both were very nervous.

Christina said to Jenna and Eddie, "If you are unsure of what to do, hold back and watch us. Do not be afraid. You will be fine."

A fancy town carriage harnessed with four horses awaited them downstairs. Ned had ordered it when they collected Eddie. They called and collected the Tindales and drove up to Government House. This magnificent building had some work still being finished but had the most incredible facade. There were towers on the top and flags flying from them. Jenna was craning her neck to look at everything.

Ned sat holding Christina's hand, and he squeezed it.

They were driven in under the stone portico, where the carriage stopped.

What followed was one of the most delightful experiences for these seven strange friends, a Duke, a Duchess, a Doctor, two blacksmiths and their wives. However, the Governor was introduced to them as "The Honourable, Doctor Gerald Winslow-Smythe; my Protege, Mister and Missus Edward Lockley, and his mentor and his wife, Mister and Missus Thomas Tindale." The Governor bowed low over each introduction.

Eddie was smiling to himself and thinking, "I'm just a blacksmith, drinking Tea at Government House." Thanks to his education at Cape's Academy, he could hold his own through the conversation. Jenna, too, could converse; she had even more confidence than he. She occasionally looked at Christina to watch her actions. She never put a foot wrong. Oh, how he loved his lady.

The afternoon passed without a hitch. Ned had the Governor almost grovelling at his whims by the time the visit had finished. All the way back to the Evans' home, they were laughing. Christina had tears of laughter running down her cheeks. "Edward, can you imagine his face when he found out who you were? His change of attitude was dramatic."She took Jenna's hand and said, "To us, you are dear friends; you are our family. Thankfully by tomorrow, we shall be on board. But you, my dears, will all have to bear his wrath. I'm sorry, but truly I can't stop laughing."

They all joined her, laughing about the prior treatment Ned had received compared to today.

Caro and Douglas greeted them all warmly on their return. Effy had prepared dinner for them all. Phil and his wife Alice, Stevie, his fiancé, May, and John were already there. They were still overwhelmed that their father and husband had returned alive and well. They sat down and enjoyed a jovial evening. The visitors retired early, as tomorrow was the final day before embarkation.

On return to The King's Arms, Christina gifted the gown to Jenna. She was overwhelmed. The beautiful new yellow sprigged muslin gown, such as Jenna had never dreamed of owning, was now hers. Gerry did the same for Eddie and the Major with the shoes and top hat. The young couple said, "But we'll never use them again."

"My dear," said Christina. "If what Gerry says is true, then neither will I. I have bought parcels and parcels of fabric to make some gowns when I am on board. These will be out of fashion by the time I arrive. Wear it to church until it no longer fits." Jenna accepted it gracefully.

Ned said, "You never know exactly what the future will bring." Ned and Christina smiled and looked at each other knowingly and smiled.

They all turned in early. The ladies were exhausted.

Ned had been up before dawn and gone for a morning walk. He had met Major Humphrey Downes and Henry Gates as they were hunting for Brodie Stewart, Henry's caretaker. He had gone missing and presumed that he had been shanghaied. Humphrey discovered Ned's title, only to admit that he, too, was the son of a Lord.

On Ned's return to the hotel, all their belongings were moved onto the ship. Ed carried their bag with their new clothing in it and left it with the Tindales as they were all returning together on the late ferry. They would return on another day and do the hospital visit.

Gerry insisted they all walk down to the quay as it would be the last stretch of their legs on solid ground for some months. They meandered down to the quay and saw that their luggage had arrived and was loaded.

Ned and Gerry saw it stowed in the correct cabins, and the excess stored in one of the spare cabins they had turned into a dining room and another into a sitting room.

Jenna and Ed had never been on a big ship, so they were taken on a tour by Captain Wallace. He apologised that he could not spare more time but must get things ship-shape before departure as they sailed in two hours.

He left them on the deck and returned to his work. Christina joined them, explaining that the men were arranging baggage. It needed to be secured, as once they were through the harbour heads, it could be rough, so everything had to be tied down tightly.

Christina leaned on the railing next to Jenna. "Will you write to me, please, Jenna? I count you as my true friend, along with Sally and Elizabeth. You all accepted me without knowing anything about me. I was just Mrs. Meadows, a widow back then. You do understand just how much that means. Edward is the same as your father, Eddie. Charles never asked him for anything. Not once, not in all those years." Christina continued, "If by any chance you can come to England, please know we will welcome you with open arms. Jenna, you are like the little sister I never had." She gave Jenna a big hug. "I really would love you to come."

They both looked at her, astounded. Speaking for them both, Eddie thanked her profusely. Knowing, however, it would probably never happen.

Ned and Gerry appeared. Everything had been secured. Captain Wallace gave them a thirty-minute warning as he walked past. He told them he had twenty passengers, including themselves, with ten more to collect in Melbourne. Very few were first-class. As the ship usually catered for one hundred and sixty passengers, there was lots of room.

Captain Wallace was excited to tell them, "I'm normally carrying passengers, but as so few are returning home, I have loaded the lower decks with the wool clip. We have over two hundred bales on board. They won't get seasick or eat much. There are no steerage passengers either; we moved them to intermediate." He laughed as he walked off. As he laughed, his handlebar moustache bounced.

They started saying their goodbyes.

Christina and Jenna were both in tears in each other's arms. Eddie shook both gentlemen's hands, Gerry, first. After Ed shook the Major's hand, the Major embraced him.

"Stay safe, lad," Ned said with a catch in his voice. "I'm so proud of you, you know," he said softly.

Eddie escorted Jenna down the gangplank. They stood on the dock in the shade until the ship slipped its moorings. Two small rowboats towed it out into the main channel of the harbour. The sails were unfurled and slowly loosened; initially luffing, they filled. Eventually, they caught with the gentle breeze, and the ship slid into movement, heading out to sea. Jenna now sobbed openly onto Eddie's shoulder. She alternately waved and sobbed.

Gerry stood a little to the side of Tina and Ned, waving. Christina stood under her husband's arm, and they could tell she was also in tears; they could see the Major wipe them away from her face. He, too, wiped his own with a handkerchief.

Eddie felt the same but held his emotions in check. They stayed until the ship was out of sight. They did not even notice when the Tindales, Captain Douglas and Mrs. Evans joined them with their luggage. They stood watching as the sails slipped from view around the headland.

Margaret Tindale walked to Jenna and touched her arm. Jenna lifted her tear-filled face to Margaret. Together they wept.

Parting with special friends is never easy.

They stayed locked together until Eddie said the ferry had arrived. The men loaded their bags and helped the ladies up the gangplank; more farewells were said to the Evans family, although much happier ones.

Captain Robert's cast off. Thomas had his arms around Margaret.

Jenna stood in Eddie's arms, miserable and unable to speak. They headed for home. They would go to the hospital sometime later.

Chapter 21   Stunning Revelations

𝒯he passage back to Parramatta was uneventful. None of Captain Roberts' four passengers felt like chatting. Ed spent the trip with his arms around Jenna. Thomas Tindale with his arm still along Margaret's shoulder. All were silent, all deep in thought.

The little ferry puttered back west, the sloshing paddle wheels splashing spray occasionally upon the deck. Arriving at twilight, they all walked up to Charles' Inn, where Captain Roberts intended to sleep the night before returning on the dawn tide.

They all greeted Ed's parents but didn't feel like talking, so they walked up the hill to the forge and went to bed. None were hungry; all were somewhat miserable.

Onboard the *Sarah Bosford*, the passengers settled into the way of life for the next four months. They discovered that they were not the only top-deck passengers. They were ten others in first-class and assorted others in the lower deck. None were in steerage as the Captain had told them. Mr. Falconer-Meade and his two grandsons were three of them.

Neither Ned nor Christina felt like being social. Gerry, however, explored the ship and then returned, having worked out a walking path for exercise. They had set up a small sitting room in one cabin, another for storage and a dining room. Christina and Ned had two cabins, as some days Christina wished to sleep, and he did not wish her disturbed. Gerry had the fifth room, which was a suite in itself. The three dined alone.

Christina was quite ill; however, on the third day, she wanted some air; she said she thought she'd like to go up on deck. Ned prepared a spot for her and then accompanied her to this secluded place, only to find another young lady had now occupied the prepared seat. Gerry returned with another seat and placed it near the first. It was one of the few areas out of the breeze. Christina sat, enjoying the fresh air, reviving her spirits.

Gerry introduced himself and left Ned to introduce themselves. He went the full title. Gerry raised an eyebrow to Ned.

"Your Grace, Your Grace, sir," she nodded to each, "I am Mrs. Annabella Derbyshire. I am returning to my family in England. My husband, sadly, was bitten by a snake and died. I am returning to my father's house." She even addressed him correctly. Christina settled back in her chair.

The men stood on the railing. "She didn't blink," said Gerry to Ned. "I wonder who she is?"

Ned glanced back, "No, you're right. Hmm, I wonder."

They stood looking at the coastline slide by as they sailed south. When they turned back, they saw the ladies talking.

Christina said, "Edward, Annabella is from Ashford in Kent. So it looks like we'll be travelling all the way with her. Gerry, Edward, would you mind if she made a fourth to our group while travelling alone? It will be nice to have some female conversation over the next four months."

Annabella soon discovered that Christina was *enceinte*, possibly with twins, and quickly fussed over her. They soon became friends.

Gerry said to Ned, "Ned, have you noticed Mrs. Derbyshire has the sweetest smiling, blue eyes that dance when she laughs? Her laugh is like tinkling chimes; it's so musical. I love making her smile so I can see her dimples. They are so sweet."

Ned said, "No, Gerry, I have not; my eyes are for another."

Gerry continued, "Her hair is a soft, strawberry blonde, and it sparkles in the sunshine and springs into ringlets at her neck," he said dreamily. His eyes were not moving from Annabella as she sat talking to Christina.

Ned finally tore his eyes from Christina and watched Gerry in amazement. He noted that when Annabella was in the same room, his eyes rarely left her, following her around the room. Later that day, Ned spoke to Christina and asked her to approach Annabella to ascertain her feelings.

Christina laughed. "Oh, Edward, I do not need to. Her feelings are as obvious as Gerry's. She watches him as much as he watches her. When their eyes meet, they cannot move, and both hold their breath."

They wondered how to reveal these two reciprocated feelings of each other without being obvious.

They need not have worried. God had this in hand. However, it took a storm later that week for Annabella to hit her head on a bulkhead of a door. The ship lurched as it slid down a massive wave as they moved to the sitting room. Annabella was knocked unconscious. Gerry was, of course, near her when the accident occurred. So close that he caught her before she hit the ground. He carried her back to her cabin, closely followed by Ned and Christina. Ned informed the Captain, but Gerry shooed the onboard physician away, allowing only Christina and himself near her.

His skills as a doctor were put to the test. He did not leave her side except when Christina and a ship's maid came to undress her and put her to bed. Hour after hour, he sat sponging her head and holding her hand. He prayed; it was all he could do. Oh, how he prayed. His medical skills were useless. He only had prayer to rely on. He was still sitting beside her holding her hand, when she roused. It had been nearly eight hours. During those hours, she had not stirred. She had not moved nor murmured any sound.

He tended her and cooled her forehead. His head was resting on her bed, and he prayed again. He pushed Ned away and only accepted Tina's presence because she did not interfere with him.

Distraught, he once again prayed. "Dear God, I have just found her. Please, Lord," he pleaded. "Do not take her from me. Please let her be all right. Oh God…" he stopped, stunned by realisation. "Oh, God, I love her." He blanched, "Oh God, I love her so much," he said in both shock and awe. As he said this, he lifted his head; he looked at her. Her eyes were open, and she held out her arms.

"Gerald! Oh, Gerald, I love you too," she said weakly.

He went to her, placing his head on her chest. "Thank you, God. Thank you."

She placed her arm around his neck, holding him to her. He enfolded her in his arms and kissed her tenderly and lovingly.

Annabella recovered quickly and was back on her feet some days later.

Gerry rarely was more than a few feet from her side.

After a week, Ned took him aside one day and pointed it out. "Now, Gerry, I realise Christina is a suitable chaperone, but would it not be better not to need one? I highly recommend the married state."

Gerry looked stunned. Gerry tore his eyes from his love to Ned's, giving him total concentration.

Ned continued, intently watching his dear friend's face. "Did you know Gerry that Captain Wallace can marry you? He is a Justice of the Peace. However, I understand he may also be an Elder of the Church of Scotland."

Gerry stood, looking at Ned. "I had forgotten that some Captains have that legal ability. I shall attend to this matter immediately." He walked off in Annabella's direction.

She was in their small sitting room with Christina. When he entered, his eyes fixed on Annabella. Christina stood and excused herself with some excuse to obtain something from her room. She departed without either person realising she had gone.

Gerry walked to her and took her hands. "My dear," he swallowed. "No, my darling; you may have guessed the depth of my feelings?" He drew closer, fell to one knee, and saw her gazing at him. "Oh my love, will you marry me? I cannot live without you. I knew I was drawn to you and enjoy your company. However, when you were injured, I realised the depth of my feelings. When you would not wake, I was distraught and panicked."

He watched a tear slowly slide down her cheek. He reached up to wipe it away with the tip of his finger.

She took his hand and held it to her lips. "Oh, my dearest Gerald, of course, I'll marry you. Whenever and wherever you wish."

He fell to both knees and swept her into his arms.

March in Parramatta was passing quickly. The sadness Charles felt was most profound. His best friend gone, Ned's place at the table on Sundays permanently empty, he asked Sal if she'd mind if the Tindales could join them each week now.

Sal was ecstatic. "Oh, Charles, could we please? Margaret and I have become quite close. She is so alone. Oh, my dear, I would love that."

Since the revelation of Ed's schooling and the whole truth of the situation was revealed, Thomas Tindale had become even closer to Charles.

Ed and Jenna moved out of the back cabin and into the Major's cottage. Maryanne stayed with them to help until the babies were born.

Repairs were started on the roof of Christina's cottage.

Plans were made for the new shopfront at the forge, but nothing had yet been started. They were busy building up stock as they knew Eddie would be in Sydney for about a month when the babies were due in August or September. The building would not start until after they were born. Eddie had taken on four of the young boys and began to teach them basic smithing skills. Wills was one of the newest apprentices, he could only use the smallest hammer, but Ed also taught him how to weld. He had shown unique skill with this.

Luke proved almost useless, but as he always had his head in a book, it didn't surprise Eddie at all. Ed still insisted that Luke knew the business and made an effort to be involved, so he employed him as a striker, teaching him the basics of adjusting a horseshoe. He also learned to re-shoe a horse and how to do basic wheel repairs. He thought, "Luke would be a Scholar and make the family proud. We're not all skilled at the same thing, thank goodness." Wills, however, had a knack for welding. Ed would sit and watch him, amazed at some of the items the lad produced. He loved the intricate fiddly things that drove Eddie mad.

He shrugged. "Well, I'll be blowed." His welding skills were better than Mr. Tindale's. Four other boys were brought in from town. After church one Sunday, Reverend Bobart had made an announcement and asked if any lads would like to try blacksmithing with the idea of training. Ten applied, but only five were chosen other than Wills. The stock built up slowly as much time was spent training the new boys.

They were skilled enough by June to let them work on orders. By August, when he had to leave for Sydney with Jenna, they would be fine.

The relationship with Margaret Tindale also grew much closer. The ladies first met when Eddie had gone to school, but they had seen little of each other. Mrs. Tindale said, "Please remember, Sal, you promised to call me Margaret or even Maggie."

Sal, embarrassed, said, "Are you sure? I would be honoured. What would you prefer?"

"Maggie, I think. My friends at home used to call me that when I was young. Yes, I'd love that," she said.

"Then Maggie it is, and I'm Sal or Sally. Either is fine," said Sal.

"Deal," said Margaret laughing.

Charles walked into the kitchen, followed by Mr. Tindale.

Margaret turned to him. "Thomas, it's time we dropped the formality. Sal and I have, so from now on, you are 'Thomas' and 'Charles'." She beamed.

"Yes, love," said Thomas grinning. "Actually, love, we have already worked that out. Charles has just invited us to Sunday dinners each week with the family. What about that?"

Maggie turned to Sal. "Do you mean that? Oh, Sal, I'd love to come. You've always been like family, the one I could never have."

Sal saw her eyes glistening, and she wiped a tear away. "Oh, Maggie, I never thought. You've always been welcome, but we're convicts. I know we had this conversation years ago. I didn't think you would want to come. I thought you were just being polite." The ladies stood in the kitchen.

Maggie reached for her and gave her a hug. "That wasn't it, my dear; I just didn't want to intrude." Maggie hugged Sal again.

Thomas turned to Charles. "Looks like we're *de trop*. Where's that ale you promised me?" They walked out.

Eddie, Jenna and the rest of the family dawdled in over the next hour. Soon they were all squeezed around the family table. The growing family were jovial. "Growing is right." She wasn't sulky; she just felt huge. She waddled everywhere. Liza didn't.

Eddie said, "Her favourite trick is to sit a cup of water on her tummy and watch the babies kick it. Watch this." He sat a glass on her tummy and, sure enough, bump. "Right on cue," he chuckled.

Liza was neat and compact. Jenna was almost jealous. They walked together every morning in summer and midday as the weather got colder.

Jenna's feet were swollen by the end of July, and she couldn't bend over without overbalancing.

They had visited Sydney a few times over the months to see the doctor. Eddie had booked the same suite at The King's Arms that they had occupied on their visit with The Major, Christina, and Gerry.

Eddie came in one day in early August after work to find her sitting on the floor. She was in tears. He sat beside her drawing her into his arms. "Oh, love, what's wrong?"

"I can't get up," she hiccuped. "I've been here for an hour and need to wee. Maryanne has gone home for the afternoon to help her folks. I'm over this, Eddie."

Ed had never seen her like this before, and he was worried. His Jenna never cried. He stood up and lifted her with ease. "Come, love, do what you must, and then we'll talk." He helped her to the commode and retired to the sitting room.

A few minutes later, she waddled out. Her face was still red from crying. He just enfolded her in his arms and comforted her. He chuckled when he was kicked.

"Ouch," She looked down. "I felt that, little Neddie," she said, patting her tummy with a laugh.

Ed sat her down. "Come on, love; we need to talk. Sit with me." She sat curled up under his arm. She brushed away another tear.

"Ed, I'm so big, I can't do anything. I'm so over this. I still have about six weeks to go." She started crying again.

Ed didn't know what to do or say, so he just held her. He'd got her into this state but could not help her. All he could do was be there for her. A shoulder to cry on. He felt helpless. "Love, before we talk more, can we have a little prayer so we can think clearly?"

She nodded.

Ed prayed, "God, we know you know what is ahead of us. We're at a stage we need help. Please give us direction and comfort too. Amen."

She was still snuggled up on the settee in the sitting room. He bent and kissed her hair. "Jen, I love you so much. What can I do? How can I help?"

"Just hold me, my love; just keep telling me you love me, no matter what I look like. Tell me it will be all right," she said.

"Oh, Jenna, are you serious? I love you so much, even more than when we married. I think you look amazing. You're growing two people in there."

She hiccuped again, and they sat in silence for some time. Her deep rhythmic breathing told him she slept. Poor lamb, she was so tired. He sat holding her for over an hour. She woke when there was a knock on their door. Ed lit the lamp before going to the door.

Sal had decided to check on her. They had finally moved into Christina's refurbished cottage two doors up from them. The light was not on, and she was worried. When Charles asked her if she knew if they had gone out, she said, "No, not that I know of." He'd walked up from the Inn and noticed the darkness as he passed to their cottage.

Sal thought she'd just check. She looked at their faces and sat on the settee next to Jenna. "Okay, what's wrong?" she said, looking at Jen. "Have you had enough of being big?"

Jenna nodded, and the tears flowed again. This time, with Sal on one side and Ed on the other, she sobbed. Mother and son's eyes met over her head.

Sal said, "Well, my dears, I think it's nearly time you went to Sydney. I used to get like this not long before the pains started. I think we'll pack and get you off to Sydney tomorrow, even if only for a check-up, but I suggest you stay until the babies come."

Jenna looked up, eyes swimming with uncertainty. "Oh, Mama, I wish you or Maa could be with me too. Eddie won't be allowed in the hospital. I'm so frightened, Mama, I'm so scared." Jenna wept again.

Eddie just held her. His own eyes were watering; he felt totally helpless.

Sal stayed for a bit, then said, "I'll go and cook you something for dinner, then we'll come and eat here with you. You both stay here." She stood and left.

Eddie mouthed, "Thank you," as she left.

Sal walked back to their cottage, deep in thought.

Half an hour later, Charles opened the door and ushered her in. They each carried food and placed it on the table. Eddie had set the table, and Jenna emerged from the kitchen where she'd washed her face. She shuffled to the table and sat in the chair Eddie held for her. She was still teary but managing to hold herself together.

Charles took one look at her and said, "Well, let's say thanks to God, then we'll talk."

They all bowed their heads, and he gave prayed.

Sal served, and Charles cleared his throat. "After talking with your Mama while she was cooking, I've made a decision. She will accompany you to Sydney tomorrow and stay with you until either Martha can join you or until the babies come, whichever comes first. Having been through this ourselves six times, I am pretty sure you're sick of being *enceinte*."

Jenna nodded, not trusting her voice. Her eyes began to sparkle through. Eventually, she managed to say, "Really, really, you'd come with me? Oh, Mama, Dar, thank you so much. Even just until we settle, then you can come back for Liza. But, oh, that would relieve me so much. Ed is wonderful, but he knows as much about babies as I do, nothing."

Ed said, "I'll send a message to Maa and Pa tomorrow and let them know and ask if Martha can come as soon as possible for an extended stay."

He looked at Jenna. "See, I knew God wouldn't let us down." He met his Dar's eyes. "We didn't know what to do."

Sal laid her hand on Jenna's mobile tummy. "Oh, love, they are fighting to get out," she laughed.

Jenna sniffed and said, "You should feel it from the inside. Feel. This one is doing pushups on my ribs." Sal put a hand on Jenna's ribs and felt what she meant. She could feel two tiny feet.

After eating, Sal and Ed cleared the dishes. Sal shooed him out, and he returned to talk to his father and Jenna.

They stayed for a while. Charles and Eddie went to the forge to let Mr. Tindale know the situation. They returned in thirty minutes and said it was all sorted.

Sal and Charles left soon afterwards, telling her to sleep while they could.

Jenna had a restless night as the babies were unsettled. Eddie slept lightly and woke up whenever she got out of bed.

They were up early the following day and packed, ready to leave. A letter was sent to Emu Plains, and hopefully, Martha could make it to Sydney before the babies were born, as Sal was needed at Liza's side for her delivery.

Charles took Eddie aside and told him how he felt at this time. So helpless and concerned too. "Hug her, touch her and let her know you love her. That's what she needs to hear. Just be there for her."

Eddie nodded.

An hour later, they slowly wandered down to the ferry. It was due at ten o'clock, and they would be in Sydney by lunchtime.

This time the trip had a tailwind.

Charles stood on the wharf, waving goodbye. For the first time in their married life, he was alone. Twenty-five years and he loved her as much as ever. He did not like this. No, he would join her too. He turned; he would seek out Charlie. He would catch the evening ferry. Sal would not be alone; he wanted to be with her. Charlie would have to step up and run the Inn alone for a week. He strode quickly towards the Inn and went straight to Charlie.

As they were having morning tea just after they became engaged, Annabella made a confession to her beloved and her new friends. She sat with them in the sitting room cabin and held Gerry's hand. "Gerry, friends, I would like to tell you something. I, like Christina, had an almost runaway marriage the first time. Before that, I was The Honourable Annabella Watkins-Harlow; my Papa is Viscount Ellison. He's a difficult man, to say the least; he cast me off when I married, as it was against his wishes. I've had to swallow my pride to crawl home."

Gerry and Ned inhaled sharply. They smiled at each other. Gerry took her hand and kissed her palm. He remembered the Viscount would be his father-in-law, aghast about the realisation.

Ned spoke. "Err, Annabella, we met your father when we were

young. I do hope he does not remember either of us." He smiled at Gerry, remembering some of the antics they had been involved in. "Trust me, we understand," Gerry said with comfort.

Ned and Gerry smiled at each other. Both knew his reputation as a more than authoritative sort of chap. His temper was volatile and thunderous. The area around Gracemere Castle and its surroundings was not that large. Having spent their youth in Kent, both men knew many of the haunts around the towns. 'The Woolpack Inn' in Ashford had been one of their favourite haunts. The Viscount had chastised them more than once for their behaviour. Ashford was only about thirty miles from Gracemere Castle, about the from Emu Plains to Parramatta. The watering hole there had been a favourite haunt for the young society men in their youth. 'The Black Horse Inn' at Tunbridge Wells was another.

Three days after Gerry's proposal, Annabella and Gerry became man and wife in the middle of the Pacific Ocean, with Captain Wallace performing the ceremony in their suite's sitting room. The only ring he had was his signet ring. They had known each other for precisely five weeks.

The two happy couples celebrated with a meal together, and they invited the Captain to join them, but he declined.

The weather held fine, the breeze stiff. The sails stayed full, carrying them across the sea in a gentle motion. Rounding the Horn had been rough but not overly so.

They hit a crosswind that gave a double-beam sea, but the sturdy ship under the skilled Captain traversed the area quickly until they tacked and proceeded up the coast. Heading north in the final months, they were occasionally becalmed for a few days. This quietness allowed the passengers to spend much more time on deck getting exercise. Mr. Falconer-Meade and his grandsons often stopped and chatted. They did not detain him.

Once their daily walk was done, the four were often found enjoying their particular spot more often as they sought out the sun, but as the trip progressed and the weather warmed, they sat in the shade.

They also watched the occasional dolphin, whale, or other sea creatures and an albatross. Standing on the ship's bow at night, they'd watch the magical phosphorescence in the waves. Captain Wallace had called them out late one evening. He explained how minute sea creatures were disturbed, but the ship would give a bright blue-white light in the water. Each splash set off a fireworks explosion of sparkles in the water, bringing oohs and ahhs from those who saw them. Soon word spread, and they shared this magical experience with others onboard. Two dolphins joined in the fun and were set off the magic with every splash.

As the weather warmed and the cabins heated, the two couples would stand for hours outside enjoying the sea spray splashing onto them. Each pair would stand with their husband's arms around their ladies, holding them tight to the railing around the ship's gunnels. Thus secure, the salty spray was invigorating. They'd watch the moon rise and stars shoot across the sky. Occasionally, a seabird would sit on the rigging. Every small thing was noted. Each enjoyed.

They did not need the companionship of other passengers on board. The two newly married couples were utterly content with their own company. They politely greeted others when they encountered them on their regular walks around the ship's deck but did not seek them out. Occasionally they saw the Falconer-Meade boys but rarely conversed with them. The grandfather just waved as they walked past him on each deck circuit. They, too, were content alone. Each couple only had eyes for each other.

Gerry and Annabella used this time as an extended honeymoon. Christina's condition improved somewhat, but Ned hovered near her. However, she continued to be ill, though not always in the mornings occasionally. Gerry was not concerned. She was eating properly where possible; Sal's powder was invaluable. She was otherwise well. The jar of sweet soda, gifted by Sally, had been refilled several times over the three months they had been on board. The ship's cook delivered a refilled jar to Christina when she required it. He had finely grated lemon peel into the powder, which was delicious. The powder certainly helped. Her condition was undoubtedly far more apparent. She was only six months along by this stage, and although the sickness had abated, it was comforting to have this when required.

Annabella saw her taking some as she entered the room. "Ahh, the magic powder," she said. "Gerald told me about this. We may soon need a double quantity. Gerald thinks so. I missed my menses. He was counting; I lost track."

Christina was thrilled. She squealed with delight. "That's so exciting; I do hope you're not as sick as I've been, though."

"I hope so too. Oh, Christina, I didn't mean it that way." Annabella said, "It is nice being married to a doctor."

Christina took her hand, "It's nice being married to a man who loves you, isn't it?"

Annabella agreed. "I can't believe how foolish I was as a girl, Christina."

Christina said, "At least you swallowed your pride and contacted your family. I didn't. If it had not been for Edward, well, I don't know what would have happened to me." Tears swam in her eyes.

Annabella took her hand. "Now look what we all have together."

Christina looked at her. "Bell, wouldn't it be lovely if we could stay together?" They both brightened and smiled.

"Oh yes, that would be a delight," she exclaimed. "Even if only until the children are born. I have no desires to ever live at home again, and Gerry doesn't own any property."

The weather became cooler again as they neared the end of their journey. They needed to don their overcoats for their evening strolls.

A little over four months after departing from Sydney, Captain Wallace pointed out England's distant coastline. They would disembark in Liverpool. There, they would say their farewells to Captain Wallace and the Falconer-Meads. The Captain had dined with them often, and they had got to know him quite well. Christina was beginning to find the room rather cramped as her size increased. Annabella was nearly over her morning sickness and was glowing with happiness, as was Gerry. He still had a spark of concern about her, but overall she was breezing through the pregnancy.

They disembarked and spent a week about the town. It was no use buying gowns for the ladies in their enlarged conditions. They could shop later. The men, however, replenished some basic needs like shirts and cravats. Sydney's style had not changed; however, the shirt points in England were now much higher. The ladies found that after four months at sea, the land moved as much as the sea. They were both pleased to be heading back on board another yacht for the final leg. Departing from Liverpool, they would travel again by sea to Whitstable in Kent.

Ned outlined the next leg of travel. "I have chartered a yacht, the *Sea Spray,* to take us on the final leg of their journey to Whitstable. I have already sent word to the Castle by land, with most of our luggage, so they will expect us. I have ordered a fleet of carriages to meet us at the dock. From there, we shall travel slowly via Canterbury and Ashford to acquaint your father, Annabella, of your new status, err, and condition and introduce him to his new son-in-law." He looked at Gerry and laughed. "Let's hope he doesn't remember us after all."

"Hope so, too," said Gerry grinning mischievously.

Ned paused, smiling. "Then we shall all travel on to the Castle at Maidstone." He looked to Annabella for affirmation.

Christina said, "I'm pleased we do not have to take a carriage ride across the country. The sea voyage would be much more comfortable. Edward, how long will it take? I'm getting so uncomfortable. I can't even walk through the cabin door sideways now," she giggled.

"Why would you want to walk through sideways, love?" Ned said innocently but with a smile in his eyes.

She threw a pillow at him.

Christina certainly had an uncomfortable gait as her pregnancy proceeded. It had become evident that she would almost certainly be carrying twins due to her size. She complained, "Oh, Edward, I waddle."

Ned chuckled and told her that she was even more beautiful than before. Secretly, he was concerned. He looked at her and thought, she still had three months to go.

Later Ned enfolded her in his arms "Oh, my love. What have I done to you? I don't care what you look like, even though you are glowing in your interesting condition. As long as you are mine." While still holding her hand, Ned explained, "Depending on the winds, we should be no longer than ten days, hopefully, less. Our cabin luggage is being transferred onto the yacht as we speak. Most of the larger items have already left with the cross country coaches with a letter for Mother."

The four were relaxing in the dining room on the yacht when Ned spoke. "Ladies, I have spoken at length with Gerry about this next issue. We have decided that for your safety and to save Gerry much travel, all the children, however many there are, shall be born at the Castle. I will hire the staff required to assist you both in any way you need. We are to be your devoted slaves." He laughed.

Ned turned to Annabella. "I hope to persuade you to stay on afterwards, too, for as long as you wish. You may have your own wing. Even if we have twins yearly, it will take many years to touch the castle's two hundred or so rooms. Please stay?"

He looked then to Annabella, then Gerry and back. "The castle is certainly large enough, and I'm sure numerous empty estate houses will be nearby." Ned looked anxious. "Gerry, I'm going to need a lot of help finding my feet. I'm out of my depth and have not even arrived yet." He loosened his collar. "Heck, man, I'm petrified." Aside, he said, "Sorry ladies," before continuing. "I need you close by, Gerry. If you go traipsing around somewhere else, we'll lose contact again. I won't let that happen."

The girls looked at each other smiling, knowing they had planted this seed themselves; they merely reached for each other's hand.

They heard movement on board and walked out onto the deck to watch the little yacht departing from the Liverpool wharf.

The trip was uneventful and transpired as Ned had planned. On arrival at the Port in Whitstable, the carriages from the castle met them. All the luggage was taken directly to the castle. They travelled on to Annabella's family seat at Ashford. After apprising her parents of her return, remarriage and subsequent pregnancy, they departed shortly afterwards towards the castle, giving her family an invitation to visit at their convenience.

Annabella relaxed, sighing as they departed, "Well, that went better than I expected. Thank you, Edward."

Gerry took her hand and said, "Thankfully, he didn't remember me." Then laughed, as they all did.

They were now all relaxed. Only Ned was tense. Was *she* still at the castle? He prayed there would not be a scene.

The carriage paused not long after entering the castle grounds. Stopping by the Dower House to acquaint Ned's Mother with his return and to introduce Christina.

Ned's mother, Susanna, The Dowager Duchess, welcomed them warmly and with relief and joy.

Ned enfolded her in a loving embrace.

The years of parting fell away. Her eyes swam with unshed tears. "Oh, Neddie, you are home." Her hand was on his cheek in a loving mother's caressing welcome. "I've missed you so much."

He hugged her, too, years of pain and loneliness evaporating.

She took Ned aside. "Neddie, she's gone. Elouise packed and left when your message arrived with the luggage last week. She did not know about your marriage. I do not think she will ever return."

Ned nodded and released a long breath.

She sent them off soon after their arrival as she could see both girls wilting. She said, "Go now, but expect me for morning tea tomorrow."

The Dowager Duchess had been informed when his message had arrived some days before. Knowing the only other option was the share the Dower house, Elouise returned to her parents' house. The castle was empty and was awaiting them.

Ned sighed with great relief. He did not have to confront her, and neither did Christina.

The last hurdle had gone. Ned could now return home in peace.

"Gracemere Cottage"
Phillip Street
Parramatta
23rd August 1842

Gracemere Castle,
Maidstone
England

Dear Sir,

I hope you have arrived home safely and that your trip and welcome were all that you hoped they would be.

I hope Christina is well. Send her our regards and love, please.

I write with Joyous news. Jenna was safely delivered of twins eight days ago on the morning of Aug 15th in Sydney. Dr Gerry was right, it was twins, and they arrived early. We were only in Sydney for ten days before the happy event. Mama came with us but returned to Liza for her confinement when Martha arrived the next week. Jenna was so big towards the end that she could sit a mug of tea on her stomach. The poor dear was so uncomfortable. She hated the waddle when she walked.

She and the babes, Edward Charles John and Christina Sarah Martha, are well. We are now at home, your house, sir, which we have named "Little Gracemere Cottage." I feel close to you living here.

The doctors in Sydney did not want us to leave so soon, but Jenna bounced back amazingly. I am more amazed every day with how she's coping, especially with feeding two babes at once. Mama found us a rocking chair, and this is a great help.

They are funny little mites. Edward, whom we call Neddie, sir, has a mop of unruly fair hair like mine. Christina is already being called Tiny Tina by Mama, as she is the smaller of the two. She has no hair at all save a curl on the top of her head.

If by some chance we separate them, they cry for each other. They sleep holding the other's hand. They normally wake together, which is a blessing as it gives Jenna time to sleep. Maryanne is an angel.

Sir, I thought I knew what love was when I met and married Jenna. I discovered this week that I was wrong. I may be a big Blacksmith, but I am jelly when it comes to this new love I feel for these two scraps of humanity. Little Tina fits in the palm of my hand. Yes, all right, they are big hands, but she is so small, and both are so fragile. I sometimes fear to touch them lest I hurt them. Mama and Jenna are in their element. Martha, Jenna's mother, is also with us for a while until we settle. To know we have help at hand is wonderful.

Maryanne has refused to return home. So she stayed with us until we build the new shop. She will be paid to work there and tend to the new store. I fear she will not want to leave us at all, but I have said she can live with us while she works at the store, so she is content. She was to share the other room with the babes; however, they kept her awake, so she is now staying with Charlie at the Inn. Martha is currently in the nursery room with the twins. Mama and Dar have moved into Christina's cottage.

The Governor came to Parramatta for a visit last month. I was requested to attend an Afternoon Tea at Government House. I went. I was quaking in my shoes lest he finds out he'd been duped. Apparently, he already knew. I have been commissioned to do much fancy Ironwork for assorted Government Buildings here and in Sydney. This will be a boon for our business. Your patronage of me was enough to secure the order. So, again I thank you. Who knew that would come out of that visit on your last day? He asked me to let him know when we heard any news from you. I shall do so when we hear.

Sir, I wish to thank you again for all you have done for me. Every step of it, you have been there protecting me. I feel God put you there as my earthly Guardian angel. Dare I call a Duke that? To me, you are the Uncle I never had. I can never thank you enough.

I have filled the paper now and dare not use another sheet.

I write with humble thanks for you and to you. I pray for you both daily.

Send my regards to Doctor Gerry too. But for him, you may still be here with us, but I feel no anger, just pride to have been able to call you my friend.

Sir, so I will keep My hands upon the Anvil. It's work I know and love. I will teach others to do the same.

With Mr. Tindale's permission, I have placed a Bible verse upon the forge wall. I think it's apt.

It's Isaiah 41 v 7

> So the craftsman encourages the smelter,
> And he who smooths metal with the hammer
> encourages him who beats the anvil,
> Saying of the soldering,
> "It is good."

I go now to post this screed. May God be with you always
Eddie Lockley
With Love
Eddie, Jenna, Neddie and Tina

PS Liza and Bertie had a boy on August 15th as well. They named him Albert George Charles, to be called Albie.

So all three were born on the same day, with Albie arriving in the afternoon.

Ed

Gracemere Castle,
Maidstone England
1st September 1842

"Jolly Sailor Inn"
Phillip Street
Parramatta

Charles, my Dearest Friend,

I write this day to let you know our happy news. My Darling Christina was safely delivered of twins. I am a father of two. Charles Edward John arrived first, closely followed by Sarah Christina some fifteen minutes later. How could I not name them thus?

Other news I should have written earlier is that Gerry is married, and they, too, are expecting a happy event in about two months. They married on board some five weeks after our departure. Call it a shipboard romance, but they are a perfect fit. Her name was Mrs.

Annabella Derbyshire, a widow whose situation was similar to Christina's; only she had enough funds to return home. She was travelling alone, so Christina adopted her in friendship. Gerry was soon besotted, and seeing her frequently hastened things somewhat. However, it took a storm and her being knocked out for him to finally declare his feelings. They were married by Captain Wallace, Master Mariner and Justice of the Peace, only three days later. He, too, has become a friend.

Annabella is from Ashford, not far from Maidstone, and her father is Viscount Ellison. They have made their home with us at the Castle. I shall endeavour to write again after Gerry and Annabelle's child is born. Gerry says if it's a boy Gerald Matthew and if a girl, Annabella Jennifer. Annabella may have a say, but Gerry said he would not concede. He has become a chucking mother hen.

On another topic, and also the reason for my delay in writing, by the way. Do you remember I was questioning you deeply for your information on the last day we were together? I can hear you replying Yes.

Did you never wonder Why I used to watch you so intently on the ship? Again I hear you say Yes. I can now reveal the answers to both, but I shall start with the latter.

On the day I first saw you, a lad of about nineteen. Your fair hair caught my eye. It was an unusual shade, the same shade as my brother, who is your age. However, it was something in your stance that was somehow familiar. I let it pass, or so I thought. Until I finally found out your name. Even then, the penny should have dropped, but that nagging feeling of familiarity came to me each time. Eventually, I put it aside. You became my friend; that was enough. You see, although Gracemere is the Title, the family name is... Lockley. I never used it. It was, however, the name Gerry looked for me under. Edward Lockley was my correct name. I thought none of the family had; it's not that uncommon. Young Charles Edward is actually Viscount Lockley.

In all those years, some twenty-three now, you never asked me for anything other than saving Sal. You accepted me at face value, and I treasure that.

Charles, when you finally revealed your back story. It shocked me. I so wish I had asked before. I do not know why it just never occurred to me. I nearly blurted out my suppositions, as did Gerry, but I needed to confirm them.

As a village lad, you may not have been aware of your surrounding area; the Castle was often referred to as 'The Castle', but it's in Maidstone on the other side of Coxheath. When you said your cottage was named 'Bramblemere', again, I started. I knew this to be one of the endowed cottages of the Estate. All of the 'Mere' cottages are. Gerry and Christina wanted me to say something to you then, but I could not until I knew all the facts.

Oh, Charles, I so wish I had asked decades ago. I am truly sorry. 'Bramblemere' was endowed to your Grandfather, Charles Lockley, and my father was named after him. He was the second son of my Great Grandfather, the 6th Duke. Your

Charles Snr had a Title conferred upon him after his involvement in Poona, India, in 1776. Although I have been unable to precisely discover what he did, I discovered he was a friend to William Pitt and Lord Temple. Therefore, I imagine he did something for the East India Company, infiltrating the enemy and so on. I have discovered that he inspired something called 'The Great Game'. Regardless, it was enough to earn your grandfather a title. He became Earl of Coxheath for being a secret spy or similar, it was hushed up, but he earned his title. I think he must have been injured somehow. Mother didn't know. He refused to use this new title, ever. He retired incognito, was happy being an artist, he only wished to paint.

He fell in love with the daughter of the Castle Chaplain. Our Great Grandfather bestowed this cottage upon them and their children in perpetuity. Yes, Our Great Grandfather! I now know that your father, John, was the only child of this union. As a small lad, John became the Earl after his father's death. His mother, the minister's daughter, was, according to my mother, somewhat of a hermit herself and took the family pension as she had no other income. She never asked for more, and it was never increased. I do not know how they survived on the pittance they were given. She obviously never discussed anything with your father, so the story was never passed down to you or your mother. My mother, however, knew their story.

Oh, how I grieve Charles.... for you ARE family; you are my third cousin. I grieve when I think of the time we have lost. This, of course, also means that although your Grandfather refused to use his title ever, he remained Earl of Coxheath until he died. He refused to use the name Coxheath but his untitled name Charles Lockley. The Earldom is hereditary; therefore, both your father and you are Earl's. Charles, you have been an Earl longer than I have been a Duke, and you were born a Viscount as Charlie is now.

Therefore, Sal is a Countess; Charlie is a Viscount; Eddie and the others are all The Honourable... the same as Gerry.

Your full title is The Right Honourable Charles, The Earl of Coxheath.

Sal is, The Right Honourable, The Countess of Coxheath.

You are Lord and Lady Coxheath. Charles, even your mother is titled, The Most Honourable Elizabeth, The Dowager Countess of Coxheath Your sister is The Lady Elizabeth... and so on.

I'll let that sink in. Ask Harry Moffatt. He'll fill you in on the nuances of titles.

I have visited your mother and sister (and yes, I have told her too). I have ensured she is now known as Dowager Countess, or Lady Coxheath (Mother calls her Elle), and your sister Lilabet is The Lady Elizabeth Lockley. They also had no idea of this. They are well and send their greetings and their love. I'm sure they will now write in their own time once the shock of it all wears off; now they know your direction.

They thought you must have perished. I checked they are both on the full family pensioner endowment list. I shall also give them the fifty years back pay they are owed. They are on the list, but for some reason, it has never been increased since your Grandfather's time; this has been corrected. She will receive the same as you, plus back-dated from her marriage as will you. This will give her some ready cash, and Lilabet has already planned a shopping trip for clothing for them both with my mother. (I am pleased not to have been invited on that trip.) I have also employed a maid, cook and gardener-come-groom for them. I have also bought her a small carriage and pair, so they are now mobile.

I shall personally care for them all my days. They will have whatever they need or want. This, I promise. They will be taken into our household if ever they wish to. Your sister Elizabeth, or Lilabet, has become an excellent companion for Christina and Annabella. She is their senior by only a few years. My mother has taken your mother under her wing. Both were lonely, and I hope your mother will eventually move into the Dower house with her. Mother is angry with herself that she never realised her situation. They are forever in each other's company with only four miles between residences.

And yet Charles, there is even more. Because of my newly found importance, I have had your case revisited. I found the owner of the flock; he still lives locally. On reflection, he realised he was wrong and has belatedly withdrawn his lawsuit. The paperwork was officially stamped yesterday. You do not need an Absolute Pardon, as your slate is wiped clean. Maybe one day you can come home, or just for a visit. I do hope that this will come to pass.

I shall be writing to the Governor with the relevant paperwork regarding the quashing of your conviction. There is more to this. I'm sure he will summon you once word is received.

I feel so guilty that I had not looked into this before, but then in God's timing, maybe things will work out better. I do not know. With this letter, I am enclosing a bank draft for the backdated allowance that was duly yours as a family member. Do with it as you will. It is yours. Each other family member receives the same. This will now be paid quarterly to you and your family in perpetuity. Do not hesitate to ask for anything more. I owe you far more than earthly money. Sadly the Title of Coxheath is merely that. Neither land nor finance accompanied it. However, I shall make over the title of 'Bramblemere' and the village of Coxheath to you and your family as a 'family seat'. I will continue to manage it for you.

A few more things I wish to write regarding Eddie. You know I have always had a soft spot for him. Now knowing my name also may explain why, as well, he was born on my birthday. He always reminded me of my youngest brother, Douglas, when he was little. Again now I understand why. I treated Eddie as the son I never thought I would have. As such I am sending him a wedding gift of £1000. I shall write to him about this, but I wanted you to know why he was getting it. Charlie will get a lesser amount when he marries as he will be entitled to much more later through you, but this will enable Ed to build his foundry. I shall endow each of the others with £100. Liza will get hers immediately and the others on their marriage.

As you know, there is no doubt about Eddie's parentage. I never looked at Sally in that way, nor did she me. She only had eyes for you from that very first day. He is truly your child, so do not think otherwise... but I will always love him like my own. I feel now that I could be referred to as Uncle Ned by all the children. What do you think?

Now for the final matter. I searched for Sal's Mother in London but sadly have been unsuccessful. I will continue to seek news of her. There is no record of her death, and one old neighbour thinks she remembers something about her returning home soon after Sal's arrest. However, she does not know where that was. She may have returned to the land of her birth. I shall send someone to Ireland to see if they can find her. If you can furnish me with more details, it will make tracing her easier.

God has been weaving His side of the tapestry all these years. We could only see the knots. We still only see the stitches, but the picture Is becoming clearer.

May He continue to uphold you in His arms as He always does.

I sign as your dear and apologetic cousin but Best Friend.

Edward / Ned Lockley

Gracemere

I enclose a drawing of Bramblemere for you.
Your grandfather did it. He was very good, wasn't he?

Gracemere Castle,
Maidstone England
1st September 1842

"Little Gracemere Cottage"
Phillip Street
Parramatta
Dear Eddie,

I write with the good news that Christina was safely delivered of twins this day, Charles Edward John and Sarah Christina. Please read my long letter to your father for full details of this and about Gerry. It will explain much.

I do hope by now that you, too, will have been blessed by a Happy Event, maybe a double one.

The primary purpose of this letter is to explain its physical contents.

I have enclosed a draft for £1000. Your father knows of this. But I wish to explain that this is a gift for you and Jenna. The Wedding Gift I could not give you at the time.

I do hope that you have taken up residence in my cottage. As I explained, I gave it to your parents, as did Christina.

Although you do not have to follow my suggestions, I would like to know that you will always have a roof over your head that is your own. I was worried that with the Tindale's return to the forge, you had nowhere to go. Thankfully our cottages were available. I would like you to use some of the money to buy or build a house with some land and have your own stable on it for the magnificent James and his future stable mates. Ensure your home has at least one guest room, as we plan to return for an extended visit one day.

There should be ample money left to build some of your dreams for a Foundry or extend the smithy shop. You might even wish to buy the Tindales out. It's just a thought.

Your father's letter will explain many things, but the family will now receive an annual endowment in perpetuity. This will ease the burden of many things for your folks.

Yours etc
Edward Lockley / The Major/Uncle Ned
Gracemere

Christina's Cottage
Phillip Street
Parramatta
13th December 1842

Gracemere Castle
Maidstone

Ned, *my very Dear Friend and My Dear Cousin,*
   Oh, Ned, I do still find this hard to believe.
   Captain Macdonald hand-delivered your letter. He arrived on a new sort of ship called a 'Clipper Ship'. It took a mere seventy-two days to arrive. He delivered it to me personally the day after docking.
   I have delayed writing until my mind settled somewhat. I am still trying to get my head around your news. I find myself walking around in a daydream. I'm not sure what I find more amazing, The fact that we Are related or that I am no longer a convict. I am also thrilled that you are not only a father but I am a Grandfather to three. My mind and heart are in a whirl.
   Tim and Anna, Charlie and Gracie, and Marc and Milly are married. They had a triple wedding on November 5th. It was the young people's decision, and all families contributed. It's silly to have three parties when one large one will do. We are all one big happy family.
   The church is still in disrepair, as is the rectory. They are now still living with Elizabeth's sister Martha and her family. The Reverend Mr. Bobart has persevered and continued holding services, most often outside, but he still performs weddings inside the Sanctuary as he did with yours. There is a possibility they may not rebuild it but construct a larger church elsewhere. Time will tell.
   Ned, as yet, we have not said anything, outside the family, about my change in circumstances. As you well know, a title is problematic.
   The Governor visited Parramatta in August and summoned Ed. He has been given a Government Commission for Ironwork just after knowing of your patronage. Imagine what it will be like for us all when we have the remainder revealed.
   My mind keeps wandering to the remote possibility of a return 'home'. It would not be permanent, as our life here is too good to leave. However, I would love to see you again, but I would dearly love to see Mother and Lilabet. I now feel so guilty I never wrote a second letter. I honestly did not think they would wish to hear from me. I wrote while in prison but had no reply. Now I realise they never received my letter; I thought they had cut me off.
   Ned, with your discovery, our children will have many possibilities here that they would not have at home, even with a title. There, the mud will stick.
   Home! I am now torn to find where exactly this is, but I think it is here.

However, the children will have to decide what is best for them; we shall send them all over in good time so they can make an informed decision.

Your letter and funds have opened the door for our two young rascals to be enrolled at The King's School. If all is well, they will start next year.

They will be the only two at home now as Charlie and Grace plan to live in your cottage after Ed and Jenna's house is finished; they are currently living in the Inn. A start has been made on Ed's home with the construction of a timber cabin at the back as a residence for staff. Tim and Anna moved into a house in town with Tim's Law Office attached. I feel he will go far. I am thinking of sponsoring him for the Legislative Assembly or the like. For this, my Title will prove useful to him. Marc and Milly live at Emu Plains at the Inn.

Eddie and Mr. Tindale (Thomas) have shelved their original plan and started building their large shop in town. It turned out much more extensive than they initially planned, but many town businesses have asked if they can sell items from there. This meant that the original site they had chosen for it needed to be rethought. They had asked for a land grant in the middle of town. However, Ed bought a double block in town for the shop. It will become a single-stop shop for many farmers. They plan to call the store 'The Farmers Emporium.' All sorts of products will be stocked. It's being built on Church Street near the centre of town. All vehicles driving through the town will pass it. It's set back off the road so that many vehicles can halt and load without blocking the carriageway. More is being added to their inventory with every passing month. Bertie's brother Robert will take over the management. As their father, George, is the tanner and saddler, Robbie knows how to answer people's questions. I wish George would teach violin I think he would make more, but he loves his chosen profession.

Maryanne works at the old shop at the forge daily; she will move to the new shop when it opens. She returns to Ed and Jenna's to help them with the babies. She refuses to accept payment for this as she said she's getting free board in exchange.

Maryanne has suggested building a small kitchen and room where ladies can have a 'Tea and Scones' while waiting for their husbands while shopping. She is becoming quite a businesswoman. Robbie also seems to like working with her, possibly even a budding romance.

Thanks to your wonderful gift, Ed will tell you in his next letter that they will build a new house. It will be on Phillip Street, not far from your Cottages. They decided not to move far from the town centre or us. This will mean they will have to employ someone to tend their garden. I have suggested that they turn a large section into a large vegetable garden, and the excess can be sold.

The plan is to have five main bedrooms, and Maryanne will have her own room at the back if she wishes to avoid being in the cottage with her parents and younger sisters. One large room will be dedicated as a special guest room; hopefully, one day, you will return for an extended visit. The other room will allow Jenna's family to have rooms available when they wish to stay. I have seen the plan, and it looks wonderful. It sits on an acre of good ground. It will be interesting to see if their plans come to fruition.

Charles

PS (December 15th)

The Governor must have received the paperwork. I have been summoned. So to Sydney, we go. Charlie and Eddie come too.

CL

PSS (December 20th)

Ned, I can afford to use a second sheet and may need a third, so I shall, as I need to relay the whole.

We have just returned from Government House in Sydney.

Eddie had warned us what to expect. We went shopping the morning we arrived, and Eddie had us 'togged' outright royally. That night you taught us to tie a cravat, I laughed. Thankfully Sally and Anna listened. The gent in the shop finally managed to get me looking somewhat presentable.

Ned, I am not cut out for this caper!

Sal looked fabulous in her new deep pink gown and bonnet. Eddie wore the outfit that Gerry left him, and Charlie was also togged out in new clothes. Eddie wore what he did last time but did buy new shoes.

To continue, Eddie arranged a fancy Town Carriage, and we were regally deposited under the portico at Government House.

As we alighted, we were announced by their Butler...

The Right Honourable, The Earl of Coxheath

The Right Honourable, The Countess of Coxheath

The Right Honourable, The Viscount Lockley

The Honourable Edward Lockley

... I nearly choked.

It finally sunk in; I am an Earl!

I think I got that right. I must freely admit I was so frightened; much of it went over my head.

Then the Governor and his wife greeted us and, would you believe, bowed to US. It's laughable. If I had not been so scared, I would have laughed out loud. The boys, too, although Eddie is now beginning to take this in his stride. As much as one can in shoes that pinch. As it was, I was so scared as I stood accepting their subservience, yet inside I was laughing.

We were ushered into the formal red sitting room and served tea by a Livered butler and maids. Very La de Da.... to think you must now do this daily. You have my full commiserations.

I now have the paperwork to say I was never a convict. My hand shook as I took it. Sal took it from me, so I would not spill my tea on it. She is breezing through with grace and dignity. Lord and Lady Coxheath.

Later the Governor's wife asked permission to address her alone. I was nearly in stitches but held my face bland. Sal Was a convict, her conviction not quashed; she served her time with you. After they had talked for some time alone, Lady Gipps said that she would have Sal's case looked into as well. It seems she had known all along that we were convicts. She apparently liked her well enough, as she asked if she may call her Sarah and would be pleased to have Sal call her Elizabeth. I gather that they have already done some investigation into us.

Meanwhile, the Governor took the three of us into his office in the adjoining room.

Eddie was given the full Government Warrant for All Ironwork for All Government Buildings. The Governor laughingly suggested that the Emporium be called 'Lord Lockleys Emporium', which would also hold the Government Warrant. I shall talk to Thomas Tindale, but I hope the name will not change. However, it may bring in more custom.

Ned, his next request floored me totally. He asked me if I would become the Viceroy for Western Sydney as his representative for Official Functions in the Parramatta area. Charlie would be in an equal position or actually as Assistant Viceroy, as he's a Viscount. He would also be paid for his duties. He would do the travelling for the more distant functions as I am unable to do this. My injured leg still worries, so I would stay locally. This, as you can imagine, is not my 'cup of tea', Charlie's even less. I can fully understand my Grandfather's decision to opt out of this lifestyle.

However, as it will eventually benefit our children, I will conform at this stage. It will take Much adjustment for us all. He said nothing about us giving up the Inn, but Charlie and I have already decided that we shall be swapping houses. Sal and I will stay in 'Christina's Cottage' until Eddie and Jenna move to their new home. We will then probably move the two doors down. Charlie and Grace take over the Inn, and I will now only assist. The two boys can choose where they wish to live, but they will probably come with us. So either 'Christina's Cottage' or 'Gracemere Cottage' will become the Viceroy's official address. House names and residences are up in the air at the moment, but for you, we'd all still be at the Inn.

My mind is even more, a whirl than it was before. The Governor saw my confusion and suggested I discuss the matter with Harry Moffatt, the Justice of the Peace in Parramatta. He has been officially informed about my change of status. Being a friend of both Gerry and you, I think he would be a good choice. He will also be on hand to advise me when the need arises.

Oh, he told me Erastus Black didn't last the first month in Hobart. He was knifed for theft by a cellmate. As you know, his term had extended to life. Well, that's what it turned out to be.

> *Charles*
> *(aka, The Right Honourable, The Earl of Coxheath)*
> *P.S I'm not so sure I like being called 'My Lord.'*

> *PP.S Ned (December 21)*
> *I have just realised that We are now Toffs too. I have spent my life working for them, jibing and ribbing them, only never realising I WAS one myself all this time.*
> *Charles ~ Toff!*
> *NB I, too, shall keep the name Lockley rather than Coxheath.*
> *However, as the Governor now knows my title, I will use it for official duties; I must answer to it. Charles*

> *(December 22)*
> *PPSS I have just purchased the middle cottage as well. We have named it 'Coxheath', So if we move there, I really can be Earl of 'Coxheath'.*

> *Coxheath*
> *No ... I shall not use this ... Except officially.*
> *Charles Lockley*

"Gracemere Cottage"
Phillip Street
Parramatta
4th May 1843

Gracemere Castle,
Maidstone
England

Dear Uncle Ned,

Sir, I have always wanted to call you thus.

I find the happenings of the past two years have had far-reaching consequences, but many of them have been delightful. Now where to start?

I did not write much in my Thank you note as I was still in shock. I shall now endeavour to cover the changes and how we've used your generous Wedding Gift. Mere 'Thanks' is never going to be enough.

I shall start with the people …

Jenna, Neddie and Tina are well. The babes are now sitting up, and Tina has already learnt to roll over and manoeuvre herself to get closer to Neddie. They do so hate being apart. My Darling Jenna is well and bounced back after her confinement. The birth, she now said, was more discomfort than pain. I could hear her screaming from outside her room. I find that in this comment from her, I am much confused. Minutes later, she's sitting up in bed cuddling two babes, her face beaming. Her willingness to undertake this pain all over again is astonishing. She is already looking forward to more of these delightful bundles of joy. I think we may end up with a large quiver of Little Lockleys.

As Dar told you, we had a triple wedding on November 5th, and the happy news is that all three couples are expecting a happy event. Both couples, Tim and Anna, plus Marc and Milly, are expecting to be parents in September and Charlie and Grace in October, but she is larger than the other two, so we're wondering if she, too, is carrying twins. I have spoken to Charlie and suggested that they have this investigated. We have recommended that they visit our Doctor in Sydney. It looks like twins do certainly run in the family. We had no idea how big that family was, though.

Everyone else is well, although still stunned. Life here for Dar and Mama has changed amazingly. They moved into 'Christina's Cottage' while Jenna was expecting and are still two doors down from us. Charlie and Gracie are running the Inn, and they have employed other staff to assist, as Gracie has been so unwell in her confinement, so life has eased for them too. Our new house, 'Bramblemere Close', is nearly finished and we will move there next month. (Milly did a drawing of it which I shall enclose). Shortly before Christmas, Dar has also purchased the centre cottage as it came up for sale. We have not worked out what this shall be used for, but it is in the process of being refurbished. It may become the 'Women's centre' that Mama has always wanted to have. He has named it 'Coxheath'.

Now to the things …

Your gift to us was overwhelming and has enabled us to buy some land, build the house, and expand the ideas of the shop. I have endeavoured to use it to benefit many, all the family and the town. (More about that later.)

The house is a two-story sandstone building; the upstairs has a verandah all around, and I have made the wrought iron for the balustrade, and it's very fancy. I have had tremendous fun experimenting with many designs. We planned on having five bedrooms but have extended the rear to include more rooms; now, eight are inside the house, not including staff rooms. The house has four tall windows on each floor, two on either side of the front door. Upstairs, the same, but they are French doors, all opening onto the verandahs. The extension out the back means that the top verandah has been extended over, as it gives a wide, flat area that is elevated. It catches all the breezes from the river.

We have been assigned Maryanne's parents, who will live in the timber staff cottage out the back. They are both 'lifers' and will never attain freedom, but we can make their lives easier. Maryanne is still with us, but only until next week when she and Robert finally marry. She is three months gone with child, much to her parent's anger, not to mention the Ellis's, and we have persuaded them to marry. We have not allowed her to move into the residence at the store until they are legally wed. Reverend Bobart is, of course, performing the ceremony. I was surprised to find they are not Catholics, although Irish.

Maryanne's parents, Patrick (Paddy) and Cara Connor have been working for a settler on Windsor Road. They were unhappy there, and Cara could not cope with the work required (she was the laundry maid). Their owner wanted younger convicts, so they are now with us. They have now made their home, where Cara will become our housekeeper and cook. Six months ago, they moved into a covered wagon parked on our land and have been on hand for everything from before building started. Paddy is an excellent gardener, so taken over the planning of the gardens. Two of their youngest girls are joining them now in the new rooms at the rear. Their two youngest boys work at the Government Dairy; they live there already. The girls will work in the house. The family can't believe that they, too, have fallen on their feet.

We built their rooms first. It's just a timber cottage to which the stables will be attached later. They needed to leave the previous accommodation. Their roof became the base for the upstairs deck of our verandah. They moved in, even though the building was going on around them. I suppose after living in the cart for some months; it's luxury. Paddy has the gardens already overflowing with produce, including our favourite… potatoes, of course.

As soon as we move out, Charlie and Gracie plan to move into our cottage, 'Gracemere Close,' but plans can change. The boys have moved in with Mama and Dar into 'Christina's Cottage.' Every time we tried to choose a name for it, we all just kept reverting to this. The boys were supposed to start at The King's School this year, but it closed due to financial problems after Scarlet Fever swept through the school. I have heard whispers that it may reopen later this year. Dar, Mr. Moffatt and others are in discussion with Reverend Forrest. If so, the boys will enrol as soon as they can. Reverend Forrest has been asked to return; he is seriously considering it. If Wills can have one or two years of good education, it will stand him in good stead. I have been tutoring them in the evenings, and they both have mastered elementary Latin and French. Luke, forever the scholar, will enjoy a more formal style of education. Again thanks to you.

Now to the Store…

The night Jenna and I married, we sat outside, looking over Parramatta and discussing the future. I told Jen my dream of building a Foundry but knew that this could not eventuate as there is no mineral mine yet in the country. One day I believe this will happen. In the meantime, I wanted to expand the sales from the forge. The afternoon after we went to Government House with you, I discussed our ideas with The Tindales. Things moved a pace on our return to town. Mr. Tindale was in full agreement. (He wishes me to call him Thomas, but I cannot. I have too much respect for him to do so.) Dar, however, does and did so before his news. We discussed plans and location of said store… Then your letter arrived. Thankfully we had not started building.

Uncle Ned, you should see it. (I do so love calling you that.) When others heard of our plan, they asked if they could add their stock too. It is now built and has grown and grown. A large shed was the original plan, and this was constructed. This quickly became too small, and we enlarged the building before completion. We more than doubled the size. However, we have ended up with a more significant stone-based building which has recently been finished. It has a three-bedroom residence at the rear and a small lean-to store joined on the side as Maryanne's Tea shop; only this, too, has grown. You can walk through from one shop to the other shop via a connecting door.

This is a thriving business in itself. Many local farmers bring in their excess produce; anyone can purchase these. Things like honey, eggs, potatoes, dried and salt meat, boiled lollies, mint bullseyes, aniseed humbugs, toffee, and fudge. More and more farmers come with products each time they visit the town. Their wives and children spend money on lollies, toffees and Tea while they stock up on items, and we load them for them.

Paddy has planted many green vegetables. So many that we cannot hope to eat even half. All the excess from our garden is placed in buckets of water and sold from the shop. Non-perishable items are sold on a 'sale or return' basis, so there is no cash outlay. Everyone is happy with this as they can come and remove their items at will. The store has a 10% commission on all nonperishable goods sold and a 15% on perishable items. We sell far more stock than each of the craftsmen in their shops. We have also raised their prices to cover the percentage commission. They can take their own goods back at any time with no penalty. It also means they do not have overhead costs. Thus benefit all around.

Maryanne and Robert have hired two more girls, and they help in the shop with her. Her idea of the Tea House has been so successful. It's brought some elegance into the town. She has made the girls light blue gingham skirts with lace-edged aprons and white lace-edged mob caps. They are clean and tidy. All Tea inside is served in fancy china teacups and saucers, but large mugs are available for men if they wish to sit outside and drink it. Each order is served with a freshly cooked giant scone, clotted cream and jam made by Mama and Jenna. Some days there is a lineup to sit inside. We have added a massive log to the front for the men to sit upon.

Uncle Ned, the shop we named the 'Farmers Emporium' though that is not what everyone calls it. It's known as 'Lockleys Emporium', even by Mr. Tindale. He wants to change the name on the front.... So, the Governor seems to have got his wish.

There are coopered barrels, buckets and drums, ironmongery of all sorts, and we have a custom-made order facility. Joinery items, like shelving, chairs, beds and all manner of household furniture. All other required articles can be made to customer requirements. Nails of all sorts, from sewing pins to 8-inch bridge nails. There are tools, sheers, clamps, callipers, hammers, and more types than you can dream about. Steel posts for fences and the ramming tool for them, fence wire and everything you can imagine for a farm, and baskets of all sorts, too, from Mrs. Walker at Windsor.

And then there are the leather goods. Oh, you should see the quality of the items that George and Bertie Ellis are making. Milly is still working, but from home at Emu, doing some unique leather carving. They are using kangaroo leather to produce some outstanding work. We are unable to keep up with the supply of saddlery. Who knew 'side saddles' were so popular? Jenna still refuses to ride on one, insisting on riding astride; however, I have said she may do so, but only if she wears a split habit instead of hitching up her skirts. There are reins, traces, collars, stirrups, girth straps, bags, belts and everything else you could imagine.

The cobbler wants us to build a room next door for his shoes. Currently, we only take his boots. If we do, we will add other clothing for farmers. I think this is the next step. We have already added a bulk loading dock at the back. This next wing be built from the profits from the store. I own 80% of the store and Mr. Tindale 20%. Others wanted to buy in, but until we have it how we want it, we shall keep it between us as we have full control. I do not want to turn it into a Co-Operative.

I'm trying to think of other things we could stock. We also now have a section for stock feed. Although most animals eat native grasses, grain, hay and other fodder are required for stables. Things like whitewash and coloured paints would be useful. Fabric for curtains and furniture. Oh, my mind never stops.

Luke and Wills wanted some pocket money, so Dar suggested they bag some manure and sell it. So this is now something else we keep in burlap bags and outside, though, as it stinks. I'm sure they will think of other things we can sell, even goods they have made. At the rate we're growing, we won't need a Foundry.

It's been a boon for all the tradespeople in town; they no longer have to worry about staffing their own store. The 10% from sold items pays for the staff wages and then some. We have a set wage, and any profits will go into the store's growth and further developments in the town. If sales are very high, the staff will get a monthly bonus.

We encourage people of all walks, from The Governor, who now prefers to have Tea here than at the Inn or with Dar, to Mrs. Moffatt, who loves to sit and have Tea with Mama at the Tea House. Also, Mr. Moffatt and many of the society ladies come regularly. Mama, Jenna and Grace often come up for tea and encourage others to meet with them for a chat. They have started a little group of young mothers so their children can play together. They usually meet in 'Coxheath' for that, as they have turned one room into a playroom and the back yard into a secure area so no child can escape, and they can yell and shout. The sitting room at 'Coxheath' has become the Women's meeting room, where they sit and sew, chat, spin or similar. Many of these crafts can be taken outside while the mothers watch over the children. The second bedroom is also a storeroom for fabric, offcuts, and the like and is set up with a bed and cots for emergency use if a woman needs a safe place to stay, rather than under the inn. Mama calls this group the 3C's, Craft, Companionship and Care. It has grown from a conversation she had with Aunt Christina. As Mama no longer has much to do with the Inn, it fills her time. Mrs. Jenkins is instrumental in its running. Hard to believe the amazing change taken place in her life.

Bill Miller's friend, Old Tom, who has almost taken up residence on hitching poles at the front door of the Emporium, refuses to leave his room at the Union Inn, but he spends most of his days at the store. He has become a popular figure; everyone now waves and stops for a chat. He has taken on the role of 'groom' at the store. Taking care of all the arriving horses. He refuses payment but loves the position. He gets to take home any leftover food from the Tea Rooms and considers this fair compensation. He still goes to Mama for a free meal. The Governor even now knows his name. You should see his face light up when greeted by name by anyone.

Oh, I could keep on and on about how the town is growing. I so wish you were still here to see it.

Uncle Ned, I let you know that Dar and Mama have made inquiries to find out if Mama would be allowed to return to England for a holiday. When they went to the Governor, he informed them that the man who had accused her of theft had made a deathbed confession that her story was true; he forgave her. Her conviction was unable to be quashed, but the Governor issued her with an Unconditional Pardon. This means they can travel at will.

So... I give you fair warning that you may well have visitors for Christmas or soon afterwards. Sadly, many ships are going to New Zealand as there is a war over there. There is a ship called 'Ragamuffin', hopefully, due sometime late this year. We sent some products back with her last year. She is due again soon. Captain Murd Macdonald is a friend of Captain Wallace. He was the Captain who delivered your letters. He brought them to us personally.

We're hoping that he will again carry some produce and products from our town on this ship. We are going to be sending some of our own honey. They are aiming to get passage on her. It would be lovely if they could accompany our stock back and see how it's received in the Motherland. They're hoping that it will be by October this year. If it's not this ship, they will try for the next one. To our knowledge, few ships are expected before this that will be heading back to Portsmouth.

We will not be able to let you know exactly when they will arrive, as so few ships are heading back...but coming they are. Can you please let Grandmama and Aunt Lilabet know too?

I would love to come back and meet my grandmother and aunt; we now write as regularly as possible. Dar is very eager to see his Mother and Sister again. We may try to come later. I would dearly love to see you all again. Mama is hoping that they will get to Cork in Ireland and see if she can find any of her family. She is thankful that you have searched in London, so they plan to try Ireland. Shannon McCarthy is an unusual name in London but not in Ireland. Her parents were Eamon (Edward) and Nioiclin (Nicola) O'Shane. It might be more challenging than they expect. I do hope that for Mama's sake, she is found or some family for her.

    I wish I could keep writing. I want to write and write and write. However, I must post this letter. 'Till we meet again, AND we will.

    Eddie,

      Your loving honorary nephew

      The Honourable Edward Lockley

    PS I think that we may well send the children to school with yours when they are old enough. Who knows, Tina may fall in love with your Chip. Tina will undoubtedly return to be presented, and we will accompany her. How many more blessings will we each have by then?

    Eddie

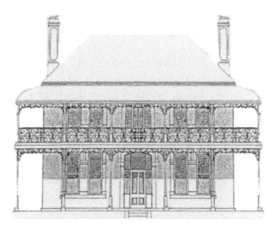

Bramblemere Close, Parramatta
(drawn by Milly)

Wills story continues in…
'Out Where the Brolgas Dance'

The criss-cross of letters across the world continued
as did the journeying of family. With the advent of Clipper ships,
the trip took only from eight to ten weeks.
Both families made the journey often.

In time, Ed and Jenna went on to have ten children.
Neddie, their oldest,
took over the forge and married Stevie Evans's daughter.

In 1858, two beautiful girls were presented at Court.
Both were ravishing blondes.
Lady Sarah and her cousin Miss Christina (Tina) Lockley
They took London by storm.
Like the Gunning sisters, one hundred years before,
one married a Duke's heir, the other an Earl's heir.
One a Duke's daughter, one an Earl's Granddaughter
Tina did indeed marry Chip, who, in time,
became the 11th Duke of Gracemere.
*(but that's another story-
Read Out Where to Brolgas Dance for that.)*

Charlie's son, Edward (Teddie-the older twin), married Annabella (Bella)
Jennifer Winslow-Smythe and eventually took his place as 5th Earl.
They lived in *Bramblemere House* in Coxheath, UK.
(read 'Once a Jolly Swagman' for that story.)
And ran the walnut farm that Charles had bought for him.
(See, *The Earl's Shadow* & *Waiting at the Slip Rails* for those stories)
His twin brother John Lockley took over the "*Jolly Sailor Inn.*"

But what of Sal's mother? Did Ned find her?
And then there is **Wills** and his discovery of gold.
However, that is another story entirely…
Book two continues the family saga.

"*Out Where the Brolgas Dance*"
And the discovery of Gold in Australia

See the brief outlines on the following pages.

Author's Note

While inspired by my Great Great Grandfather, **Thomas Ellison**,
this story does not follow his life. He was a blacksmith who did go to Cape's
Academy with James Martin and George Thornton, and he, too, was also a
convict's second son, there the likeness ends.

As to the other people's characters and lives, they are mostly
fictitious, although names may be similar.
St John's Parramatta did get severely damaged by a storm
on the evening of December 21st 1841, as did the Rectory.
What happened to the Bobarts after the storm is pure supposition.
I do not know if the church was usable after the tornado.

The geographical description of Parramatta has been described
with some artistic license.
The three cottages I have described are still in Phillip Street Parramatta as
Cafés (in 2020). I am not sure when they were built.

The **safe room** that the Ellisons had at their inn was also a fact. It came to
light when John was charged with running a brothel and serving drinks on a
Sunday. Rev's Marsden and Cowper gave him character references and
endorsed his work.

The *Jolly Sailor Inn* was true, but its description was inaccurate; it was a two-
story timber cottage. **John Ellison**, my GGG Grandfather, ran it and the
Government Stores.
But John was convicted of stealing shirts.
Another Innkeeper, **Joseph Huff**, another GGG Grandfather,
was convicted for stealing a lamb.
They became in-laws when their children married.
John Ellison's son, **Henry**, took over when John died in 1832, aged 66.
The Inn was on George Street on the Parramatta River.

Captain **Leopold George Wallace** was, in fact, real and was a
Master Mariner and Captain of various ships, including the
'*Sarah Bostford*,' although the 1842 trip, she only sailed to Singapore.
He, too, was another of my GGG Grandfathers
(maternal side), arriving in the 1850s on the '*Kestrel*.'
and ending up in Ballarat, Victoria, on the gold fields.

If you loved this book, these are similar.

Unlikely Convict Ladies - Trilogy

Dancing to her Own Tune

Co-authored by Sheila Hunter and Sara Powter

Sydney 1790s to England 1830s

Annie White is released after serving seven years as a convict in Sydney. She gets a visitor who, with his help, she can start a baking business. She is then asked to assist another sick man, **Sam** Corbett. Annie nurses him back to health, and a relationship develops. They settle into a life together, barely making ends meet; she realises she's expecting a child. Sam has his past laid bare and must adjust to the revelations. They both must face their accusers and find that the answers to their questions are not what they thought. Their life experiences seem to cling to them, and unable to shake them off, they end up back in England. They must face their ghosts and discover they are not who they think they are. How can they turn their anger and spite into love and forgiveness? The Dance of Life goes on.

ISBN 9780645110715   ISBN9780645110722

Long-listed in the Historical Fiction Company Competition 2022

October2021

https://amazon.com/dp/064511071X   https://amazon.com/dp/B09JC378YV

Amelia's Tears

Parramatta 1828 – England 1840s

In the Parramatta Female Prison, **Amelia** awaits her assignment. Forced to leave the relative safety of gaol, she is assigned and now faces her worst nightmare. A foul man claims her and makes her life a living hell. Then, her world goes black. A glimmer of hope arises when she hears from her brother, Jim, who has enlisted a friend to help her. She writes to Jim, pouring out her heart and telling him of the horrors of her new life. He encourages her to stay firm in her faith. All she can do is pray. When Major **Ned** Grace, her brother's friend, enters her life in Parramatta, he starts to ease her path. Things have changed, as now she has a child in tow. How can Amelia forge a new life for herself? What man could want her with her background and a child at her side? Who is the gentleman who turns her tears of sadness into tears of great joy?

ISBN: 9780645110739   eISBN: 978-0-6451107-4-6 Hard Cover ISBN 979-842061-7953

April 2022

https://amazon.com/dp/0645110736   https://amazon.com/dp/B09SS855BR

A Lady in Irons

England 1800s - Parramatta 1808+

Katy is mourning the death of her husband after he died in a shooting accident. Barely coping, she awaits the birth of their child. If it's a girl, she must hand the family home to her husband's brother. The day after giving birth to a daughter, she and her daughter are left on the side of a road. She collapses and is found by someone she thought had died in a fire ten years before. **Perry**, badly scarred himself, nurses her back to health. They marry and move in with her widowed friend, Mary.

After some years, she discovers her husband and friend in each other's arms. Now living in a love triangle, she flees. Grasping the only straw available, she intentionally gets arrested and is sent to a colony far away. By doing this, her marriage can be annulled.

What happens in the Colony is different from what she expects. Governor Macquarie comes to her rescue.

But what of Perry and her children?

ISBN: 9780645110784   eISBN:9780645441505

November 2022

https://amazon.com/dp/0645110787   https://amazon.com/dp/B0BCWSXB9Z

The Convict Stain Collection
(All stand-alone stories)
NO MORE, MY *Love*

Hunter Valley, NSW 1820s

Jess Elkin is distraught when tragedy ravages her family. She becomes the victim of a carriage accident and is nursed back to health by the driver, **Marcus Ryan**. Marcus was not expecting to fall in love. Yet, when Jess's fortunes suddenly turn for the worse, Marcus must decide how far he will go to pursue her. As time passes in Newcastle, Australia, Marcus must take a business trip and is taken by pirates. Jess is left wondering if her will keep his promise to return to her… Will she ever see him alive again?

ISBN: 9780645441536   eISBN 9780645441581

April 2023

https://amazon.com/dp/0645441538   https://amazon.com/dp/B0BSBH143Q

The Vine Weaver
Hawkesbury River area 1820s+
New Beginnings and Old Threats

In the 1820s, Australia, **Joel and Hetty Walker** live on a secluded farm on the Hawkesbury River, which becomes a healing haven for the protection of young convict women. A series of events brings **Fran Rea** to the attention of Hetty, and she is taken to the farm. Fran and Hetty develop a cottage industry under the compassionate eye of farmhand **Hector Macdougal;** Hector's loving words change lives. It is to him that Fran turns when threatened.

The vines now must draw them close to survive the future revelations, and of those, there are many.

ISBN: 9780645441512   eISBN: 9780645441529

June 2023

https://amazon.com/dp/0645441511   https://amazon.com/dp/B0C6Z552Y2

The story continues in Scotch at The Rocks…

SCOTCH AT THE ROCKS
Glasgow, Scotland, early 1800s to The Rocks, Sydney 1830s

Orphaned children Brodie Stewart and Heather Anderson live on Glasgow's streets. Although hungry, somehow they survive and keep out of trouble. Heather finds a job and looks to be settled; things go pear-shaped for them both. Eventually, they marry by declaration, yet even that gets messed up, and they are both arrested soon after they make their vow. In 1838, they were transported to Sydney as convicts. Heather arrives within weeks of Brodie, and they are assigned close to each other. They are now living on the docklands in Sydney, called The Rocks. They now have to forge a new life halfway across the world from their homeland.

Adventures abound, and Brodie gets press-ganged. While he's away, Heather's life changes and soon, she's officially selling Scotch Whisky at a shop in The Rocks.

You can take a Scot out of Scotland, but where did the Scotch come from?

ISBN 9780645441550   ISBN ebook 9781923097001

November 2023

Waiting at the Sliprails

The Bathurst Road 1830s
A Convict's Tale

Bea Dawes's term of conviction nears an end, and she has few options other than marriage to a stranger or going on the street.

Jack Barnes, the hired drover, wants a wife. Bea accepts his offer; then, she discovers that he could be gone for months, leaving her alone with **Billy and Netty**, part of the tribe of Aborigines who live on his secluded farm. Bea learns to love her husband and also this wonderful aboriginal couple.

Drought ravages the farm, and Jack must hit the long paddock with the flock. In his absence, a visitor arrives, threatening to destroy everything she has worked so hard for. Can Bea touch her heart? Can she cope? Will the drought ever end? And when will Jack return?

ISBN: 9780645441543   eISBN: 9781923097032
August 2023

Convict Shadows of the Past

Two Jennifers, two hundred years apart

When aged eight, **Jenny** Kellow learns of her convict family history and discovers that she was named after a convict from nearly two hundred years ago. Her grandfather's stories inspire her to dig deeper into her ancestors' convict past. From her grandfather, she hears stories of bushrangers, convicts, and life in the infant colony of Parramatta. She sets about retracing the footsteps of her convict great-great-great-grandmother to honour her. Jenny's search starts with microfiche back in the 60s, and she learns about the small tin mining town in Cornwall and the production of a cheese that sets London afire. Then she discovers her ancestor, **Jennifer Kellow,** has brought these cheese-making skills to Parramatta, where she taught others her craft. Echoes of the past can still be heard if you know where to listen. But who was the first Jennifer? Why is she so elusive?

ISBN: 9780645783315   ISBN ebook 9780645783322
A NaNoWriMo 2022 book winner

January 2024

In Defence of Her Honour

London 1800s to Parramatta 1819

Bill Miller had been raised and educated with the sons of the family. The youngest, Bert, had been his best friend. However, jealousy intervenes when Bill's excellent schoolwork curtails their friendship. He wins a scholarship and enters Oxford University. When Bill's father, the old butler, dies unexpectedly, Bert insists that Bill take over the position, but it's more to oppress him. Bert's jealousy grows and festers. Now looking for a way to rid themselves of their new butler, a ruckus ensues, and Bill is arrested for assaulting Bert. The housekeeper and her daughter **Molly** vouch for him, but it's too late; Bill has been arrested and sentenced to be transported. With Bill gone, Molly now needs to defend herself from Bert. After hitting him with a pan, she is arrested and sent to Sydney. Bill and Molly arrive with letters of introduction and compensation from Bert's father. Soon, they are running the best Inn in Parramatta with an endorsement from the Governor.

ISBN 9780645441567 ISBN ebook 9781923097049
April 2024

Gentle Annie Soames

A 1788 First Fleet Convict Story

Her dreams lead to unexpected outcomes. An Australian First Fleet story.

Annie Soames is shattered by the cancellation of her debut into society, so when she hears of a position as a carer for the nearby Marchioness, she grabs it.

Oliver Quilpie, the recently married Marquess, discovers his arranged union is not to his taste; he is drawn to his wife's companion. Unfortunately, he is unable to keep his hands off her. For revenge, Annie mimics his every move while riding but is dressed as a highwayman. However, she had now fallen in love with him. This action finally leads to her arrest and transportation to a faraway land.

After some years, Oliver's wife dies, and his thoughts turn to Annie. He seeks to find her, but she has vanished. He is horrified to discover she was transported to New South Wales as a convict on the Lady Penrhyn. He follows with a shipload of supplies.

Will Annie want to see him?

ISBN 9780645441574 ISBN ebook 9781923097063

July 2024

J can't stop Tomorrow

Irish Famine 1840s to Avoca Beach, Australia

Escaping bigotry and prejudice in Ireland, the **O'Shane** family lives on a secluded farm on the west coast of Ireland. The potato blight soon decimates their farm. It's always darkest before dawn, and the two remaining girls cling to the hope of a new life. With the kindness of strangers, the oldest girls, **Clare** and **Kerry**, head to their cousin, Sal Lockley, in Parramatta, Australia. A new, wonderful life awaits them both.

Shéamus Connor is the annoying teenage boy who reluctantly draws Clare's affection. However, living in a convict town means ruffians abound.

John Moore is an angry and troubled Irishman, content to live alone on another secluded farm until he discovers Clare and two other lads need rescuing.

Can John protect her from the pain inflicted by an evil world?

Can Shéamus find his lost love who had fled?

ISBN: 9780645441598   ISBN ebook 9781923097056

October 2024

Madeline's Boy

England 1830s to New South Wales 1840

All is not straightforward when money and a title are involved.

Madeline is asked to care for her best friend's son when his life is in danger.

Christopher is the pawn between a greedy, unscrupulous uncle and his inheritance. Maddie must do everything she can to keep him safe, including moving halfway around the globe to take Chip to his guardian, Major Humphrey Downes, in the Australian Corps in Sydney. Humphrey's best friend, another soldier, Major Tim Hinds, meets Maddie, and with the support of these two men, a chase around the colony ensues.

Will Maddie and Tim be able to find happiness together?

Can the three adults keep Chip safe until he's old enough to claim his inheritance?

ISBN: 9780645783308   ISBN ebook 9781923097094

January 2025

Early Colonial Days Trilogy
WHEN UPON LIFE'S BILLOWS
Sydney 1795-1800 - Governor John Hunter

Captain John Hunter is born to a life at sea. The wind blows where no man knows, and John is caught up in the gale. From the wrecking of his ship, the HMS Sirius, in 1790 to become the second Governor of the colony of NSW, John seems to always be in the wrong place at the wrong time.

Helena Rosedale is not a typical female convict. She fights tooth and nail to stop The men from abusing her. She gains the name of Helena Hellcat.

Crispin Milroy is one of the Governor's security detail. Can he win the fair lady's heart? Life in 1795 in Sydney Cover. I it raw at best. Food is scarce, and disease often raves the settlement. Life throws them everything possible except death. Somehow, they survive. What trials will the young couple face to make a new life in this raw town? How can John ease their path?

ISBN: 9780645783339   ebook ISBN: 9780645783346
Coming April 2025

Tuppence to Pass
London 1800s to Parramatta 1820s - Governor Lachlan Macquarie

Josh Callan is a London lad who makes the best of the life that has been dealt to him. Stealing from the man who killed his father gives the family a change of direction. Josh is arrested, but the judge belittles him and says he's not worth tuppence. He is sent to the penal colony of Sydney as Governor Macquarie's term starts. He proves his worth and falls on his feet, becoming the Governor's groom. Life in the Colonial town opens opportunities they could never have dreamed about in England, but can Josh find his niche in life?

Where will this new life take Josh and his family?

ISBN : 9781923097070 eISBN: 9781923097087
Coming July 2025

Saddler's Song
London 1790s to Parramatta 1840

George Ellis is a tanner's son living on the outskirts of London. When disease takes his family, he seeks to find a new life for himself. Hearing from a friend about the possibility of setting up a business in New South Wales, he sells up and leaves all he knows. His beloved violin is the most valuable item he has, and his talent for making beautiful music is hidden from all but a few.

Ben Parker is a saddler and, like George, is now alone in the world as his father is dead, Ben also sells up to head to the new colony. Having booked passage on the same ship, the two meet up and combine their skills to start afresh in a new world. On the journey out, George's skill on his instrument is revealed.

On arrival, the two find accommodation with a family who have many lovely daughters. Two lovely ladies steal the hearts of the lonely lads, but how will the business survive in an animal-started land? Access to their primary material is limited. Where will this lead them?

ISBN : 9780645783353   eISBN: 9780645783360
Coming October 2025

A 100-year, six-part Australian Colonial series

The Lockleys of Parramatta

Hands upon the Anvil

A blacksmith's life and love are more than work

Parramatta 1830s

Eddie Lockley's parents were transported for their crimes. Can a steadfast lad rise above his origins and guide others to succeed in a land of opportunity?

Ten-year-old Eddie longs to help his mum and dad. Living in a convict town with his family, the keen youngster has been working with the local blacksmith since his sixth birthday. But when a lieutenant doesn't stop abusing his older brother, the young boy yearns for the day when he can stand up and end the torment. Though he's thrilled when his mentor offers to send him off to learn his letters, Eddie fears he won't be around to watch his sibling's back. But as he takes on the biggest adventure of his life, the brave believer soon discovers God is looking out for everyone he loves. Does this young man in the making have what it takes to change everything for the better?

ISBN 9780994578235 Ebook ISBN 978-0-9945782-5-9 Hardcover 9798496177368
Released 2021
https://amazon.com/dp/0994578237 https://amazon.com/dp/B08TB51L19

Out Where The Brolgas Dance

Gold is found, and so is love

Parramatta 1840s

How can a question change so many people?

It's the 1840s, and discoveries across the Blue Mountains continue. Major Mitchell's new road is complete, and towns are planned and being built. Abundant land is available for those who want it.

William "**Wills**" Lockley, 18, has laid a solid foundation for a respectable career as a blacksmith, but the Lockley lust for adventure flows deeply within his veins. He dreads the monotony of work at the blacksmith's forge and yearns for adventure in a new frontier. Wills meets six Englishmen who have the means to make his dreams come true. What they discover changes the Colony and their lives forever. Gold fever ensues. In the West, Wills has to deal with an uncertain romance. Does she even want him?

ISBN 9780994578242 Ebook ISBN 978-0-9945782-6-6 Hardcover ISBN 9798755445504
Released 2021
https://amazon.com/dp/0994578245   https://amazon.com/dp/B08T6NS3XX

Diamonds in the Dirt

Diamonds, love and money… but there is much more to life.

Parramatta 1850s

Luke, the youngest Lockley son, has completed University, and his life has no direction. No job, no money, and no love. Desperately alone, he prays for guidance. How can Luke trust that God has a plan for him if he can't even find a job? He does the only thing he can … he prays. Within a week, life has changed … oh, how it has changed as his brother Wills turns up with a suggestion. Would Luke be interested in joining the expedition with John Evans? Reverend William Clarke needs assistance on a Government Mineral Survey. The challenge, adventure and finds are life-changing for many. However, it gives Luke meaning, purpose and direction. The condition of his heart problems also takes a turn. Can he walk away?

ISBN:9780994578273 Ebook ISBN: 978-0-9945782-8-0 Hard cover ISBN 979-8788011141
Released 2022
https://amazon.com/dp/099457827X   https://amazon.com/dp/B09NH1MLXZ

The Earl's Shadow

Who or what is the 'shadow'? How does it affect so many?

Parramatta 1860s

Charles is the Earl of Coxheath and spends his youth as a convict in Parramatta; he had no idea he was an Earl. He had minimal education and few social skills. His eldest son, **Charlie**, is no different.

Now faced with his own mortality, Charles has to work out how to live the remainder of his life after a near-death experience. He is called to step way out of his comfort zone in London. His action will change the world for many. The echoes from the past still haunt Charlie. London is calling the family, and they can't postpone the trip. How does **Jim**, the Cobb and Co. coach driver, fit in? And precisely what is '*The Earl's Shadow*' that he speaks about? What happens if the 'Shadow' is gone?

ISBN: 9780645110708 Ebook ISBN 978-0-9945782-9-7
Released June 2022
https://amazon.com/dp/0645110701 https://amazon.com/dp/B0B158SKSK

Once a Jolly Swagman

An old black Billy Can contain the secrets of an incredible life

An Australian Historical Novel

Set in 1870s Parramatta and Kent, UK

Rick Lockley, battling his family's expectations, runs away to become a swagman. Jack, a jolly swagman takes him under his care. Even after years together, Rick knows little about the old man.

On his death, Jack leaves Rick his precious Billy Can; the contents reveal Jack's identity. Stunned, Rick must travel to England to finalise Jack's wishes. There, he uncovers Jack's life of love, betrayal and a link to his own family. Rick discovers there is much more to learn about this enigmatic man.

ISBN 9780645110753 Ebook ISBN 978-0-6451107-6-0
Released Sept 2022
https://amazon.com/dp/0645110752 https://amazon.com/dp/B0B5JN1WCV

Jonty's Journey

Gems, Love, Artists and a Golden Lion

Australia and South Africa 1880-1902

Sydney Jeweller, **Jonty** Evans' passion for gems takes him to Africa at a volatile time. He finds the diamonds he wants and gets given a lion cub. Jonty gets all but kidnapped. His experiences in the Transvaal plunge him into questioning everything he knows of life. Soon, nightmares haunt him.

On return home, he nearly messes up his love life with **Lottie** before it even starts, and he struggles to settle. Lottie's father, **Luke** Lockley from Parramatta, takes him in hand and points him to someone who can help.

Jonty is then recalled to Africa as a liaison and reconnects with his lion, Chimbu, when he saves the life of his security detail. His life journey introduces him to the most amazing Heidelberg artists, politicians, poets, rebels, and the scapegoat soldier Harry Breaker Morant. Can Jonty bury the past and regain the peace he's lost?

ISBN 9780645110777 HC ISBN 9781923097124 Ebook ISBN: 978-0-6451107-9-1
Released Feb 2023
https://amazon.com/dp/0645110779 https://amazon.com/dp/B0BLJ7ND1Q

Australian Colonial Trilogy

By Sheila Hunter

Co-Winner of 1999 NSW Senior Citizen of the Year, In the Year of the Senior Citizen

Mattie

Coming of Age in Convict Australia

Twelve-year-old London street urchin **Mattie Paul** is convicted of petty theft and sentenced to seven years of transportation to the penal colony of Port Jackson, NSW. Peg, another female convict, takes Mattie under her wing and gives her a chance to make something of her life by teaching her to read. Mattie seizes every opportunity that comes her way. Though life is not particularly kind to her, she battles through earning her freedom, marrying and becoming a mother in her homeland. On this journey, she encounters bushrangers, is widowed, and becomes an entrepreneur in the Bathurst goldfields. She mixes with escaped convicts, but her spirit is indomitable, and she becomes a pillar and much-loved treasure of her adopted community. Mattie may be a fictional character, but her experiences are only too real and invest us in immersing ourselves in the lives of those remarkable women who helped to make Australia what it is today. *(Mattie's story continues in The Lockleys of Parramatta - bk 2+)*

ISBN 9781503252370 & ebook AISN BOOTTEDBTO
(The Story continues in The Earl's Shadow)
Released 2015

https://amazon.com/dp/150325237X   https://amazon.com/dp/B00TTEDBT0

Ricky

A boy in Colonial Australia

Ricky English and his mother immigrated from England to join his father in the new Colony of Sydney. On arrival, there is no sign of his father. Ricky's mum uses the tiny amount of money they brought to get lodgings in a run-down building. Things go from bad to worse when his mother dies; he is thrown out of the rooms, and the caretakers confiscate all their possessions.

Ricky lives on the streets of Sydney Town as a street waif. Ricky finds safe places to sleep and befriends freed convicts who can help him survive. One day, he encounters a lost child and helps reunite her with her family. These people try to help him, but because of his stubbornness, he insists on doing things his way, but he has found a mentor and confidante. The story follows him through his life. He survives and turns his life around, helping others along the way.

Paperback ISBN 9780994578211   Kindle ASIN: B00MLYN6IG
(The Story continues in Jonty's Journey)
Released 2014

https://amazon.com/dp/1500770574   https://amazon.com/dp/B00MLYN6IG

The Heather to The Hawkesbury

Four Scottish families brave a new life in a strange land.

Mary Macdonald and husband **Murd** and family; her brother **Fergus MacKenzie**; sister-in-law **Caro** MacLeod; cousin **Alex** Fraser and all their families who have had to emigrate from the Isle of Skye during the "Clearances."

The story follows the four families from Scotland on the ship out to the NSW colony in the 1850s. Mary does not cope with the changes and losses that occur in the first months in the colony. The other women in the family rely on her, and she nearly crumbles. The families struggle together through accidents, losses, trials, floods, and hard work and forge a strong bond with their new country. Trials, tribulations and triumphs see the four families make a firm mark in their new homeland. The immigrants from Scotland helped make Australia what it is today.

ISBN 978994578228   ebook AISN B01A21JYWQ   Large Print ISBN1533473641
Available on Amazon/Kindle & Large Print
Released 2016

https://amazon.com/dp/1503251438   https://amazon.com/dp/B01A21JYWQ

Author Bio

Sheila Hunter and Sara Powter were a passionate mother-and-daughter team of amateur genealogists. While working together on their family tree, Sheila and Sara made many captivating discoveries. The greatest of these was finding four convicts, and these four had very different perspectives. They were sent to Australia from 1792 to 1814 during the height of Convict transportation. Before her *passing* in 2002, Sheila adapted some of these histories into enchanting stories, her Australian Colonial Trilogy. Sara later had these published. A fourth she left unfinished, and this inspired her to finish it. However, before she did, **The Lockleys of Parramatta** were created. The first two in the series were completed before she completed 'Dancing to Her Own Tune' for her mother.

Vividly living through the Colonial Era, these books delve further into the theme of overcoming adversity in Colonial Australia and how it developed, the demise of the Convict system and the discovery of mineral wealth.

Sara intricately weaves accurate archival data and a charming narrative to create a series of tales of faith, love, loss, and redemption.

And so, two hundred years after her family arrived in Australia, Sara continues the Australian Colonial stories started in **Lockleys of Parramatta,** followed by the **Unlikely Convict Ladies** Trilogy.

No More, My Love, The Vine Weaver and **Waiting at the Sliprails** are stand-alone novels, and all are part of my *"Convict Stain Collection."*

More Historical Fiction books are to follow... as eight more are already in the editors' queue.

Amazon Aus QR

See her web page to keep up to date with more stories.

With an online store available for a signed copy of Sara's books.

www.sarapowter.com.au

(Australian Postage only)

Feel free to email me at
saragpowter@gmail.com

BOOK BUB
https://partners.bookbub.com/authors/6273615/edit

FACEBOOK
https://www.facebook.com/profile.php?
id=100063887262514

FREE Newsletter signup
https://preview.mailerlite.io/preview/41388/sites/
77987646202184961/wCAAcK

Bibliography

Marsden's mill cover picture (cover)
https://historyandheritage.cityofparramatta.nsw.gov.au/blog/2015/08/12/
reverend-samuel-marsdens-mill-and-mill-dam-farm-1812
Marsden's Mill and Cottage, 1820, J Lycett, SLNSW PX*D41F1

Mr. William Timothy Cape
http://adb.anu.edu.au/biography/cape-Bill-1880

The King's School, Parramatta
http://www.kings.edu.au/about/history.php

Tea
https://scroll.in/article/959944/how-indian-chai-became-the-drink-of-choice-
in-20th-century-australia?fbclid=IwAR01-
D048ANtbsUBHoUhV3aDu_FDfc6KjB8Oh3SmfasoqGEFq0Dy6BOHR00

Parramatta and Sydney history
http://www.visitsydneyaustralia.com.au/history-5-first.html

Emu Plains History
https://www.aussietowns.com.au/town/emu-plains-nsw
The 'Inn' in Emu Plains is actually the *"Arms of Australia,"* first known as Mortimer
House. My Grandfather, Norman A Hunter, was born there in 1879. His
grandparents, Thomas and Betsy Ellison, ran it as an Inn for decades. My Aunt sold
it in the 1960s. They also ran Ellison's Pinch at Linden. They were not related to
any Peers (see book 4)

Dawson's Sydney Foundry
https://dictionaryofsydney.org/organisation/australian_foundry

Shipping information
https://trove.nla.gov.au/newspaper/article/12873755?searchTerm=passengers

Parramatta storm extract
https://trove.nla.gov.au/newspaper/rendition/nla.news-article12872982.txt?
print=true

Parramatta history, book
Parramatta, the cradle city of Australia: its history from 1788 / by Frances
Pollon

Barque picture
https://commons.wikimedia.org/wiki/
File:StateLibQld_1_110988_Drawing_of_the_barque_Newcastle_under_full_sail.jpg

Convict ship 1820
https://www.mq.edu.au/macquarie-archive/lema/1820/1820sept.html

Parramatta map 1812
https://historyandheritage.cityofparramatta.nsw.gov.au/sites/phh/files/wp-
images/2014/10/Parramatta-Town-Map-1812_Meehan_LSP00431.jpg

Duke's Family Tree

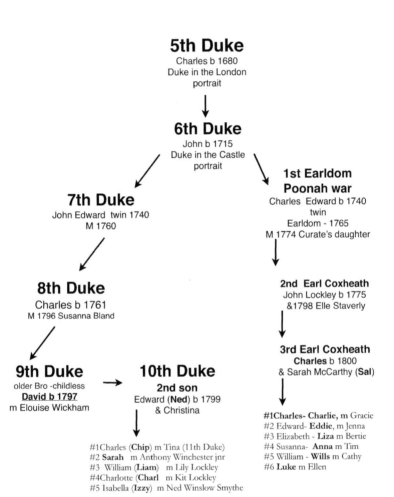

5th Duke
Charles b 1680
Duke in the London
portrait

6th Duke
John b 1715
Duke in the Castle
portrait

7th Duke
John Edward twin 1740
M 1760

**1st Earldom
Poonah war**
Charles Edward b 1740
twin
Earldom - 1765
M 1774 Curate's daughter

8th Duke
Charles b 1761
M 1796 Susanna Bland

2nd Earl Coxheath
John Lockley b 1775
&1798 Elle Staverly

9th Duke
older Bro -childless
David b 1797
m Elouise Wickham

10th Duke
2nd son
Edward (**Ned**) b 1799
& Christina

3rd Earl Coxheath
Charles b 1800
& Sarah McCarthy (**Sal**)

#1Charles (**Chip**) m Tina (11th Duke)
#2 **Sarah**   m Anthony Winchester jnr
#3 William (**Liam**)   m Lily Lockley
#4Charlotte (**Charl**   m Kit Lockley
#5 Isabella (**Izzy**) m Ned Winslow Smythe

#1Charles- Charlie, m Gracie
#2 Edward- **Eddie**, m Jenna
#3 Elizabeth - **Liza** m Bertie
#4 Susanna- **Anna** m Tim
#5 William - **Wills** m Cathy
#6 **Luke** m Ellen

Characters

Lieutenant Simmons, Soldier in the 48th, served under Major Grace in Parramatta.

Mr. **Thomas** Tindale b 1800 - (bro to Caroline Evans)
Mrs. **Margaret** Tindale b 1801 no children

Charles Lockley b 1800 and parents Elizabeth and John, "*Jolly Sailor Inn.*"
Sarah Shannon b 1800 (**Sal/Sally**) McCarthy (Dar and Mama)
Sally's mother :- Shannon McCarthy
Charlie b 13 Nov 1820 m Gracie
Eddie b 16 Oct 1821 m **Jenna** - Jennifer Martha Turner m Dec 4 1841
Liza b1823 m Albert (Bertie) Ellis m Nov '41
Anna b1824 m Tim Miller Nov 1842
Wills b1826
Luke b1828

Bill Miller b 1800 (Bill) "*Rear Admiral Duncan Inn*"
Molly Miller (Par and Ma)
Timmy b 1822 (lawyer, Ed's Best friend) m Anna Lockley
Gracie b 1824 (Anna's best friend) m Charlie Lockley
Samuel b 1828 (Sammy)
Ellen b 1830

Caroline Evans 1798 (**Caro**), sister of Thomas Tindale m Margaret
Captain **Douglas Evans**, 1795 supply ship captain, lives in Pitt Street, Sydney.
Phillip b 1819 **Phil**; Law married to Alice
Stephen b 1821 **Stevie**; Law engaged to May
John b 1822, loved bugs etc
Effy b 1816, their convict maid

Major Edward (Ned) John Charles Grace b 1799 Parramatta
His Grace 10th Duke of Gracemere, at Maidstone 48th Batt
Mother **Susanna** Bland, Dowager Duchess
m Dec 25, 1841, **Christina** Hunt Meadows
b Charles Edward John (**Chip**) 1 Sept 1842 twin Viscount Lockley
b **Sarah** Christina, The Lady Sarah Lockley b 1 Sept 1842 twin
Brother 9th Duke David b 1797 of Gracemere and
wife Elouise Wickham - no issue
Paul b 1800 Twin, Charles died at birth
Douglas b 1802

Reverend William Branwhite **Clarke**
married Maria Moreton - children

Major Humphrey **Downes**, Sydney Troop Major, Hyde Park Barracks
Captain Stephen **Roberts** Ferry Captain 'PS Surprise' (1831)-
Mr. **Iles** the Bookmaker, Sydney b 1790

John (Jack) Turner b 1799 arrived "Shipley" with Charles Lockley
Martha Turner b 1800 (Pa and Maa) Arms of Australia Inn, Emu Plains,
Marcus b 1820 (called **Marc**),
Alexander b 1821 (**Alex**) (saddler Ben Parker - daug Mary Parker),
Jennifer Martha b 1822 (**Jenna**) (met in 1840 aged 18)
Victoria b 1825 (**Vicky**)
Catherine b 1827 (**Cathy**)
Nicholas b 1830 (**Nick**)
Malcolm b 1832 (**Calum**) baby

George and Charlotte Ellis, Father is a tanner and Sadler, in Parramatta
Albert George (**Bertie**) b 1819 m **Liza** Lockley
Robert (**Robbie**) b 1821) m **Maryanne** Connor
Amelia (Milly) b 1822 m **Marc** Turner
Isabella (Belle) b 1826 m **Sam** Miller

Mr. Benjamin and Kathleen (Kath)Parker, Alex's boss, a Sadler
Mary b 1826 m Alex Turner
Violet b 1828

Finn and Maureen Murphy, lots of kids … Colleen and Shamus + more

Dr **Gerald Winslow-Smythe (Gerry)** b1799, the Dr who helps Eddie
(Emily dead wife) daughter Charlotte
Bro George, Sister Genevieve Sheridan, Orchard Hills farm

Mrs. **Christina Meadows** Lady Christina Catherine Meadows, née Hunt (daug of Edmund
William, Earl of Riverdell at Tunbridge Wells & Catherine

Mr. Henry (**Harry**) **Moffatt**, b1799 Justice of the Peace, Parramatta & Wife, Emily

Annabella Derbyshire - husband died of a snake bite from Ashford, Kent
Honourable Annabella Watkins-Harlow (maiden name) Papa is Viscount Ellison
Bro Matthew **Watkins-Harlow,** The Honourable Matthew
Gerry and Bell's daughter Annabella Jennifer, Bella b 1842

Charles Mother Elizabeth (**Elle**), The Most Honourable, The Dowager Countess of
Coxheath
Lilabet, the Lady Elizabeth **Lockley**

Shannon McCarthy, her parents Eamon (Edward) & Nioiclín (Nicola) O'Shane.
Samuel James Corbett Garney (Lord Garney/Viscount Clarestow then 6th Earl Meldon)
Meldon Hal
-mother **Anne** Corbett, served time West's farm arr *Royal Admiral* 1792 b 12 July 1773 d Dec
1864
#1 **Daniel** James Corbett Garney b 1803 Sydney

(see 'Ricky' by Sheila Hunter)
Mr. Joshua Falconer-Meade
looking for son Matthew, Martha (& Theodore (Tad) b ca 1835) lost From Meade Park UK.
Mr. Fishbon knew his son. At "The King's Arms" 2 g.sons Joshua UK & Tad Aust

(From Amelia's Tears)
Jimmy Westaweller b 1800 (Ned's friend & Amelia's brother)
Amelia Mary West/Westaweller/Black b 1804 Aylesford Kent.
Arrested and Convicted 1827, Shipped on "I" 1828
m2 22 Oct 1835 **Robert Styles** (Ned's friend)

REAL PEOPLE:-
Rev William Branwhite **Clarke** see *'Out Where the Brolgas Dance' & 'Diamonds in the Dirt'*
married Maria Moreton - children
Timothy Cape
Reverend Bobart & Elizabeth
Rev Samuel Marsden
The Kings School Parramatta

All the Governor's mentioned - incl
Governor Gipps

Printed in Great Britain
by Amazon